Mrs. Eliza Fletcher

Autobiography of Mrs. Fletcher

Mrs. Eliza Fletcher

Autobiography of Mrs. Fletcher

ISBN/EAN: 9783337027933

Printed in Europe, USA, Canada, Australia, Japan

Cover: Foto ©Raphael Reischuk / pixelio.de

More available books at **www.hansebooks.com**

AUTOBIOGRAPHY

OF

MRS. FLETCHER

WITH LETTERS

AND OTHER FAMILY MEMORIALS.

EDITED BY

THE SURVIVOR OF HER FAMILY.

" We live by Admiration, Hope, and Love,
And even as these are well and wisely fixed,
In dignity of being we ascend."
The Excursion.

EDINBURGH:

EDMONSTON AND DOUGLAS.

1875.

PREFACE.

In going through the first issue of my Mother's Autobiography (which was intended solely for private circulation), with a view to its publication, I have found it extremely difficult to make any change in the book without injury to its interest. I therefore let it go before the public with very little alteration, from the feeling that although unknown as a writer of books, *the use* she made *of Life* has an interest of its own which makes the publication of this volume less presumptuous than it would otherwise have been.

I confess that it is a great pleasure to me to feel that one whose estimate of her own place in the world was always so modest, and who never anticipated the circulation of her Autobiography beyond the circle of her friends and descendants, should still excite so much interest in " the city of her affections" as to make the call for this publication one I was glad to yield to, and I have therefore left the book very much the same as it was, except with the addition of some letters from those among her friends not unknown to the world by their own words and works.

M. R.

Lancrigg, *April* 1875.

CONTENTS.

PART I.

PART II.

AUTOBIOGRAPHY OF MRS. FLETCHER.

PART I.

I WAS born on the 15th of January 1770, at the village of Oxton, near Tadcaster, in Yorkshire. My father was descended from a respectable race of yeomen, his grandfather having purchased a small estate in the township of Oxton, in the time of Charles II., as appears by the titledeeds. His father, in addition to his paternal property, rented a large farm at Wighill Grange, the property of the Stapletons of Wighill Park. My mother was the eldest daughter of William Hill, Esquire, of Oxton, who inherited a considerable estate, which had lineally descended to him from the time of Queen Elizabeth, his ancestor being a younger brother of the Hills of Marston.

My father was a man of quick parts and ingenuous dispositions, but having a disinclination to the learned languages as a boy, and a strong preference for figures, he studied geometry and mensuration under the Rev. Mr. Atkinson, of Thorp Arch, and was, at fifteen, apprenticed to Mr. Lund, a land-surveyor and land-valuer, at Dring Houses, near York. He was the eldest of four children, and his father dying when he was about twenty, he succeeded to the small estate at Oxton, which, with industrious attention to his business, enabled him to marry Miss Hill in 1768, when he established himself at Oxton. My father and mother had been acquainted from their childhood; for though her condition was somewhat superior to his, yet his sister and she being at the York Manor Boarding School together, and being neighbours in the country, they were early thrown together, and could scarcely remember the time when they did not love each other better than they loved any one else. My mother's early attachment was put to the test, for at the Manor School she became intimate with a young lady of ancient family and aristocratic connexions, and, moreover, an heiress, with whom my mother afterwards visited the then fashionable places of resort, such as Bath and Clifton, as well as London and Windsor, when Miss Hebburn occasionally visited these places under the care of her maternal aunt and guardian, Mrs. Johnstone. My mother's personal attractions and pleasing manners brought many admirers round her, but her first love made her indifferent to their attentions, and in October 1768, when she was twenty-four years of age, she rewarded my father's constancy and worth by becoming his wife. Their happiness was not of long duration. At the end of the first year she had a still-born male child, and at the beginning of the year 1770 she died of milk-fever, after child-birth of me.

Thus early deprived of the blessing of a mother's care and tenderness, I became the object of my father's concentrated affections, and not of his only, but of those of his mother, brother, and sister, who, on the death of his wife, all became inmates of his family. Perhaps there never was a more cherished infancy and childhood than mine; and if this did not make me selfish in the worst sense of the term, I escaped that misfortune from having my affections and sympathy constantly exercised by feelings of love and gratitude towards those around me. My grandmother, "eldest of forms," was a woman of violent temper and strong affections. She exacted obedience and habitual attention from all her family, and I was accustomed to see her treated with the greatest respect by her sons and daughter. She was kind and beneficent to her poor neighbours. She used to send me with her tea-pot to the sick cottagers, for tea was then a luxury confined to the upper and middle classes—it formed no part of the diet of the poor. The village people consisted of eight labourers' families, three of whom had married from my grandmother's service. It was a little patriarchal community. They treated her with the same respect as if she were still their mistress. She was always doing them some little offices of kindness, in which she employed me likewise. I had one favourite little village playmate, Polly Bovill. I never was allowed to tyrannize over my humble companion, and I think she died before I felt aware that there was any distinction of rank between us. I visited her many times a day when she was on her death-bed, and I remember being struck by her saying " I shouldn't like to be buried in Wighill Churchyard, it is so lonely."

When I was about six years old, an event occurred which probably had a considerable influence on my future character and fate. My mother's early friend, Miss Hebburn, had married (I think two or three years before she did) the Rev. Edward Brudenell, a descendant of Lord Cardigan, and nearly related to the Duke of Montague. Mr. Brudenell had served as aide-de-camp to his father in the German war, and was induced to quit his profession of a soldier and to enter the service of the Church for the sake of a good living, the gift of which was in his family. This unworthy motive for engaging in the profession of a clergyman was followed by such consequences as might have been expected. The habits of dissipation he had acquired in the army were not forsaken, and his marriage to an heiress was a further step to the gratification of his expensive pleasures. He was a man of insinuating and accomplished manners, but totally without moral or religious principle, and the selfish hardness of his heart showed itself in utter disregard of the happiness of an affectionate wife and in the grossest indulgence in illicit amours and profligate habits of expense. His wife brought him two sons; they both however died in infancy, and after suffering every species of unkindness and indignity, Mrs. Brudenell came to the resolution of parting from her ungenerous and cruel husband. This resolution was not hastily formed, and it was resolutely executed. She was on a visit at my father's house at Oxton, and while there wrote to inform Mr. Brudenell of her determination to insist upon her separate maintenance or pin-money, as fixed in her marriage settlement, and to part from him whom she could no longer respect or love. Mr. Brudenell suddenly appeared at Oxton, and after some conversation, in which he opposed the resolution she had formed of a final separation, saying that he chose "to keep up appearances," they retired separately for the night. My grandmother, who was in Mrs. Brudenell's confidence, promptly arranged that in the middle of the night two horses should be in readiness to take this injured woman to a place of concealment, accompanied by my aunt Miss Dawson. Accordingly at midnight the fugitives escaped. My uncle and aunt accompanied Mrs. Brudenell along a private road about half a mile from my father's house, at the end of which Mr. John Hartley (a trusted neighbour) was waiting with two horses. Each of the gentlemen took one of the ladies behind him on a pillion, and took the road to Moor Monkton, a very sequestered village about nine miles distant, where a relation of my grandmother's lived. In that family they were hospitably received, and the gentlemen returned to their respective places of abode, without any one suspecting that they had been concerned in the adventure. Mrs. Brudenell had left a letter with my grandmother for her husband, repeating her determination to live with him no longer; and threatening that, if he attempted to molest her or refused the separate maintenance provided by her marriage settlement, she would throw herself on the protection of the Duke of Montague, and disclose the cruelty with which she had been treated. The reverend gentleman knew the spirit and firmness of his wife's character too well to risk such a disclosure. She had borne much, for she had loved much; but when she lost her children, she felt that there would be meanness and degradation in living longer with a man who had violated every principle of honour in his cruel infidelity to her, and who no longer regarded her but as an object of convenience.

On quitting her place of concealment, Mrs. Brudenell visited some of her mother's connexions in London, while Mr. Brudenell made some arrangements with respect to her estate of Hebburn in Northumberland, and he finally agreed to allow her £100 a year. From the deranged state of his own affairs, he found it expedient to accept the appointment (obtained for him by his half-brother, General Philips) of Chaplain to General Burgoyne's army, along with a detachment of which he sailed for America in the year 1776.

My father felt a strong interest in the friend of his late wife. Her generous and affectionate disposition made her cling to his young child as her mother's representative, and my father offered her a small cottage on his property at Oxton, if she could find repose and comfort in so humble a dwelling. She gladly accepted this asylum, and having much taste for the elegancies of life, she soon converted her little thatched house into a cottage *ornée*, and established herself there with two maid-servants, when I was between five and six years old. She devoted some hours of every day to teaching me to read and work, but this was the least part of my education from her. She cultivated my taste for poetry, exercised my imagination and heart by the history of her own eventful life, and by other narratives calculated to excite and interest a child. In truth, she supplied too much excitement to one who was perhaps predisposed to strong emotions and keen sensibility. She unwittingly supplied excitements to vanity, by making too great a display of my slender acquirements. I was brought forward on every occasion to recite passages from Pope's Homer or the Plays of Shakespeare, and was accustomed to hear and to expect high commendations of my wonderful powers and extra-ordinary accomplishments! If these dangerous stimulants had not been counteracted by the simple habits of a village life, and by the cultivation of the affections, I must have become an intolerable mass of conceit and pretension.

But here I must indulge in retracing more at length the affectionate family group round our cheerful fireside in the little parlour at Oxton. My grandmother, a beautiful old woman, of quick and sensitive temper, uniting much generosity of feeling with homely and frugal habits; my father, her eldest son, of a remarkably cheerful and hos-pitable disposition. He became a widower at thirty years of age. He had been an adoring husband to his first love, and for many years he had so cherished his grief on losing her that her name was never mentioned in his presence, nor had he ever been able to enter the chamber where she died. This gave to her character, and to his affection, a sort of mysterious sacredness in my young imagination, and excited in my mind a deep and tender interest in everything that related to my mother. The loss of this dear mother's tenderness was, however, supplied to me in no common degree by my excellent aunt Dawson, one of the most single-hearted and unselfish of human beings. She was my father's only sister, and she took a special charge of me from the time of my mother's death, which happened ten days after I was born. Night and day this kind aunt watched over me. She had a meek and submissive temper, with a considerable portion of early romance. She had good looks and gentle manners, and she was sought by many lovers; but, though in favour of one of these her young heart was deeply interested, she resolutely determined not to marry lest in that case my father might give me a stepmother, who might not treat me kindly. My poor grandmother was tormented with that apprehension; and listening at one time too credulously to gossips' tales, she took it into her head that my father's visits to a lady in the neighbouring market town would end in marriage. Not being able to extract a serious denial of this report from my father, I well remember the old lady's indignation rising to a high pitch at the notion of this impending evil; and one day, taking me by the hand, she said: "Child, you and I will beg our bread through the wide world together rather than you shall submit to the cruelty of a stepmother." With this we set out together to leave my father's house, and were trudging away to Wighill Grange, where her second son lived on his farm, about three miles from Oxton. We were in high heroics, for I remember—though then not more than seven years old—thinking it would be a fine thing to beg one's bread rather than submit to cruelty and injustice. But we were soon overtaken in our Quixotic pilgrimage by Mrs. Brudenell and my aunt, who prevailed on the old lady and her companion to return to their comfortable home, where an explanation soon took place

between her and my father. These " cataracts and breaks,"
however, did not often interrupt the serenity of our lives.
Such exhibitions of temper might have lessened my love
and veneration for my father, against whom they were
most improperly directed, but such was his invariable
kindness that they had no such effect. My father's
youngest brother, William Dawson, also formed part of
the family, and was as indulgent to me as the rest. He
was passionately fond of music, and played beautifully on
the German flute. My aunt had a pleasing voice and a
good ear, and she sang sweetly. I had no young companions in the family, but I was "mirth and matter" to
them all. I spent the early part of every day with Mrs.
Brudenell, and she spent the evening with us ; and music
and story-telling, recitations from Pope's Homer, or Shakespeare's Plays, with sometimes a pool at commerce, or a
game at blind-man's-buff, were our evening recreations.

Mr. John Dawson, my uncle, at Wighill, had two
children, a son three years older and a daughter half a
year younger than me. That he might have the advantage of attending a school at Tadcaster, my father took
his young nephew for a time to live with us. This boy
was a sad plague to me. He did not easily lose his own
temper, but he delighted to vex and put me in a passion,
and I attribute it somewhat to my early association with
him that it has cost me so much all my life to combat my
besetting sin—the being too easily provoked to anger.
His sister, Elizabeth Dawson, had the sweetest temper
possible. She and I never had a quarrel in our lives.
Her visits at Oxton were long and frequent. We were
delighted to be together. Though six months younger
than me, she could read well, when I could only say my
alphabet : the emulation she excited at six years old made
me give my mind to reading, and having once attained

that difficult art, I devoured every book that fell in my way. There were then no books for children but fairy tales and Æsop's and Gay's Fables. My father's library was upon a small scale—the Spectator, Milton's Works, Shakespeare's Plays, Pope's and Dryden's Poems, Hervey's Meditations, Mrs. Rowe's Letters, Shenstone's Poems, Sherlock's Sermons, with some abridgements of history and geography, filled his little book-shelves. To these Mrs. Brudenell's store added a few other works, such as Robertson's History of Scotland, Sully's Memoirs, Pope's Homer, etc. My cousin Elizabeth and I cherished the fondest friendship for each other. We contrived little stories and acted them together, often weeping and laughing heartily over our own tragi-comedies. I returned her visits at Wighill Grange, the only visits in which I had then any pleasure, because there was no restraint. The sheepshearings there were days of great festivity. We milked the ewes, and had our dairy in a hollow tree, and gathered garlands to celebrate the first of May, and cowslips for making wine. My visits to my maternal grandfather's house were not exactly of that description. Mr. Hill was a man of very superior understanding, and an elegant classical scholar, a perfect gentleman in manners, with a mildness and quietness approaching to Quakerism. He had an utter contempt for the vanities and frivolities of life. He lost his wife when his four daughters and his only son were very young, and he then took as inmate, a niece of his own, to be their guardian and companion. My mother, his eldest daughter, was the only one he ever sent to a boarding school. He cultivated in them all a love of reading, a taste for simple pleasures, and a strong sense of usefulness and public good. He gave his son a liberal education, having sent him to Westminster School, and entered him a student of Gray's Inn, preparatory to his being called to the Bar. This young man, whether from his mother's injudicious kindness in early childhood, or from naturally headstrong passions, proved a great grief to his family. With talents and acquirements of a high order for his profession, he became such a lover of pleasure, and such a slave to sensual habits, that without violating the estimation of men of the world, he sacrificed professional eminence and domestic respectability by his passion for hunting and his indulgence in licentious dissipation. Mr. Hill's three daughters were exemplary in their dutiful attention to their father, and in their unwearied devotion to the moral and religious education of the poor. They established the second Sunday-school that was taught in England, as early as the year 1784, having read in " The Gentleman's Magazine " an account of the first experiment of the kind made by Mr. Raikes, a public-spirited printer at Gloucester. My visits to these excellent relations when I was a child were rather those of duty than inclination. They were strict in their notions of duty and self-denial. They had been educated themselves in a stoical school, and neither claimed for themselves nor exercised towards others much indulgence. Their notions were of too severe and strict a cast to please a child accustomed to sympathy and fond caresses, as I was at my father's house. The day I was to spend with them was looked forward to as a day of trial, and got over as a day of penance. Never shall I forget how, at the end of a passage leading from their back-yard, I used to watch for John Copeland, an old man who passed that way every evening to milk his cow at Oxton, and beseech him to tell my grandmother to send for me home, be the night ever so wet or stormy. These messages were never neglected. John Bovill, an old Oxton cottager, a favourite tenant of my father's, was duly despatched on his grey mare, and, muffled in a red cloak, I rode before him, often through rain or snow, to the bright fire-side, where a kind and cheerful welcome always awaited me. My grandfather and aunts Hill were not unkind to me, they were only reserved, and the ladies admonitory. They gave me plenty of advice, but no sympathy ; they were intelligent, just and good, but they saw in me the faults of a spoiled child, and thought it their duty to point them out. I do not remember my grandfather's having ever in his life taken me on his knee or kissed me. He was to me a very awful person, one before whom I was always on my good behaviour. At that time I liked my uncle Hill (by far the least deserving of the family) much the best of them all, because he used to play with me, and once he took me before him on horseback a hunting, which I then considered the height of human happiness. But I was cured of my passion for that sport by hearing the shriek of the poor hare when the hounds pounced upon her. I screamed louder than the hare ; the sportsmen laughed at me, and when poor puss was dead they swung her across my shoulders, and I toiled home, half a mile, crying bitterly, half-proud, half-ashamed of my trophy. I could not forget the pitiful shriek of the poor hare, and never more wished to go a hunting.

As I advanced in life I learned to make a juster estimate of the worth of my mother's family, and looked up to my grandfather with real respect, and to my aunts with much regard, especially the youngest, Miss Mary Hill, who, at the time I am writing these reminiscences, is in her 85th year. She has as strong and original a mind as I have ever known, of high principle, and most extensive benevolence, with more habitual self-denial than I have met with in any other person. She bestows three-fourths of her income to feed, clothe, and instruct the poor. She is not indiscriminate in her charities, but devotes herself in Christian love to her

Master's business. If she had been placed in circumstances to exercise the smaller sympathies as well as the
virtues of charity and self-denial, hers would have been a
more attractive character ; but I have much personal cause
of gratitude to, as well as of veneration for her, and am
often reminded of the false estimate I see others make of
the value of things, by comparing it with her practical
wisdom. At eighty-five, she declares old age to be the
happiest period of human life, because the most free from
cares and worldly anxieties, and the nearest to its heavenly
destination.

[Letter from Mr. Hill to his Son in January 1767.

DEAR TOM,—I am glad thou hast so far conquered the
pride and self-conceit that so commonly prevails over mankind
as to acknowledge thou hast thy share of it : this is a great
step, but thou must not stop here. A good general must not
only know how to gain a battle, but likewise how to turn it to
advantage, for pride will be always up in rebellion, and the
weeds and brambles are as constantly to be plucked out of the
mind as they are out of a well-cultivated farm. Self-conceit
has a like ill effect on the body by its close connexion with the
mind, as from this source all that train of maladies called hyp
and vapours are derived, and the self-conceited man quarrels
with the world because it does not pay that regard to his merits
he thinks he is entitled to, whereas the humble man is happy
in meeting with more respect than he thinks he deserves. As
these two different tempers have such different effects with
regard to mankind, so doubt not but they will have the like
with respect to the Author and wise Governor of the universe,
whose protection thou must always seek, and whose guidance
thou must always rely on if thou hopest for happiness and
comfort.—I am thy affectionate Father,   WILLIAM HILL.][1]

---

[1] [There was a tradition in the Hill family which should not be omitted,
although not recorded by our mother herself, but kept in remembrance by
me in the form of a sword presented to me in one of my early winters at

My father was at this time, 1778, much employed as a commissioner under various Acts of Parliament for enclosing and dividing common land attached to townships, while my uncle took the surveying department. This took them much from home; and I well remember the joy which my father's return, especially, diffused through all his little household. I used to be on the watch for him at our garden gate, listening for the tramp of his horse, hours before his arrival. I had been diligently employed weeding or watering his favourite flowers, or seeing his pointers fed, and doing everything I thought would give me a claim to his approbation. He was fond of his garden, and made me a partaker in all his amusements there. On returning home, he had always something new and amusing to relate, and generally some little present to bring to each of us: perhaps some fairy tales for me, a matronly ribbon for his mother's neat mob-cap, or a new song for his sister. At this time the American revolutionary war was at its height. My father felt strongly on the Whig side of that question, and he and my grandfather Hill agreed in reprobation of taxing the colonies without their own consent. I understood, of course, nothing about the matter, but I listened with intense interest to these discussions, and picked up some notions of national justice and injustice.

Tadcaster, by my great-aunt Mary Hill. This basket-hilted sword was said to have belonged to an officer of the Hill family, behind whom the Lady Fairfax rode when she was taken prisoner on her way to Cawood Castle. Hartley Coleridge, in his Life of Sir T. Fairfax, mentions this, in the words of her husband, which he quotes, and it is there said that the name of this officer was "Will. Hill." What, however, made this so interesting to me at the time was this, that a certain Grace Hill, belonging to this family of Hills, went to the field of battle after the field was won, to look for the body of her brother, who could not be heard of, found him wounded but alive, brought him home and he recovered, and that is unfortunately all that I could ever learn of this, to me notable, heroine of my early days. The sword is still to be seen.]

I think it was in the year 1779 that my father took us all to a review of the West York Militia, on Chapeltown Moor, near Leeds. The regiment was at that time commanded by Sir George Savile, whose speeches I had often heard my father read with peculiar emphasis and satisfaction, considering him as the most patriotic and honest man in the House of Commons. He happened to be personally acquainted with Sir George, and meeting him accidentally that day he invited us all into his tent, and regaled us with wine, fruit, etc. He took me on his knee, and his good nature found amusement at my childish delight in all the "pomp and circumstance" of the review. For many a day after I enacted the glories of that day in the little garden at Oxton, shouldering my musket, rushing on to the charge, marching in quick and slow time. But the greatest glory of all was having sat on the knee of Sir George Savile. At that time Sir George's hair was thin and grizzled, and stood off from his face, and it much amused my father to find me often frizzling, or, as I said, "Sir George Saviling" my hair in the weeks after I had seen him. Sympathy with my father's high esteem for that good man's public virtue laid perhaps the foundation of my hero-worship.

[Another little tradition of our mother's child-days must, as we think, have belonged to this time, though not given in her written record. It was lodged in the faithful memory of good aunt Dawson, who was fond of telling it to us. She had taken her young charge, on medical advice, for a few weeks to Harrogate, and during their abode there the little girl's beauty had attracted much notice from a childless lady of fortune who was an inmate with them of the same hotel, and who sometimes begged to have her in the carriage to take drives along with her. One of these included a visit to the best furnished toy-shop of the place; but this, as the lady observed on bringing her back to aunt Dawson, had not proved so successful in the way of amusing her little friend as she had hoped. "She was bright and lively," she said, "as usual on setting forth, but has been out of spirits on our way back, and I have returned the sooner to you thinking she may feel unwell." It was not illness, however, only a sad disappointment to the eager little spirit, as she soon told when the ill-judging lady had left them. "Oh, aunt, if you had seen the drums, and the trumpets, and the guns and swords in that shop—and see (unwrapping a costly article from its paper covering), see, she has given me nothing but this stupid doll."

To us who knew the dear subject of these memorials as none else could, and who also knew most of those with whom her early days were passed, it has often been curiously interesting to note how strongly were met in her the hereditary instincts derived from both sides of her parentage. The quick, almost fiery temper—the affectionate, forgiving heart—the plain household integrity and sense of duty of the one,—her father's side ; and the more intellectual cast, and (with nothing less of "plain living") more "high thinking" tendencies of the other,—her mother's side, which, as she has told, led her aunts Hill to a sympathy with all purposes of *public* good, and to deeds of their own in accordance. From neither parental side, as we think, came her hero-worship (in military sense), which we saw as keenly alive in her eighty-fourth year, during the Crimean war, as it could have been in her ninth. This, if indeed it be not a part of every impulsive nature, must have been early engrafted on hers in her morning readings and talks with Mrs. Brudenell, herself a soldier's daughter, who, as we can remember in her talks of after years with us, delighted to show how fully she inherited, as well she might, her father's chivalrous Northumbrian pride in his descent (collaterally) from that hero of Chevy Chase memory, the Widdrington, who

> "When his legs were smitten off
> Still fought upon his stumps."

One point of woman's taste which seemed in her instinctive like the other, Mrs. Brudenell quite failed to impart to her pupil, the love of needlework.   Plain work, indeed, was not her *forte ;* the skill and practice in it which enabled aunt Dawson on one renowned occasion (the only self-boast that, I think, we ever heard her utter), to begin and finish a fine shirt in one day, never was attained by the more aristocratic family friend.   Indeed, as aunt Dawson used to tell us, Mrs. Brudenell always maintained that plain hemming or stitching gave her a disabling pain in her thumb ; but in the higher branches of the needle's doings she would gladly have taught her pet pupil to excel.   It was in vain, however, that precepts were uttered by her on this matter, or that her goodly examples of cross-stitch or tent-stitch, reaching even to hearth-rugs and carpets in these kinds, were set before our mother. One small token only of her having attained even the art of marking letters with the needle has been preserved amongst us —a sampler ; and we infer that she had been induced so to employ her fingers by being allowed a little expression of hero worship at the end of the toil, there being inscribed by her needle on the canvas (after the usual alphabet in letters great and small, and some not very happy imitation of flowers in worsted) a favourite passage from Pope's Homer, ending with the sounding couplet :

> " Who dares think one thing, and another tell,
>   My soul detests him as the gates of Hell." [1]

From her ninth year, her age at the date of the "glorious" day of the review and Sir George Savile's entertainment in his tent, there is a break in the thread of our mother's written reminiscences of her happy child-life, till she takes it up again to tell of what was in truth her first sorrow, the being sent to school.   The even tenor of those village days left her probably

---

[1] The second couplet inserted in the now moth-eaten sampler which I lately inspected is quite as prophetic of her future constancy in friend-ship as the first is as to her moral standard of truth and falsehood.   It is this—

> " The friends thou hast and their adoption tried,
>   Grapple them to thy soul with hooks of steel."

Certainly no one ever did more fully follow out the good advice of Polonius on this point than she did from youth to age.

little to note down concerning the two intervening years, but her vivid recollections of all this young time, so often the subject-matter of her talks with us, and good aunt Dawson's also, whose village annals had a simple, truthful quaintness about them very pleasant to hear and to remember, and our own knowledge of the localities, enable us well to imagine, almost to see, how those years went on, with "working day and holiday," in wholesome interchange. Oxton was a hamlet rather than a village, its cottage homesteads lying apart from one another for about a quarter of a mile along the right and left sides of the lane leading from Tadcaster (distant a mile on one side) to Bolton Percy, about three miles farther on the other side. It had no village green, but there were grass fields on all sides ; those on the right (as you entered from Tadcaster) stretching down from behind the cottages to the banks of the river Wharfe, those on the left to the York turnpike road, from whence a cart rather than carriage-way led to the village at its entrance. There was nothing, in tourist phrase, very "attractive " in the surroundings of Oxton, or in the place itself. Our grandfather's dwelling, the only one above those of the labourers' sort, was, and is, confessedly ugly in outward aspect, a brick house, somewhat narrow for its height, with a square low-walled and hedged garden in front, opening by a little gate on the village lane. An old porched house which once stood on the side nearly opposite, constructed of brick interspersed with beams of black oak and plaster, which might have been a Franklin's hall, was in our time but a tradition of the past. And yet, though there might be little that was picturesque at Oxton, hardly anything, as modern ladies say, to "sketch" (save a fine old walnut tree standing about midway on the side of the irregular village street just before John Bovill's cottage), there was much to enjoy. Each cottage, besides having the needful comforts within, had the free air without, and nearly all had a little orchard as well as garden ground behind. The place always had a "heart-some" look, as we used to come upon it from under the shade of some fine trees overshadowing the lane at its entrance on the Tadcaster side ; and there was a field just there that looked like a fragment of park scenery. Some stately oaks grew in its hedgerows, and a few noble elms within the enclosure at its lower

end.   But our mother's favourite fields were at the other end
of the village, beyond Mrs. Brudenell's cottage.   They opened on
a pretty bit of bosky lane, in the direction of Bolton Percy.   All
the fields round would probably have been open to her wanderings; many had footpaths through them, but these as her father's
possession, were her own more especial domain for violet-
picking in March, and birdnest-seeking (to look into reverently)
later on in the spring, and for large cowslip-gathering when
wine-making time was at hand, and for that most cherished of
all her young holiday joys, the flower-collecting for her garland
to be hung over the house door early on the first day of May.
Oxton did not boast of a May-pole.   So far as we have heard
her say, garland-making there was for household adornment
only, in which on May-day no cottage home was to be found
lacking.   Often has she recounted to us, and sometimes in
the same scene and season, when the primrose tufts and the
"nodding forests" of blue hyacinths were rife in the hedgerows of those fields, and the cowslip was scenting the air
everywhere, the true story of these May-day preparations;
how, on the last day of April, she and her cousin from Wighill Grange, or failing her, some young playfellow of the
village children, were set free from all tasks directly after
breakfast and allowed to follow their own devices till well on
in the afternoon, no home dinner hour to be observed; their
midday meal, a standing meat pie and some sweet articles,
being packed up for them in a covered basket by the unfailing
provider aunt Dawson.   Aunt D. did not fail to *recommend*
that the basket should not be opened till fair dinner-time, but
this, like much other good advice, our mother used to admit
was not always followed.   It *was* difficult to help peeping in,
just to see what aunt Dawson had put in besides the meat
pie, and then a little tasting followed, more than once perhaps,
before the flower-gatherers sat down to their dinners in good
earnest.   But the business of this happy day was not neglected.
All that was wanted for the garland was ready before tea-time
(not much after four o'clock in those days) brought them home
to sort and tie up the posies, and with Mrs. Brudenell's help
make all right for fastening them on to the large osier frame-
work (something of globe fashion) which was to display their

beauties next morning. No wonder that we should like to dwell even to tediousness (we are growing old ourselves) on the "sunny memories" of our mother's child days, for to the last hour that she was permitted *here* to enjoy anything, the thought of them never failed to light up her face with a peculiar joyousness. Another cherished reminiscence of those days was the dance and supper of the haymakers on the last evening of their season's work. The Oxton festivity of this kind was held in a field close to Mrs. Brudenell's cottage, and she supplied the music, by drawing a barrel organ which stood in her parlour close to the window that looked into that field, at which she stood turning the handle with unwearied good humour till the dancers were tired and ready for the good supper cheer that followed. Much less was said and written then about the amusements of the people than in our days, but it was a clear part of our mother's remembrances that the labouring poor had lighter spirits than we see in them now, not only that they had more taste for the periodical play that lightens toil, Christmas mumming ("ploughstott" processions as they were called in those parts), and the village "feasts" at Whitsuntide or Midsummer, but that they were more habitually cheerful in their domestic ways. She often recalled with heart-pleasure the sight and sound of John Bovill's young family when gathered round the father and mother under that walnut tree aforesaid, on summer evenings all singing together "lustily and with a good courage."

No wonder that school in exchange for such home and village life looked a dolorous prospect, though its terror was not increased to her by any child timidity or bashfulness; and it could have been no cheerful prospect for those left behind either, so much of each day's "mirth and matter," as she has said, to be taken away from her father, grandmother, uncle William, and her mother aunt Dawson also. But we, who knew her unselfish ways and works, can well fancy how, when the matter was once settled, her thoughts were bent on the needful preparations for school apparel, and how well stored was the "goody box" on the last day's packing. Mrs. Brudenell had her kindly cares and anxieties also ; but these related chiefly to the effect her pupil was to produce in the eyes both of the teachers and the taught at the Manor School by her young attainments. It was she, as our mother used to tell us, who took her to school and made the awful presentation to the presiding governess.

The Manor House at York was, and is still, a fine building in the old city, and had its royal traditions, having been used as a resting-place, and sometimes as a dwelling-place by kings of England in the olden time, when occasions led them north of the Humber. It is well and worthily used now as the "Wilberforce School for the Blind," a fitting memorial chosen (on Lord Brougham's suggestion) for the honoured man who, as one of the county Members for Yorkshire, had so long pleaded the great interests of humanity in his place in Parliament. If sorrowful feeling had not quenched fancy, our mother, even at eleven years old, would have liked the place, at least of her banishment. A photographic picture of its venerable door-way and a window over it, that of the room in which she and an amiable schoolmate, a friend for life afterwards, slept, is of interest to us to look upon now. Her own record, however, gives but a comfortless picture of the time passed there, and of school ways at the place in best repute for the instruction of young ladies in her time in the North of England.]

At eleven years old I was sent to the same boarding-school at York, at which my mother and Mrs. Brudenell had contracted their early friendship. It was a place in which nothing useful could be learned, but it did me some service, because I had something to unlearn. It taught me that all my reading was not to be compared with the graces that other girls had acquired at the dancing-school, and my rusticity subjected me to many wholesome mortifications. The dull restraints of a school life were extremely irksome to me; everything was artificial, flat, and uninteresting. One great reason of this, no doubt, was that whereas at home I was everything, at school I was nothing—self-love was in a perpetual state of subjection and humiliation. The four years I spent at that school were not without their use, because if their experiences did not convince me that the making a graceful curtsey was the chief end of human existence, and that an awkward gait was worse than a bad action, they did convince me that, if the acquirements I valued myself upon were not to be more admired by the world than they were by my school companions, I had made a very mistaken estimate indeed of the value of my own knowledge and literary attainments. I formed, however, some friendships at school which both at the time and afterwards permanently contributed much to my happiness. Of these were Miss Forster and her sisters, Miss Ann Cleaver, afterwards Mrs. Chapman, and Miss Beckwith, afterwards Mrs. Craik. But reflecting on my experience of a boarding-school as then conducted, I cannot but wonder how any one could escape the peril of such association as might have been met with there. The Manor School was in the hands of a very well-disposed, conscientious old gentlewoman, but of so limited an understanding that, under her rule, mischief of every kind (short of actual vice) was going on without her even suspecting it. Lessons were said by rote, without being understood; servants were bribed to bring in dainties clandestinely; in short, every kind of dissimulation was practised to indemnify the subjects of this petty despotism, for the restraints unnecessarily imposed upon them. During the four years I was at this school, two chapters of the Bible were read every morning by two of the young ladies as a reading lesson. Prayers were regularly drawled out by the husband of our governess, a choleric old man, who thumped our fingers so often for bad writing, with his mahogany ferule, that we listened to his prayers with any feelings but those of love or devotion. I do not remember to have received a single religious impression at this school, though creeds were repeated, and catechisms taught, and all the formalities of religious service regularly performed. Four volumes of the Spectator constituted our whole school library. But besides the negative evils of such school life, was the misfortune of having as daily associates some girls of thoroughly depraved character. Two of these, the most remarkable for dissimulation and all evil characteristics, who afterwards married, eloped from their husbands.

[" Such," our mother adds, "were the dangers to which the inmates of a boarding-school were then exposed." In thinking of her, well may *we* add—such were the healthy instincts that saved her from danger, and led her in that young school-world to "refuse the evil and choose the good." Her own intimate schoolmates, all of whom were well known to us in after days, —pleasant it is now to remember how much we inherited of their kindly friendship,—were no less marked than herself by purity of thought, word, and deed. It was one trial of those weary years, a minor one certainly, and only matter for merry recollection with her friends afterwards, but sorely felt at the time,—that in the daily school walks she was coupled with a girl of uncommon stupidity, whose ideas ran on tarts and puddings only. She supposed that the lady at the head of the school had a special dislike to her, and that this infliction was a proof of it. A burst of tenderness from the old lady on her leaving school, however, brought forth an *éclaircissement* on this point. Tears were shed on both sides. "Why," said the pupil, "did you always make me walk with Miss ——?" "My dear, I thought you might do her good, and she could do you no harm." And so it might be. We do not know what brightenings might come in after-life to that dull girl. As to the limitation of the school library, and the authorized reading, the Manor School girls of course indemnified themselves in the usual manner of sufferers from undue prohibition. Our mother's school friends in after-days had happy remembrances, along with her, of the little reading parties gathered together round a fire, over some smuggled article of dramatic, and commonly of tragic sort—in one case indeed made doubly tragic, when, in the midst of a scene in the pathetic play of Sir Thomas

Overbury, one of the listeners, lifting her arm in high excitement, dashed the little paper *tome* out of the reader's (our mother's) hand, and it flew into the fire, from whence hardly a fragment could be recovered. The " stolen pleasures" of such reading, in spite of occasional mishaps, were doubtless " sweet," and school dulness was sometimes, as she relates, otherwise diversified.]

My father had many friends at York who were kind to me. It was at Mr. Forster's house [the father of her school friends of that name] that I was most at home. The family were old friends of Mrs. Brudenell. They had moved from their country seat, Bolton, in Northumberland, to live for some years at York for the education of their daughters. By Mrs. Forster I was always treated as one of her own children; but I never reflect with pleasure on my school-day life. I had more of the home sickness than most of my companions. From our play-ground on the "Manor shore" I could see Bilbrough Spring, a tall clump of trees within three miles of my father's house. That clump of trees interested me more than any game at play, and it was only when I mounted my pony to trot homewards that I knew what real happiness was at that period. I left school finally at the midsummer of 1785. So fond was I of my newly-acquired freedom and command of time, that so long as the early mornings were light I rose at four o'clock, and with some favourite book, generally of poetry, I sauntered in the lanes or fields till our eight o'clock breakfast-time.

[These were days of chosen remembrance with our mother. We can all recollect how, in our walks round Oxton together, she used to linger at one particular stile leading from the lane into a field footpath, and tell us of her sittings there on those early summer mornings. Like most ardent young readers of poetry, she wrote not a little verse in those days, the said stile being her seat with pencil and note-book for that pleasant rhyming work which Southey says " no one ever practised without being the better for it." We can well believe that she *was* the better for such expression of her young summer joy ; from any vanity that might have made her the worse, she was saved by a high and true sense of poetic beauty, an imagination already fed by the mind and the music of Shakespeare (her father's recitation of nearly the whole play of "Romeo and Juliet" was among her earliest recollections), and an ear trained by the graceful flow of Pope.]

About this time (in the same year of happy freedom), a friend of my father placed at my disposal £20 to make some addition to my slender stock of books. Well do I remember with what exultation of delight I entered old Tessyman's, the bookseller's shop at York, to make my purchases. Warton's Edition of Milton's Lesser Poems, Cowper's First Edition of his poems, Hayley's Works, and Brydone's Tour were amongst the number. There lived at that time in the neighbouring village of Bolton Percy a family of the name of Ewbank. Mr. Ewbank, a man of good private fortune, was Curate of the parish, and lived at the Rectory. His wife was a truly devout and exemplary woman, of cultivated mind and great refinement of manners. Mrs. Brudenell and I often visited this family. They formed my *beau-idéal* of domestic happiness, and they presented religion to me in its most engaging form, " carrying it (as Dr. Chalmers would have said) into their week day as well as their Sabbath ministrations."

The very summer I left school an incident occurred which afforded interest to a romantic imagination. Mine had been little cultivated by novel-reading, but that seductive amusement had not been wholly resisted, and I had a great admiration for the military heroic. The addresses paid me by an officer whom I met at Thorp Arch*

* A watering-place on the banks of the Wharfe about five miles from Oxton.

while on a visit there, was the first episode of the kind in my simple annals. My notions of filial duty were of the strictest kind. I was wretched till I imparted my secret to my father, and more wretched still when he desired me at once to put a negative on the hopes of my adoring lover. Not that I was in love myself, but I never doubted that the gallant captain would, as he said, forthwith die of grief and distraction if I did not give a favourable answer to his suit. I am amused now by the simple credulity of a village girl of fifteen fifty years ago. There is not now a girl of that age, of capacity above an idiot's, who would not quiz the notion of a man's dying of love. A succession of admirers furnished me for the next two or three years with *serious* occupation, for I had nothing of the coquette in my disposition, though a good deal of the heroine of romance. I never could make light of the sorrows of the heart. My suitors were dismissed without the self-love of any being hurt by scorn or impertinence. One youth I could have loved; the eldest brother of my school-friend, Miss Ann Cleaver. I met him in the year 1787, when I was on a visit at his father's house. His appearance was prepossessing, his mind manly and ingenuous, and his manners pleasing. He had finished his Cambridge education, and was entered a student of law at the Inner Temple. I allowed him to ask my father's permission to pay his addresses to me. The displeasure he felt at my father's unfavourable reception of his proposals proved that he had more pride than tenderness of heart, and this enabled me to conquer my attachment and to acquiesce without a murmur in my father's better judgment.

[In the same page that tells of her young " passages of love," our mother tells also of her deep sympathy with its fictitious woes in her first reading of " The Sorrows of Werther."]

This touching book fell into my hands (while staying

with the Forster family at York) on the morning of the day on which I was going to my first ball. I had anticipated as much delight as girls commonly do from this event, but my swollen eyes, red with weeping, and my grief for Werther and Charlotte, obliged me to give up the ball. I never cared enough for dress to make much impression in a ball-room, neither did I at all excel in dancing. My pleasure was in the conversation of an agreeable partner. I never was gratified by complimentary admiration of my personal attractions; vanity lay in another corner of my heart. I ambitiously desired to be distinguished for mental superiority, and had no objection to a little sentimental flirtation, though I do not remember ever wishing to inspire a passion for the sake of conquest.

At the balls given during the Lent Assizes at York, my uncle Hill used to take a great charge of my dancing with *proper* partners, and generally introduced to me some of his younger brethren at the Bar, whom I found better educated and more conversable than the young men I was in the habit of meeting at the York evening parties. It was at one of these parties, however, at Mr. Forster's, that I had the long-wished-for gratification of seeing the poet Mason. He was then Precentor of the Cathedral. Many a time had I walked before his door in the Minster Yard, to get a peep of the author of Elfrida and Caractacus. But to be in the same room with him, to watch his countenance, and hear him speak, the anticipation was delightful! I figured him an interesting-looking man worn with deep affliction, for I had read his beautiful "Monody" on his wife, who died at Bristol of consumption. But when he entered Mrs. Forster's drawing-room, what was my surprise to see a little fat old man of hard-favoured countenance squat himself down at a card table, and give his whole attention to a game at whist!

[It was in the year previous to this, before her taste of the gaieties and incidents of the "York Lent Assizes," that our mother made her first acquaintance with the land north of the Tweed, and with the English highlands of our lake district, those places of her habitation in most of her after-years of life.]

In the summer of 1786 my kind father indulged me with an excursion to the Highlands of Scotland. I had my choice either to go for six weeks to London or to Scotland; I chose the latter. I was much attached to Miss Stewart, a young lady who had married the year before (from the Manor School) Mr. Meliss, a gentleman of Perth, her native place. This and some romantic associations with Scottish scenery decided my choice. My uncle William Dawson, my cousin John, and I, set out on this excursion on the 23d of July, and after a visit of three weeks to my friend Mrs. Meliss at Rosemount, a pretty villa near Perth, where I witnessed much domestic happiness and received much kindly hospitality, we proceeded through Perthshire and Argyllshire by the ordinary tourist route, and returning by the Westmoreland and Cumberland lakes, we completed our expedition by the 5th of October, on which day we returned to Oxton.

My taste for and enjoyment in picturesque scenery were much increased by this journey. From Bamborough Castle, on the coast of Northumberland, I first saw the sea. It was on a tempestuous day, and the foaming surge and roaring billows of the German Ocean astonished and affected me. I have never looked on the sea since without a recurrence of the same emotion of dread, which philosophers consider the source of the sublime. It would be impossible for me ever to feel familiar with the sea; I have no feeling of happiness connected with it. I was greatly struck with the noble situation of Edinburgh, and interested in the historical associations of the place, but we did not then know any one there. The frankness and urbanity of Scottish manners were very agreeable to me. I was not discriminating enough to be a good judge of character, or refined enough to be fastidious. I had no very high standard of manners, but I returned gratefully impressed with much personal kindness. I had an unaffected wish to please. This feeling was, I think, compounded of benevolence and a great desire of approbation. I never could flatter or say what I did not think ; but I was disposed to think well of others. I had no turn for ridicule, no very quick perception perhaps of the ludicrous, no pride, I think, or assumption above others ; but I had plenty of vanity, and great—much too great—desire for the estimation of others. If it had been the estimation of the good and the wise only, it would have been a desire that all rational beings ought to have ; but I was more voracious, and less discriminating in my love of approbation.

This delightful Highland tour filled my mind with many new thoughts, both respecting scenery, national character and manners, and various subjects, which a wider field of observation afforded. I was then sixteen ; and for my father's amusement I kept a journal of each day's adventures. This was afterwards transcribed in a book, which held a favoured place in my father's book-case, and yet now-a-days a very ordinary girl of sixteen would be ashamed to write so bald, so affected, and so absurd a narrative of a six-weeks' tour in Scotland ; I could sit down and laugh at it from beginning to end, there is so much attempt at fine writing in it, a thing never thought of now, I presume, by a girl of sixteen. It abounds in the bad taste of the time ; it is a sort of " sentimental journey." My fondly indulgent father, however, and all my little family circle, were delighted with it, and thus my love of approbation " grew by what it fed on."

[This judgment, often pronounced by our mother's later-formed self-knowledge on her early self, was doubtless true ; but quite as true was it that an earnest benevolence, that best natural antidote to the poison of selfish vanity, was as much a part of her nature as the love of approbation. She knew that her love of doing good was far stronger than her desire to be thanked or praised for it. *This* love grew with her growth, from an impulsive sentiment into a working habit, a principle of her life. The next two notices in her own words, relating to incidents of this or the following year, are very characteristic.]

It was about this time that I read somewhere of a dispute between Mrs. Hannah More and Ann Yearsley, the Bristol milkwoman. The poor woman's " narrative " struck me as having a strong claim on the reader's sympathy. It appeared that after Mrs. Hannah More had introduced her to the public, by a very high and eloquent eulogium on her genius and her virtue (in a letter addressed to the celebrated Mrs. Montague), she quarrelled with Mrs. Yearsley for her requesting to have the uncontrolled disposal of the interest only of the money which, chiefly through Mrs. Hannah More's influence, had been raised by subscription for her poems. Mrs. Yearsley had readily agreed that the principal sum, about £350, should be vested in the funds for the benefit of her family, under the trusteeship of Mrs. Hannah More and Mrs. Montague. Mrs. Yearsley's " narrative " made a great impression on me. I thought it showed a case of direct attempt by the strong to oppress the weak. My father and all our little household sympathized in this feeling, and authorized by my father, I wrote to Mrs. Yearsley offering to collect subscriptions for her new volume of poems advertised for publication. Mrs. Yearsley, who had been highly irritated by what she conceived to be Mrs. Hannah More's injustice, received the offered assistance of a stranger with exaggerated, but I believe sincere expressions of joy and gratitude. I enlisted with all the zeal of partisanship, as well as the feelings of justice and benevolence, in her behalf, and seldom had I felt more delighted than when my father put a £50 bank note into my hands to give immediate help to the Bristol milkwoman in bringing out her poems. This sum was nearly replaced by the five hundred subscribers I obtained for her. She afterwards addressed some complimentary verses to me in that volume, and, not being then much given to the practice of self-examination, I daresay I was not aware how much of vanity and self-love mixed with better feelings in my patronage of Mrs. Yearsley. The correspondence with this remarkable woman afforded me much interest for several years, and I carefully preserved her letters. When, in the spring of 1834, I visited Bristol and Clifton for the first time, I tried in vain to trace any vestige of her or her family.

It was in his generous indulgence, and sympathy in such impulses as these, that I felt my father's kindness so deeply. It was about the same time that he encouraged me in my strenuous exertions to save a poor friendless girl from vice and misery. When on a visit to my friend Miss Beckwith at Ripon, as we were on our way together to attend as visitors at a Sunday School, we observed, through a grated window of the lock-up house, the face of a modest-looking girl not above seventeen years of age. She looked very sorrowful. In answer to our inquiries, she said that, on her way from Sunderland to join her mother in London, she fell into company with two other poor travellers, a man and his wife, and accompanied them to a beggar's lodging-house in Ripon, where they committed a theft, and she, being with them, was committed to take her trial along with them at the Quarter Sessions. There was so much apparent artlessness in her story that my friend and I interested ourselves deeply in her fate. Her name was Elizabeth Anthony. She was acquitted of participation in the theft, and her companions were sent for six weeks to the House of Correction. A respectable service was obtained for her by Mr. Beckwith in a farmer's family near Ripon, and my friend and I had the satisfaction to think that we had saved the poor girl from ruin. What was our disappointment to find, six weeks afterwards, that she had absconded from the farmer's service, and had taken the road to York with her former companions when liberated from prison. My friend Ann Cleaver was staying with me when I received this grievous intelligence. At once we mounted on horseback, and full of Quixotic enthusiasm we rode full canter to York, where we prevailed on a good man to search all the mendicant lodging-houses for our fugitive. He found her, and brought her to our inn. Again she imposed on us by saying that her quondam friends had frightened her into leaving her good master's service by telling her that they would set fire to his barn if she refused to accompany them. We credulously believed her, and again found, in the house of Mr. Potter of Tadcaster, a respectable service, and a kind roof to shelter her. But "a begging she would go," and although most kindly treated in Mr. Potter's family she again absconded, without however committing any theft or breach of trust in either of the families who had given her shelter.

[One of our mother's favourite heroines in humble life belonging to this period was a person of the name of Sarah Watson, who lived in the village of Grimston, near Tadcaster, where I

often saw her as an old woman.   I well remember the respectful and affectionate manner my mother had towards her, when
she took us to her cottage on a fine summer evening during
one of our visits to Tadcaster, when we were children.   On
our walk home across the fields, she told us that Sarah had, in
her youth, when they first knew each other, been a single
servant in a clergyman's family of small means; that the
master of the house was killed by an accident, and left his wife
in great poverty and some debt.   Sarah, who had married a
labourer, took a cottage and fitted up her best room with all
the comforts she could collect from her mistress's old home, and
which she would much have missed, moved her into it, and
waited upon her for years, as she had been accustomed to do,
but without any remuneration ; showing her more respect than
ever, and bearing all the irritability of illness and age with the
utmost gentleness and forbearance.   Sarah had one child, which
died young ; and in the cottage on that fine summer evening,
I remember there was a little chair with a large Bible on it.
I have still a distinct impression of that cottage, its beautiful
cleanliness and comfort, the roses about the open lattice, the
little chair and the Bible on it, the grave refined look of the
venerable Sarah,—and then the history of her beautiful self-
devotion, related to us as we walked home, in the glowing words
we loved best to hear.   All this made an impression on us that
no written annals could have done.   It was a remembrance of
her own youth that she conveyed to us, as the history of Ruth
might have been related in the walks at eventide of a Hebrew
mother ; and such histories of goodness and mercy sink deep
into the hearts of children.   We afterwards heard in our visits
to Sarah (which continued to be one of the pleasures of our
Tadcaster life so long as she lived) that our mother had thrown
her loving energies into this village history at the time it
occurred, and had assisted Sarah to collect the articles of
furniture which were essential to the comfort of her old
mistress.   It was evident to those who saw them together
that there was a link of old remembrance and regard between
them which broke down all the barriers of condition and made
them feel as friends living in the presence of a loving Father.
Where our mother recognised the presence of God's spirit in

others, the humility of her own nature appeared in a re-markable degree and gave a deferential grace to her manner quite apart from the ordinary courtesy of society. One of the sayings of her old friend, Mr. Clowes, early entered her soul, and expressed what she felt to be a great happiness to herself to exercise and cultivate in others. "To delight in good is the temper and disposition of angels."]

My good old grandmother died in the winter of 1787, an event all her grown-up sons, and her only daughter, felt deeply at the time, and none of the family more than my-self; for, with many infirmities of temper, she had a noble generosity of heart, and had always treated me with most affectionate indulgence. It was a little later in the same year that a circumstance occurred upon which perhaps hinged the future condition and happiness of my life.

In the spring of 1787 Mrs. Meliss wrote to tell me that her husband, who had become a zealous borough reformer, was going as a delegate from Perth to attend before a Com-mittee on Borough reform in the House of Commons, along with a distinguished Scottish patriot, Mr. Archibald Fletcher, of Edinburgh, who had written "The Principles of the Bill for Scottish Borough Reform," now to be brought into the House of Commons, and that, if I chose, she would accompany the travellers as far as Oxton. Nothing could exceed my satisfaction on receiving this intelligence. I had very dim and imperfect notions concerning politics, but during the American war I had caught many liberal opinions from my father, and my grandfather, and uncle Hill, all of whom detested the arbitrary and unjust prin-ciples of that war, by which England lost her colonies in North America; and from the admiration General Washington's conduct excited, and the estimation in which Sir George Saville's character was held, I had conceived the loftiest opinion of a disinterested lover of his country, and my curiosity was strongly awakened to see the reformer in whose praise my friend Mrs. Meliss wrote in such glowing terms. The party from Scotland arrived some time in April 1787. Mr. Fletcher was then about forty-three, of a grave, gentleman-like, prepossessing appearance. There was an expression of intelligence and benevolence in his countenance, with great mildness and gentleness of manners. I was flattered by the pleasure he seemed to take in conversing with me. I remember that the conversation turned much on Ossian's Poems. He was a great admirer of the works ascribed to the Celtic bard, and, to a certain extent, a believer in their authenticity, having heard several of them (or poems of the same description) recited in his youth, before Macpherson translated and gave them to the world in their present form. Mrs. Brudenell gave a little musical party at her cottage to our Scottish friends. She always contrived to give these simple entertainments a tasteful and elegant appearance. At the end of three days the reformers left us to pursue their route to London. I don't remember any impression of what is called love at first sight from this interview with Mr. Fletcher, but it would appear that I had made some impression of this sort on his mind. Mr. Meliss wrote to his wife that his companion could think and talk of nothing but Miss Dawson. Mr. Meliss returned some time sooner than his friend, and brought me a handsome copy of Ossian's Poems from Mr. Fletcher, with a letter containing some critical remarks upon them, and a request that I would honour him with a letter to say how I liked the work. My vanity was flattered by the respect paid to my opinion; some letters passed between us, and though the correspondence was confined to literary subjects, I found it extremely interesting. Some time afterwards I remember to have felt somewhat piqued and mortified to find that Mr. Fletcher had passed through Tadcaster, on his way northwards, without so much as calling at Oxton. On explaining how this happened, it appeared that he had, with two companions, arrived at Tadcaster at twelve o'clock at night, had taken a chaise to Oxton, and had walked round and round my father's house, in the dead of night, without daring to disturb the family, and had then returned to the inn at Tadcaster to be ready to set out with his companions early next morning for Scotland. I was not displeased with the romance of this incident, but I thought if he had cared much about seeing me he would have contrived to accomplish it. This was not the disappointment of one who loved, but of one who fancied that she was more beloved than she now appeared to be. There was some interruption to our correspondence : it languished on my side.

In the spring of 1788 Mr. Fletcher again paid us a short visit at Oxton. He was accompanied by the Hon. John Douglas, afterwards Earl of Selkirk, who was also a borough reformer, and they were on their way to attend the Parliamentary Committee on that subject in London. On his return from town in June we had removed from Oxton to a house in Tadcaster ; and I do remember that when I received his note from the inn, saying that he would do himself the honour to call and spend the evening with us, I did resort to the toilette to curl my hair with rather more care than usual. I was more struck even than before with the good sense and good taste of his conversation, and much interested in his animated account of the splendid speeches he had heard at Westminster Hall, at the trial of Warren Hastings. My own mind had perhaps made some advance in knowledge and reflection, and I enjoyed this visit more than I had done before. The correspondence which had grown languid on my part was resumed with more spirit, but was still confined to literary and general subjects.

In the summer of the same year, while visiting Doncaster in the company of two Scotch acquaintances, a Mr. and Mrs. Anderson, who went to place their only daughter at a boarding-school at that place, I accidentally became acquainted with the Rev. Edmund Cartwright,[1] who had lately published "A Legendary Tale, Armine and Elvira," along with some other poems of considerable merit. Mrs. Anderson was a great proficient in music. We had accompanied some ladies at Doncaster, whose names I now forget, to see the old church there, and Mrs. Anderson was allowed to play some sacred music on the organ. While she was so employed I was struck with a simple and elegant inscription to the memory of Mrs. Cartwright, the wife of the Rev. Edmund Cartwright. I asked if that was the poet. I had no sooner asked the question than I was introduced to that gentleman, who, attracted by the music, had strolled into the church. He was a grave-looking man, considerably turned of forty, of very gentle and engaging manners. He was acquainted with the family with whom we had spent the day, and he accompanied us to their house to pass the evening, and next day he took us to see some power-looms of his invention,—set to work, not by steam or water, but by a large wheel turned by an ox. We dined that day with Mr. Cartwright, and were all much pleased with the good taste, animation, and variety of his conversational talents. We proceeded next day to Matlock, promising him another visit on our return from that place. At Matlock and Buxton I had some opportunity of mixing in more miscellaneous society than I had been accustomed to. I was not insensible to the admiration I met with, but it was not of a kind to gratify or interest me; and much as I admired the natural beauty of the scenery about Matlock, and marvelled at the wonders of the great cavern in the

---

[1] Mr. Cartwright was also the inventor of the power-loom.

Peak of Derbyshire, I wearied of the heartless frivolity of watering-place society, and longed to return to my affectionate and happy home. Mrs. Brudenell had by this time become an inmate of my father's family, and though subject to irritability of temper from bad health and a life of disappointment, she was always affectionate and sympathizing, or lively and amusing. The very limited society of a small country town did not compensate to us for that quietness and repose we had enjoyed at Oxton, but we were so united and attached a family that no place was so dear to me as home.

My second visit to Mr. Cartwright confirmed our mutual prepossessions. He soon distinguished me with his friendship; and, in the autumn of that year, I think, he brought his gifted friend the Rev. George Crabbe, and his amiable wife, to pay me a visit. I accompanied them all three to York Minster, and at the distance of half a century I have still a vivid recollection of the gratification I then enjoyed in the society of such elegant and cultivated minds. Mr. Crabbe made me a present of his "Village Library," and "Newspaper," two poems which had been printed in quarto separately by Dodsley, in St. Paul's Churchyard, the former in 1783, the latter in 1785. I continued to correspond with Mr. Crabbe for several years, and had the honour of being godmother to his second son, now the Rev. John Crabbe. Mr. Cartwright placed his two eldest daughters, Mary and Eliza, at the Manor School of York, and they sometimes spent part of their holidays with me at Tadcaster. His correspondence was considered by me as a great privilege. He honoured me with his confidence and friendship so far as to wish me to become the mother of his five amiable children by uniting my fate to his. I had not confidence in my own worthiness for such a trust, but in refusing it, I neither forfeited his good opinion nor his friendship. In the winter of 1788 he introduced me to his excellent friend Mr. Woodison, the learned and amiable Professor of Law at Oxford (the successor of Sir William Blackstone), with whom Mr. Cartwright had been a fellow-student at Magdalen College.   Mr. Woodison was a man of singular modesty and refinement of manners; so diffident of his own merits that he inspired diffidence in others, not of his, but of their own pretensions.   This sensibility of temperament was to him, I believe, a source of much disquietude, in the active and busy life of a professional lawyer in London.   He was, in truth, better fitted to be a Lecturer in a University than a Wrangler in Westminster Hall.   I was occasionally honoured with his correspondence from our first acquaintance till the time of his death, which happened, I think, in 1806 or 1807.

[Her intercourse with Mr. Cartwright and the chosen friends to whom he introduced her never was recurred to in after-life by our mother without warm interest, grateful interest, such as we can well believe was called forth in her young days by the opening thus given her for observing new aspects of life, and for an interchange of thought much above that which an ordinary country town affords. And with her, at this as at all times, such variety from the usual current of home life might be as safely as it was heartily enjoyed. No home languor or unneighbourly fastidiousness followed from that contact with "metal more attractive" which she might occasionally find elsewhere. We can all testify from our earliest childhood how habitually she practised the sentiment of a favourite quotation—"The joy of seeing is to tell." We are very sure that it was so then, and that the home she loved so dearly was always the brighter on her return by what she gained when away from it. Meantime she found or fastened life friendships in the place of her habitation. The nearness at this time to her grandfather and aunts Hill, whose house, "The Grange," stood in a pleasant field on the left bank of the Wharfe, edging close to the town of Tadcaster, brought her more into daily intercourse with them than formerly, and with the youngest of the three sisters especially, whose influence henceforth became a telling one.　The stately maiden aunt, who for lack of indulgent tenderness had no attraction for her love as a child, had much in her to draw out admiring regard when advanced tastes were to be met and ministered to.　She read more than was common with ladies of her date ; and though her reading was desultory enough, ranging without any plan from " Baker's Chronicles " (" the nearest " approach to a story-book, she used to tell us, that came within the children's reach in their father's house in *her* child days) up to the " Emile " and the " Nouvelle Héloise " of Rousseau, and down (if we may so speak) to Mrs. Trimmer's " Economy of Charity,"—the three latter books were almost equally her favourites at the time now mentioned,—an instinctive taste for the noble and the practical at once, had always led her to make her mind's food and possession out of the best quality to be found in her somewhat curious variety of book-companionship.　But even more than her love of books did her habitual practice of wise benevolence to the poor meet the growing earnestness of our mother's growing character, helping much at this time to strengthen in her a value for the " good of uses," according to a phrase of old Cotton Mather, which aunt Mary Hill often quoted, and to deepen her sense of this large part of life's highest purpose.

We have often wished that our mother could have told us more from her own local observation of that great awakening of religious life in England in which the founders of Methodism bore so large a part.　As an era in our country's history, no one regarded it with higher interest in after-life than she, and not a few members of the Methodist community were at all times objects of her loving honour ; but the phase of faith in her own home could not well assimilate with Methodism. Her father's joyous temperament repudiated the gloom he often saw associated with early convictions in followers of the new sect.　His old English churchmanship made him impatient of long extempore prayers and sermons outstepping all accustomed limits, and the wild extravagance often attendant on the new services either disturbed his love of order or furnished matter for his ready mirth. Mrs. Brudenell, from somewhat like taste and temper of mind, agreed with him fully, and aunt Dawson was at all times more given to doing for, than differing from those about her. All three were alike incapable of bitterness in their hostility ; but on the whole, the household tone was more that of mistrust than of charity as to the genuineness or worth of Methodist pretensions. Our mother had a very early but quite distinct recollection of having gone once from Oxton with her grandmother to hear John Wesley preach in the parish church of Tadcaster, then (in consequence of the favourable dispositions of the Vicar) not closed against him. The venerable beauty of his look never was forgotten by any one who saw him ; the subject of his sermon—the alarming advance of luxury in England—was doubtless fixed in her memory by one illustration, which she used to report to us, given on the preacher's own experience, viz., "that in his young days his mother used to make one apple serve for the family dumpling, whereas he found that many apples were used for that purpose to satisfy the tastes of the children of the time in which he then addressed them." Wesley died in 1791, at a very advanced age ; and at the time now spoken of, many of his early helpers must have gone before their master to the grave. The machinery of Methodism was complete, and at Tadcaster it was in very active exercise ; but probably much of the living interest and fervour spread abroad in almost every part of our land by its first teachers had evaporated. It was, at all events, not from this "administration" of revealed truth that our mother received, as she has noted in the following passage, those views of the Christian message which were through life her abiding ones.]

It was in the winter of 1788 that I met, at the house of the Misses Hutton (two excellent maiden ladies) at Tadcaster, the Rev. John Clowes, Rector of St. John's Church, in Manchester. The bond between these pious and primitive old ladies and Mr. Clowes was, I believe, their mutual admiration of the writings of Emanuel

Swedenborg. Although I could not participate in their enthusiasm for that visionary writer, I think it was from Mr. Clowes's conversation and writings that I first became interested in the spiritual sense of true religion, or, in other words, felt its experimental truth; and I wish here to preserve the following transcript of the conversation which I made from memory after passing the evening with Mr. Clowes at Miss Hutton's. Several ladies, some of the Methodist persuasion, were present. His views have always appeared to me to contain much of the true spirit of Christianity.

Being asked his opinion of Mr. Law's[1] works, Mr. Clowes said, " I read them, madam, with great diligence and much affection, and I found that they tended to produce a pure, holy, and peaceable frame of mind, but I found likewise that they disqualified a man for the duty of his calling. I could not even go to perform my duty in the church without finding something to disturb me. This made me conjecture that all was not right in Mr. Law's doctrine, and I conceive it to be this : that it is admirably suited for the contemplative but not for the active life of man, inasmuch as it does not bring the outward man into entire subjection to the inner man, for man has two lives, or two beings, in his very best state while on earth."

Speaking of regeneration, Mr. Clowes said he conceived the vision of Jacob's ladder to afford a beautiful figure on this subject, and that we should do well to consider that the descent was a much more difficult and arduous task than the ascent. The ascent was the desire of knowledge, or the love of truth, which made us climb the ladder, that we might know God and the things of His kingdom; but when we have reached the top of the ladder it will avail us nothing unless the love principle, or the love of good,

---

[1] Author of " Serious Call."

descend with us, penetrate to the very bottom of our hearts, and purge them of all unclean affections, so that the natural man should act under entire subordination to, and entire conjunction with, the spiritual man. Thus is the descent much more difficult than the ascent, as it is said, "And he dreamed, and behold a ladder set upon the earth, and the top of it reached to heaven, and behold the angels of God ascending and descending."

Asking him how we should know that we were in a safe state without deceiving ourselves, he said, " Let us carefully examine what is our delight. If our delight be in good, then may we certainly conclude that our state is safe, because all good is from God and the things of His kingdom."

When asked what he conceived to be the state of the blessed, he replied in a calm, but animated tone of voice, " I conceive the state of the blessed to be a total forgetfulness or absence of *self*, and to consist in beholding the good and happiness of others, so that every individual will enjoy the whole happiness of heaven." He afterwards said, " It was a principle in the old law, that if any man should kill his neighbour unawares, he might abide for a time in the ' City of Refuge.' This he conceived a beautiful figure to represent the mercy of God. We often engaged in action from a principle of good, but in the performance of it were overtaken unawares by some evil or uncharitable inclination. The good principle which at first operated was from God, and this is the city of refuge in which we may abide until the enemy which thwarted us is overcome." He added, " The state of man is a state of absolute dependence upon God, and the most desirable frame of mind is that in which the Psalmist saith, ' I am poor and needy, but the Lord careth for me."

Being asked what was meant by justifying faith, he said, " It is to be feared many deceive themselves in this matter. It is dangerous to rest our salvation on the bare belief of the death and sufferings of our Lord. That is indeed resting in the first attainments of religion. Belief enlightens the understanding, but it is love which regulates the affections and produces obedience to the commands of God, without which no man can enter into the kingdom of glory. Works are not in themselves meritorious, but as being tests of obedience, for without works the spiritual world would stagnate."

" I conceive," he said, " that the great evil of life arises from a contempt of others in comparison with self. A strict and resolute self-examination, therefore, and supplication for Divine assistance, will enable us to expel this evil, for evil affections must be expelled before we can receive good ones. Who would put lambs among wolves?"

On being asked if he thought fear and doubt of the favour of God consistent with true faith, he said, " Most certainly ; for it is impossible to arrive at any degree of favour with God but by the state of deep and sincere humiliation, which produces fear and doubt, and which proceeds from a clear conception of the beauty and holiness of the Lord's kingdom. This is, perhaps, the best state man can be in, because while he is under the influence of these fears he will be continually labouring to grow better, and be continually dependent on God for grace and favour. This is the cross which we must all bear if we would be followers of the Lamb and partakers of His kingdom. We are commanded not to resist evil, for the fierce and violent spirit of opposition which this resistance would demand is hurtful to us. When evil assailments come our only security is in our dependence upon God. He will give us strength to overcome evil, though we should perish in attempting to resist it. Every man is according to his own desire, for assuredly the Lord wills the good and happiness of all His creatures. If a man say he desires to be better, and that he is unhappy because his desire is not fulfilled, let not that man be impatient; he has begun to bear his cross, and if he bears it patiently, humbly waiting for a better state, he will certainly obtain his desire. The good he did, because he saw it was commanded, will soon be his delight; and to delight in good is the temper and disposition of angels."

I renewed my acquaintance with this truly pious and amiable man twenty years afterwards, when on a visit to Miss Kennedy at Manchester, in 1808. He was much beloved and honoured by the large congregation of St. John's Church, Manchester; and when he had been fifty years their rector, they erected in that church a marble tablet, with a design and inscription expressive of the affection of his flock towards him, and of their gratitude for his labours of love in the promotion of Sunday Schools, and in the moral and religious education of the poor. Soon afterwards he removed, on account of his state of health, to Warwick, where I saw him again in 1829. He told me that he was then in his 84th year,—employed in translating the Psalms from the Hebrew, and that his motive for such undertaking was "to control the activity of his thoughts, and to give them a profitable direction."

In the spring of 1789 my father allowed me to accompany Mr. and Mrs. Wright, of Lawton, in Perthshire (who had come to place their eldest daughter at school at York), to pay a second visit to my friend Mrs. Meliss, in the neighbourhood of Perth. On our way through Edinburgh I called on Mr. Fletcher at his lodgings in Parliament Square, along with Mr. and Mrs. Wright. His servant told us that he was at the General Assembly. We left our Edinburgh address,—Captain Inglis, George Square; and in the evening Mr. Fletcher joined us there, and accompanied us on horseback next morning part of the way to the Queen's Ferry, but was obliged to leave us to attend his duty in the General Assembly of the Church, of which he was an elder, and where he was then most warmly engaged in supporting the claims of Professor Dalzel to be Clerk of the Assembly. I meantime proceeded with Mr. and Mrs. Wright to Perth, and took up my residence again at the house of my friends Mr. and Mrs. Meliss, at their pleasant villa of Rosemount, near that place. My impressions of the hospitality, kindness, and superior information of the Scotch, in comparison with those of the same rank in England, were confirmed by my second visit to Scotland. As soon as his engagements admitted of his leaving Edinburgh, Mr. Fletcher came to pay a visit at Mr. Meliss's, and then the opportunity of conversing much together confirmed the attachment he had entertained for me from our first acquaintance in 1787, and converted the sentiments of respect and high esteem I had felt for him into those of a tenderer nature. I thought I had never met with a person of such real elevation of mind, and such independence and worth of character; and a happy union of thirty-seven years as his wife served to confirm me in that opinion. It was agreed that he should come to Harrogate in the autumn of that year, and from thence pay us a visit, when he had my permission to make his wishes known to my father. In the meantime we were to correspond as friends, as we had formerly done. His letters were always shown to my father; and perhaps a person much versed in the language of the heart might have discovered more in them than the lectures of a philosopher or the epistles of a friend. The autumn arrived, however, and the *éclaircissement* was made. My father positively opposed the union. We were willing to wait till he thought Mr. Fletcher's circumstances justified the prudence of it. But no!—my kind, fond, and hitherto most indulgent father had formed splendid expectations for the child on whom he doated. He could not think of parting with me to such a distance. He could not think of my marrying a man altogether without fortune, and where there was so great a disparity of years, —one, too, who had made no provision for a family. These were sound and rational objections. I admitted that they were so, and I promised to remain unmarried, but I felt that I had so far encouraged Mr. Fletcher's attachment, that I could not, either with honour to him or satisfaction to myself, marry any other person. I was not, perhaps, what in the language of romance is called in love with Mr. Fletcher, but I was deeply and tenderly attached to him. He had inspired a confidence and regard I had never felt for any other man. I could not bear the thought of marrying in opposition to my father's will, but I was resolved on principle never to marry so long as Mr. Fletcher remained single. This did not satisfy my father. For the first time in his life he was unjust; he attempted to effect that by authority which he had failed to accomplish by reason and kindness. He became stern and severe in his conduct towards me. This produced its necessary consequence, evasion and concealment. I received Mr. Fletcher's letters clandestinely. I was decidedly wrong in doing so, but either I must have sacrificed Mr. Fletcher's happiness without satisfying my father's prejudices, or I must have continued the correspondence. I chose the latter, with the sincere intention of prevailing on Mr. Fletcher to give up the engagement, for it would then have been less painful to me to have done so than to have offended my father. But I was unacquainted with the history of the human heart; at the end of two years I found that Mr. Fletcher had reasoned me into a conviction that it would be best for the interest and happiness of all parties that we should marry; that my father's objections, though quite natural, were not founded in truth and justice, since he had nothing to object to in Mr. Fletcher's character or position in society.

In the winter of 1789-90 I paid a visit to a friend at Ripon,—Mrs. Harrison,—and there became acquainted with Lord Grantley. He was then, I should think, bordering on fifty, a man of insinuating address and of cultivated taste and accomplishments. He distinguished me by marked attention, invited my father to accompany me to visit him and his mother at Grantley, and showed me a preference, which, had my heart been untouched and my faith unpledged, might, by flattering my vanity, have made some impression on my heart. But happily I had nothing of the coquette in my disposition, and the attentions of this nobleman, though flattering, were indifferent to me. I had, besides, no good opinion of his moral character, and in all the partialities and friendships I have had in life, either towards my own sex or the other, I never could found friendship on anything but solid esteem and moral approbation. I might be pleased or amused with, but I could not like, far less love, any one I did not thoroughly respect. Report and gossip, even so far as paragraphs in newspapers, gave my hand to Lord Grantley. Certainly he never asked me to do so in words; his attentions were always delicate and respectful. He visited me frequently at my father's house, but I took care to save his pride by requesting a mutual friend,—Dr. Kilvington,—to acquaint him with my engagement to Mr. Fletcher. From that time his visits to my father's house were discontinued: Mr. Fletcher was made acquainted by me with every visit this noble person paid me; and I believe it was owing to my virtuous attachment to him that I was saved from sacrificing my happiness to a splendid but miserable fate.

Lord Grantley might, or he might not, have had serious intentions to make me an offer of marriage. Had I been free, it is possible that the vanity of my character might have led me to encourage his addresses. I never did so, however, but I perceived that my dear father was gratified to see me so distinguished ; and though he would never have consented to sacrifice me to a bad man, of any rank, had he known him to be such, he could scarcely persuade himself that one of that condition, who preferred his daughter, could be undeserving. My excellent aunt, and my attached friend, Mrs. Brudenell, pleaded my cause and Mr. Fletcher's with my father : still he remained inexorable. My health began to suffer from the alienation of my father's confidence and kindness. My home was no longer cheerful or happy. Since he would not be satisfied with my remaining unmarried, all my hope now was in his becoming reconciled to my marriage to one, whom I was sure he would find worthy of my confidence,—and on the 16th of July 1791 I became the wife of Mr. Fletcher.

[The marriage ceremony took place in Tadcaster church, and though her father did not sanction it by his presence, he did not on that day refuse a loving farewell to his child, nor did he refuse to see the husband to whom she had given herself with a rightly assured heart. "Be kind to her, sir, she has been tenderly brought up," were his parting words to him, as aunt Dawson used to tell us. Never were words lodged in a more faithful heart, or acted on more tenderly.]

And here (our mother continues, after giving the date of her marriage) I am inclined to review the circumstances which had hitherto formed my character. My mother having died soon after giving me birth, that event gave a melancholy interest to my life from its very commencement. I became an object of the concentrated affections of all the family, and this acted in two ways—as a great stimulus to the desire of approbation and as a powerful means of cultivating the kindly affections. I became early acquainted with the happiness of being tenderly beloved, and was reared and nourished by the "law of kindness." I was wholly governed by that law, and knew no other authority. I had no temptation to violate truth, because I was treated with openness and justice, but so great was my fear of giving offence, that I remember, at four years old, to have pinned on the head of a beautiful tulip which I had inadvertently broken, and instead of frankly acknowledging the mischief I had done, I tried artfully to conceal it. My father's stern reproof at this little instance of deception and concealment made a deep impression on my mind. It was the first time I had done anything to forfeit his confidence, or to feel the disgrace of having acted a lie. The excessive pain his displeasure gave me, and the degradation of being convicted of meanness, made me thenceforward ready to confess my faults, and I was rewarded with the praise I dearly loved for being open and ingenuous. My religious education in childhood was simple and impressive. I was early taught to love God because He was good, and to desire to be good myself that I might not offend Him. My father's scriptural maxim, and that which he considered the test of religion as well as morals, was " to do to others as we would be done unto." This sacred axiom formed my only code of morals. My father's life was an illustration of this principle. Much as I was praised, indulged, and excited, I never was suffered to domineer over or to act unjustly or unkindly towards others ; and I do think that the selfish passions were early curbed and brought into subjection by the example as well as precepts of those I lived with. As I was an object of much tenderness and affection, so nature and education gave me an affectionate and grateful disposition. I remember my

D

friend, Dr. Kilvington, in writing to me once said, " I have known as beautiful, as attractive, and more witty young women, but I have never known any one so tenderly, and truly, and universally beloved as you are, and I believe it arises from your capacity of loving others." I had nothing satirical in my disposition, no wish to detract from, or to see others mortified. I had little merit in this, having, as I said before, no very quick perception of the ludicrous. I was sufficiently vain of my own good qualities, and sufficiently blinded by self-love to the defects of my own character; but this did not lessen my respect for, or admiration of, the excellence of others. I never was tormented with any of the passions that belong to "the family of hatred." I was too easily provoked to anger, but it was momentary, and I almost instantly sought reconciliation when I had given offence. I had not been brought up in the school of fashion, which so sadly hardens the heart and limits the understanding. The great error of my education was, that it excited too great a desire of general approbation. This led to something like a love of display, and it cost me much in after life to conquer the mischief of this propensity. Mrs. Brudenell early culti-vated in me a high-toned and poetical turn of mind, and if vanity was mixed up with this feeling, it saved me from the vice of gossiping, from the love of finery, and other vulgar propensities. I had been a happy and indulged child in my father's house. I was going to enter on a new and a wider sphere of duties. When leisure serves I will endeavour to set down faithfully how they were performed.

[*From Mr. Fletcher, explanatory how Eliza Dawson acquired the name of Sophia in April* 1787:—

" From repeated observation of the character of my own mind, I think it is distinguished by some contradictions. Not incapable of submitting to dull and dry studies, it can also travel with delight, even with romantic wildness, into the fields of fancy and imagination. No young lady with the warmest imagination ever read plays or novels with more pleasure or more avidity than I have always done, and still do. I take the keenest interest in the ideal characters I like, and conceive the hottest resentment against those whose manners I disapprove. I am, in fact, agitated in the same manner as if I were acquainted and concerned with such persons in transactions in common life.

"In 1779 or 1780 I was confined for many weeks to the house. I spent my time partly in reading novels. Among these there fell into my hands, I think for the first time, the beautiful novel of 'Tom Jones,' by Fielding. I was struck with its variety of incident, its striking delineation of character, and its inimitable manner of describing the secret springs of human conduct. Sophia was too beautiful and too brilliant a figure not to attract in a most peculiar manner my attention. I was astonished. Sophia, painted by the inimitable pencil of Fielding, was just the woman I desired to see. She was in every respect so. Her person, her manners, her sentiments, her disposition, were such as it was impossible not to admire. She never uttered a thought of which I did not cordially approve, nor disclosed a passion with which I did not instantly sympathize, and her manner of saying and doing everything was unspeakably graceful; the more surprising, too, that she never appeared to have been away from the house of her father, a country gentleman. In this lady, from almost the first moment I was introduced to her acquaintance, I took the warmest interest. I was perfectly uneasy when she was out of sight. I passed over parts of the book until I came to those parts where I was to be introduced to her company. In short, I loved Sophia with sincerity, and although I am ashamed almost to confess it, as it seems so ridiculously romantic, yet the truth is that this ideal Sophia made so deep an impression on my imagination that it never was effaced till the second or third day of my visit (I know not yet whether to call it fatal or fortunate visit) at Oxton, in April 1787 ; and since you have desired me to tell why I have given you the name of

Sophia, you must excuse me if I relate the time and manner in which you completely erased from my mind every trace and impression of the ideal Sophia, who had been so long the object of my adoration, but whose place you have ever since occupied with additional advantages.

" You know I set out on my journey from Scotland to London in 1787, in company with your amiable friends, the Melisses of Perth, at a time when I was ignorant that such a person as Eliza Dawson existed in the world, far less that she was so very dangerous a personage as I have since found her to be. In the course of our journey I heard my agreeable fellow-travellers often mention the name of Eliza Dawson, with expressions of peculiar regard and esteem, but without saying anything of her person or accomplishments.   I therefore paid little or no attention to the conversation, so far as respected her, and expecting to meet with nothing at Oxton (for I had on the road learned the name) that could either amuse or inform, I was extremely unwilling to go there at all, being very impatient to push forward to London.   Besides the pressing nature of our business, which was urgent and important, London —a new and great scene—presented to my imagination the strongest inducements to despatch.   I proposed to Meliss that I should wait at the inn at Tadcaster, or some other place, until he should leave Mrs. Meliss at Oxton, and that we should proceed to London as soon as possible ; but Meliss then told me, I think for the first time, that he intended to make a stay of some days at Oxton.   I was surprised, and not a little displeased, at this unexpected interruption.   However I resolved, though with reluctance, to accompany my friends to Oxton, but not in the best humour.   As I am rather irritable than sour, it soon went off, I believe before we reached Oxton, at least I am sure it did not continue long after.   Mrs. Brudenell was there at tea ; she was the person who first engaged my attention ; her frankness was uncommon, and soon removed any little remains of discontent I had felt at being stopped in my progress towards the metropolis.   I knew the reserve of the Scotch character, I had heard much of the open frankness of the English ; Mrs. Brudenell, I thought, proved it to be true, and I was pleased without being surprised.   Before I was an hour or two in the house I knew, I think, from this lady herself, a great part of her history, though it was rather peculiar. For a long time she exclusively, or almost exclusively, occupied my attention and conversation. When she was gone (for I think she went away before supper), or when her discourse was exhausted, I had time to observe Miss Dawson, of whom, I think, I had not before taken the least notice, unless by once or twice glancing towards her, which produced no effect but a pretty strong curiosity to be better acquainted with her. We exchanged some words ; without any skill in physiognomy or pretending to apply its rules, I was soon prepossessed. The conversation proceeded. Miss Eliza gradually unfolded herself ; she riveted my attention more completely than Mrs. Brudenell had done. I listened with greater surprise and pleasure. I soon discovered in a beautiful form an elegance of mind and sentiment, and an easy gracefulness of manner, which I thought were not natural to the little village of Oxton. I began to be interested in Eliza ; I felt a very particular desire to sit beside her at supper, and I think I contrived to do it. I was still more and more pleased with her manner and conversation. Her easy affability was such that I think we were tolerably well acquainted before supper was done. Nothing could be more pleasing to me than Eliza's frankness—nothing more delightful than her elegant turn of manner and conversation, and the peculiar intelligence by which it was conducted. 'There is,' I said to myself, 'something very uncommon about this girl ; I wonder Meliss never spoke of her in a more particular manner.' When the ladies retired after supper I felt an uneasy sensation, as if I had been deprived of something which contributed extremely to the pleasure of the company. I could not enjoy the company afterwards, though in any other circumstances it would, I think, have been agreeable, for it was distinguished by every mark of politeness and hospitality. Meliss went with me into my room, on which I instantly turned and said, rather peevishly (though surely that was absurd), 'Meliss, why did you never speak of Miss Dawson in a more particular manner on our journey ? or did you never discover anything superior about her ?' Meliss laughed, and said he believed Mrs. Meliss wanted to surprise me. 'If that was her object,' said I, ' it is completely accomplished, for I never was more surprised in my lifetime.'   Meliss again laughed, and maliciously asked me whether I wished to be off for London next morning.   I bid him go to his bed, and I should think of that after I had slept.

"I awoke next morning without the least desire to leave Oxton. My impatience to be in London was greatly diminished.   A few days sooner or later, I thought, did not signify much, and the state of our public business, though it was pressing, did not require absolutely that we should be in London on a precise day.   All the anticipated enjoyments of London vanished.   I became quite reconciled to a longer residence at Oxton.   My only anxiety now was to see Eliza again in the morning, and I felt an irresistible desire to place myself beside her at breakfast.   She appeared to still more advantage ; I was indeed charmed.   When breakfast was about over and I took a view of Eliza's form, manner, and conversation, the character of Sophia Western instantly flashed on my mind.   The resemblance was in every feature striking.   I began from that moment to lose sight entirely of the ideal Sophia who had so long figured in my imagination, and to transfer the name, for which I had so peculiar a fondness, to Eliza Dawson.   I mentioned the circumstance to Meliss.   I baptized Eliza by the name of Sophia, to which I had ascribed every amiable quality.   The more I became acquainted with Eliza, the more I was convinced of the truth of the resemblance between the two characters.   I grew quite uneasy when Eliza was not present : I was unhappy if I did not sit beside her at table. The mind of Eliza every day gradually and occasionally unfolded itself with peculiar force as well as elegance.   If I had found brilliants on the wild and rugged mountains among which I first drew my breath, I could not have been more surprised and delighted than I was by meeting such a person as Eliza. ' Fielding,' said I, ' you have drawn your heroine, it must be confessed, with a fine pencil, but here is in real life, at a little country village, a character every way equal, in some respects far superior.   Without saying anything of external form, the mental accomplishments of Eliza Dawson are above those of the amiable and intelligent Sophia Western.   You seem to

think, Fielding, that knowledge of books is no ornament to a
woman ; but had you known Eliza Dawson, you would have
altered your opinion.   She would "have taught you how
compatible literary acquirements are with the most engaging
feminine manners, and when so blended you would have seen
how much they must contribute both to the ornament and
the happiness of life.'"   Such were my sentiments of Eliza
Dawson, early adopted, and since confirmed by indubitable
experience.

"Every hour of my residence at Oxton increased my esteem
for Eliza Dawson.   I could not endure to call her by any other
name than that of Sophia, so deeply fixed in my imagination
was the resemblance between her and the ideal Sophia, with
the advantage every way on her side.   One incident had, ·
however, one day piqued me not a little.   I had been pretty
free of my censures on Pope's Translation of Homer, which
unluckily had been a favourite with Sophia, but she listened
with at least apparent satisfaction to what I had said.   Some
time afterwards, during our residence at Oxton, on conversing
with Meliss on the subject of my criticisms on Pope, Meliss,
without any design I believe, mentioned that Sophia, in
allusion to my criticisms, had observed that some people were
very ill to please, and made criticisms merely to show that they
could make them, or something of that kind.   I was, I confess,
seriously offended by this remark of Sophia, to whose good
sense and clear intelligence I had meant to pay a compliment
by entering at all on such a subject, but I said nothing to
Meliss about my taking Sophia's observation ill.   I, however,
positively determined never to make to her another observation
of the same or a similar kind, and to keep a profound silence
and reserve, and to converse as little as possible with Sophia
during the remainder of my stay at Oxton.   In this resolution
I thought myself fixed and unalterable, but I no sooner saw
Sophia than it was violated, and I conversed with her with as
much openness and as little reserve as ever.   I was surprised at
my weakness, but could not help it ; and every trace of my
resentment was effaced by Sophia's sitting beside me almost the
whole night of Mrs. Brudenell's concert at the cottage.   It is
amazing how easily the imagination embraces what one wishes

to be true.   I thought Sophia took some satisfaction in being with me rather than with any other, but I immediately checked this idea by asking myself how weak it was to mistake a mere mark of polite attention to a stranger for a partiality which could not exist.   I, however, sincerely declare I was *so* happy, that I thought I never could wish to separate from Oxton. But the hour now approached when I perceived I must leave it, with whatever reluctance.   Sophia accompanied us to the coach, and in going there, I know not by what accident or power of sympathy, but we certainly walked arm in arm—a little circumstance which increased beyond measure my reluctance at leaving Oxton.   When we arrived at the coach, and I contrasted the form and manner of Sophia with a female figure to whose company I saw we must for some time be sacrificed, I own I was shocked.   I could scarcely think them of the same species.   I was mortified beyond measure when I sat down in the coach—my change of situation was too sudden and too violent.

"Misery, however, is often ingenious in relieving itself.   I soon learned—I know not how—that Meliss had got Sophia's watch to get repaired in London.   I immediately seized on the watch as the only representative or substitute for Sophia I could have, and gave Meliss mine.   This watch of Sophia's was my darling companion by day and night;   in the possession of it I took the most extreme delight, and kept it the whole time, except when I was reluctantly obliged to part with it, to send to the watchmaker.   When I was possessed of it I felt, I thought, some connexion between Sophia and me. It is astonishing what trivial circumstances affection will lay hold of to gratify itself.   Stripped of this watch, I really knew not what to do, how to get anything belonging to Sophia, or how to begin a correspondence with her, without which I felt I could not be happy.   I resolved to make her a present of Ossian's Poems, in the view of giving rise to some correspondence.   What has followed since, Sophia is acquainted with, and I need not repeat it.   It depends on her whether I am . to be rendered for ever happy or miserable by that visit at Oxton which gave her the name of Sophia, a name to which I own I am still partial, because I know no other word that

brings so forcibly and so clearly before me the accomplishments
and perfections of Eliza Dawson.   A. F."

I cannot resist inserting parts of two letters to my father
before their marriage, in the same year in which it took place
(1791), as marking the entire confidence and trust she placed
in the man who had won her affections by the depth and
constancy of his own.   The old-fashioned mode of speaking of
herself as Sophia, the name he gave her after their first meeting
in 1787, is sometimes kept up in the correspondence of four
years' continuance.   This letter is dated January 1791.

"Sunday Morning.

" Having put me in possession of your religious sentiments,
and of your opinion that nothing but a life of active faith and
obedience can assure to us the blessings of eternity, you will
think, perhaps, the circumstance Sophia was led to mention
at the beginning of this letter savours something of Romish
superstition, as on perusing it herself, Sophia really thinks it
appears that she was arrogating to herself the monkish office
of absolution.   As she believes that is the very last character
her friend would wish her to assume, she is desirous of explaining the motives that carry her every day to the bedside of the
dying woman she mentioned, and as often to read to her the
evangelical writings.

" This poor woman is above eighty ; her character in early
life is said not to have been immaculate.   However, about seven
years ago, she came, laden with infirmities, to ask relief from
this parish (to which she belongs), and was accordingly sent
to the town workhouse.   She fell sick about six weeks ago,
and has no friend or relation near.   This circumstance accidentally came to my knowledge, and I went to see her, and
found her in a nice clean bed, in a very comfortable little room
(for, to the credit of this place, the poor-house is admirably
conducted) ; an old woman had been hired to attend her.   ' I
want nothing, madam, that money can furnish ; but I am on
my deathbed, and I have not *one* creature in the world that
cares for me.   I have endeavoured to make my peace with God
and my Saviour, but I want somebody to read to me ; *I want*

a comforter.' These, my dear friend, were her very words, uttered in a voice scarcely audible. Every day since I have read to her those parts of Scripture where 'The Comforter' is promised, and the mercy of God to the repentant sinner is most fully revealed and manifested. Did you see how she stretches her withered arm to put by the bed-curtain when she hears me open the door—how she points to the Bible that lies on a chest of drawers near the bedside, then points to a chair, which Sophia draws close to the bed, then listens while she reads slowly and distinctly, and, without speaking a single word, when any passage strikes her, raises her hand quietly, an impulse of devotion which Sophia observes and always repeats the passage—did you see all this, my dear friend, and perceive how hope brightens her countenance, marred as it is by the hand of death, you would, I know, for such a scene, relinquish almost every other that imagination can conceive to give comfort here. She told me to-day, in a whisper, she had no fear of death, and added, 'You have indeed comforted me.' I promised to see her every day while she lived, and the last word I heard her utter was a blessing on me, raising herself a little in bed, and putting by the bed-curtain to see me as long as she was able. My dearest friend, what a tale is this to relate to a profound politician and a learned lawyer! but *my* politician has a heart and a mind which I value above all his profundity and all his learning, for he has a heart and mind that can feel an interest in every story where Nature and simplicity form a part, and, above all, wherein his Sophia is concerned."

" This moment I have come from performing my evening service in the kitchen, reading and explaining to the servants the words of Christ. I find the parlour empty, the good folks having all adjourned to our father's apartment, and this leaves me leisure to converse with you on paper. I am never more disposed for this gratification than when I have been discharging an important duty : the delightful impression this leaves upon my mind never fails to make me more sensible of the happiness of loving and being beloved by you. I have felt this very forcibly and very often, without inquiring into the cause, as, on the other hand, I reproach myself much more severely for every fault that I commit than I used to do, prior to our unequalled attachment. What a preservative, or rather what an incentive to virtue is such an attachment; it is composed of sentiments that have exalted us above ourselves— I say above ourselves, for we should never have known what we were capable of, we should have remained ignorant of ourselves, if we had not known each other. We have, if you will allow me the expression, been mirrors to each other. Had we formed other connexions we possibly might have glided through life like common lovers and fashionable married people, and have been totally unacquainted with our own extensive capacity for disinterested friendship, and deep and delicate affection. You would have continued mounted on your hobby-horse, and have loved fame better than your wife. My character was far less decided, I think,—as Pope says, 'I had no character at all,'—before I knew you, therefore it is hard to say how I should have turned out.———I am interrupted—and I find this interruption has broken the thread of my story.

"The only conclusion we can deduce from the above is, that no two persons were ever so happily destined for each other.

"E. D."

Part of Letter to Miss Cleaver, afterwards Mrs. Chapman.

". . . . You tell me never to expect a regular letter, and complain you are 'tasteless and uninteresting to yourself.' I am certain you can find no other person to whom you are uninteresting, and least of all to me, so write to me often, and give *me* leave to judge whether or not your letters are insipid. Dear Nanny, you were formed for activity and exertion, and you suffer your powers to lie confined and dormant. I send you a little book, simply written, from which, I think, more real benefit may be deduced, both to yourself and others, than from ten thousand folio pages of subtle disputations and philosophical reasonings: such authors are read and admired; their precepts in theory are excellent; but Mrs. Trimmer recommends a practical system, which, if persevered in with ardour, will effectually prevent you from feeling 'uninteresting to yourself.' She drives away *ennui* by teaching you to become a truly useful member of society. I declare to you I speak from conviction. I used to substitute sentiment for activity ; and though I had a silent gratification in the indulgence of my feelings, I was not happy. 'The Economy of Charity' pointed out to me an easy method of being useful to others, and I of course became more important to myself, and therefore happier ; for nothing is more necessary to happiness than a certain portion of self-importance. All this you know as well as I can tell you, only I can affirm that I can speak from experience. If possible, continue personally to interest yourself with your little flock, and contriving schemes for their improvement : if they never answer, the disappointment won't give you so much pain as the conception gave you pleasure. I know you too well, and have known you too long, to be deceived. With a heart so susceptible, and a mind so sanguine, you cannot exist without exertion. There are few people I should write to in this manner, because few people are like you. If this letter is welcome to you, write next week and tell me so.—Yours, ELIZA DAWSON."

Inscribed on a blank leaf of Lavater's Work sent to Eliza Dawson by Mr. Cartwright.

When on Eliza's face I fix my sight,
That living page I read with most delight,
I ask thee not, Lavater, to impart
The rules fallacious of thy idle art.
Without thy aid, untutored, there I find
Each perfect trace of her inspiring mind ;
There Wit and Fancy's rays united shine,
And Sense and Genius mark each varied line ;
There Taste and quick Intelligence appear—
Intelligence as intuition clear.
Nor less the moral features can I trace
In the sweet lines of that expressive face.
How rich the radiance of that bright expanse !
Where every virtue beams in every glance—
Affections such as angels feel reside—
Soft without weakness ; firm, yet free from pride.

There, too, see sensibility of soul,
Enchanting grace diffusing o'er the whole,
That, scorning dull cold Apathy's disguise,
Glows in her cheek and sparkles in her eyes.
What explanation, say then, can I need
Of characters that he who runs may read ?
Yet this I'll own—could thy pretended skill
In prompt obedience to my ardent will,
Instruct me how to read her inmost heart,
Provided there in some dear tender part
My favoured name, by Love's soft trembling hand
Imprinted deep, were suffered to expand,
Then, then indeed, thy art would I adore,
And freely own, while every doubt was o'er,
Thy visionary dream derived from Heaven,
" And, though no science, fairly worth the seven."]

PART II.[1]

It has pleased God in His great mercy to bring me to my sixty-eighth birthday, and I am now writing in that cottage in my native village which was for some years inhabited by my aunt, Mrs. Fretwell, opposite to the house in which sixty-eight years ago I first drew breath, and where for eighteen years this day was annually celebrated as a day of rejoicing amongst friends and neighbours. All the merry-makers of those days are now in the grave except my aunt, Miss Hill, now in her eighty-sixth year, and myself, now well stricken in years; and the house is empty and desolate and falling into decay. It will be half a century next April since we left it.

My marriage day, the 16th of July 1791, was one of the most sorrowful of my life. The pang of parting from my father and all my family had almost broken my heart, but I was not of a morbid temperament. Youth and hope, and affectionate confidence in my husband, soon reconciled me to the separation. I was received by Mr. Fletcher's circle of friends in Edinburgh with a warmth of hospitality and kindness I had never before met with among strangers. Each vied with the other who should show most kindness to the young bride of their friend. An English stranger, too, was at that time (nearly fifty years since) a novelty in Edinburgh compared with what it is now. Our circle was not wide, or fashionable, or highly polished, but it was intelligent and warm-hearted.

[1] Our mother's continuation of her domestic memorials in her own handwriting is dated Oxton Cottage, January 15th, 1838.

[The following letter, preserved by our mother's early friend, Mrs. Laycock, to whom it was addressed about a month after her marriage and arrival in Edinburgh, gives happy testimony, then and there, to the cheering influences which awaited her, both in and out of her new home. It tells, too, what it was in these which cheered her most—the true and kindly estimation in which she found her husband held, and his tender consideration for her, not only as a wife, but as a daughter. He had never allowed himself to feel resentment for her father's opposition to his suit, always admitting that, in so far as worldly considerations went, it was natural and reasonable. There can be no doubt that this generous forbearance in him advanced his cause in her heart, making her the more steadfast during the trying period of her engagement, and strengthening her as to the rightness of fulfilling it.

To Mrs. Laycock.

"EDINBURGH, *August* 1791.

"You have known me long enough to find out that my hopes were always extremely sanguine; yet believe me, I had formed no conception of the happiness I have enjoyed, and continue to enjoy, in the society of my husband; nor could I have conceived that tenderness was so ingenious, for he absolutely contrives to be continually giving me new and additional proofs of his affection. In addition to the attentions which constitute my happiness, I have the satisfaction of seeing his character universally esteemed, and his talents universally respected. Without troubling himself about the selection of society, he seems to be acquainted with none but good people, for he has so nice a sense of honour, and cares so little about any distinctions but those which arise from character, that persons of unsound principles must feel uneasy with him. The concern he feels on account of my father's illness affects me very sensibly. He is very sanguine in the hope of some benefit arising from the prescriptions of the Edinburgh physicians. I wish my friends at Tadcaster could have seen the eagerness with which he convened the medical men upon that occasion; I wish it because I think it would have given them a better knowledge of his character than they could receive from any other circumstance, especially the representation of a wife."

Our mother's written reminiscences thus go on to tell of two persons among the friend-circle of her past years in Edinburgh, who were indeed no common ones.]

Chance placed me in the neighbourhood, in Hill Street, of an Ayrshire family, the Fergussons of Monkwood;[1] and Miss Fergusson, the eldest daughter, became the earliest, as she has always been the firmest and fondest, of my Edinburgh friends. Mrs. John Craig Millar, the young wife of an advocate,[2] an intimate friend of my husband, soon fascinated me with the brilliancy of her talents and the charms of her conversation. She was the youngest daughter of the celebrated Dr. Cullen. Her father's house was for many years the resort of all the men of talent and literature in Edinburgh, and of many women of rank and fashion. David Hume, the historian; Adam Smith, author of "The Wealth of Nations;" Black, the celebrated chemist; Henry Mackenzie (often called, from' his well-known book, " The Man of Feeling"), were frequent visitors at Mrs. J. C. Millar's early home, at the foot of the Mint Close, Canongate, where Dr. Cullen then lived; and in their society his highly-gifted family had acquired a taste for all that was intellectual and refined. Mrs. Millar had singular quickness of parts, with great sweetness of disposition and elegance of manners. We became intimate friends, and our sympathy in the political sentiments of our husbands was a great bond between us. At this time, 1791 and 1792, the grand principles of the French Revolution occupied the thoughts and stirred the passions of all thinking and feeling men. Mr. Fletcher

---

[1] At Mr. Fergusson's house where Walter Scott was intimate, my mother often met him in her early married life ; he did appear in the drawing-room in those days, which very few did.

[2] Eldest son of Professor Millar, of the Glasgow University, author of some works of well-earned repute.

was an ardent admirer of the first principles of that revolution. He loved liberty from an enlarged sense of philanthropy, not out of party spirit, but because he firmly believed that a free government was the only means of promoting national improvement and happiness. He had devoted the last ten years of his life to obtaining for Scotland that borough reform which he conceived would lead to Parliamentary reform, and to the emancipation of Scotland from that vile system of irresponsible municipal government, and Parliamentary corruption, which disgraced and depressed it, and made it a by-word among its English neighbours. This feeling was so strong in my husband's mind that it might be called his master-passion. I believe he would have gone to the block in defence of his political principles as cheerfully as any martyr that ever bled in that good cause. But his sound judgment tempered his enthusiasm, and prevented his ever doing any rash or foolish thing. He never did that which he feared to avow. He was solicited in the winter of 1792, by the celebrated Thomas Muir, to join the Society of the "Friends of the People." I remember Mr. Muir's calling on him one evening in Hill Street, and I heard them at high words in an adjoining room. When his visitor went away, Mr. Fletcher told me that Muir had quitted him much dissatisfied because he could not persuade him to join the Society. Mr. Fletcher added—"I believe him to be an honest enthusiast, but he is an ill-judging man. These violent reformers will create such an alarm in the country as must strengthen the Government. The country is not prepared to second their views of annual Parliaments and universal suffrage."

The country did become exceedingly alarmed, as he predicted, and the subsequent atrocities committed in France by an unprincipled faction,—the worst enemies of liberty,—produced such a horror (amongst the higher orders especially) in Scotland, that every man was considered a rebel in his heart who did not take a decided part in supporting Tory measures of government. Mr. Fletcher, however, kept firm to his Whig principles. Though abstractedly he admired Republicanism, and wished that form of government to have fair play in America, he did not by any means desire the subversion of the British Constitution at home. He was a staunch reformer, not a revolutionist. At that time, however, and for several years afterwards, such was the terror of Liberal principles in Scotland that no man at the Bar professing these could expect a fair share of practice. There being no juries in civil cases, it was supposed that the judges would not decide in favour of any litigant who employed Whig lawyers. Mr. Fletcher always treated this opinion with scorn, as a foul calumny against the Scottish judges, though he suffered under it, being told by some sincere friends that under such an impression they dared not employ him as their advocate. We were often at that time reduced to our last guinea; but such was my sympathy in my husband's public feelings that I remember no period in my married life happier than that, in which we suffered for conscience' sake.

A great happiness occurred to us in the summer of 1792. This was a visit from my dear father, my good aunt Dawson, and Mrs. Brudenell. That my father should come and see with his own eyes how much my husband was honoured in his own place and country, and how happy I was in my new relationship, had been the height of my hopes and wishes. Soon, indeed, this happiness was increased by the birth of my eldest son, Miles Angus Fletcher, which took place on the 6th of September 1792. In the following spring we took our beautiful boy to cheer his grandfather in Yorkshire, and after his weaning I left him there; while later in that year (1793) I accompanied Mr. Fletcher to pay his mother a visit at his early home among the "Braes of Rannoch," after passing some weeks at the hospitable house of Mr. Fletcher, of Dunans, in Argyleshire.

We proceeded from thence to Rannoch, in Perthshire, where my mother-in-law lived with her second husband, Mr. Macdiarmid, a true-bred Celt, who disdained to speak a word of the Sasenach tongue, or to wear any dress but the philabeg and belted plaid. She was a devout and gentle-hearted woman, refined by the purity and depth of her religious feelings. She claimed hereditary descent from a certain renowned Highland chieftain, M'Naughton, known as the "Black Knight of Loch-Awe." He was hereditary keeper of the King's castles before the Campbells had established themselves in that district. But she allowed no pride in this alliance with Highland chieftainship to make her forget her duty to God and her neighbour. The parish of Rannoch was perhaps thirty miles in extent. On a Sunday she used to convene her unlettered neighbours, the tacksmen and the cottars' families, on the shady side of a hill, and there translate aloud for them portions of the English Bible into Gaelic. They came to her in all their troubles and difficulties, for she was a woman of strong understanding and admirable temper. She twice became the second wife of men who had families by their first marriages. She had six children by her first, and five, I think, by her second husband, and these four families of children lived under her maternal government in perfect harmony with one another. She loved my husband, the eldest child of her first marriage, with pride and fondness. She had bestowed all his little patrimony on his education, and from the age of sixteen he had worked out his own honourable independence, and had besides done much to help his family. She had, at the time I first saw her, when between seventy and eighty, resigned all household cares to her widowed daughter-in-law, Mrs. John Macdiarmid, but she was treated with respect and deference by all who approached her; and, though living in a simple farm-house, she and her old Celtic spouse (known by the name of Baron Macdiarmid, an old patronymic of the Highlands, which survived the possession of departed lands) dwelt in ease and comfort, on an extensive sheep farm, then tenanted by the widow of her son.

I had then never seen a state of society so primitive as that at Rannoch. My husband and I were cherished guests there, and it would have said little for my heart if I had not loved and honoured the good old lady who at once took me into her warmest affections.

Soon after our return to Edinburgh from the Highland visit, my good uncle, Mr. William Dawson, and my cousin, Miss Dawson, of Wighill, brought us home our darling boy. He walked stoutly, though but one year and a week old.

In the spring of 1794 my father made us a present of an excellent house in Queen Street, No. 20, and came down himself in the summer with my aunt and Mrs. Brudenell to spend a month or two with us. His little grandson, Miles, was now able to talk to him, and such was his delight in looking on this child that I could not find in my heart to refuse his request to take him along with them when they left us. I think my dear father enjoyed his second visit to Edinburgh even more than his first. He saw me surrounded with many blessings. He enjoyed the pleasant house he had given us to live in. He received much respect and attention from all Mr. Fletcher's friends. He saw that I had confided my happiness to one most deserving. On leaving us, he and Mrs. Brudenell took Miles with them to Tadcaster, and my good aunt remained to be with me at my second confinement, which took place on the 31st of October 1794, when my eldest daughter, Elizabeth, was born.

Not many days after her birth the newspapers were full of the proceedings on the State trials in London—the trial of Thomas Hardy and John Horne Tooke, etc. etc., for high treason—and the joyful news reached us that these persecuted men were acquitted by a jury of their countrymen. Mr. Fletcher considered this verdict as the noblest proof of the excellence of the British Constitution. Had the juries of England truckled to the Tory Government of the time, as those of Scotland had unhappily done in the convictions of Muir, Joseph Gerald, Fysche Palmer, etc. etc., he thought that Great Britain would not have been a country for a free man to live in, because not one in which a man could fearlessly avow his sentiments on political subjects. This assertion of the right of private judgment in matters of State policy being established by the glorious acquittal of Hardy and Horne Tooke, put hope and confidence into the hearts of all true and honest reformers.

My husband read at my bedside the very interesting details of these trials, and so highly did I sympathize in his delight that the excitement was followed by a sharp attack of fever, and newspapers, juries' verdicts, and all triumphs of Liberal opinions were for a time interdicted to the lady in the straw, who had a somewhat tedious confinement. I was able, however, to suckle my lovely infant, as I had done her elder brother, and this privilege was amongst my most cherished maternal duties. I was a good nurse in the true sense of the word, never denying my infant its natural food, night or day when called for. I never allowed any other occupation or amusement to interfere with this first claim of duty. My child grew and prospered, my home was happy. Political animosity around us was increased by the bitter disappointment of the Tory party, but this never cooled the friendship between Miss Fergusson and me, and her gentle spirit was often brave in defending me against the aspersions of political rancour.

[It is hardly possible to credit now, save as having been uttered in jest, the things gravely said and as gravely believed at that time in Edinburgh concerning those who were generally held to be on the wrong side in politics. That our mother had provided herself with a small guillotine, and exercised the same in beheading poultry, or perhaps " rats and mice and such small deer," in order to be expert when " French principles," and practice in accordance, should prevail in our land, was one of these. It reached our father's amazed and amused ears by the question asked him in sad earnest by a kindly old Highland clergyman (when in Edinburgh on the business of the General Assembly), whether it was possible that a lady he so much respected could be so " awfully misled"? We can well believe that Miss Fergusson had often to defend her friend against grievous aspersions in those days ; but this was not the only service gratefully numbered as fruit of the intimate communion which then and long afterwards they enjoyed with one another. It was from her, above all others, that our mother found the sympathy she needed in those deep religious affections, which were never warmer in her than in days of gladness,—from her that she most gained that living support to her Christian faith and hope, to be had only from one whose friend-love, like all the other blessed uses of her "charity," came "out of a pure heart and a good conscience, and faith unfeigned." All our mother's friends had something of a lover-like regard for her—Miss Fergusson as much of this as any—for hers was a very fervent as well as a very gentle nature. She abounded in natural, genial sympathy ; she could, in no common sort, make *all* the joys and the sorrows of friends her own ; but, as free from vanity herself as she was free from selfishness, she never dangerously ministered to the vanity even of those she admired most. In later days, when our mother read those passages, as true as they are beautiful, in which Jeremy Taylor gives *his* sense of the quality and the uses of a " brave friend," it was to this first intimate neighbour of her wedded life that she always specially applied them. As young children, we can all recollect being not a little jealous of Miss Fergusson. She and our mother used to have such earnest talks—often too long ones we thought—with one another, at times when we had rather have had the companion we loved best all to ourselves ; but very precious to us was that inherited love in after-days, as precious as to her who counted it among her blessings to look upon the growing and the matured friendship of her children with one she so entirely loved and trusted.]

In the spring of 1795 our friends Mr. and Mrs. Millar took their departure for America, banished thither by the strong tide of Tory prejudice which ran so fiercely against Mr. Millar. He had joined the Society of "The Friends of the People." He lost his professional employment, and though a most able and honourable man, was so disgusted with the state of public affairs in Scotland that he determined to seek peace and freedom in the United States of America. I felt Mrs. Millar's departure as a great loss. In two years she returned a widow, and our friendship continued till her death.

In the summer of 1795 we took our infant daughter to see my father at Tadcaster, and stayed there till the winter Session of that year brought us back to Edinburgh in November. Our boy Miles seemed so essential to my father's comfort that we consented to let the child remain with him for the winter months. Much occupied in my home with nursery pleasures and hopes, and taking a strong interest in public events, my time passed on in placid contentment. I had by no means an extensive circle of acquaintance.

[At an after time, when our mother's circle was somewhat large, we can all remember, even in the midst of much bright enjoyment of society in Edinburgh, how often she would recall with a loving memory this quiet home season of her early

wedded life.   It was, she used to say, her most bright, most
satisfied, and satisfying season.   She looked back to it thankfully, as having been then withheld from any large indulgence
in what she honestly called her "besetting sin," the love of
popularity, in the days when spirits fresh, unjaded by the
often toilsome claims of wide social intercourse, are so specially
needed, and so dearly prized, round the hearth of a young
mother's home.   There she was indeed the light and the life
of our young lives.   We knew that we were her joy, and we
felt that she was ours.   But as all her care for us, constant
as it was, did not in the least interfere with a true wifely
sympathy in our dear father's public interests, so did neither
the one nor the other hinder her from taking to her heart and
her providing thoughts, the case of any needing help who
might come within her reach.   Of silver and gold she had
indeed very little to give in those days.   We have often
thought since that this must have been to her a severe form
of self-restraint in the days when strict frugality was necessary
at home, for never was there a more cheerful bestower of what
she could justly spare, and largely did she give of that earnest
sympathy which in many cases is above all other help.   She
had a friend during the period of her active Edinburgh life
who ought not to be passed over, although it is difficult sometimes to select from the many of all classes who came and
went as familiar helps about our Castle Street home.   We
have a feeling that the person who then went among us by the
name of "Susan the Good" was very valuable to our mother, and
acted indirectly on the minds of her children, who were often
observant and silent listeners to the conversations which took
place between them.   This friend lived in a very obscure
street not far off, and for the sake of supporting her mother
(a reduced Highland lady), and assisting in the education of
her sisters, exercised the craft of dressmaking, without the
skill to do it well.   Her mind was occupied with great and
good subjects and objects, such as negro emancipation and the
relief of the poor and needy, while her fingers vainly attempted
to make a good fit.   To this excellent person our mother
always adhered as a dressmaker so long as it was necessary,
and their friendship lasted through life.   Many were the

interesting conversations listened to while the so-called fitting-on proceeded. They were both gifted talkers in their different ways, and both were impressed with the hopeful truth of the power of good to overcome evil. This friend was especially useful to our mother in enabling her to find employment for the many unfortunate persons who came under her notice. It was some years before this that she had been led to join in a work then first entered on by a good man named Campbell,[1] for the purpose of reclaiming some of those poor women whose fall from woman's virtue had made them outcasts in the saddest sense. No home of shelter and kindly instruction had then been formed for such in Edinburgh. The one then opened was on a very humble scale, in an obscure close of the Old Town leading from the Nether Bow, a place unknown by sight to the present generation, having been swept away—rightly, perhaps—in the course of modern improvements; but poor as the asylum was, it was carefully tended, and our mother could long afterwards recall with comfort and hope several cases in which the work effected there had been manifestly blessed. One history, which occurred I believe early in my mother's married life, we have heard her relate with peculiar satisfaction and thankfulness, and ought to be recorded in these memorials of her life. The name of this person was Nelly Wilson. Our mother first saw her in one of her visits to the Infirmary to see a sick child. On her way out, she was struck with the fine appearance of a young woman at the door of one of the wards, dressed in a white wrapper, and she asked the nurse who conducted her out what illness that young person had. The nurse shook her head, saying, "Oh, mem, she's here for an ill cause; but she's better, and goes out to-morrow, and back to 'her ill ways, nae doot." My mother felt strongly impelled to speak to this unfortunate and erring sister; and having requested the nurse to allow her to do so, they were left together in a small empty ward. She spoke all that was in her pure and loving heart on this sad subject, but without appearing to make the least impression on her hearer.

[1] John Campbell, ironmonger, foot of the West Bow, afterwards the Rev. John Campbell of Kingsland, London, and author of "Travels in South Africa."

She said she was herself so strongly moved that she even went down on her knees to Nelly Wilson, imploring her to renounce her life of sin and degradation, and go into the asylum which she told her of, where she might find employment and support ; but all in vain.　On that day she made no impression, at least to her own perception : the proud, bold look never relented— the manner, although not rude, remained quite hard.　They parted, and my mother lost sight of her of course.　Some months after this, late one evening, only a day or two before a journey to Yorkshire, my mother was told a person wished to see her.　It was the nurse from the infirmary, who said she had come by the earnest desire of Nelly Wilson, who was. again ill, and could not rest night or day without seeing the "leddy" who had spoken to her some months before ; and, said the nurse, in her broad Scotch, "If you'll believe me, mem, she's no' like the same cratur she was ; her bolster's wet wi' her tears, and she'll do what you bid her noo."　The "leddy" went the following morning, and found Nelly Wilson in a loathsome state of disease, but in a broken and contrite state of mind—the stony heart had become a heart of flesh, and she listened with eagerness to the words of hope and warning.　The poor penitent gave her solemn promise that she would henceforth renounce the life she now loathed, and enter the asylum as soon as she could be admitted.　She faithfully kept her promise, and ever after led a life of faith and obedience, and assisted others to enter the same course. Many years after this occurred, Nelly Wilson became the object of a virtuous attachment.　A respectable tradesman asked her in marriage, but she would not consent to become his wife until she came to my mother to request her to relate to her lover *the whole* history of her former life ; that after knowing that, if he was still disposed to make her his wife, she felt that she could make him happy, but that she set him entirely free to do as he felt right.　The man was deeply affected, my mother said, but so touched by Nelly's fine sense of honour and truthfulness, that he said he loved her more than ever.　They were married, and went to live in London, where her husband had a profitable business, and where my mother saw her a happy wife and mother more than once afterwards. This was one of the many incidents which made her life in Edinburgh one of real missionary work, when it might be supposed by those who saw her only in society that that was her chief vocation. She was so little of an egotist, that, except to those who were deeply interested in such annals, she never introduced them ; she could not abide a half-interest in a soul-stirring subject, and the purity of her own nature gave her an intense feeling of the degradation of this form of vice, and indeed for all the fallen ; she felt that Christ's followers were especially bound to hope, and pray, and do " what they could."]

On the 23d of May [1796] my domestic interests were increased by the birth of a second daughter, my dear Grace, so named after my husband's excellent mother. My good aunt Dawson on this, as on former confinements, came to be with me on that occasion. My infant was singularly thriving, and at the end of a fortnight I had perfectly recovered from my confinement. In the autumn of that year I took our two little girls to Tadcaster. We found our dear Miles grown in size, strength, and beauty, and again left him to gladden the winter of the affectionate circle at Tadcaster. He was a child of quick parts, and of ready combinations, with a warm temper and a very affectionate heart. He was too much an object of concentrated attention in his grandfather's home, and used to say, in after-life, that his temper never recovered the spoiling of Tadcaster. I do not remember that the winter of 1796-7 was marked by any particular event in our domestic history. Of my two little girls, the eldest, an uncommonly beautiful child, was of a hasty temper, but truthful in a remarkable degree, and quick of apprehension. The second was less attractive in appearance, but gentle, reflecting, and exceedingly affectionate and unselfish. Again we took them to my father's house in the summer of 1797. He had begun to perceive that our boy

Miles, then five years old, required more discipline than he had resolution to enforce, and proposed that we should take him back to Edinburgh with us. The parting scene I never shall forget. The child shrieking and clinging to his grandfather's knees,—the old man sobbing with grief, and yet insisting that he should go, since it was for his good. He was carried by main force to the carriage, an unwilling prisoner in the custody of his parents,—his heart knit to the friends he had left. The sorrows of a child have been aptly compared to April showers, but this sad scene made me feel, more than ever, the evil of being so far separated from the home of my youth.

On the 8th of January 1798 I was blessed with another daughter. We called her Margaret, after our kind and affectionate friend Mrs. Brudenell, with whom she became an especial favourite, having, as she said, the dark eyes of my mother.

It was in March 1798 that I prevailed on several ladies of my acquaintance to join me in the institution of a Female Benefit Society in Edinburgh, and after much difficulty and opposition this club was established for the relief of maid-servants and other poor women in sickness. Such institutions among men had long been in operation in Scotland, but this was the first Female Benefit Society attempted, and as all innovations at that time were looked upon with suspicion, and especially where ladies suspected of democratic principles were concerned, this poor "sick club" was vehemently opposed by the constituted authorities,—namely, the Deputy Sheriff and the Magistrates, when these were legally applied to, to sanction the rules of the Society. I mention this to mark the spirit of the time at that period in Edinburgh, both as regards politics, and with regard to the condition of women. For ladies to take any share, especially a leading share, in the management of a public institution, was considered so novel and extraordinary a proceeding as ought not to be countenanced. This "Female Friendly Society" has however been in operation now in Edinburgh for forty-six years, the late Miss Wilson (of Howden), my much-valued friend, having kept the accounts with such accuracy that it has been considered a model for other Societies of like kind to form their rules upon, and to conduct their establishments. It has by the blessing of God relieved much distress, and has been the means of doing good to working people, mainly at their own expense, thereby cultivating habits of forethought and economy, as well as attention to good morals in other respects.

In the autumn of 1798 we had distressing accounts of my dear father's increasing infirmities, and Mr. Fletcher and I resolved to take our little son Miles to see him. Dropsical symptoms had begun to appear; his breathing was much affected, but he was not too ill to be cheered by our visit, and especially by the sight of his darling boy, now six years old, and, for that age, most companionable. We remained till the middle of October, and the parting was sad indeed, for it was without the hope of meeting again in this world. But our visit had soothed some hours of languor, and had cherished warm feelings of affection. In less than a month after we parted, my dear father was released from his sufferings. A man of more sterling worth of character I have never known, or one of higher principles of truth and honour. He had great natural quickness of parts, a liberal heart, and a most happy temper,—diffusing cheerfulness wherever he went. When he lost my mother, his strongest affections became concentrated in me; and though nothing could exceed the happiness of my married life, I often marvelled at myself for having left such a father.

[We can remember how, for many years after this bereavement, our dear mother, on her birthday (though she always tried to make it the bright holiday looked forward to by us) used to take out some memorials of her old home and weep over them. We did not, in those young child days, well understand "why mamma always cried on her birthday morning." We do quite understand it now.]

In the summer of 1799, during the vacation of the Courts, Mr. Fletcher's health, as well as my own, seeming to require change of air, we repaired with our children to a very inexpensive cottage, in the Morningside district to the south of Edinburgh, called "Egypt" (so named in memory of a gipsy colony who, as tradition said, had made their head-quarters in its immediate "whereabouts," by virtue of a grant of land given to them there by one of the Scottish kings). It was the first time that we could afford ourselves the luxury of a country house, and we enjoyed it greatly, seeing how much it promoted the health and happiness of our children. Our friend Mrs. Millar had by that time returned from America, a widow, with all her hopes and prospects blighted. She came to visit us at "Egypt," and interested us much by her animated and graphic descriptions of America, and of men and manners in the United States. She had often seen and conversed with the greatest man of his age,—General Washington, Philadelphia being then the seat of the Federal Government. She described his demeanour as calm, mild, and dignified, and his domestic character as excellent. I should not omit to record that it was in the latter part of this summer, when we were living very quietly at our country house, that my dear friend Miss Fergusson, and her very agreeable sister Ann, brought me to read, for the first time, Wordsworth's "Lyrical Ballads." Never shall I forget the charm I found in these poems. It was like a new era in my existence. They were in my waking thoughts day and night. They had to me all the vivid effects of the finest pictures, with the enchantment of the sweetest music, and they did much to tranquillize and strengthen my heart and mind, which bodily indisposition had somewhat weakened. My favourites were the "Lines on Tintern Abbey," the "Lines left on a Yew Tree at Esthwaite Lake," "The Brothers," and "Old Michael," and I taught my children to recite "We are Seven," and several others.

In September of 1799, Mr. Fletcher and I returned to 20 Queen Street, leaving our children under the care of Miss Fletcher of Dunans. We were joined by dear aunt Dawson, and our good friend Mrs. Brudenell,—the latter, however, preferring to remain in the country with the children. On the 6th of October I was confined of my youngest son Angus, my aunt cheering and attending my sick-bed, as she had affectionately done four times before under the like circumstances.

In the spring of 1801 I accompanied Mr. Fletcher to London, leaving our children under the care of Miss Deas, a respectable nursery-governess, with a promise from my kind and faithful friend Miss Wilson, that she would see them daily, and report progress frequently. This, my first expedition to London, was partly one of business, partly of curiosity to see the great city. We were in lodgings in Albemarle Street, and made good use of our time in seeing all the sights and the distinguished people that were within our reach. It was then I first became acquainted with Joanna Baillie and with Mrs. Barbauld. Miss Millar (a kind friend then and always) introduced me to the former; Lord Buchan gave me a letter to Mrs. Barbauld. I was taken by Dr. and Mrs. Baillie to Hampstead to see the gifted Joanna. I found her on a Sunday morning reading the Bible to her mother, a very aged lady, who was quite blind. Joanna's manners and accent were very Scottish, very kind, simple, and unaffected, but less frank than those of her elder sister. She seemed almost studiously to avoid literary conversation, but spoke with much interest of old Scotch friends, and of her early days in Scotland. I was much interested in her, having but a short time before read her "Plays on the Passions" with deep interest.

With the brilliancy and power of Mrs. Barbauld's conversational talents my husband and I were greatly delighted. She took the same views that we did on public affairs, and had felt deeply, as we had done, disappointment in the disastrous turn of the French Revolution. We saw Mr. Barbauld also, and thought him remarkably intelligent and agreeable. We visited my quondam friend Mr. Woodison, whose introduction to me in 1789 by our mutual friend Mr. Cartwright I have already mentioned, and who still honoured me with his esteem and friendship. He lived in a small house in Chancery Lane, where his mother had lived for many years along with him, and where she had died a short time before. Mr. Fletcher had at this time some interviews with his political friend Mr. Sheridan, whom, however, I did not see.

I well remember after the fatigues of sight-seeing the pleasure and refreshment I had at our lodgings in reading Miss Edgeworth's admirable novel, " Belinda "—some of the hours so spent were among the pleasantest of our London visit. We were happy to return to our home and to our children, after passing a few days with our friends at Tadcaster on our way.

In the October of this year, our dear Miles, then nine years of age, went to the High School. I well remember his bright, animated face, in returning home in the frosty days of winter, without any great aspirations after scholarship however, but exhilarated by the enjoyment of mixing with many play-fellows. In the May of the year following (1802) our home happiness was increased by the birth of our youngest daughter Mary. She was a beautiful infant, with bright large eyes and curly brown hair. On the fourth or fifth day after Mary was born, I became very feverish and unwell : my milk left me, and my distress in not being able to nurse this dear infant, as I had nursed my other children, was unreasonable. We procured a wet-nurse, a respectable married woman, whose husband was at sea ; and when we removed to Dalmeny for country air and quiet, a month after my confinement, we had the nurse's child lodged in the village that the mother might see it daily, and feel satisfied that it was taken care of. My dear aunt remained with us till I was quite strong, and then took dear Bessy, our eldest daughter, back with her to Tadcaster. Our summer at Dalmeny was a very pleasant one, spent in a cottage, which was small and homely, as suited our fortunes. After our eldest boy's return to school to Edinburgh, Grace, Margaret, Angus, and the infant Mary, formed our little household; and it was this summer, when Grace was the eldest of the young party, that I observed her mind to take a spring of advancement which quite surprised me. It was here, too, that I observed good promise of strength in little Margaret's character. Being one day hurt by a fall out of doors, she came home, and, without alarming me, quietly put herself to bed. When I looked for her, on hearing of the accident, an hour afterwards, I found her fast asleep. She rose no worse for the misadventure.

After a year's experience of the High School for our dear Miles, we found that the dissipations of idleness in a large companionship were too strong for his power of resistance. Some misleading school friends, and some evasions of truth, made us decide before the close of this year on removing him, to be placed under the private tuition of a respectable clergyman, the Rev. William Thomson, at the manse of Dalzell, near Hamilton. His new master had not above six little boys to look after, and he performed his duty conscientiously, so that we had reason to be satisfied with the step we had taken.

The latter part of the year 1802 was interesting to us in a public way by the commencement of the Edinburgh Review. We were fortunate enough to be acquainted more or less intimately with several of the earliest contributors, Mr. (now Lord) Brougham, Mr. Jeffrey, Dr. John Thomson, Mr. John Allen, Francis Horner, and James Grahame, the author of "The Sabbath." James Grahame was a much-valued friend. He united to a highly refined and cultivated taste much general information, a very sincere and elevated piety, and the greatest simplicity of manners. I, who knew Edinburgh both before and after the appearance of the Edinburgh Review, can bear witness to the electrical effects of its publication on the public mind, and to the large and good results in a political sense that followed its circulation. The authorship of the different articles was discussed at every dinner-table, and I recollect a table-talk occurrence at our house which must have belonged to this year. Mr. Fletcher, though not himself given to scientific inquiry or interests, had been so much struck with the logical and general ability displayed in an article of the young Review on Professor Black's Chemistry, that in the midst of a few guests, of whom Henry Brougham was one, he expressed an opinion (while in entire ignorance as to the authorship) to the effect that the man who wrote *that* article might do or be anything he pleases. Mr. Brougham, who was seated near me at table, stretched eagerly forward and said, " What,

Mr. Fletcher, be anything?   May he be Lord Chancellor?"
On which my husband repeated his words with emphasis,
" Yes, Lord Chancellor, or anything he desires."   This
opinion seems to confirm Lord Cockburn's words in another
place concerning the young Henry Brougham of the Specu-
lative Society, that he even then " scented his quarry from
afar."

James Grahame, the gentle poet of " The Sabbath," and
" The Birds of Scotland," was so susceptible of the tender
passion that he fell in love at first sight with a young lady
whom he saw first ringing at our door, then No. 20 Queen
Street.   He came in a little afterwards, and asked me many
questions about the dark-eyed beauty, who, he said, had
cast the glamour " owre him."   I invited him to meet her ;
she completed her conquest, and at the end of two months
they were married.   It was about this time our excellent
friend Dr. Anderson brought Thomas Campbell to our
house, and a firm friendship between us was formed, which
stood the test of time and London, and fame, on his part
to the close of his life.   I have often lectured him, and
made him angry, but he never wavered in his friendship.
Life at this time glided on with us calmly and satisfac-
torily.   My husband's professional emoluments, though
very moderate, were amply sufficient for us, combined with
my inheritance from my father's property which was left
to me in liferent, and was entailed on our children.   We
had no vanity to lead us into expense, our circle of acquaintance was very limited, consisting chiefly of old professional friends of Mr. Fletcher, their wives and families,
—with occasional *gleams* of more literary and distinguished
persons.   Of these was the Hon. Henry Erskine, whose
wit, and whose graces of mind and manners, placed him
at the head of good society in Edinburgh, while he was
confessedly the honoured leader of the Liberal or Whig

party. I do not remember to have had any stirrings of worldly vanity or ambition. My delight in feeling that my sympathy in my husband's public feelings contributed much to his happiness, and my just pride in the lofty integrity of his character, and the affectionate kindness of his heart towards me and our children, formed my happiness. These children, too, were my "mirth and matter." I was wrapped up in them,—and though I never could command the patience that qualified me to be their teacher, I delighted in making them my happy and confidential companions. I seldom required to use any other punishment for their offences than exiling them from the sitting-room, and they became very contrite in the nursery. My principle of education was sympathy, and truthfulness in my dealings with them.

In the spring of the year 1803 our kind friend Mrs. Brudenell came to see us, accompanied by Mrs. Laycock. We had great pleasure in showing them all that was worth seeing in Edinburgh, and Mrs. Brudenell afterwards went with Mr. Fletcher to see a small property in Stirlingshire —Park Hall—which he wished to purchase. Their excursion extended to the house of Mr. Stewart of Garth, in Perthshire, where Mrs. Brudenell was delighted with the beauties of Highland scenery, and with the kindness and hospitality she met with. It was on her return home after this visit to us, and while at the house of her old friends Mr. and Mrs. Wilkie of Foulden, in Northumberland, that I received alarming accounts from Mrs. Wilkie of Mrs. Brudenell's dangerous illness. I should immediately have gone to my kind old friend, but at that very time our eldest little girl was taken ill of fever,—so ill that I could not leave home. I thought it a hard trial, but it was afterwards matter of thankfulness to me that I could not be suspected of having influenced Mrs. Brudenell's mind in the disposition of her affairs at that time. It was when she was alone in a sick-chamber, at a distance from us, that she reflected how she owed all the happiness and protection she had sought since her separation from her husband to my father and his family; that she had no connexions by her father's side, and that her mother's relations had never shown her any affectionate consideration or regard. It was from the force of these reflections, operating on a grateful heart, that she determined to leave the bulk of her fortune to the daughter of her earliest and dearest friend, my mother, and to testify her gratitude to my father for all his kindness. I believe that her affection for me personally was very great, but I always thought that it was as my father's and mother's child she left me her estate at Hebburn. She happily recovered from this illness, and the next summer she and my uncle and aunt brought our dear Miles (who had then been placed at school at Thorp Arch, near Tadcaster) to spend the midsummer holidays with us. We had then (June 1804) removed from Queen Street to No. 51 North Castle Street, for the sake of additional house-room, and a larger back green as playground for the children. For their home instruction I had then engaged a governess, Miss Rattray, strongly recommended to me by Mrs. Elizabeth Hamilton, who about this time established herself in Edinburgh. I was introduced to her by our friend Hector Macneil,[1] and soon found in her a warmly-attached friend. She was a woman of liberal mind, with much cultivation, with very considerable liveliness and quickness of apprehension, with great kindness of heart.

In the same summer, and before they left us, Mrs. Brudenell heard of the death of her most unworthy hus-

---

[1] Author of the well-known ballad, " Scotland's Skaith," a poem worthy of all circulation, and of some other poems of merit.

band. She put on no mourning, she affected no grief, but she was greatly agitated, and deeply concerned to know that his last illness had given him time for reflection, in the hope that at the eleventh hour he had been enabled to make his peace with God. By his death she became possessed of her hereditary estate of Hebburn, in Northumberland; and, at her earnest desire, Mr. Fletcher and I accompanied her to take possession of it. I think one of the most melancholy days of my life was that on which I accompanied this once gay and light-hearted woman to the hills and ruined castle of her ancestors (the charter of the estate had been granted to them in the time of King John). She who in her youth had bounded over those fields the heiress of a fair domain, full of life, hope, and promise, now, at the age of 66, came back a shattered, feeble old woman,—without strength or spirit to enjoy the goods of fortune. She felt this incapacity of enjoyment with an intensity proportioned to the exquisite pleasure she would have had in being able to exercise hospitality, and to spread cheerfulness around her. Now she felt that it was all she could do to prolong a feeble existence. With this view she determined on spending the following winter at Bath, in the hope that a southern climate might do her good.

In the winters of 1805 and 1806 I had much agreeable intercourse with Mrs. Elizabeth Hamilton, at whose house I met with a greater variety of people than I had yet mixed with. She did much to clear my reputation from the political prejudice which had, during the first ten years of my life in Edinburgh, attached to all who were not of the Pitt and Dundas faction there. She had good success in persuading her friends that Mrs. Fletcher was not the ferocious Democrat she had been represented, and that she neither had the model of a guillotine in her possession nor carried a dagger under her cloak.

In January 1806 Mr. Pitt died.　It was said that the battle of Austerlitz killed him.　Mr. Fox was " sent for " to form a ministry.　His health had become infirm, but he accepted the foreign department, with two purposes very near his heart,—to make peace with France, and to abolish the slave-trade.　He tried to accomplish the first of these objects by sending Lord Lauderdale to Paris to treat for peace; but the terms insisted on by Napoleon were such as could not be granted without loss of national honour to England.　The ambassador was recalled, and all parties were united in prosecuting the war, confident that a Whig Cabinet would take the first opportunity of bringing it to an honourable conclusion.　The second great object of Mr. Fox was most happily accomplished,—the abolition of the slave-trade.　Mr. Wilberforce had laboured in Parliament, and Mr. Clarkson out of it, with untiring perseverance to accomplish this great measure; but even with Mr. Pitt's professed approval of the principle of abolition, the Royal Family and Mr. Dundas had overruled the Premier on that one point.　It was reserved for the Whig Administration of 1806-7 to have the glory and the happiness of putting an end to the British trade in slaves.

In the summer of 1806, Mrs. Brudenell, always, even in her days of poverty, a " deviser of liberal things," carried out a long-cherished purpose of bringing together the friends for whom love and gratitude were warmest in her heart, to spend a few months round her in the district of England's mountain beauty.　She engaged a house of ample size—Belmont, near Hawkshead, in Westmoreland—to which we from Edinburgh repaired early in June, Mrs. Brudenell joining us from Bath also very soon after, and Mr. Fletcher when the rising of the Law Courts in Edinburgh set him free.　The good uncle and aunt Dawson, from Tadcaster, came to us, with Miles in their company, as soon as his midsummer holidays began.

[To our dear mother and to us this was indeed a summer of new, bright, and busy enjoyment. "It was," as, she has written, "the first time that my children expressed any great pleasure in natural beauty. They had what they called a cave in a bit of rocky copse-wood behind the house, where they carried on all manner of rural devices when Miss Rattray's stern school hours were over." Our mother understood too well the true child way of being happy to disturb our pleasures near the home doors, by expecting us to delight as she did in the wider scenes beyond. A large July sheep-shearing held at the Yew Tree Farm, a statesman's dwelling near at hand, was however a pleasure quite as much to her taste as to ours. We had our family picnics too, now and then to Coniston on the one side and to Windermere on the other, and to a little tarn which lay between Belmont and the latter, where we first saw the water-lily, and also the yellow poppy growing wild on its shore. But generally we were better pleased to keep to our devices about the cave, sure of our mother's abundant sympathy in them always,—and of her bright company often, at the little fruit feasts we used to get up there, or in a stone-built summer-house of the old-fashioned kitchen and orchard garden, which last made no small part of this summer's felicity to us. Her eldest boy Miles was always ready to mount a white pony presented to him here, and called " Belmont " in honour of these happy holidays, and to canter off in any direction along with her for riding's sake. Our mother possessed no proper lady's palfrey either then or at any time of her wedded life, but she had nowise lost her early courage and skill on horseback. It was a delight to her to return to the favourite exercise of her youth, and, quite indifferent to appearances, she mounted any available steed that was to be found at the near farms,—the variety and quality of her stud giving no small amusement to the neighbours whom in her day's ride she visited. Of these the nearest were the Harden family at Brathay Hall on Windermere side, friends whose kind intimacy we have all inherited. Mr. Harden, a true lover of nature, and well accomplished as an amateur artist, was attractive to neighbours of all ranks and ages from the genuine and genial kindliness of his nature. Mr. Lloyd and his family then lived at Old

Brathay, also near us. Charles Lloyd was known beyond the Lake district as the author of some sonnets of poetic worth, and he was much beloved in and about his home from the gentle social qualities so fully inherited by and so dearly prized in his son Owen.[1] A little more distant lay the abode of Dr. Watson, then Bishop of Llandaff, but who still made Calgarth on Windermere side his ordinary residence with his family. Lower down the lake, Fellfoot, then the property of Mr. Dixon, was a house of much social resort, and always, as our mother found, of pleasant intercourse,—Mrs. Dixon having an intelligent taste for bringing round her persons by cultivation, or pursuits, companionable to her and to one another. Our mother had always much to tell us on her return from the boating parties or indoor hospitalities of Fellfoot. Wordsworth's dwelling in Grasmere was somewhat too distant for frequent intercourse, but an introduction to him was no common event, and a day's visit from him at Belmont was among the very "white days" of this pleasant time. Our mother had, as she has herself told, led us all to share with her, so far as might be, in the good, and the enjoyment of his verse. She used to record with pleasure that her younger son, Angus, not then above six years old, marked his interest in the poet's deep, sonorous recitation of his "Lines to the Spade of a Friend," by coming close to her ear, and saying, in an earnest whisper, "Do ask him to say it again." Wordsworth's impressive "Lines on the Expected Death of Fox," which belong to this summer, show that one subject of very deep interest common to him, and to both our parents, would not then have been wanting to the increase of intimacy if their neighbourhood had been nearer. We can all remember the saddening effect, on our dear father especially, when the tidings came that Fox was indeed gone, and at the very time when his country seemed to need him most. His "public passion" (an expression our father often used in speaking of him) had, in the feelings of those to whom his name had long been the

---

[1] Afterwards the pastor of Langdale, early taken thence by illness and death, but still well and affectionately remembered. His remains, brought to Langdale from the place—at some distance—where he died, rest under a yew-tree in the churchyard of the vale.

symbol of enlightened patriotism, redeemed in some degree the errors of his private life. Our mother has, in writing of his death, truly said—"The warm generosity of his heart, and the genial sweetness of his temper, left him without one private enemy." A few days after his death, she adds—"We dined at Calgarth (the Bishop of Llandaff's), when he, who had been the personal friend of Fox, on drinking to his memory after dinner, pronounced a very true and eloquent eulogium on his character."

Of another neighbour of this summer—an object of warm interest to her for many after-years—our mother thus writes : "It was then I first became acquainted with Mrs. Smith of Coniston. She visited me in compliance with her daughter Mrs. Allan's request, but under the impression that she would find me a violent Democrat, and distasteful accordingly. However, it so happened that, bating the Democracy, we became great friends. She loved me in spite of my politics, and I both admired and loved her for the high principles of rectitude and honour which had supported her through many trials ; while the gracefulness of her manners, and the spirit and vivacity of her conversation, were most engaging to me. She lost her daughter, Elizabeth Smith, this summer. We were engaged to pass some morning hours with them[1] the very week before her death ; but she became worse, and the visit was deferred. Elizabeth Smith died, and when we heard from Hawkshead church-tower the sound of her death-bell, we regretted that we had not seen one who seemed to have lived so much with God."]

Mrs. Brudenell remained some weeks at Belmont after my uncle and aunt left us. We accompanied her (on her way to rejoin them) as far as the town of Settle, and there

---

[1] The residence of Mrs. Smith at the time mentioned above was a small cottage by the road-side, near the gate of Tent Lodge, her well-known home in after years, on the banks of Coniston Lake. It was built soon after Elizabeth Smith's death, on a spot greatly delighted in by her, and where a tent had been pitched during her illness, in which was often her morning sitting-room, commanding (as the house raised " in memoriam " now does) one of the finest views in the Lake district.

I parted for the last time with my mother's earliest friend, and one who certainly had a considerable influence in the formation of my character. She had a high moral standard; and though there were many inconsistencies in her character, the generosity of her heart and the truthfulness of her gratitude were the prominent qualities that made an impression on me. She was full of sympathy, a most engaging quality to the young. She cultivated my taste for reading, as well as taught me to read in her little cottage at Oxton; and her sensibilities did not evaporate in sentiment. She was a kindly friend to the poor, and by example impressed upon me early the force of a very favourite passage of hers from Beattie's "Minstrel"—

> "And from the prayer of want, and plaint of woe,
>   Oh ! never, never turn away thine ear ;
>   Forlorn in this bleak wilderness below,
>   Oh ! what were man should Heaven refuse to hear !"

We all returned to Edinburgh in the October of this year, and Mrs. Brudenell died at Tadcaster in the December following. My uncle and aunt followed her remains to Hougham Church, in Lincolnshire, where she was buried in the chancel, between the graves of her two children, according to her expressed desire. She left me her family estate of Hebburn, subject to the debts and legacies specified in her will. This was a considerable accession of fortune, at a time when the education of our children made such increase important.

[Aunt Mary Hill's wise views on Education.

"GRANGE, *October* 1807.

" MY DEAR NIECE,—I am very glad that you intend Grace should have her full swing (excuse the vulgarism) in reading. I know a very superior woman who laments to this day the starvation her mind underwent from the person under whose

care she was placed, being possessed by the ill-founded prejudice that a literary turn tends to give a disrelish for domestic
duties.

" Grace has interested us all very much with her account
of Angus and Mary's little cave, and the full enjoyment they
found in it. I wish you could convince Miss R——, and all
the friends to artificial and premature instruction, that one
hour in this cave, employed in their own way, will strengthen
their faculties and invigorate their minds more than twenty
lessons. These good folks never consider that when the
faculties of children are exercised with most pleasure to themselves, they are receiving their best lessons, and that God Himself is their Teacher."]

Our winter of this year was unmarked by any domestic
event except Miles's entrance on the classes of the Edinburgh
College. My daughters went on with their school-room
education under Miss Rattray's tuition. And here I must
enter my protest against any one's continuing to tolerate
such faults in a governess as may interfere with the happiness of children. Miss Rattray was truthful, pious, considerate of the poor, and very industrious ; but she had a
sternness and want of sympathy, a harshness of nature which
made the school-room irksome, and which was alike unfavourable to the temper and to the happiness of the children. It was a great mistake to inflict on them this
unnecessary discipline, and I have often bitterly regretted
it. It was my custom then (not a very common one with
Edinburgh ladies) to walk with the children before breakfast, they taking their little tins to get milk at a dairy-
woman's field on the Queensferry Road. I liked to
cultivate in them an early taste for simple habits and
simple pleasures. These morning walks in spring were an
emancipation from school-room rigidity, which they and I
enjoyed together exceedingly.

In the summer and autumn of this year we all spent

some months at Hebburn. Our kind old friend Miss Forster exerted herself to get the house there furnished for our use; and though it was small—little more, indeed, than a shooting lodge, built by Mr. Brudenell for his own use, and therefore by no means convenient for a large family—these months were spent by us very happily. Two Shetland ponies of small dimensions, whose arrival was a great event amongst us, gave our younger children their first experiences on horseback, and I often availed myself of Miss Forster's kindness by trotting over to her house at Bolton, a few miles distant, on the horse and pillion which she sent for me. Old Lord Tankerville spent that summer, as his wont was, at his baronial residence, Chillingham Castle, not far off, and, with his daughter, Lady Mary Bennet, had the courtesy to call upon us, and to invite Mr. Fletcher and me frequently to dinner. He was a fine specimen of the old English aristocrat, punctilious in the observance of courteous manners, strong in his regard for constitutional Whig principles. With this bond between them, Mr. Fletcher and he became good friends. He had that summer, for the first time, overcome a strong reluctance to the marriage of his eldest son, so as to receive Lord Ossulston and his beautiful young wife at Chillingham Castle. This was done at the dying request of a favourite daughter: and his heart was softened and his happiness increased by it. He told me that he had disapproved of his son's marriage, not because his wife was a foreigner and without fortune, but because she had been educated amidst all the dissipation of Devonshire House, which he feared might make the union fatal to his son's happiness.[1] Another baronial Castle—that of Alnwick—

---

[1] This Earl of Tankerville purchased in the year 1817 the estate of Hebburn, which adjoined his own estate of Chillingham, and added the wild part of Hebburn to his range for the celebrated white cattle.

we were introduced to this summer, by Mr. Burrell of Broom Park.[1] It was worth seeing for once the stately remains of ancient hospitality at the castle of the Percys. At that time, when the Duke of Northumberland was present there, a flag was every Thursday unfurled on its highest tower, as an invitation to any who had been previously introduced to come and dine there. The gentry of the county did not slight this invitation. About forty guests sat down to table on the day we dined there. On entering the dining-room, Miss Forster pointed to me where I should sit—next to a vacant space. The old Duke was presently wheeled into the room, and his chair filled that space ; so I had much of his discourse during dinner : it was lively, courteous, and good-humoured. He spoke, but not tediously, of his infirmity from gout ; he had tried, he said, every remedy for it, as he believed, except one, which, in the case of a friend of his, proved efficacious, viz., the bastinado. This had been applied to his friend when travelling in Turkey, and disabled by gout from descending from his palanquin to pay the required homage to the Grand Vizier, and it actually cured him!

[The Hebburn summer had by no means the charm that belonged to our Westmoreland sojourn of the year before ; but it was a happy one, as our mother has said (for country life was in itself enjoyment), and for us children it had its bright days of adventure, too, out of the common course, one especially —an expedition taken in a cart, with well-filled provision baskets for the day, the elders of the family party riding on horseback along by our side, all save aunt Dawson, who jolted along amongst us, leading the tune and words of the " Jolly Beggars " and other old ditties, given forth in full, if not

---

[1] A sister of Miss Forster, and, like her, one of our mother's early school-fellows at the Manor, York, was the wife of this gentleman.

harmonious, chorus by all round her, to beguile the long morning's journey to Bamborough Castle. Our first sight of this fine old place when we reached it—the flash of the blue sea, and the rush of its white foam as the waves broke on the rocks under the Castle at full tide, and the long stretch of white sand and shingle which, at its ebb, lay between Bamborough and Lindisfarne, " The Holy Isle " of St. Cuthbert,—are not forgotten by us now ; the less so, that the memories of this day as to scenery were richly brought back a few years afterwards by the vigorous poetic pictures of Scott in the finest canto of his " Marmion."

In another excursion, one more soberly conducted, we also accompanied our parents to Haggerston Hall, then occupied as a nunnery, having been granted as a house of refuge by Sir Carnaby Haggerston, an ancient Baronet " of that ilk," to some French nuns who had been dragged from their convent, and for some time imprisoned in Paris during the Reign of Terror. They told us, but with no bitterness, simply as a matter of history, that it was only the death of Robespierre that saved them from being victims of the guillotine themselves. After their arrival in England, and their establishment at the place where we found them, a Highland cousin of our father, one of the Miss Fletchers of Dunans, had taken the vows and joined their community. She was permitted by the Abbess mother to see her kinsman and give kindly welcome to our mother and us for his sake. She had preserved a token of him (whether of familiar kindness or something tenderer we know not)—a Latin motto in praise of friendship—which, as she reminded him, he had given to her when they met last, or rather parted, after crossing a burn (for she noted the time and place) near her father's house. There was no reserve in showing this to him, which she drew forth from an embroidered pocket-book, and we thought the sisters looked on very benevolently as she did so. We often recalled this visit to our Catholic cousin and the good sisterhood with pleasure.

Of other matters at Hebburn, and other interests in which our dear mother led us cordially to share, the following letter to a much-valued friend speaks in her own words :—

To Mrs. Stark.

"Hebburn House, near Belford,
Northumberland, *July 26th*, 1807.

" The kind wish you expressed to hear from me, my dear Mrs. Stark, was too gratifying to be for a single day forgotten, although a fortnight has passed away since we arrived here. I wished, however, to be able to tell you how we liked our dwelling and all its accompaniments. Fate (as if to punish me for coveting your sequestered cottage) has placed us in a house at the summit of a bleak, bare hill. It was built by the late Mr. Brudenell, who pulled down an old baronial castle which 'time had spared,' and fixed upon precisely the only part of the estate which affords a prospect utterly devoid of picturesque beauty. The Cheviot Hills form our boundary to the south-west, and we hope it is no treason against the Epic Muse, if we rejoice that this far-famed scene of martial prowess is now covered with bleating flocks and peaceful shepherds. The peasantry of this country are not less simple, though they are far less independent, than those of Westmoreland : we have none of that erect deportment and that proud civility we used to meet with in our wanderings last summer, when we were obliged to ask permission of the statesmen (ploughing their own fields) to walk through them. Here property is in the hands of the few rich. The country is thinly inhabited ; the farms are extensive ; and the cotter's hold of the farmer (not the proprietor) is a sort of feudal heritage. His cottage, cows, grass, potato crop, and some bolls of corn are given him in exchange for his labour. His wife, or some one member of the family, is obliged to work at fixed wages for the farmer the year round. This is called *working bondage*, and it is felt as a great grievance by the people ; but it is an ancient custom in Northumberland, and though attended with personal grudging and private feelings of oppression, which never fail to hurt the character, it secures the cottager's family a maintenance, and there seems to be little abject poverty or wretchedness in our villages. The village of Hebburn is a short mile from us. There has not been a school there in the memory of man. Last Sunday we assembled about twenty children in the remains of the old castle, read a little appropriate address to them, and prevailed on them to accompany us to church, about a mile distant from the village. They had never been in any place of worship. Their parents were chiefly Dissenters, and their chapels and tabernacles were many miles distant, too far for the children to travel barefooted ; so they were suffered to run wild on Sunday. I was much pleased with the liberality of the parents ; there was no bigotry among them, for, though of many different persuasions, they all willingly sent their children to accompany us to the nearest place of worship. The children on their part were delighted ; most of them could read ; and we agreed that ' the Sermon on the Mount ' was good for us all. You would have been pleased, my dear Mrs. Stark, to have seen how earnestly my children took a part in this interesting project. Much did I wish for three or four whom I could name to have enjoyed it with us, and, believe me, you were among the number. You perceive that, notwithstanding the bleak, bare hill, we shall contrive to be very happy. You will not, I am sure, refuse your contribution to make us so ; do let me hear from you."]

From Tadcaster, in the course of the summer 1808, our eldest girl, Bessy, and I went to visit an old friend—Miss Kennedy—in the neighbourhood of Manchester, and she made us acquainted with the family of Mr. Greg at Quarry Bank. We stayed a week with them, and admired the cultivation of mind and refinement of manners which Mrs. Greg preserved in the midst of a money-making and somewhat unpolished community of merchants and manufacturers. Mr. Greg, too, was most gentlemanly and hospitable, and surrounded by eleven clever and well-educated children. I thought them the happiest family group I had ever seen. Miss Kennedy also took me to visit her friends, the Rathbone family, at Green Bank, near Liverpool, and we there met Mr. Roscoe, the elegant-minded author of the " Life of Lorenzo de' Medici." Mr. Roscoe took us to his beautiful

residence at Ollerton Hall, and charmed us by the good taste
of his varied and agreeable powers of conversation.   He
had been returned member for Liverpool during the Whig
Ministry of 1806, and both he and Mr. Rathbone had taken a
decided part in the cause of the abolition of the slave-trade.
We were taken to see the last ship which had sailed from the
port of Liverpool for trade in human beings.   It was then
undergoing a change for the stowage of other goods than
those wretched negroes who had formerly been crammed
in the space between-decks not more than four feet high.
The iron hooks remained to which they had been chained.
It was a sickening sight,—but those chains were broken.
We stayed some days at Green Bank, where we enjoyed the
society of the venerable William Rathbone, the zealous
friend of civil and religious liberty.   It was he, and Mr.
Roscoe, and Dr. Currie, who by their personal influence
and exertions established the first literary and philosophical society at Liverpool, and induced their fellow-towns-
men to think and feel that there were other objects besides
making money which ought to occupy the time and
thoughts of reasonable beings.

For the summer of 1810 we took a pleasant country house,
Frankfield by name, about a mile above Lasswade, on the
banks of the Esk, where our eldest daughter, with the
three younger children and I, repaired early in the spring,
Mr. Fletcher joining us at the end of each week before the
Courts rose, to have his Sunday rest among us.   It was
here that Mr. and Mrs. Simond and Miss Wilkes, afterwards
Mrs. Jeffrey, first visited us, introduced by Mrs. Craig
Millar.   Mr. Simond was a grave, misanthropic Frenchman,
who had emigrated to America during the stirring period
of the French Revolution.   He was a man of refined and
literary taste, became a merchant at New York, and married there a lively and agreeable woman, Miss Wilkes, a

niece of the celebrated John Wilkes, the agitator of the early part of George the Third's reign.

In the autumn of that year I well remember our watching one fine evening the expected arrival of our dear Miles and Grace from Yorkshire, and I could even now fancy I see their light active steps on the wooden bridge that crossed the Esk near to our garden gate at Frankfield. It was a happy meeting, and our Grace, whose love of home and love of nature partook of the poetical enthusiasm of her character, often mentioned it as one of the brightest spots in her happy life. She found her sister Margaret, then twelve years old, much advanced in companionable qualities, their tastes and pursuits were similar, and her little sister Mary had all the beauty and the shyness of a most interesting child, the plaything of the family. The peculiar reserve of Bessy's character made me think that she would benefit by being thrown among strangers, and it was at this time fixed that she should go and spend some months with Mrs. Barbauld, where a new view of society, and the great advantage of living with that most excellent and highly-gifted woman, might excite her to more energetic aspirations after knowledge and all thât was praiseworthy. Her personal beauty at that time was most remarkable, but her manners were so cold and distant that she had few intimate friends, and yet she had deep feeling. I remember that she could hardly recover composure after reading the last chapters of " Clarissa Harlowe." It was on a fine summer evening at this time, when we had just finished that powerful book, and when our eyes were red with weeping over it, that we sallied out to talk it over, for we could think and speak of nothing else. We were sauntering about on a bank above the Esk called the Whinny, when who should we meet but Professor Playfair, his then pupil Lord John

Russell, Mrs. Apreece, afterwards Lady Davy, and Miss Hannah Mackenzie[1] (a daughter of the " Man of Feeling," Henry Mackenzie).　Mrs. Apreece had brought me a letter of introduction from Mr. Banks Cleaver.　This very agreeable party returned with us to drink tea at Frankfield, helping us to forget the creations of Richardson's genius in the sparkling vivacity of Mrs. Apreece, and the taste and refinement of her companions.

[Those of us who survive well remember our enjoyment of this beautiful locality, known to us before only by occasional visits to Roslin or Hawthornden.　Our possession of the dear mother's daily company was more complete than in any former summer spent in the country ; and as that district was much less a place of villas than it has since become, the wood walks of the surrounding glens, with the steep banks of their streams, the tiny feeders of the Esk, were as quiet and free as they were beautiful.　"*Paidlin'*" and even bathing in these "burns" were often incidents of our walks—to town children an especial delight.　So was our intimacy with the whole succession of flowering plants that grew in those nooks, from the earliest primrose to the latest harebell.　We never became botanists in any systematic sense, though (as our mother has recorded) " Sinclair Cullen, a grandson of Dr. Cullen, a young man of unquestionable genius, and of manners the most lively and engaging, used to come from Edinburgh as a frequent visitor, and give us botanical lectures in those woods ; " but it was at Frankfield that one unfailing pleasure of life became a habit with us—to observe minutely in their own haunts, and thus to share the "innocent mirth" of wild-flowers.　It was there, too, that we first held intercourse with the labouring people of our own country.　Many of them not engaged in farming work were employed in some paper-mills near at hand, but the hours of work there were not so long as in most other factory toils.

---

[1] This lady died many years ago, and none who had ever known her can forget the charm of her social intercourse.　In this it was difficult to say whether her play of genuine humour in conversation, or her quick sympathy and comprehension as a listener, were the most attractive.

The workers had time for the cultivation of their kail-yards, and for no small cultivation of their minds besides. The boys and girls came readily to some evening classes for instruction such as we could help our mother to give them, and we learned fully to respect the intelligence and to enjoy the conversible qualities of the elder people when we visited them at their frugal homes. Though we never returned to Frankfield as summer residents, it was long afterwards a pleasure to us to keep up the friendly intercourse of this time with a good many of our village neighbours. The kindly welcomes we found at the hearths of those we knew best well repaid the long walk we sometimes took from Edinburgh in frosty days of the following winters to see them, and to admire, hardly less than in summer, the glen streams of those parts in their garniture of icicles and frozen spray.]

In December of this year I set out with our eldest daughter for London, where my old friend, Miss Forster, met us. Previous to my leaving Bessy with Mrs. Barbauld, I saw a good deal of that remarkable woman,—remarkable not more for genius, taste, and feeling, than for great elevation of mind, lively wit, and playfulness of fancy. Her manners were very pleasing, without the polish of fashionable life, but with much of refinement and perfect good breeding. I wished my dear child to have a high standard of intellectual and moral perfection, and in placing her with Mrs. Barbauld I had my wish accomplished. I think it was Mrs. Barbauld's admirable essay on "The Education of Circumstances" that gave me so great a desire to place my daughter under the enviable circumstance of being her inmate.

The winter of 1811 was not marked by any home event that I can specially remember, except that our son Miles's attendance at the Moral Philosophy class of the Edinburgh College was the means of making us acquainted with Dr. Thomas Brown, who had the year before been appointed

successor to Dugald Stewart.   Mrs. Elizabeth Hamilton was
still resident in Edinburgh, and at her house we always
found most agreeable society, as well as at that of Mrs.
Grant of Laggan, who two years before had established
herself in Edinburgh, proving a great acquisition to our
little circle.   The society of Edinburgh at that time was
delightful.   The men then most distinguished in social
intercourse, alike by literary reputation and amiable manners in society, were Walter Scott, Mr. Jeffrey, Dr. Thomas
Brown, Mr. Mackenzie, Mr. Thomas Thomson, Professor
Playfair, Mr. Pillans, the Rev. Dr. Alison.   A little before
this time the forms of social meetings had somewhat changed
from what they were when I knew Edinburgh first.   Large
dinner parties were less frequent, and supper parties—I mean
hot suppers—were generally discarded.   In their place came
large evening parties (sometimes larger than the rooms could
conveniently hold) where card-playing generally gave place
to music or conversation.   The company met at nine and
parted at twelve o'clock.   Tea and coffee were handed about
at nine, and the guests sat down to some light cold refresh-
ments later on in the evening; people did not in these
parties meet to eat, but to talk and listen.   There you would
see a group (chiefly of ladies) listening to the brilliant talk
of Mr. Jeffrey; in a different part of the room, perhaps,
another circle, amongst whom were pale-faced, reverential-
looking students, lending their ears to the playful imagina-
tive discussions of Dr. Brown,—while Professor Playfair
would sometimes throw in an ingenious or quiet remark,
that gave fresh animation to the discourse.   On other
occasions, old Mr. Mackenzie would enliven the conversation
with anecdotes of men and manners gone by.   It was this
winter that Mrs. Apreece and Mrs. Waddington divided the
admiration of the Edinburgh circles between them,—the
one attractive by the vivacity of her conversation, the other

by her remarkable beauty and the grace of her manners. Her eldest daughter, then an intelligent girl, was afterwards the wife of Baron Bunsen. I may remark that it was in this society that Lord John Russell, then the inmate of Professor Playfair, used to spend some of the evening hours that he could spare from hard study. The enlightened philosophy of Mr. Playfair's mind, when brought into close contact with his own youthful aspirings, may have contributed to give Lord John's mind that high tone of political morality for which he has since been so distinguished.

It was during this period also, when my children were growing up and able to enjoy variety of intercourse, that several English families of intelligence and agreeableness were attracted to Edinburgh, for the sake both of its society and the advantages it afforded as to education for both sons and daughters. It would be in vain now to enumerate all the new people that came and went among us, some leaving permanent friendships behind them, and others most kindly feelings and not infrequent interchange of letters after they left Edinburgh. Among those whose acquaintance in those days ripened into friendship (which was continued without interruption to the close of her life), Lady Williamson, the widow of Sir Hedworth Williamson of Whitburn, should be especially mentioned. She had a house for many years in Queen Street, a few doors from North Castle Street. Her daughters attended classes along with mine, and a strong theatrical friendship was formed among our young people, both sons and daughters, which led to most pleasant meetings for rehearsals at our respective homes. Lady Williamson's house was large, and one of the drawing-rooms was converted into a little permanent theatre during one winter, when the play of "Douglas," and some of Joanna Baillie's dramas were got up with great effect, and large audiences sometimes gave their applause *con amore*. After the friendly family party left Edinburgh, we were always urged to make Whitburn Hall a resting-place on our way to Yorkshire, and frequently did so. The youngest Miss Williamson married the Hon. T. Dundas, now Earl of Zetland, and she never failed in showing me the most friendly kindness in my dull Tadcaster life, when attending on my aunt Dawson.

[Part of a Letter from Mrs. E. Hamilton to Mrs. Fletcher, dated 1808.

"I long to hear of your meeting with Grace, and of the improvement you found in the dear girl, and I know your account will be a faithful one; for this I can say of you with truth—that I have never known so fond a mother so perfectly candid and impartial, neither have I ever known one to whom I could so freely speak on the peculiar character of a child without any apprehension of being mistaken by her in what I said. This I consider as the greatest blessing to your children. It permits you to make use of the eyes of your understanding as well as your heart, and the consequences to them must be great beyond expression."

Relating to my daughter Elizabeth, from Mrs. Barbauld.

"DEAR MADAM,—I cannot let Miss Fletcher make up her *pacquet* without adding a line to say—in truth, what I said before, yet a mother, I fancy, will allow me to repeat—that her child is well and lovely, and the darling of every one who sees her. I am every day more and more pleased with her intelligence and the justness of her taste, as well as with the sweetness of her manners. You would have been amused with a dialogue that passed between us the other day. We were reading Paley. 'But,' says she, 'I do not want all this evidence, for it never entered into my mind to doubt of any of these truths.' I observed to her, that there were those who had made objections and had written books against them, and that it might occur to her, at some time of her life, to be asked for a reason of the hope that was in her; 'But,' replied she, with great *naïveté*, 'I think it would be the best way, then, to read first one of these books that are written against Christianity.' You may believe I did not recommend one, but I felt the conviction that we do not even wish our children to inquire without a bias on their minds.   Nor ought we; if we think ourselves to be in possession of important truths, it is both right and kind to impress them on the mind of youth without waiting for the uncertain process of their own crude reasonings.   There is a great deal of unjust prejudice against prejudice.   Miss Fletcher has no doubt told you that we have seen 'Berenice' performed, and very well, at a private party.   It is wonderful that a Play should support itself, as this does, without change of situation or anything that can be called an incident, and with the miserable expedient of three confidants created for the sole purpose of being so; but 'Berenice' has many pretty lines, which one has often heard quoted, and it has the remembrance of the interest excited by the loves of Louis XIV. and Mancini.   The French Plays are better than the English for private representation, as they require no change of scene.   I see, dear madam, you have been struck as well as ourselves with the uncalled-for severity of the Edinburgh Review against my niece—I say uncalled-for, because they were not reviewing her; and if they did not choose to bring her book before the public, I think they had no right to bring her name.   The cause of their unfounded sarcasm appears pretty evidently in the next page, where they mention Montgomery.   I wish my niece had not inserted her address to that poet.   'They are too proud and too generous,' said Mr. Hamond, some time ago, when I was expressing a fear that it might influence their notice of her; but it has not proved so. I wish the Reviewers would ask me for a motto; I could give them one from Shakespeare :—

<blockquote>'And, like the tyrannous breathing of the North,
Shakes all our buds from blowing.'</blockquote>

"I must have tired you, dear madam, with this long letter.

"A. L. BARBAULD.

"STOKE NEWINGTON, *April* 1811."

To her daughter Grace, from E. F.

"*Sunday Morning, November* 1812.

"The Napiers leave town on Tuesday, and I must prepare my packet for you, dear child. Colonel George Napier is a most interesting and truly heroic man. It was Miss Craig's letters to her brother, so full of good sense and affectionate solicitude, that won his heart ; then her brother used to dwell on the sweetness of her temper and the goodness of her heart, and with his dying breath he besought his friend to see his sister whenever he returned to England. Under these impressions, Colonel Napier was in the truest sense in love ; and before he left London this summer, to fulfil young Craig's dying wish, he told his mother, Lady Sarah, that if Miss Craig corresponded with the expectations he had formed of her, she was the only woman on earth he could love. His mother sanctioned what the world would call his romantic passion. He came, saw, and was completely conquered. You may remember how deeply she was interested about him when she was here last winter. To hear him talk of General Moore would do you good, dear child ; he was his *aide-de-camp*, and had been receiving orders five minutes before the General received his fatal wound at the battle of Corunna. Napier was at that moment sent to bring up some fresh detachments, and did not return in time to see him while consciousness lasted ; he was just expiring when Napier entered the tent. He said Moore's heart was broken, and that he exposed his person with desperate courage that day on which he fell, but that during all his misfortunes his courage, firmness, and magnanimity never forsook him, and it was only his peculiar friends who saw what was passing in his mind. Napier says, 'We shall never look upon his like again.'

"I hope, my dearest Grace, you enjoyed your last packet ; believe me, you cannot have greater pleasure in hearing from us than I have in preparing them for you. Your kind heart and affectionate attentions are a constant subject of sweet recollection to me, and nothing pleasant occurs without my earnestly wishing you were here to share it with us. We shall hope to hear from you at great length by Mr. Marshall, when you will give us a narrative of all your proceedings, thoughts, feelings, and opinions. I expect much gratification this evening in our meeting with Sir James Mackintosh again, who is a man of very distinguished talents and great conversational powers. He has been for the last ten years in India. His conversation is full of interest and instruction. The account he gives of the Hindoo character is very curious; he says in refinement of manners, cultivation, and politeness, they are equal to Europeans; that they talk of truth, honour, and moral obligation, as if they felt it, but that, in fact, they neither act upon these principles themselves nor expect you to act upon them. Sir James knew a Hindoo Rajah, a man of great acquirements and of the most polished manners, who, when he was disappointed in the collection of his taxes of the sum he expected, ordered a pound of eyes to be brought him of those who had refused to pay the taxes. Such horrid barbarity can only be attributed to the want of the humanizing power of Christianity. The rites of Juggernaut accustom the people to believe that their deity can be pleased with human suffering; how, then, can they be persuaded that the exercise of cruelty can be displeasing to him? Mr. M'Neill dined with us yesterday. He has just been on a visit to Walter Scott, and hears that ' Rokeby ' is a domestic tale : the scene, Mr. Morritt's, Rokeby ; the time, during the wars of York and Lancaster. It will be published about Christmas. I have been much pleased with some of Crabbe's Tales—they are so true to nature, such beautiful pictures of the common and every-day joys and sorrows of humanity. There is not a particle of poetical romance in them, but they are often very touching. Pray tell Mr. S——, with my best compliments, that since I saw him we have seen a speech of Mr. Fawkes, so full of wisdom, truth, and public spirit, that I am convinced the report of his being deranged is nothing more than a political calumny. I wish there were five hundred such madmen in our House of Commons. I believe we should all be the better for their measures, from the King to the lowest of his subjects."

Parts of Letters to Mrs. Stark, 1813 and 1814.

"PARK HALL, 1813.

" No changes have happened since you left us except that our autumnal tints are of a browner shade, and that we draw closer round our fire in the evening, and that our picture grows more like every touch we give the canvas.

" If Grace had a temper to be spoiled by commendation, my delight in this picture would make her conceited, but though she has pleasure in the art, it is with her a very secondary pleasure—what she most feels is the reflected enjoyment she affords to me."

To the Same.

" *December 15th, 1814.*

" I could not write till I heard of dear Grace's safe arrival at Tadcaster after a journey in the mail during the severest weather we have had this winter. She set off with Mrs. Macnab last Thursday.   I cannot tell you what it cost me to part with her for so many months, for even your indulgence would condemn my weakness when so peremptory a duty required the sacrifice.   Miles's illness and our consequent anxiety has prevented us from knowing what has been going on in Edinburgh since we returned, but it has given us frequent opportunities of seeing Dr. Thomson.   He gives a sad picture of the demoralization of Paris.   He thinks this is greatly owing to the unprincipled ambition of Bonaparte's government.   It was a government of expedients and not of general principles, and, of course, no man of integrity could obtain or keep a situation of public trust or national importance, because if a more enterprising or bold adventurer started a more daring project of ambition he was always preferred, hence character lost its value and fidelity its reward. · Dr. Thomson seems to think this corruption of manners pervades all ranks, nor are the literary and scientific men exempted from it.   It makes one sad to think of these things, dear friend, but I still hope that the great division of property in France will in time establish a middle class, and that this middle class will exercise a wholesome control over public opinion favourable to private morals and general happi-

ness.   Dr. Thomson says there are now in France three millions
of landed proprietors.   We have been reading Wordsworth's
'Excursion' and Mrs. Brunton's 'Discipline.'   Wordsworth's
Poem, of 423 pages quarto, has some exquisite passages, but is
on the whole far too long.   It is marked, however, by that
high tone of moral sensibility and devout aspirations after goodness for which his other works are remarkable.   His hero is a
pedlar, a Scotch pedlar, too, who carries his sublime morality
as well as his pack to the native mountains of the poet, and
there holds converse with Wordsworth.   The critics may sneer,
but the lover of nature, and of mankind, will find much to love
in the 'Excursion.'   We are delighted with 'Discipline;' I
will not anticipate your pleasure in reading it, but I am sure
you will find much to commend.   The saintly purity of Miss
Mortimer's character is the finest illustration of genuine piety
that I have anywhere met with in fiction."

To the Same.

"*May* 19*th*, 1814.

" Although I have not written to you, my dear friend, I have
been rejoicing with you in spirit and in truth at the great
events which have immortalized the past month, and have given
a new interest to the destinies of mankind ; never again did I
expect to feel the same interests in politics, the aspirations of
hope, or the same confidence in national virtue.   The precepts
of La Harpe have not been as the good seed that was sown in
stony places.   His illustrious pupil, the good Alexander, has
nobly proved the pre-eminence of virtue.   How beautiful is the
simple and unostentatious manner in which he has acted !
Joanna Baillie writes to me that when the Duke of Clarence
asked the Duchess of Oldenburg what her brother would do when
he entered Paris, she said in broken English, ' He will first tank
God, and then he will seem as if he had noting to do in the
matter.'   Count Orloff told Dr. Baillie that he had on his
estates in Russia about 40,660 peasants, all of whom could read,
and most of them write, that they could carry their complaints to
three different courts if they thought themselves injured, and that
the expense of law proceedings would not exceed fifty shillings.

" We are now upon a visit to one of my earliest friends, Mrs. Laycock, in the sweetest of Yorkshire villages, where beautiful woodland scenery, the loveliest freshness of spring, and the happiest domestic intercourse contribute to our enjoyment. How I wish we had you in this pleasant village, where every-thing wears the aspect of gladness, and harmonizes with the festivity of nature in her gayest season ! An English village is in my mind the best commentary on the English constitution, the independence, comfort, security, industry, and opulence of its inhabitants are the blessed fruits of peace and liberty."

From G. F. to her Mother.

VISIT TO SARAH THE GOOD SERVANT, WHOSE STORY WAS TOLD IN THE FIRST PART OF THESE MEMORIALS.

" TADCASTER, *March* 1813.

" MY DEAREST MOTHER,—On Monday, immediately after breakfast, I set out on my delightful errand to Grimston.   I happily escaped all our Argus-eyed neighbours, and therefore had the satisfaction of walking alone.

> ' It was the first mild day of March,
> Each minute sweeter than before.'

Those beautiful lines of Wordsworth were strongly recalled to my memory, for there was in truth ' a blessing in the air.' I found Sarah alone in her cottage, excepting her little silent friend and companion, her infant's chair, which you know always stands beside her.   She spoke much of you, and told me she remembered well the first day you went to visit her poor mistress. When I gave her Lady Williamson's generous present, she seemed almost overpowered, and she told me after-wards, when I asked her to dictate to me what she wished to say I would write for her, that at the moment she received the £5 her heart was so filled with gratitude that she could not speak. She said that, not having learned to write, she could not indite properly to a lady, and I did not press her to do so, lest it should perplex her and make her think I doubted her gratitude ; but she repeatedly begged me to tell the good lady how very much she felt her kindness, for it had been a hard winter, and that she was growing old now and not able to work as she used to do. With admirable delicacy she never mentioned her conduct to her mistress in expressing her thanks to Lady Williamson, not even to depreciate it ; she seemed to feel that touching on her own merits would have been like giving herself a claim to the generosity of the 'good lady.' When I told her that you wanted a picture of her, she said certainly, it was her duty, and without making one excuse seated herself where I wished her. I was delighted to find one human being at least free from vanity, for though Sarah was in her common working dress, she did not seem at all discomposed ; she was much pleased that you should think of her, but did not concern herself how she appeared. Indeed, she submitted to it as a sort of duty, and thought, as you desired it, it was the only little return she could make for all your kindness. When she had sat some time I told her I feared she would be tired of sitting still so long ; with great simplicity she mildly answered, 'Oh, thank you, I can sit still very patiently.' The sketch I have taken does not altogether please me, but as I have caught some of the expression of her countenance I will send it in the next frank. I should have much pleasure in introducing our good Sarah to Dr. Brown if he comes this way in spring, and can spare time. She is an admirable creature, when I see her in dress and manners, so simple, uncultivated, and uneducated, with a soul filled with every excellence, and when I contrast her with many of the great worldlings around us, Shakespeare's words constantly come into my mind—

'A ministering angel shall she be when they lie howling.'

It is difficult to give in a drawing the peculiar expression of placidity and resignation in her countenance. This is another proof among many of the wretched limitation in human power when inspired—almost poetically inspired—by the character, the mind of the person whose countenance you are to delineate ; if, unfortunately, your pencil has not a sharp point and you have forgotten your knife, vainly will you seek to give to each varying beauty of the human face 'its local habitation.' There is great vexation of spirit in this, a vexation from which Sarah has been saved, as she cannot draw.

" Among the late subjects at the Forum, would it not be a good one to discuss whether accomplishments are of essential advantage to the happiness of rational beings ? and though for my own part I should much plead in favour of them, yet a good deal might be said on the other side of the question."

Parts of Letters from Grace Fletcher to her Mother and Sisters.

                                        "*January* 15*th*, 1815.

" When this reaches you, dearest mamma, you will be sitting with them all—Miles telling you about Bourtree Hill, and all those pleasant little minute histories so interesting to ourselves. It is your birthday, and they have all wished you many, ah ! how many, joyful returns of the day.   I remember we used all to try to be the first to run into your room, and give you the wish, and receive the first kiss.   I must content myself with being the last this time, but now from my heart do I send you my little tribute of affection.   We enjoy at this moment, I trust, the only true happiness, the only happiness I think we much prize, the wellbeing of those we love—dearest papa's good health, yours, and all of us ; how few are so blessed—for a continuation of these do I hope and pray, and poor indeed after these would be any wishes of worldly benefits.   Accept then, dearest of mothers, this best wish, and think of me on the 15th as thinking only of you.   Dear aunty, she spoke of you this morning, with tears in her eyes—tears of love and memory.

" Your kindness has furnished me with a great gratification ; two or three days ago I received 'Discipline.'[1]   I have read the greater part of it twice over ; common sentiments of admiration and liking do not suit a book which is so uncommon, —a book which, independent of its interest, has precepts and opinions which must be chronicled in the mind,—a book, in short, the aim and object of which is so noble.   I rose from the perusal of it better, at least in the desire of being better. Miss Mortimer seems to me a character perfectly new ; hers is a soul and a spirit which sets commonplace at defiance ; how

[1] By Mrs. Brunton.

beautiful is her tenderness, her piety, her generosity ! Maitland is the only sort of hero I admire ; splendid, dashing heroes I cannot endure ; perfect heroes, such as my dear Sir Charles, are a little tiresome, not from their goodness, for it is unpleasant even in speaking of the hero of a novel to hear goodness objected to, but from the minuteness with which their charitable deeds are related, which gives them the air of being busybodies ; but in Maitland, the noble intellect, the force of mind, and those feelings which make you know he must be good and charitable, with a certain (I hardly know what to call it) want of detail in the delineation of his character, present to us a being altogether admirable, altogether worthy of love. I like the manner in which Mrs. Brunton has treated the Highland part of the book. She has seized on those features in the manners and character of the Highlanders which are descriptive and picturesque, not those which are ludicrous. She has not taken from the nature of her picture by giving a too brilliant colouring to the scenes she presents ; she has mellowed the background, and touched the prominent and interesting parts with feeling aud genius. To me she has as much surpassed the author of ' Waverley ' in taste as she has in sentiment. Is it not more pleasing to soar than to sink almost buried in the mire ? It is as if a person in describing man said that he was an animal, prodigiously like an ouran-outang ; this is a bodily comparison taken from the earth. There was a poet who, glancing from heaven to earth, exclaimed, ' What a piece of work is man ! in action, how like an angel ! in apprehension, how like a god !' This was a transient burst of exultation, not of arrogant self-confidence ; thinking of great things must always make us humble, because such thoughts lead to the fountain of all greatness. But there is no end of these reflections ; my solitary musings make me very tedious, dearest mamma.— Fondest love to all. G. F."

From Miss Aikin.

"Stoke Newington, *July 1st,* 1815.

" My dear Mrs. Fletcher,—I must not lose the opportunity of writing to you by our dear Grace, yet what can I write that she will not be able to tell you far better ? On one subject only you will find her information defective, and that is herself. She never can, or never will, tell you how very much she has delighted us all by her sweet manners and most interesting conversation, and how deeply we have all regretted her very hasty departure, which has left us tantalized rather than satisfied with her society. 'She is all soul,' says my father. 'She pleases me,' says my mother, 'more than any young woman I have seen ; she is all one could wish.' She is everything, say I, that I hoped and expected she would be, when I saw her three years ago at her own home, already a being that I could make a companion and friend. How exquisite must be your feelings, my friend, who can look on such a creature and say, This is mine ; mine her manners, mine her tastes, her talents, her principles, her feelings. Who can think of you without envying a little the privileges of a mother of such a child ?

"But you will expect me to quit this theme of domestic interest for those public events which nothing can long banish from a mind like yours. What shall we hope or fear, welcome or deprecate, for a nation where revolution succeeds revolution with a rapidity which baffles all speculation and all example ? For my part, I imagine myself sitting in a theatre, where, with eyes riveted on the stage, I watch with eager curiosity and intense interest the unfolding of a grand and complicated drama. Sometimes I smile, sometimes I weep or shudder, often I am surprised, not unfrequently disappointed, but through all successive changes I look with impatience to some end, some great catastrophe, which is to wind up all and show me why this or that incident was made to turn so or so, and what was really to have been wished at such a particular point of the history. Meantime I scarcely feel justified in rejoicing or lamenting, and all my abstract principles seem to be swept away by the resistless current of events. Never, indeed, have I seen the friends of freedom in general so divided, so perplexed, so much in danger of falling into a dilemma on whichever side they speak or act. Bonaparte, the Republican General, was an object of fond admiration to all whom the atrocities of the reign of terror had not previously disgusted for ever with the French cause and nation ; of those some ceased to wish him well after the plundering of Rome, others after he deserted his army in Egypt, and all the consistent ones, as it appears to me, abjured him at last when he assumed the throne; but some, either from a fanatical belief that he was destined to overthrow the Church of Rome, or from the habit and passion of opposition to the ruling party at home, have clung to him in all fortunes. It was difficult for us to hail with cordiality the return of the Bourbons, and some acts of Louis have certainly tended to show that it was truly said that the family had learned nothing and forgotten nothing. On the late restoration of Bonaparte, which had something in it very imposing, it appeared as if the voice of the nation was again heard, and you were by no means singular in indulging a hope that a constitutional party would arise and convert this military despot into a lawful sovereign. I, however, cherished no such expectations. I expected that the Prætorian guard and their emperor, if successful against their foreign enemies, would soon overpower the feeble resistance of the Senate, and I anticipated nothing in such a case but a restoration in full force of his odious tyranny, and ten years of bloodshed and devastation for Europe. In the triumph of the allies and the expected second return of the old dynasty, I therefore rejoice as in the triumph of peace over war, a legitimate sovereign of mild character and pacific disposition over a soldier of fortune, insolent by temper and arbitrary by habit, while his rival is likely to be only haughty by birth and absolute in theory. If, indeed, a constitutional party worthy of the name survives at Paris, by whom will its voice be most willingly heard, by Napoleon the military emperor or by Louis the lawful king? I think unquestionably by the latter. I even hope that he may find it his interest to throw himself into the arms of this only sound portion of the nation as a support against the enmity of the army, which I hope to see under his reign unemployed and consequently disaffected. That the last great battle has thinned its ranks I regard as happy for France and for Europe. Under the terror of such a standing army devoted to such a leader, could civil rights exist in security?

"Thus have I given you my whole profession of faith on this momentous subject, on which in general I think much and speak very little, conscious of my imperfect knowledge, and the many, many chances of erring in my judgment.

" Grace will tell you that I am on the wing for Brighton, and I every moment expect her to claim this letter with our reluctant adieux.—Believe me, ever yours,

" L. AIKIN."

To Mrs. F. from Mrs. Brunton, author of " Self-Control " and " Discipline."

"LONDON, *June* 1815.

" G. left me on Wednesday, and has carried with her more of my esteem, as well as affection, than I ever bestowed upon any person in the same term of acquaintance.   Perhaps I like her the better that she affords me occasion to applaud my own penetration.   She is precisely the being I expected her to prove. She tempts me to the sin of covetousness ; and is, at this moment, the only possession of yours, or any other person's, for which I am inclined to break the tenth commandment.   If I do not absolutely, as the Catechism says, ' envy and grieve at the good of my neighbour,' I cannot deny that I have ' inordinate motions and affections ' to what is yours.   I am ready to quarrel with you for taking her away from me before I had time to steal any part of the kindest and gentlest of hearts from you.   I have seldom seen any one whom I was more desirous to attach ; but she is gone from me before I had time to counteract the ill impressions she would receive from my stiffness and my Calvinism.   This last, you know, you gave me permission to expose ; and accordingly I have not concealed it.   On the contrary, I have spoken out my convictions strongly, though, I hope, not harshly ; and have even solemnly adjured my dear young friend to give them her deliberate and candid consideration.

" She will probably tell you this, and all which has occupied our discourse and attention.   But she will not tell you that the modesty and candour—the singular mixture of simplicity and acuteness, of enthusiasm and gentleness, which she was every moment unconsciously exhibiting, have made her the most interesting show which I have seen in London."

From Mrs. Barbauld to Mrs. Fletcher.

"Stoke Newington, *June 23d,* 1815.

"I must write, I must tell you how much I, how much all of us, admire your daughter. It is but seldom that expectations highly raised are gratified. The imagination has been at work, and the first feeling, at least, is disappointment, but I do assure you your dear Grace is everything I expected, and everything her friends can wish her. The stores of her mind are evidently large, her knowledge not vague, but clear and accurate, and generosity and sensibility seem the leading features of her mind. Her manner is, I think, equally remote from shyness and from a love of display, and has all the graces of youth and modesty. To this she adds all those obliging attentions which youth, confident in its attractions, sometimes neglects ; but now, my dear madam, do you think we can soon resign such a treasure, just look at it and say farewell ? Indeed we cannot ; and the object of my letter is to say that I do hope you will alter your intentions of having Miss Fletcher home so soon, as to our sorrow, no less than surprise, she talks of. So near London, and with your extensive connexions and those of your friends, there cannot long want opportunities of an escort home ; and if our own dear Grace can make herself happy here, I hope you will not refuse to let her prolong a visit on which we have thought so long and with so much pleasure ; and now, I will say no more, but leave it to your generosity.

"Are your friends in Edinburgh rejoicing or mourning over our late victory ? I should suppose there are few families that have not lost some relation, some endeared friend, in the last bloody day. O what a pugnacious animal is man, and what prospect for Europe in so many hordes of fighting men, who, if they please, may cut and carve it amongst themselves. I should not wonder to see France divided as Poland was. A portion in the middle, perhaps, left for the Bourbons; they could secure nothing by their own prowess."]

In the summer of 1812 Mr. Fletcher and all the family went to Yorkshire. The following winter my husband found himself less able for the labours of his profession ;

though nothing could exceed his industry, he became
more frequently attacked by feverish ailments. He had
weathered the political storm most manfully, without
truckling either to judges and men in power on the one
hand, or courting popularity by any subserviency to the
party of the people on the other. He held his course
right onward, and nothing could exceed his interest in the
public good. It was always the subject next his heart,
and the most animating topic of discourse at his own fireside in the midst of his family. He had no turn for
frivolous conversation, and though no enemy to cheerfulness, and most indulgent to the tastes and feelings of his
wife and children, to whom I never heard him utter a
harsh word or unkind expression, he was less personally
disposed to mix in large parties than he had once been.
In the summer of 1813 he was prevailed on to take his
whole family to Park Hall, our small and most incommodious dwelling in Stirlingshire. The interest he took
in his planting and improvements at Park Hall led us
after this to pass the greater part of five summers there,
where he was free from the fatigues and cares of business,
and by this means, I think, added some years to his valuable life, as well as afforded him great interest and amusement. Our summers at Park Hall were made cheerful and
agreeable by the friendliness of our neighbours and the
novelty of the situation. We were twenty miles from
post and market, and I remember in the summer of 1813
a man used to go round among the carnivorous inhabitants
of the parish to ask if they would bespeak a quarter of lamb
or leg of mutton before he ventured to kill the animals in
question. There was a carrier once a week from Glasgow
who brought our bread, our groceries, and our letters ; and
often our impatience for news from the distant world
made us walk miles on the Glasgow road on fine summer

evenings to meet the carriers, and the contents of the bag for the village of Balfron were turned out upon the road, while by the light of the carrier's lantern we picked out our letters and hastened home to read them. Balfron was a most lawless village. There was a cotton-mill in it, and the workers in it were among the best people there. It was illicit distillation that demoralized the district. The men of the place resorted to the woods or to the sequestered glens among the Campsie Hills, and there distilled whisky, which their wives and daughters took in tin vessels in the form of stays buckled round their waists to sell for a high price at Glasgow. This fraud against the Excise led to many other frauds, as these poor people were tempted to steal the articles from which they made the whisky, and a gang of that desperate description lived upon the plunder of their neighbours' goods. One Saturday night the contents of our larder were carried off by some of these marauders, and we were left to make shift for a Sunday dinner, but our hapless condition being noised abroad, legs of mutton, cheeses, butter, and all sorts of good cheer were heaped upon us by the neighbouring gentry. These were diverting incidents at the time, and the summer of 1813 passed most happily away, although quite without the luxuries or almost the ordinary comforts and accommodations of persons accustomed to polite society. We had several friendly visitors, and among others, a distinguished stranger, the brother of my dear friend Mrs. Henry Erskine, Colonel Monro, who after a life of honourable warfare in India had the year before come home to see his friends. Sir Thomas was a man of stern appearance but of most gentle and kindly dispositions, with great talents and high principles of integrity and honour. His sister afterwards told me that the object of his visit at Park Hall at that time was to gain our eldest daughter for his bride. He had the previous winter often met and admired her at Edinburgh parties, but the fates, or rather Providence, willed it otherwise, for she was then, when he came to visit us, on a visit to Mrs. Glasgow in Ayrshire, and there became engaged to Mr. Taylor. Sir Thomas married and returned to India, and died Governor of Madras.

I have said little yet of my younger children, whose characters were by degrees becoming more and more developed. If I had any system in education, it was to lay as little restraint as was consistent with their good on the wishes and pursuits of my children. They equally shared my sympathy and confidence. I had no pleasures which they did not share, no amusements in which they did not take part. I thought that in making them happy I should make them good; but I think I erred in encouraging amusements of too exciting a character, such as private theatricals and recitations. In dear Grace they had perhaps a tendency to increase an excessive sensibility and enthusiasm of character, which, while it made her a most attractive and delightful human being to every one who could appreciate her refined taste and varied talents, would, had she lived, have made her too susceptible to the disappointments of life. I think I did not help my children sufficiently to strengthen their minds by self-discipline; and though I endeavoured to teach them the religion of the Bible, still I think their religious home teaching was too vague and unsystematical to impress habits of self-restraint and self-government from the fear of offending God constantly on their minds. To girls educated at home this is not an unsafe religious education, but to sons, educated as all men are by the world, it is not strict enough to enable them to avoid the seduction of the passions, and the evils of bad example, to which they are so soon exposed. It was on principle, as well as from a feeling of deep gratitude towards the kindest of aunts, that I consented that my three dear girls—Grace, Margaret, and Mary—should take it each in turn to spend their winter half-year with my good uncle and aunt at Tadcaster. They all loved home intensely, and it was no small sacrifice for them to remain in a small dull country town with two old people, without variety, and with no society, or such as they considerèd worse than none; but such was their sense of duty, and such their desire to repay the debt of gratitude their mother owed to this good aunt, that they never complained, when their turn came round, to give up their happy home, and all the pleasures and delights of an Edinburgh society, which they could so fully and richly enjoy, but went cheerfully into their exile; and by frequent letters to and from home, cultivated an ease and liveliness of letter-writing which exercised both mind and heart. This was not the only use of these Tadcaster winters,—it abstracted them from the constant whirl of amusement in which other girls of their age were engaged, it proved a seasonable aid to reflection, and enabled them to live contentedly without excitement, for never did an expression of discontent escape from any of them under these circumstances. Fortunately they had no ready access to books of mere amusement, and were thus thrown on solid reading such as Miss Hill's library, aunt Dawson's book-shelves, and the York library offered. Another advantage this seclusion afforded was, throwing my dear girls among a different grade and description of people from any that they had been accustomed to. It is a comfort to me now to think that my dear aunt owed much of the cheerfulness of her latter years to the interest she took in her young companions. The sweetness of her temper, and her exceeding indulgence towards them, secured them from all trials of temper so far as she was concerned ; and then the joy of coming home more than compensated for the privations they had experienced. It was a good school for them ; it threw them on their own resources ; it gave them individually the happy consciousness that they were doing good, making their mother's best friend happy, and that at the expense of some amusement and pleasure which they sacrificed. It taught them to venerate old age in the sweet example their good aunt's happy temper afforded them, while by the useful employment of their time, they were making more solid acquirements than they could have found leisure to do in Edinburgh.

On the 16th July 1814 our eldest daughter was married to Mr. William Taylor, who then lived at a place belonging to the Earl of Eglinton, called Bourtree Hill. He had unfortunately left the Bar, and a life of considerable usefulness in Parliament, where he belonged to the party of Huskisson and Canning, for the sake of superintending some collieries which his father had left him, and which proved the cause of much after-embarrassment and distress.

[*From Allan Cunningham.*

" LONDON, *April 20th,* 1815.

" MADAM,—I scarcely know how to address you after such a pause in our correspondence, and lest your eye should have forgotten my hand, allow me to forsake the common path of letter-writing and say it is Allan Cunningham who writes to you—one whom you have honoured with your friendship and your counsel, and who never associates your name but with all the words that are generous and exalted and soul-warm in the language. Since I wrote to you last, I have made an important alteration in my mode of life, having forsaken the newspapers and returned to my original vocation. Do not attribute this to fluctuation of temper and love of change. It was a premeditated step, and my peace of mind, my health, and the welfare of my family, alike demanded it. When I left the papers I entered into the employment of Mr. Chantrey, a sculptor of eminent natural abilities, who intrusted me with the management of his work, and gave me a comfortable salary. With him I enjoy the greatest repose of mind. After observing all day the marble assume elegance and grace beneath the chisel of the sculptor, I return to a neat and convenient house, and amuse myself in cultivating cabbages or bachelors'-buttons till the twilight, after which I edify my youngest son, and sometimes my wife, by humming over remains of ancient song. This I hope is an amusement as harmless as babbling in rhyme, and as pleasant too, and what heightens my enjoyment still more, is the prospect which I have of seeing you in Edinburgh in the course of a twelve-month, for we are carving statues of President Blair and Lord Melville for decorating your good town, which I will have to erect. My mind is now free from the delightful but bewitching entanglements of poesy. Acquaintance with the world has sombered the rosy and romantic colouring with which my youth had decked the vista of future years. It has given me right notions and a knowledge of myself, and pictured the path of my life with an austere but a truthful hand."]

1816.—It was during this winter that we were led, by strong feelings of sympathy with dear Miles's happiness, to see clearly that his attachment to Miss Clavering, and the attachment he had inspired, called upon us to make some sacrifice to enable him to fulfil his engagement. Nothing could be more reasonable and less selfish than his feelings and conduct. When, upon being asked what he meant to do, he frankly avowed his engagement, and said—"I intend to work and wait ; I know you cannot afford to make me a separate establishment." I should here mention, with contrition, how severely I felt Mrs. Taylor's misfortunes, not with thankful submission that no part of them was owing to any misconduct on her part,—that ought to have consoled me ; but it was my first great sorrow and disappointment, and, like the spoiled child of fortune, I took her reverses of fortune so desperately to heart that I seldom awoke in the morning without finding my pillow wet with tears.   I was most rebellious under this dispensation ; but it pleased God to send me sorrow in another shape, coming not through human intercession, but directly from His chastening hand ; and when that sorrow came, though I did not feel less for Mrs. Taylor's blighted prospects in life, the character of my grief was changed : it ceased to be rebellious, and was subdued by a feeling of conscious impiety in having rebelled against the will of God.

The winter of this year (1816 and 1817) was quietly and peacefully spent; but as I have narrated it more particularly in a short memoir of my beloved Grace, written three months after her death, which happened on the 16th of April 1817,[1] I shall not here repeat the details, as the narrative contains more traits and characteristic incidents of the last six months of Grace's life than my memory would now enable me to supply.—Dated March 6, 1844.

[*Letter to Miss Aikin, from Miles Angus Fletcher.*

" *April* 19, 1817.

"I write, at the desire of my dear and afflicted mother, to let you know of the irreparable loss we have sustained.   It is not yet three weeks since our dear Grace was attacked by a fever, which soon showed itself to be typhus.   The progress of the disease was rapid, but Doctors Gregory and Thomson said it was not attended with any peculiarly bad symptom.   On Sunday last she was much better, and on Tuesday so well as to allow me, with some comfort, to set out upon the Western Circuit. On Wednesday she became rapidly worse, and that evening

---

[1] See Appendix.

closed her sufferings and her blameless life. When I tell you that we have lost Grace, I am sure I need not attempt to describe the affliction of this unhappy family. My father seems to have acquired strength from the necessity of exertion, but my mother's grief is at present beyond the reach of consolation. Dr. Thomson was with Grace at the last moment ; till all was over he had not abandoned hope ; he even thought some favourable symptoms appeared within the last hour, and when she did expire, her departure was so quiet that he could hardly observe the change.

"Will you communicate this afflicting intelligence to Mrs. Barbauld and to Miss Benger ? My mother will write to them and to yourself when she becomes more composed. I trust all those dear to you are well—I am, yours faithfully,

"Miles A. Fletcher.

"North Castle Street."

At the end of April 1817 we all went to Park Hall. After such a sorrow, the return to a place where Grace had been so happy, so useful, and so beloved was a new trial ; but the quietness and retirement of our country home was greatly preferred by all of us to remaining in Edinburgh at that time.

We all tried to support each other in the best way we could, and I had the comfort of seeing Mr. Fletcher regain both health and spirits while occupied with his farm. We were soon joined by our eldest and youngest daughters. Mrs. Taylor was at that time living at Newcastle, where dear Mary, under Mrs. Millar's kind escort from Yorkshire (where she had spent the winter), joined her sister, and they proceeded together to Edinburgh, after we had come to Park Hall.

[LETTERS FROM AND TO MRS. FLETCHER, ON THE SUBJECT OF
GRACE'S DEATH AND CHARACTER.

To her daughter Mary.

"PARK HALL, *April* 27, 1817.

"Papa, Margaret, Angus, and I, with Robertson and little
Spinky, arrived here safe and well at 8 o'clock last night.   It
was a fine day; and if we could have enjoyed anything, it
would have been the mildness of the air, the freshness and
verdure of the country, and the beauty of the setting sun and
western sky.   We have had the only refreshing sleep that we
have got for nearly a month past, for having all walked for
several miles at different parts of the road, we were much
fatigued.   We have been sauntering about for three or four
hours this morning in one of the brightest and warmest days
I ever remember at this season.   The little shrubbery that
Angus, you, and I planted, is thriving well, the garden in good
order, and the Ayrshire rose, clematis, and woodbine in most
luxuriant beauty.   The woodbine near the little parlour window
was planted by our darling Grace, when we came here on the 15th
of June 1813.   You and Bessy will remember that we all
arrived late on the night of the 14th, I and my four dear girls.
It seems strange to me now that we did not then think ourselves the very happiest of human beings.   I think we did
enjoy the blessings of each other's affection, but we did not
prize it half enough.   What would we not now give to be as
happy as we were on that 14th of June!   These reflections,
my dearest Mary, have no other use than to make us deeply
and sensibly thankful for what remains to us.   They cannot
recall what we have lost.   Tell dearest Mrs. Millar that Park
Hall is not gloomy, nor does it recall half so many painful and
heart-breaking recollections as the house in Castle Street did,
where the sound of her mournful and delirious voice was never
absent from my mind one moment.   She is here indeed, and
must be carried everywhere in my heart, as long as it shall
beat ; but she is here, tranquil and happy, such as I saw her
two years ago when she arrived from London.   Your father's
health will be greatly improved by coming here, and so will

dear Margaret's, whose paleness and melancholy have sometimes alarmed me, though she has made the most wonderful efforts to support us all. I have had a very excellent and gratifying letter from Miss Clavering, and indeed if sympathy could have availed us, we have met with more than I can tell you. It has been soothing, as a testimony to the virtues of your sister; which, modest and unobtrusive as they were, seem to have been noted in a remarkable degree. My dear child, do not afflict yourself about us : you will find your father and me wonderfully composed, and your and Bessy's coming is a joyful anticipation to us all. We long, too, to see dear little Archy also."

*Copy of a Letter from the Rev. J. Clowes to Mrs. Fletcher,
on Grace's Death.*

"MANCHESTER, *May* 13, 1817.

" MY DEAR MADAM,—A few days ago our excellent friend Miss Kennedy brought me a letter which she had lately received from you, from which I soon perceived that your pen was dipped in tears, and that you rank at present amongst the number of those blessed ones who are distinguished by the holy title of mourners in Zion. Let me not then be thought an impertinent intruder into the sanctuary of your sorrows, if I wish on this occasion to mingle my tears with yours, by entering into partnership with you, both in your afflictions and in all those heavenly consolations which the Father of Mercies never fails to mix in the cup of His afflicted children. Charity, we know, which is the spirit of heaven, is never so happy as in the opportunity of pouring into the troubled bosom the oil of joy and gladness, and he knows at the same time that this oil comes only from the God of heaven, whose high and holy name is Jesus Christ. I might therefore say to you, as the king of Israel said to a mourner in his day, 'If the Lord do not help thee, whence should I help thee ?' Nor should I conceive that the words contained anything of repulsion or of discouragement, for is not our God a present help in trouble, and do not all His dispensations as well as His declarations prove Him to be so ? Is He not also above all trouble, and this in such a sort, that He not only controls it, by saying to its waves, 'Hitherto shall ye go, and no further'? but He also compels it to administer to His own purposes of blessing, so that every trouble opens the gate of some new joy, which otherwise could neither have been seen nor tasted. I please and flatter myself with thinking that you have already experienced the truth of this sentiment, and that even in the loss of your dear child (if it may be called a loss) you have found a more than proportionable gain, through the communication and admission of some heretofore unknown consolation. And how do you know but that your dear child may have been the minister of that consolation? We cannot indeed see with our bodily eyes that this has been the case, but the eye of faith we know possesses a more quick and penetrating vision, and being enlightened by the light of this eternal truth, sees things as they are, not as they appear to be. To the eye of faith therefore the invisible world is near and visible as this world is to the eye of the body, and therefore it sees all that the Word of God has revealed respecting that invisible world, and how the souls or spirits of the deceased are still alive, even more alive than when in the material body, and also are still near to those they loved and by whom they were loved, and even nearer than heretofore; and further, that they are endowed with greater power, as well as stronger inclination to comfort, support, and protect those whom they have left behind them. Jesus Christ accordingly informs His disciples, previous to His departure out of the world, 'It is expedient for you that I go away, for if I go not away, the Comforter will not come unto you; but if I go away I will send Him unto you:' and again, 'I go away and come again unto you;' thus instructing them that although He was leaving them as to bodily presence, yet He would still be virtually and really present with them as a Holy Comforter, to guide, protect, and console them. Doubt not therefore, my dear madam, that what was true respecting Jesus Christ is true also respecting His children, so that when they quit this world they enter immediately into a state of being in which the capacity of intercourse and of blessing is indefinitely increased. In devout prayer that you may feel all the comfort of this sentiment, and still enjoy both the presence and the society of your beloved child, I remain, dear Madam, affectionately yours,

" J. CLOWES."

Joanna Baillie to Mrs. Fletcher.

"*June* 30*th*, 1817.

" I wrote to our friend Miss Millar some considerable time after your severe loss, to inquire for you and Mr. Fletcher and the family, and had the satisfaction to hear by her answer as good an account of you as I could expect. May I now be permitted to make inquiries immediately of yourself?—not, however, expecting an answer from your own pen, if it should be painful to you, but only hoping that Mrs. Taylor (who, I learn, is with you), or some member of the family, will have the goodness to send me a few lines. Your sorrow for the loss of a child so excellent in head, heart, temper,—in everything that is most desirable in one of God's children,—has been sympathized with in no common degree. It has been a sensation deeply felt by many, who on their own account also lamented the sad event. I have never known any young person so universally admired and beloved, and few, I believe, have lived in the world, unconnected with any remarkable circumstance, that will be so long and so tenderly remembered. This is soothing to your grief; and with the greatest of all consolation—the hopes of religion—and the family blessings that are spared to you still, your heart cannot be desolate, but must be comforted. May you indeed feel every comfort and consolation that your heavy affliction will admit! My sister begs to join me in condolence and all kind wishes to you and Mr. Fletcher, Mrs. Taylor, and all the family. I hoped to have heard of you last week by Mrs. Barbauld, but I was prevented from going to Newington, which I regretted. Dr. Aikin's recovery from such a decided palsy, a recovery so speedy and so complete, at his advanced age, is extraordinary. Mrs. Barbauld's spirits are quite raised by it, for at the first, I understand, she was like one stunned and knocked down. How few brothers and sisters have been to one another what they have been through so long a course of years! When they must part, it will be a dismal thing for the survivor."

I

From Mrs. Barbauld, on G. F.'s death, to her Mother, 1817.

"It has been the impulse of my heart to write to you, and yet I hardly know how. What can I say, how can I express the shock this awful, this most affecting event has given me, has given all of us? How are the fairest hopes destroyed, how are the dearest ties severed! when was the uncertainty of life, and all its hopes, exemplified in a more solemn manner? Dear Grace! I had hoped myself some time, perhaps this summer, to see more of her, to see her open the stores of her mind, to see the modest flower expand and show all its lustre; but it is shut up for ever here, to blow, I trust, in a brighter climate. Young as she was, she has seen perhaps the best of life. Like Young's Narcissa, 'she sparkled, was exhaled, and went to heaven.' No long sickness to wear the mind as well as body; none of the decays incident to a more advanced period; she leaves life, it is true, in all its freshness, but without having tasted its cares or sorrows. And is it not something to have raised and cultivated such a mind? Is she not fitter for another state, with higher powers than many a one who has passed sixty years of a drowsy existence? Oh, but I think I hear you say, the mother's heart must bleed. It must; I know it. God comfort you, my dear Mrs. Fletcher, and Mr. Fletcher, and all your family! Your mind will turn, I know it will, to the promising children you still have. One jewel has fallen from your maternal crown, but many remaiu; you are still rich. May God enable you to bear what He has laid upon you!"

To Mrs. Stark.

"PARK HALL, *April* 30*th*, 1817.

"MY DEAR FRIEND,—I do know what you have all felt for us, for you were among the few who knew what we have lost. Your kindness in offering to come to me at that dreadful time will never be forgotten. Time may and will do much, not in removing her from our hearts, but in enabling us to take an interest in present things, and softening those recollections which are now so overpowering. Even now you—no, not you, but those who do not know what grief is ; grief made up of tenderness and affectionate sorrow without one atom of bitterness—would be astonished at our composure, and doubt whether we had yet begun to feel. Yes, my dear friend, I must see you at Park Hall. Perhaps you can come to us the latter end of next week, when Mr. Fletcher and my sons return to Edinburgh to meet Bessy and Mary, who are to join us here about the 16th of May. Bessy and her children are to spend the summer with us, and our poor Mary needs the comfort of her home, such as it now is. She is a very precious child, and Margaret—my generous, kind-hearted Margaret—what should we have done without her ? God Almighty bless you ! Write to me, dear friend.—Yours, E. FLETCHER."

From Mrs. Fletcher to Miss Aikin.

"PARK HALL, *June* 23d, 1817.

" If I were to delay writing to my dear Miss Aikin till my paper should be unblotted by my tears, I know not when I should write to her.

" I have to the utmost of my power, both for my own sake and for the sake of those who are very dear to me, resisted all unreasonable indulgence of grief. I have endeavoured to derive consolation from all those considerations which you and the rest of my affectionate and sympathizing friends have suggested—from the elevation of her character, from her purity, sweetness and heavenly-mindedness ; but there is so much tenderness associated with every recollection of her life, that my very pleasures are now so many sorrows, since she can no longer share them with me. Perhaps there never was a human being so much alive to enjoyment. This is a feeling of thankfulness of which nothing can deprive me—the unalloyed happiness of her life. There never was one so ardent and so sensitive who knew so little sorrow. Had she lived, this uninterrupted happiness could not have continued, but this, while it ought to reconcile me to the dispensations of Providence, and while it takes from my loss all its bitterness, adds powerfully to the tenderness of my regrets. The energy and activity of her mind during the last six months of her life were remarkable. She had applied herself diligently to Italian literature. She painted two portraits, one the copy of a picture of young Wolfe Tone, and one of her father, which last however she did not live to finish. She passed several hours during three days of the week in the superintendence of a Female Lancastrian School, and enlivened our domestic circle by her invariable sweetness and cheerfulness of temper. At her special request (made in consideration of her father's delicate state of health) we neither gave nor accepted of invitations to large parties during the whole winter, but enjoyed the society of more intimate friends. She was truly grateful for your distinguished kindness, and loved you with the sincerest affection. With what pleasure and exultation she anticipated the success of your historical work, and how proud she was of your friendship! She used to speak of her visit at Stoke Newington as the most gratifying period of her life, and repeatedly thanked me the very week before she was taken ill for having promoted that journey ; but home and home affections were her delights. The support I received from my dear Margaret during that miserable fortnight can never be described. She is worthy of your regard, worthy of having had such a sister."]

Miss Clavering and her brothers paid us a visit that summer at Park Hall, 1817, and arrangements were made for her marriage to our dear son Miles, which was to take place in the December following. Miles's tenderness of feeling came out towards me in a marked manner during this mournful summer, and contributed much to soothe my grief.

PART III.

On the 27th December 1817, Miles and Miss Clavering were married at Ardincaple Castle, Lord John Campbell's residence. Lady Augusta Clavering and her daughter had lived there for some years.

Miles took his very lovely bride from this lordly castle to his father's homely dwelling at Park Hall, where they remained until the winter Session began, when they took possession of the house in Queen Street which had been settled on them as part of the dowry by Lady Augusta, who showed great kindness to and sympathy with her daughter in this marriage of affection.

We mixed little that winter of 1817-18 in general society, and went as early as we could to spend the last summer we were to be at Park Hall. Mr. Fletcher found it was most expedient to part with that property. It involved him in money difficulties, having now more claims upon him than he could easily meet. Miles, on whose account he chiefly wished to retain this estate, assisted me much in persuading his father to sell it; and we both rejoiced in the repose of mind which was gained by parting with this favourite but expensive farm.

My husband continued to take the liveliest interest in public affairs, and employed his daughters by turns in writing for him, both on Borough Reform and other subjects, to his dictation, after he gave up his clerk. In this way he was of use to many poor clients who consulted him, and prevented many lawsuits by advising them to arrange their affairs by arbitration. And here I must remark, how much it contributes to happiness and independence of mind in aged persons to have some object of science or literature that lightens the lassitude of daily life, and gives animation to existence beyond the family circle, when age or infirmity prevents any active participation either in the business or the pleasures of life.

The science of politics, which, according to my husband's views, may be called the wellbeing of mankind on earth, when unmixed with sordid or selfish aims, seems to me to elevate the mind above every other science. I mean that enlarged view of political wisdom which is unfettered by party spirit, untainted by selfish or personal views, and has its foundation in a profound love of mankind, and a desire to promote, not only their happiness, but their moral and spiritual good, by keeping justice and mercy constantly in view. Such were my husband's politics; and neither age nor infirmity abated the interest he took in every measure which had public good and enlightened freedom for its object.

[These remarks were written in 1844 ; and such being her feeling about my father's public life, it may be imagined with what delight she afterwards read the cordial tribute to his character in Cockburn's " Life of Jeffrey," and also in the " Memorials of his Time." I seem to see her countenance before me, as one of my brightest recollections, when I read to her, in May 1856, the following sentence from the 261st page of Lord Cockburn's book :—" The pure and heroic Fletcher knew not what jealousy was, and would have cheered on a personal enemy, if he had had one, provided he was going before him in the public cause."

In looking back on our father's dignified and benevolent old age, I think none of his children can recollect a single expression

of wounded pride or disappointed ambition escaping from him
in the almost daily discussion of public events, great or small,
which took place in our family circle.

During the few years we remained in Edinburgh after the
first great sorrow of her life, Grace's death, our mother withdrew in great measure from general society and large parties,
and gave the time and strength thus gained to an increased
occupation among the poor and needy. During this time
she gave much time to attendance at the office of the Beggar's Society, where the benevolent John Forbes (afterwards
Lord Medwyn) and she first came into close personal acquaintance.

My mother used to say it was very pleasant to her to see
the good Tories she met there smile upon her in her endeavours
to do good, and how much even party rancour died away in the
common interest felt in the sufferings of the poor.]

During this summer of 1819, Margaret, Mary, and I
went to London ; Mr. Fletcher preferred remaining at
Tadcaster. We saw many very interesting people. We
passed some days of great interest with dear Mrs. Barbauld
at Stoke Newington, admiring her for her genius, and
loving her for the truthfulness and kindliness of her disposition and the sweetness of her manners. We had also
the privilege of passing some days with Joanna Baillie and
her sister, at Hampstead. The remarkable simplicity of
Joanna's manners, and entire absence of all pretension,
struck my daughters much, and while they were awed by
the meekness with which she bore her faculties, they
admired and loved her. Mrs. Opie and Jane Porter also
passed before us, as dissolving views ; along with the Smiths
of " The Rejected Addresses," the Miss Berrys and Sir
Lumley Skeffingtons of the day. It was on this visit to
London that we had the happiness to pass some hours in
Newgate with Mrs. Fry. We heard her read and expound
to the female prisoners the third chapter of St. John's

Gospel. Her voice was melody itself, and the earnest sweetness with which she explained the doctrine of regeneration to her attentive hearers found its way directly to their hearts; many of them shed tears, and all were attentive and appeared deeply interested. She conducted us through the different wards. The women flocked round her, several of them telling her their little wants, and expressing their gratitude for what she had told them. She lent a kindly ear to their complaints, and it was plain her sympathy and kindness did them good. The faces of many who did not speak revealed this. Robert Owen, the notorious socialist, accompanied us to Newgate. He was then intimate with Mrs. Fry, and we had known him for many years. He had always appeared to us a benevolent and zealous reformer, and we bore with the intense though quiet egotism of his conversation from the belief that he had the good of his fellow-creatures at heart. He had not then openly avowed those opinions, so fatal to moral and religious truth and happiness, which he has since so unfortunately promulgated. It would be unfair perhaps to refuse him credit for wishing to promote the present good of mankind, but when he cannot but perceive that a consideration for present good, even when accompanied by a belief in a Divine Judge, is not sufficient to enable man to regulate his passions and abstain from evil, how is it likely that when those restraints are removed, as Owen desires, the sovereignty of reason alone, a vegetable diet, and one loose garment, will transform the human race, as he expects, from misery to happiness?

The same day we visited Newgate Robert Owen took us to call on William Godwin, the celebrated author of "Political Justice." Godwin, then an interesting-looking old man, lived at a small bookseller's shop on Ludgate Hill, with a figure of Æsop above the door. We sat half an hour with this mild philosopher. His countenance was benevolent, as were his writings. Thirty years before the time we saw him, his "Political Justice" was thought to have allayed the insurrectionary fever produced, as some imagined, by the writings of Thomas Paine; but now that the days of alarm were over, Godwin was more known as the author of "Caleb Williams" and "St. Leon" than as a political writer. He had a beautiful portrait of Mary Wollstone-craft, by Opie, above the chimney-piece of his little parlour. We were pleased with our interview with this distinguished man and very eloquent writer.

We all rejoined Mr. Fletcher, well satisfied with the sights of London and its environs. Dear Mary remained that winter with our aunt.

[*To her daughter Mary from E. F.*

"EDINBURGH, *January* 1820.

"We despatched the *Scotsman* for you on Saturday, which would afford you much amusement. We have been greatly complimented and congratulated by our friends on your father's appearance at the meeting in honour of Lord Erskine's arrival in Edinburgh. Miles says that when his father appeared there on the platform there were thunders of applause, and his speech was much cheered, especially that part of it relating to his being one of the thirty-eight who had the honour of voting for the Honourable Henry Erskine, when he was expelled from the Deanship of the Faculty of Advocates because he presided at a public meeting held to petition against the continuation of the war.

" On Friday morning we were honoured by a visit from Lord Erskine. He sat with us more than an hour, and was very agreeable and entertaining. He has a strong family likeness to his late brother,[1] but is less gay, bland, and engaging; his countenance bears strong marks of a life of great emotion,— of much wear and tear. He is less courteous than his brother

1 Honourable Henry Erskine.

Henry; his manners are plainer.   We talked of the State trials
in which he was formerly engaged.   He asked me if I had
ever read his speech on the trial of Williams, the publisher of
Paine's 'Age of Reason.'   He was engaged by the Society
for the Prevention of Vice as counsel for the prosecution.   He
got a verdict against Williams, which proved, he said, that there
was no occasion to make new laws against blasphemous publi-
cations.   A few days after the trial, as he was walking through
Holborn, a woman seized him by the skirts of his coat, and
dragged him to a miserable room, where Williams the bookseller was laid on a sick-bed with three children in the confluent
small-pox.   He was so much struck with the poverty and
wretchedness of the man's condition that he wrote to the Society
for the Prevention of Vice, telling them that, as they had
gained a verdict prohibiting the sale of Paine's blasphemous
book, now there was a noble opportunity to show a truly
Christian spirit, by praying the Court to mitigate the punishment of this miserable man, already afflicted with disease and
poverty.   The Society, he said, wrote him a letter full of
compliments, but declined to relinquish their victim.   The
next day their agent called on Lord Erskine with a brief and
fee, desiring him to crave the judgment of the Court upon
Williams.   He refused to take the fee, and asking for his brief,
he drew his pen through the retainer as counsel for that Society,
because 'they loved judgment rather than mercy.'   He said
he had lately found some of his speeches on this trial in a
pedlar's basket, and he left us one of them.   It is a most
eloquent defence of Christianity from the attacks of infidels.   I
should mention that Williams was sentenced to two years'
imprisonment."

To the Same.

"*February* 1820.

"Lord Erskine called with Lord Buchan on Saturday, and
sat a long time.   He has a fund of amusing political anecdote.
It was he who introduced the present King to Lady Hertford;
and it is, he says, to this unfortunate introduction that many
of the disastrous measures of the Regency are owing, for she

governs the King with despotic sway. When Lady Hugh Seymour died, she left the guardianship of her only daughter to Mrs. Fitzherbert. The testamentary guardian applied to Lord Eldon as Chancellor to take the child from Mrs. Fitzherbert, on the ground of her being a Roman Catholic. Lord Eldon pronounced judgment in favour of this separation, it being contrary to the law of England that a Catholic should be appointed guardian to a Protestant child. The Prince Regent sent for Lord Erskine, and said that it would be the death of Mrs. Fitzherbert and the child if they were separated. Lord Erskine advised the Prince to apply to Lady Hertford to use her influence with her husband, the eldest uncle of the child, to allow her to remain with Mrs. Fitzherbert. He did so, and from this accidental acquaintance has arisen the influence Lady Hertford has obtained over the mind of his present Majesty. This 'is a curious piece of secret Court history. Lord Erskine attributes to this his Majesty's change of politics, the continuance of the French war, and in short all the. disastrous measures of the Regency."]

As the spring approached, now that we were free of Park Hall, and also of the Court of Session, we were more able to wander, and our excellent friend Mrs. Grant of Laggan recommended Callander to us as a pleasant residence within easy reach of many Highland beauties; and early in the summer of 1820 we took a house called the Old Manse at Callander.

I think it was the end of June 1820 that we took possession of our summer quarters. I remember the beauty, and courtesy of our hostess, Mrs. Campbell, a young widow, impressed us favourably on our first arrival, and the appearance of her house was more comfortable-looking than we expected to meet with in those days. There was a little green bank sloping down to the clear bright waters of the river Teith, in front of the house. The course of that beautiful river was more flowing and gentle at that place than either above or below our house, but still it had enough of life, " to discourse most eloquent music," and we took it to our hearts at once. We were then a large family party, and our one spare room was seldom untenanted. We took exploring walks daily when the weather improved, and each selected a favourite seat at the Roman Camp, a place full of wooded knolls and chequered shade, a short distance from the town of Callander, then, before railway days, a very primitive Border Highland village.

Our first visitor there was dear Mary Grant, who came to refresh her soul in the Highland air she loved so dearly. She was at that time more able to enjoy than I ever remember to have known her. There had been some respite in the family sorrows, and whether in grief or joy she was equally welcome to all of us.

Our family party was often enlivened by the arrival of agreeable English and American strangers, introduced to us by different friends. I think it was that year we first became acquainted with George Ticknor,[1] from Boston, U.S., and a friend of his, Mr. Cogswell. We thought them among the most cultivated and agreeable Americans we had ever known, and have since kept up our friendship by occasional correspondence with Mr. Ticknor. We also saw a good deal of Mrs. Smith of Coniston, and "*the* Joanna" and her sister, Mrs. Agnes Baillie, from Hampstead, who were at Callander part of that summer, and joined us in many exploring expeditions.

I should not take leave of this summer without recording our pleasant intercourse with Farmer Buchanan, whose character had more of the Lowland than of the Highland type. He united the virtues of both—great cultivation and independence, with the courtesy of Highland manners. He was a very fine specimen of human nature, and we used to enjoy a talk with him much when he was binding up

---

[1] Author of " Life of Prescott," and " History of Spanish Literature."

his sheaves, or when the labours of the day were over he returned to his cottage and the enjoyment of his books. His knowledge of what was passing in the literary world was kept up by his five sons, who had all been distinguished students at Glasgow College. The only one who had not shown any thirst for knowledge assisted him in his farm. The others had all been sent off with their winter supply of potatoes and meal to Glasgow, where, after the first year, they never cost their parents anything, being able to save by summer private tuition what defrayed their expenses in winter. Farmer Buchanan's eldest son, who afterwards became Professor of Logic at Glasgow College, was, at the time I speak of, minister of Peebles, and came during the summer to visit his parents, and delight himself in his old haunts about Callander. We heard him preach a very beautiful sermon during this visit in the parish church of Callander, and it was delightful to see and to sympathize with the joy of the venerable Elder on this occasion, and to watch his face in church.

One of the old man's chief pleasures we found to be reading Milton, and so great a master was he of Gaelic lore that he had translated several books of Paradise Lost into Gaelic verse. Mr. Fletcher took to his Gaelic studies again this summer with great zest, and we concluded the pleasures of the summer by paying some visits to old friends in Argyllshire, accompanied by our youngest son and daughter, who enjoyed this introduction to the land of their fathers as much as we could possibly desire. They were then in the freshness of their youth, and were pronounced by their Highland kinsmen to be worthy representatives of the clan.

[*Letter to Mrs. Stark, Edinburgh,* 1820, *after the
Callander summer.*

"Mr. Fletcher had indeed a great triumph in making us complete converts to what we used to think his partial estimate of the Highland character. There is a kind of chivalrous romance in it of which I had before no conception. I think this arises from the absence of those gainful speculations which are open to the operative and middling classes of the English and Lowland Scotch. The gentry in the Highlands are not a bit higher-toned than the same class elsewhere. It is the Highland grazier and his clansmen the shepherds who count kindred to men of high degree, and dwell on the ancient traditions of their clan, till the whole character is elevated. A poor Highlander has no counteraction to those feelings of hospitality by which he is so much distinguished. This graceful quality is not checked by sordid calculation of any kind, not even by making a provision for his own old age; he relies with affectionate confidence on the provision his children will make for him, when he can no longer climb the hill or gather the sheep into the fold. The respect paid to old age is one of the most beautiful features of the primitive state of society. Age is not merely tolerated, but it is honoured. I saw a woman of near eighty living in a neat cottage, with an acre of land and a cow, purchased for her by five sons, who were simply Highland shepherds. Proud she was, and well might she be so, of her little possession. I never saw so much real virtue in humble life as this view of society afforded me. It made me detest poor-rates more than ever, and manufacturing districts; it made me, I fancy, a bad political economist, but a greater lover than ever of my fellow-creatures."

From Mrs. Wolfe Tone Wilson to Mrs. Fletcher.

"George Town, *September* 23*d,* 1820.

"Yes, my beloved friend, you judge like yourself—truly, nobly, delicately. The warmth and sincerity of my affection for you can never alter: it was sealed by sympathy; but before that heartrending sympathy existed, when you could sympathize with sorrow without having tasted it, my love to you was founded on esteem, on admiration of the pure and generous loveliness of your mind, and its expanded, enlightened benevolence. Speaking of you one day with Eliza Wilkes, I was observing how well your appearance corresponded to your character, and, amongst other follies, I said you were a full-blooded animal of generous breed. Eliza laughed, and said you really had the qualities of a noble horse. I observed how delightful it would be to investigate the world mounted on a horse of your character. 'Oh,' said Eliza, 'indeed I could never ride Mrs. Fletcher.' 'Ride Mrs. Fletcher ! ride Mrs. Fletcher ! !' the sound pulled up my ideas. Eliza went on saying, if you *were* a horse she would put you in a park of clover. . . . I instantly sprang upon you, and declared you should never be condemned to uselessness and plenty, and oh what a scamper I took with you through the universe ! " [1]]

The summer of 1821 we spent very pleasantly at Coniston, in Mrs. Smith's cottage, opposite the gate of Tent Lodge, which we had secured for three months. This second residence at the Lakes, at the distance of fifteen years, renewed our admiration and delight in the scenery of that district.

I was then in vigorous health, and I remember, in a pony expedition my two daughters and I took, escorted by Joseph Harden, I generally rode foremost of the party, by Hard Knot and Wry Nose to Wast Water, Calder

[1] Mrs. Wolfe Tone Wilson was one of my mother's very dear friends, and she says of her in a letter to me : " I admired and loved her for the union of magnanimity and tenderness she possessed, and it will always be a pleasing reflection to me that I believe my sympathy in all she had done and suffered was some comfort to her when she came into a land of strangers."

This lady was the widow of Theobald Wolfe Tone, and lived in Paris till the return of the Bourbons, when she and her son went to America. She married at this time her generous friend, Mr. Wilson, who gave up his country and friends for her sake.

Abbey, Buttermere, and Borrowdale, and back to Coniston across the Stake, which was thought, in those days, a perilous adventure for female equestrians. It was upon that expedition that I heard, with a degree of surprise that amused me at the time, that the landlady at Calder Bridge designated me as the "old lady." It was a wholesome truth that flashed upon me : I was then fifty-one, and had not begun to think myself an old woman. Our visit to Seathwaite and the Duddon on this occasion interested us much. Wordsworth's Notes to his "Sonnets on the Duddon" had made us acquainted with the simple annals of Robert Walker, who exercised the office of priest, schoolmaster, will-maker, wool-spinner, and brewer of ale for the whole village. Mrs. Smith's kindness and hospitality towards us could not be exceeded. She had many jokes with my daughters at my expense, as she thought I exceeded in attempting the duties of hospitality in so small a dwelling. Her graceful wit amused me, but did not improve me on the points she desired—exclusiveness as to society. She loved my children, and I was not jealous to see them more than rival me in her affection and admiration.

It was this summer we became intimate with Mrs. George Martin and her daughter, Mrs. Buckle. The latter was then lately married, and, with her husband and mother, enjoying a first acquaintance with the Lake district. The ladies were most agreeable and cultivated people. They were nearly connected with the good old Whig Member for Tewkesbury, James Martin.

The intimacy formed at this time led to much after-intercourse and enjoyment to my daughters, who paid them frequent visits in Gloucestershire, and saw many interesting places and people in a part of England they had before been unacquainted with. Many points of sympathy attracted us to each other. They were not at all political, but they were simple in their habits and tastes, entirely free from that false estimate of things which so many persons inherit who are born in a good social position, and so many assume who are not so born, and who think it necessary to keep up appearances at all times and seasons, and thus lose a great deal of innocent enjoyment. Mrs. Buckle had great artistic powers, and her mother was an excellent botanist, and one of the most refined, unselfish, and cultivated persons we have ever known, a very fine type of the English lady of the old school.

It was during this summer of 1821 I heard of the sudden death of one of my oldest and dearest Manor School friends, Mrs. Craik of Arbigland. She was a woman of excellent talents and very warm affections. We loved each other truly at school, and ever after cultivated a friendship which contributed much to each other's happiness. We had the comfort to know the same feeling descended to our children. After her marriage to Mr. Craik of Arbigland (a beautiful place on the Solway, about fifteen miles from Dumfries), we frequently took that route either to or from our visits to Yorkshire. It might be about the year 1810 or 1812, when returning from a walk, that Mrs. Craik directed my attention to some young masons who were engaged in the erection of some stone pillars of a new gateway in the approach to the house of Arbigland. She said, "One of these young men is, I do not say a Burns, but certainly no inconsiderable poet; you must find out which it is." I looked for a few moments at each, while she was speaking to them, and at once decided that the tall, thoughtful, stalwart youth who gave respectful attention to what she was saying was the poet of the party. It was Allan Cunningham, and from that time he and I became fast friends. I found some of his MS. songs on my table when I went to my room at night. When he came to Edinburgh to improve himself in his trade, we were able to be of use to him in supplying him with books and giving him introductions; but he made his own way by his wisdom and good sense, as well as by his talents, steadily and continuously. He was engaged at that time to marry an excellent young woman well known to Mrs. Craik, and he was soon able to fulfil his engagement; and a better wife no poet ever had. Allan's career in London is well known. He wisely secured for himself a certain income as Chantrey's secretary and the superintendent of his works, and gave his leisure time to the cultivation of literature and composition.

[*To Allan Cunningham.*

"EDINBURGH, *April* 15*th*, 1820.

"MY DEAR SIR,—You must not judge of the pleasure your letter gave me by my dilatoriness in answering it. You are right in saying that I am interested in your pursuits, and rejoice in your happiness. Of all the persons I saw in my last summer's visit to London, I know not one whose temper of mind, and condition altogether, pleased me so much as yours did. I saw you pursuing an occupation the most elegant and tasteful, I saw you high in the estimation of a man whose genius you revere; your children were playing round you, your wife had the countenance of a happy and contented woman, your home bespoke comfort and respectability, and all that you possessed you owed to your own talents and industry. You preserved the erect independence of your character, and were the same honourable and unsophisticated being as when I first knew you. The stirrings of ambition you speak of have rather stimulated than misled you. I hope they will continue to spur you on, but never take the rein from the hands of your better judgment.

"The information you give me of Mr. Chantrey's observations in Italy, and your own comparison between his endowments and those of the Roman artist, pleased and instructed me extremely.

I never had an opportunity of seeing any of the works of Canova but the one you showed me; and certainly the impression it made was far short of that produced by the matchless work of Mr. Chantrey, which we saw afterwards at Litchfield. I shall be glad to know if you have had leisure or inclination to retouch and remodel your 'Geraldine.' Have you any thoughts of visiting Scotland this summer? We have taken a cottage on the banks of the Teith near Callander, where we go the first week in June, and propose remaining there till October. My address will be Mansfield, near Callander, Perthshire. We shall be in the midst of that beautiful scenery described by Sir Walter Scott. The King has done *himself* honour by conferring the title on a man of genius. Mr. Campbell writes to me that he has a poem on the anvil—but he is going to spend the summer with his family on the banks of the Rhine, where his imagination will be assisted by the magnificent scenery of nature. Let us hear from you in Perthshire. Write to me of your family, and of all that interests you. Remember me very kindly to your amiable wife, and give my blessing to your children. If I were nearer to them I would recommend them to read Mrs. Barbauld's prose hymns, the best book I know for cultivating devotional taste and feelings. Farewell, dear Allan. Go on as you have begun, and you need envy none of the great ones of the earth.—I am, your faithful friend,

"ELIZA FLETCHER.

"MR. ALLAN CUNNINGHAM,
    Eccleston Street, Pimlico, London."]

Before Allan Cunningham left Dumfries I had introduced Mr. Cromek to him, who was going to that district in search of ballad lore; and this led to the curious literary fraud which my friend Allan confessed to Sir Walter Scott about this time, when he was sitting for his bust to Chantrey, and also to me, in an interesting letter, which I have since returned to his family. In that letter, Allan said that he was so piqued by Cromek's manner of receiving some of his own songs which he took to him, that he composed the ballads he had been employed by Cromek to collect, and these actually form the greatest part of the Nithsdale and Galloway songs. On hearing this, Sir Walter courteously replied, "I always suspected this, Mr. Cunningham ; they are far too good to be old."

The ·stirring public event of this summer was the approaching Coronation of George the Fourth. Then followed the tragic death of Caroline of Brunswick, whose previous persecutions and death on the 7th August had called forth the generous feeling of England, and the popular burst of indignation against her husband found an honest response even in the Tory heart of the graceful lady of Tent Lodge, as well as among her tenants of the cottage. It was well, perhaps, for the peace of our intercourse that summer that such was the case.

Led by Mrs. Smith, who was a sort of queen at that time of the society she lived in, we attended a ball at Ambleside, annually given as the gaiety of the district, at the Salutation Hotel, and testified our sense of Queen Caroline's wrongs by going in somewhat grotesque mourning procured at the little town of Hawkshead. My daughters have often since declared it was the most amusing ball they ever attended.

My aunt Dawson's health was at that time so infirm, that Mr. Fletcher kindly proposed that we should spend the following winter at York, so as to prevent the necessity of a divided family ; and this was rendered more easy as Angus had been indulged with a foreign tour, after the conclusion of his clerkship, and before entering on his professional life as a solicitor. A house was taken for us in the Minster Yard at York, where my husband and part of the family established themselves after we left Coniston ; while I, with my two unmarried daughters, went to pay a visit to my dear old friend Miss Kennedy, near Manchester, and also to Mrs. Greg of Quarry Bank, in Cheshire, where, after the lapse of many years, I found the same hospitality, benevolence, and cultivation which had struck me many years before during my first visit. The large family of boys and girls had now grown up. The sons were travelled men, full of pursuit and intelligence. Grandchildren were there to enliven the scene of this patriarchal household; death had not then visited that happy home.

At Miss Kennedy's pleasant little villa I renewed my intercourse with Dr. Henry and his agreeable wife, whom I had known well in Edinburgh when he came to study there, after his marriage to a niece of Miss Kennedy.

Miss Kennedy had also asked her favourite T. E. Currie to meet us at her house. He was the youngest son of Dr. Currie of Liverpool, the biographer of Burns; and it was a great pleasure to us to see our pet " Robin " (as we used to call him, from his bright eyes and confiding nature) expanded both in mind and form, from a somewhat silent youth of eighteen into a most intelligent and agreeable man of twenty-one. He was then a Cambridge student, and accompanied us to Quarry Bank, to meet his honoured friend Professor Smyth of Cambridge, who was staying at Quarry Bank at the time, and with whom our " Robin " was evidently a great favourite.

We did not find the society of York comparable in point of variety or intelligence to that of Edinburgh. We saw a good deal of Sydney Smith, who was frequently in York " for a short course of noise, dirt, and bad air," as he expressed it, and, as usual, he made incomparable mirth out of my alleged love of revolutions, and his society was certainly a great alleviation; to what there might be of stagnation in the air of the cathedral city. Mr. Wrangham and his family were also very agreeable; and a Highland family (the M'Leans of Coll) made a pleasant addition to the circle that winter, besides being old friends of ours.

[*From Mrs. Fletcher to Allan Cunningham.*

HER REASONS ON PUBLIC GROUNDS FOR PREFERRING A BUST OF SIR
SAMUEL ROMILLY TO ONE OF SIR WALTER SCOTT. 1822.

"MY DEAR ALLAN,—I am exceedingly glad that you communicated the history of this curious volume ('The Nithsdale and Galloway Songs') to Sir Walter Scott. No man more generously and liberally knows how to estimate the merits of contemporary genius. He does, indeed, possess too large a share of that imperishable gift to envy other men's possessions. No one can admire his powers of invention, his matchless vigour of imagination, playfulness of fancy, and quick perception of all the varieties of human character more than I do, and yet will you not think me ungrateful for all the amusement and delight his writings have afforded me, when I say that if you do send me a present of a cast of one of Mr. Chantrey's busts, I had rather it were one of Sir Samuel Romilly than Sir Walter Scott?

"You must find a solution of this puzzling preference in the importance which my husband and I attach to the public principles of public men. I believe Sir Walter Scott to be an excellent private character, as well as a man of consummate genius, but then he is a writer in support of public principles which we think injurious to the purity, dignity, and elevation of the national character, while Sir Samuel Romilly spent the whole of his valuable life in advocating that cause and those principles which have raised England to the high rank she holds in the scale of nations. What is it that has made our country great, but that the Government has always been influenced by public opinion? You may say, perhaps, Will you prefer a bust of Lord Byron, whose sentiments are those of ultra-Whiggism? I answer, No, because Lord Byron has trampled on private morals, and shamefully violated the charities of private life, and not all his powerful genius can redeem him from dishonour."]

When we returned to Edinburgh, in the summer of 1822, the whole community there, rich and poor, were agog in expectation of a visit from George the Fourth. He appeared there in August; and if he had been the wisest, bravest, and most patriotic of kings that ever wore a crown, he could not have been received with more loyal devotion than was shown him by the good town of Edinburgh. My sons were both called upon to get up their military duties and accoutrements, for the occasion of the public entry into Edinburgh from Leith. I went with my three daughters to a window above Trotter's shop, in Princes Street, to see the royal cavalcade come down St. Andrew Street to cross the Calton Hill to Holyrood. It was certainly a most imposing and gorgeous sight; but it was not the gilded coach or the fat gentleman within it which made it an affecting one : it was the vast multitude assembled—some said a hundred thousand people—animated by one feeling of national pride and pleasure in testifying their loyalty to their Sovereign. Sir Walter Scott had so admirably arranged the reception, that the poorest and humblest of his subjects had an opportunity afforded them of bowing to their King. Mrs. Grant of Laggan, a great lover of Kings, was of our party. The good old lady had, for this joyous occasion, put off her habitual black dress, and robed herself in a salmon-coloured satin, and, with the rest of the party, waved her handkerchief as the King appeared. They had all a good laugh at my expense, who, somewhat notorious for being no lover of Kings, was actually detected shedding tears and waving my handkerchief "like the lave," as the pageant passed. The fact is, I have always found the sight and cheer of a multitude, when animated by one kindly or patriotic feeling, quite irresistible in its power to command my sympathy and make me weep; and, for the time, it is an exciting and pleasurable feeling. I have never seen a multitude mischievously assembled, or disposed to evil, and hope the inexplicable emotion I have acknowledged would not lead me to follow "a multitude in doing evil."

Mr. Fletcher was then so infirm in health that we wished to persuade him to go quietly with us to Princes Street to see the procession; but no—he insisted on taking his seat on the platform prepared for the gentlemen of the Bar, and cheered the chief magistrate of a free people with all his heart.

And here I must record an instance of Highland gratitude creditable to the feelings of that country. A valued servant of ours, who had married from our house, and who then lived in the High Street, had two or three windows to the front, and, some time before the King came, I asked her to let us have one of them to see his Majesty's procession on its way from Holyrood to the Castle. Before the King came, however, I heard that all the windows in his line of progress were letting at high prices, from five to ten pounds for each window. Not being willing or able to pay any such sum for looking at a King, I called to release Mrs. M— from her promise, and begged she would let her windows for the best price she could get. The warm-hearted woman said, with tears of emotion, "'Deed no, Mrs. Fletcher; if you won't come to the window, it must stand empty." Of course we went to her window, not daring to offer payment for it, but contriving to remunerate her in some other way. Alas! what contrasts did her home on that day of the procession exhibit; her only child then, her little Mary (called after my Mary), was in its cradle dying of exhaustion from whooping-cough, and she watching by it in hopeless grief, while the tumultuous acclamations of the people as the royal *cortége* moved slowly to the Castle Hill filled the air with rejoicing.

Mr. Glassford, an intimate friend of Sir Walter Scott, was walking with us past Sir Walter's door in Castle Street when he was ringing his own bell, having just returned from Holyrood, where the King had held a levee. "Well, Sir Walter," said Mr. Glassford, "what does the King say of his good town of Edinburgh?" "Say!" said Sir Walter, "he says, 'I always heard the Scotch were a proud people; and they may well be proud, for they are a nation of gentlemen, and they live in a city of palaces.'" It was a kingly speech; and, indeed, it was a gorgeous sight to walk about the streets of our "ain romantic town" in those days of well-organized festivity. It was during that festive time I had the pleasure of renewing a personal acquaintance with my old friend, the poet Crabbe. He was on a visit to Sir Walter Scott, a few doors from us. It was in the year 1788 that he and his wife passed some days at my father's house along with Mr. Cartwright. At that time he was a slender, pensive-looking man, about thirty; in 1822, when we met again, he was a white-haired, interesting old man, old-looking for his years, but his cheerfulness had improved with his fame and fortune, for he was then one of the most popular and admired poets of the day, and in comparatively affluent circumstances. He had, indeed, lost a treasure of a wife not many years after I first knew them. She left him two excellent sons, and they were the solace of his latter years. His son George was his biographer, and a more interesting record of the struggles and triumphs of genius in overcoming adverse circumstances can nowhere be met with. Mr. Crabbe had evidently as much pleasure as I had in the recollection of our first acquaintance, and came whenever he had an hour to spare for a quiet talk about old times. He honoured us with his company at dinner several times, and one day met at our table the celebrated Mrs. Somerville, whose unaffected simplicity of manners was as remarkable as her uncommon attainments in science. My much-loved friend, Mrs. Wolfe Tone Wilson, and her son, William Wolfe Tone, were also of the party that day. They were for some time in Edinburgh that summer on a visit from America. I still found in Mrs. Wolfe Tone the same vigour and originality of mind, with as much warmth and tenderness of heart, as in my former intimacy with that delightful woman. She was happier because her son, the idol of her heart, was with her ; but they thought our good town had gone *daft* about George the Fourth.

[One of the diverting incidents of this period occurred during a forenoon visit when Mr. Crabbe and young Tone met at our house. Tone was sitting with us when the old poet was announced, and he had scarcely taken his seat in his quiet composed manner when Tone rushed towards him, went down on one knee, took his hand, kissed it, and, without saying a word, resumed his chair. When he went away we explained to Mr. Crabbe who he was, and that his Irish blood and French education accounted for this departure from ordinary manners. It seemed a relief to the gentle old man to find " that the young gentleman was not out of his mind."

Note from George Crabbe to Mrs. Fletcher in August 1822.

" MY DEAR LADY,—I have now more time to reply to your obliging note, and yet know not what more I can say. I deferred my answer because I was uncertain with respect to my engagements, and would not write till the last minute, in the hope that I might indulge myself and accept the invitation which you so obligingly placed in my way, but not entirely in my power.

" We cannot always, my dear madam, as you are well assured, do that which we would. I meet with nothing but kindness in Edinburgh, but how often does it happen that even kindness prevents us the doing as we would !

" I am convinced that I make very awkward apologies ; nay,

apologies they are not, and I am quite sure that I am writing to a lady who comprehends all that I would say.

"It would have been highly pleasing to me if I could have heard Mr. Alison preach, and to have been introduced to a gentleman of whom I know so much, and of whom so much remains to be known. I will not dwell upon my disappointment.

"Let me at least take this occasion of giving you my best thanks for the kind attention which you have shown to me. I am very sure that while I remember anything I shall remember that I remain, my dear lady, your old friend,

"GEORGE CRABBE.

"39 NORTH CASTLE ST."

This note from the poet Crabbe, written from the celebrated "poor 39 Castle Street," where Walter Scott lived so long, is curious from showing the distraction produced in the mind of a "quiet lion" when introduced suddenly into such a motley scene as the time of the King's visit to Edinburgh presented. It shows, too, such a complete difference in the style of note-writing, having much of the stately stiffness of the dedications of the days of Crabbe's youth, and not being able to depart from that, even in the prevailing bustle which might have excused a shorter apology.

To Mrs. Stark from E. F.

"EDINBURGH, 1822.

"We grieve more than I can express for the alarming state of our dear T. E. Currie. I have never known a loftier or purer mind, or a warmer heart than his.

"We always admired and esteemed him highly when he was a student here three years ago, but last autumn he stayed with us at dear Miss Kennedy's, and the intimacy of domestic intercourse made us feel towards him a much livelier interest than we had done before. He is a noble creature, a most unworldly one, and though his imagination and buoyancy of spirit imaged out successful and bright prospects, the delicacy of his character and the sensibility of his temperament would have disqualified him for the rough conflicts of life. He is better fitted for the world to which he is going than for the one he leaves ; but bright hopes go with him, and I am very sad for those he leaves behind to mourn such a loss."]

In the winter of 1822 and 1823 I had prevailed upon some friends to join me in an attempt to reform some young delinquents in a House of Refuge. This had been a favourite project of mine for many years, and I do not remember any work of usefulness in which I ever engaged with more heart and hope. It was my thought night and day how these poor boys, the children of wicked parents, themselves nurtured in crime, might be reclaimed from their evil ways. It pleased God to prosper the undertaking. For several years Lady Carnegie of Dalry House was the main support and encourager of it. Circumstances which neither she nor I could control led to its being merged into a larger Institution, but during the seventeen years our small experiment in Dalry Lane existed, 116 boys had been admitted from prison and Bridewell, of whom the manager could give a most satisfactory account, 105 being reclaimed and having become useful members of society. They were taught the trade of shoemaking, and lived as one family under the kind rule of their master and his wife.

In the spring of 1823 Maria Edgeworth and her two younger sisters spent some time in Edinburgh. We met first at my dear friend and pastor's house, the Rev. Mr. Alison. It was the first time I had been introduced to the author of " Simple Susan," though we were not unknown to each other, as she told me her brothers had often mentioned the agreeable society they met at our house when they were students in Edinburgh. Miss Edgeworth's personal appearance was not attractive ; but her vivacity, good humour, and cleverness in conversation quite equalled my expectations. I should say she was more sprightly

and brilliant than refined.   She excelled in the raciness
of Irish humour, but the great defect of her manner, as it
seemed to me, was an excess of compliment, or what in
Ireland is called "blarney;" and in one who had moved in
the best circles, both as to manners and mind, it surprised
me not a little.   She repelled all approach to intimacy on
my part by the excess of her complimentary reception of
me when we were first introduced to each other at Mr.
Alison's.   I never felt confidence in the reality of what she
said afterwards.   I do not know whether it was the absence
of good taste in her, or that she supposed I was silly and
vain enough to be flattered by such verbiage.   It was the
first time in my life I had met with such over-acted civility;
but I was glad of an opportunity of meeting a person whose
genius and powers of mind had been exercised in benefiting the world as hers have been.   I feel sure from the
feeling of those friends who loved her, because they knew
her well, that had this been the case with me, I might
have been also one of her friends; so that I only give my
impression as arising from that of society intercourse of a
very superficial kind.   Miss Edgeworth and her two very
agreeable sisters were pleased to meet at our house Sir
Robert and Lady Liston.   They accompanied us some
days after this to dine at Millburn Tower, the Listons'
country-house, near Edinburgh.   Miss Edgeworth's varied
information and quick repartee appeared to great advantage
in conversation with the polished ex-ambassador of Constantinople, who always reminded me of the couplet :—

> "Polite, as all his life in Courts had been ;
> Yet good, as he the world had never seen."

In the month of June 1823 Mary accompanied her
friend Catherine Laycock to Yorkshire, where Margaret
had spent the winter, and soon after these dear sisters set

off with their great-aunt Mrs. Fretwell, the eldest daughter
of Mr. Hill, to pay a visit to our friends Mrs. Martin and
Mrs. Buckle, near Cheltenham.

My aunt, Mrs. Fretwell, was a singular character, highly
principled and highly prejudiced. She had an old-fashioned
notion of the authority to be exercised by age over youth,
and she set out by telling her young companions that *she*
must rule and they must obey. This was quite proper as
she franked them in her post-chaise; and travelling only
two stages a day, and one of those before breakfast, they
had much time to explore the different towns they visited
in their progress. My daughters found her government a
very pleasant one; in fact, she allowed them to have their
own way quite as much as they desired, and they parted
the best friends imaginable, at the house of her stepson, in
Worcestershire.

Mr. Fletcher's feverish attacks had been so frequent
during this winter, that soon after my daughters left us
we secured the best lodgings we could procure between
Dalkeith and Lasswade, and there my husband and I,
with Mrs. Taylor and her children, went for country air.
Mr. Fletcher's health soon improved, and we were kindly
attended to by our friends in the way of a supply of books
and morning visits. Our incommodious dwelling prevented
our enjoying any society otherwise; but I shall always feel
thankful to have been sent there, as it were, by the force
of circumstances, as it enabled me to be of some use to
three most deserving young people, the children of the
unprincipled market-gardener from whom we took our
house. We returned to town early in September, with
minds made up to take a more comfortable residence in
the country the following year.

[From letters to her absent daughters relating to
the gardener's family.

"CASTLE STREET, 1823.

" I had intended to write to you to-day from Almondale, but have put it off till Monday, as your dear father had a slight attack of fever, but is kindly desirous I should go to see Mrs. Erskine. On the whole, he has been much better since we came to our home comforts than he was the two wet, dismal months we were at Viewfield, in which, however, we had some gleams of sweet scenery and much repose, and our going there I look upon as providential, since it has afforded us the opportunity of rescuing the two poor girls who were the victims of their father's brutal tyranny. Through Miss Howell, I have got one of them a situation as nursery-governess. Their brother's gratitude to me is most touching, for coming between them and their father's most unnatural cruelty. I think I gave either you or Mrs. Martin a history of this interesting family, where the virtues so peculiarly Scotch—of self-denial, submission to severe hardship without repining, education and refinement much beyond their condition, with considerable ambition and aspiring thoughts on the brother's part—form the conflicting elements of the character of this family. These are also engrafted on deep piety, and such a sense of filial duty, that although we have reason to think these young women were often in danger of their lives from the drunken fury of their father, they never once complained, or uttered a murmur against him."

"ALMONDALE, *October* 8, 1823.

"I came here on Monday, to enjoy, with dear Mrs. Erskine, the last lingering days of autumn. They have been bright and mild, and the colouring of the trees on the banks of this beautiful river,[1] that rushes past the window where I am writing, gives a richness and variety that belongs only to this season. I left your father remarkably well; he even proposed that I should remain here till Friday; but I thought it best not to try his patience too far, and am to return to-morrow.

[1] The Almond.

"Last night was the anniversary of the day Mr. Erskine died, and my friend, who is a great observer of seasons, is much depressed by the sad recollections of that event. She is pious and amiable in no common degree; but oh ! she is desolate. She has no children to expect home from Gloucestershire. I grieve for her want of objects on whom to dwell with joy and thankfulness. Perhaps when the last hour comes she will find it merciful to have so few ties to earth ; but affections such as good children afford are not earthly—they are gifts of Heaven—only bestowed to be fully enjoyed hereafter. God bless my two precious children, prays their affectionate mother,   E. FLETCHER."

Letters to her daughters absent in Gloucestershire.

"EDINBURGH, *September* 11*th*, 1823.

"I received your very cheering letter last Saturday, the day after I had despatched mine to Margaret; and though I begin my chat with you now, I think I shall not send it till after Saturday's post, that I may leave room to reply to your next letters. I can fully enter into your disappointment about 'The Fall of Jerusalem.'[1] It is impossible not to form poetical expectations of a poet—a *beau-idéal* which is, I believe, less often realized on a slight acquaintance than any other illusion of the imagination. I cherished it, forty years ago, about Mason, and have not been cured after half a century's experience of the fallacious nature of such expectations; but I must hasten to tell you how highly and truly I have been gratified by dining in company with Brougham and Denman. It was last Monday this good fortune befell me. We had heard they were at John Brougham's for a day or two, but had no expectation of seeing them when Mrs. John Brougham called early to ask your father and me to dinner that day, as they wished Henry to see his old friends. I was at the meeting of the Female Friendly Society at the time, with good Miss Wilson, and deep in the accounts there, when Angus goodnaturedly came to tell me, as an answer was required. I came home and wrote my acceptance, and your father's regrets in

---

[1] By Mr. Milman, afterwards Dean of St. Paul's.

not being able to go. Brougham met me most kindly and cordially, but the party of twenty at dinner was too numerous for general conversation, and I was not well set between Sir John Beresford and Sir Alexander Keith, but Denman's face opposite was a treat. I never saw a more noble physiognomy, morally and intellectually. He was silent. When the gentlemen came up to the drawing-room, Brougham stationed himself beside me ; Dr. Thomson joined us; and I never heard a more animated, pleasant, unforced conversation than that which flowed on for more than an hour. One had but to touch the string, and it always vibrated the very chord one wished. It was not brilliant sayings or pointed *bon-mots*, it was information given with frankness, energy, and good-nature. He said he had met with Clarkson at Penrith, and bade him go and tell Southey it was a shame that Negro Emancipation had never once been advocated in the Quarterly Review; that Clarkson told him he had got the promise of fifteen hundred petitions from the principal towns in England in favour of that measure. He said the friends of Emancipation were determined to debate and divide the House upon every petition, so as to force Ministers to adopt some efficient measure in the next session. He said his Education Bill was rendered abortive by the prejudices of the Dissenters in England, who refused to send their children to schools where the parish minister had a veto on the choice of the schoolmaster; and the ministers of the Establishment hated the Bill, because they were, generally speaking, averse to educate the people at all, and were only driven to do so by fear of the Methodists and other Dissenters. He said it was proposed to bring forward individual cases and instances of oppression and injustice exercised by magistrates and Orangemen in Ireland, rather than argue any longer on general principles of misgovernment in that country; facts would produce an effect upon the House when argument and reasoning were disregarded. Brougham's manner of treating subjects of interest is quite different from our Edinburgh Whigs. There is no affected indifference on subjects of vital importance, no contemptuous sneer at rational conversation. He speaks with animation and deep interest on the subjects I have mentioned. I met both Brougham and Denman next morning at breakfast at Dr. Thomson's. Denman is the most graceful of human beings; admired Edinburgh extremely, but was still silent; looks deferentially at Brougham, and benevolently at everybody. Brougham spoke with enthusiasm of Granville Sharp. He said he had seen him dining on bread and cheese, while at the same time he knew he was supporting many miserable human beings. He (Granville Sharp) wrote some pamphlets to prove that Melchisedek was Jesus Christ. His life was divided between relieving the poor and oppressed, and expounding the Revelations. Brougham seemed to have been greatly amused with his simplicity. B. says the Opposition are never so strong as when a Scotch job is brought before the House of Commons. The English Tories are ashamed to defend them, and generally slink away and leave the Minister to brave it out as he best can, but (added he) Ireland is as much worse than Scotland in political liberty as Scotland is worse than England. He inquired after Miles in a tone and manner that showed he liked him. Miles was much vexed he could not attend the public dinner given this day at Glasgow to Brougham and Denman, but his jury case of some importance was to come on to-day at Inverary, and he could not leave it.

"Your delightful joint-letter arrived this morning. I sent for it by eight o'clock, so impatient was I for it. It is truly the food that feeds my spirits and sustains my cheerfulness. I, too, have weary longings to have you both home again : this increases upon me as the time approaches. Your father keeps finely, and enjoys your letters as much as I do."

To her daughters Margaret and Mary, absent in Gloucestershire.

"*24th September* 1823.

"While Bessie and I were sitting *tête-à-tête* on Sunday evening, the children having just gone to bed, the door-bell rang, and a gentleman, unannounced, was ushered into the drawing-room. He walked close up to me, and it was not till his dark countenance relaxed into a smile that I half screamed out 'Sinclair Cullen!' He had arrived in the mail that morning, and was on his way to Kinfauns Castle. He sat with us an hour, and was much like what you saw of him in London, only some shades less splenetic in his opinions of men and things. He has, however, a hero, and I have therefore a hope he will come right yet. His abstract of perfection is Sir Francis Burdett. He says he is without a particle of selfishness ; that it is a beautiful character—calm, concentrated, benevolent, and purely disinterested, entirely without vanity or personal ambition ; that nothing disturbs the calmness of his temper but acts of cruelty and injustice.

" Cullen called the next day, and met here accidentally the Marquis and Marquise de Bossi. He is an expatriated Italian patriot ; she, a Swiss lady, who has followed the fortunes of the banished man, and came to marry him in England, for the Holy Alliance, she said, would not permit him to marry in Switzerland. They have established such a system of espionage in that once free and happy country, that the Marquis was obliged to change his name, and conceal himself in a cottage near Geneva, and visit his betrothed bride by stealth. She is the intimate friend of Sismondi, of whom she speaks in terms of the warmest and most affectionate friendship. Her broken English does not lessen the effect of her eloquence. I never saw so engaging a foreigner. They like Edinburgh so much, they talk of returning here for the winter.

" Sinclair Cullen was to dine with us that day, and called to say, if we would allow him, he would bring with him John Cam Hobhouse, the M.P. for Westminster, whom he had met accidentally in the street on his return from Lord Glenorchy's, and being engaged to dine with us, Sinclair thought the addition of this ultra-Whig would be agreeable ; and so it proved. Mr. Hobhouse is remarkably entertaining—quick, lively, communicative ; not interesting (he is too much a man of the world for that), not nearly so commanding and impressive as Brougham, or so dignified as Denman. He remembered dining here and meeting young Betty the actor in 1804. He told us many diverting stories, the most tragi-comic of which was the narrative of Shelley's death, which he had heard from Lord Byron. [As this is now so well known, it is omitted here. The letter goes on :] Mr. Hobhouse had a letter the other day from Lord Byron, saying that ten thousand pounds would save the liberties of Greece. Mr. Hobhouse said it was wonderful how circumstances formed character. Lord Byron and he were in Greece in 1810, long before any revolutionary movements. They had an Athenian servant named Demetrius, whose excessive timidity and cowardice furnished them with amusement. They used to set him on a spirited horse, that ran away with him, and Demetrius shrieked and screamed with terror. The barking of a dog made him cry out with fear; and yet, some years after, this very man led the assault at Athens, and, after prodigies of valour, took that city from the Turks."]

In April 1824 we all went to live at Auchindinny House, an old and odd-looking chateau on the banks of the North Esk, nine miles from Edinburgh, and within a walk of Penicuik. Mr. Mackenzie (the "Man of Feeling") and his family had lived there many years before; and although it had nothing of the neatness and order of an English villa, it suited our taste, and the walks about it were a never-ending pleasure to my daughters and to my grandchildren; while in the enjoyment of a large garden and a small pony gig, my desires, as to the means of amusement, were completely gratified. We all enjoyed the repose and freedom of a country life, and Mr. Fletcher's health and happiness were greatly promoted by it. I found my early taste for country occupations return upon me. We had several poor neighbours who interested us much, and our nearest neighbours (the Hills of Firth) were truly kind and pleasant associates. Then our more intimate friends from Edinburgh and elsewhere visited us frequently, not in a formal or ceremonious manner, but in a friendly fashion. Mr. Fletcher delighted in the quietness and freedom of our life there; he was able to read for hours, and to be read to; he bore the infirmities of age with uncomplaining submission, and his interest in public events was undiminished. The frequent visits of our grandchildren, Miles's three boys, were a great delight to us both, and Mrs. Taylor and her two children formed an interesting addition to our family circle. We had no hankerings after what were called the gaieties of an Edinburgh life. If I—the most gaily disposed member of the family—had felt any yearnings of that kind, I should have been ashamed to have yielded to them before the better regulated habits and tastes of my daughters; but in fact, though naturally a lover of the pleasures of society, and somewhat spoiled, perhaps, by the place which an indulgent circle of friends had given me in the society of Edinburgh, it had been at times difficult to keep up the expenditure such circles involve, so that it was a cheap purchase of repose to give up evening parties and their confectionary horrors.

In October 1824 Mrs. Taylor, her sweet Elizabeth, Angus, and I, went to Yorkshire, to pay dear aunty a visit before winter set in. Angus was on his way to London to commence his studies as a sculptor. He had never been able to fix his mind on law and its unpleasant details, since his visit to Italy, and as his father and I had little hope of his ever doing so, we thought it better that he should begin at once the occupation he desired, than waste time as he was then doing. It was decided that he should board and lodge in Allan Cunningham's comfortable house for a year, that by working in Chantrey's studio he might learn under Allan the rudiments of the art before going to study at Rome.

In the summer of 1825 we saw a good deal of some agreeable Italian exiles, who had been attracted to Edinburgh by our friends the De Bossis. To Madame de Bossi we were indebted for the honour of a visit from Sismondi. I remember it was a long bright summer day they came.

The Jeffreys met them, and we had a wander, after dinner, in the glen and old quarry of Auchindinny, which all enjoyed. We were all struck by the union of power and simplicity in the conversation of Sismondi, and, above all, by his remarkable benevolence and hopefulness of nature. He was a believer in the good faith of such as truly loved the welfare of mankind. He had come on a mission of love and liberty, from the friends of Greece in Switzerland to the friends of Greece in England ; but he was grievously disappointed by the coldness of English feeling on the subject. He told us he doubted whether there was a single citizen of Geneva who had not contributed his mite to this great cause, but that he had not been able to make any impression on the Greek Committee in London corresponding to his hopes and expectations.

It was not without deep emotion, though regret made a small part of it, that I learned from Miss Aikin that dear Mrs. Barbauld had been taken from us. She died on the 9th of March 1825, without much suffering, and retained her faculties to the very last. She was a woman of much deeper feeling than the world imagined ; but the great peculiarity of her mind, together with the extent of its powers, both when we consider the brilliancy of her imagination and the depth of her understanding, was the remarkable diffidence of her character. This arose from an exquisite sensibility, which never was displayed, but constantly escaped. I consider it one of the greatest privileges of my life to have been in habits of intimacy with this incomparable woman, and never felt so humble as in her society. Her own modesty of character inspired this feeling in others ; and as reverence is only a modification of the devotional feelings, it was impossible to be with Mrs. Barbauld without feeling the better for it.

[*To Mrs. Laycock.*

"AUCHINDINNY, *April 16th*, 1825.

" The severe blow you met with so lately, although it will have made all other sorrows light in comparison, and chastened even the happiness that may be in reserve for you, will make you feel the sentiment of thankfulness more sensibly than you ever did before. I speak from experience. It is eight years this day since we lost our precious Grace. It was a stroke that gave a reality to every succeeding event. It made every other sorrow sink to its proper level. It made every remaining blessing more than ever valued. It taught that most important truth—a constant dependence on the providence of God, and a thankfulness, never before properly understood, for His merciful support in the hour of bitterest trial. It took away much of the fear of death, and made life a thing so very precarious and uncertain as to be valued only for the *use* that was made of it in reference to another state of existence. You and I, my dear friend, have met with similar trials iu our family, and we know better than ever how to feel for each other. But oh ! how many mercies are spared to us, and how sinful would be our unthankfulness ! "]

We took the variety of a three months' stay in Edinburgh in the winter of 1826-27, which, from my husband's improved health, he was also able to enjoy in a quiet way, seeing his old friends in the morning, and we doing so in the evening. It was during one of these small evening parties, when I remember Sydney Smith happened to be in Edinburgh, and spent that evening at our house, that my son Miles, returning from the Theatrical Fund dinner, joined our party and announced that "The Great Unknown" had, on Sir Walter Scott's health being drunk, risen and acknowledged himself to be the author of " Waverley," " Guy Mannering," etc. Though the fact was as well known, as if he had proclaimed it at the market cross, ten years before, this public and unexpected acknowledgment produced a great sensation not only on the people present, but throughout every circle in Edinburgh. The secret had been extracted from him by the unfortunate state of his affairs, involved as he was in Constable's bankruptcy. Sir Walter was one of those great men who had an undue estimate of the "pride of life." He did not care for money, but he cared much for baronial towers and aristocratical distinction ; and yet this taste was unaccompanied with haughtiness of disposition or manners. It was rather the romance of his character that had led him to add acre to acre, and to found the family of Scott of Abbotsford ; for there was nothing sordid in his nature ; he was frank and kind-hearted, as much beloved by his poor neighbours as he was admired and courted by the great. It must always be regretted that the labours of his busy life failed to secure him an honourable independence in his advanced years; and yet he was never more truly great than when he said, on declaring himself insolvent, "But this right hand shall work me out of my difficulties;" and so it would, had his life been prolonged. There can be little doubt, however, that the painful excitement of the difficulties, which he met so bravely, broke down his constitution and shortened his life.

We spent an agreeable three months in Edinburgh, and returned to Auchindinny in the month of April 1827. We had not long returned there when we had very distressing accounts of Angus being taken ill at Rome in May 1827. We sent our kind relation, Lieut. M'Nicol, to travel home with him, and the following winter he spent with us in complete retirement, and gradually recovered his health of body and mind in the spring of 1828. At this time we were not without much anxiety about Miles's health, which began to decline, and Mr. Fletcher became visibly more feeble and less cheerful. I remember his saying that he thought he had now lived as long as life was desirable, on which I reminded him that not many years ago he had said that he should like to live his life over again. He smiled, and said, "Yes, my dear, my married life." His tenderness of expression seemed to increase towards all connected with him, and he often spoke of me to his children, and of them to me with the fondest affection. That summer, the last of his life, several old friends came to pay their respects to him; among others Mrs. Ker, Miss Forster, Mrs. Spiers, and her daughter Mary. He continued to take the warmest interest in public events, and at this time the Greek Revolution occupied his thoughts, and his daughters used to read to him and write for him whenever he desired it. He never used spectacles, and was able to read easily till within five or six weeks of his death. Towards the middle or end of November of that sad year our dear Mrs. Taylor took his loved grandchild Elizabeth to stay, as we thought, some months with my aunt at Tadcaster. I still think I see our precious Elizabeth with her brother in the little pony-carriage, attended by Lunnan, the gardener's wife, leading the pony through the avenue at Auchindinny, she taking her last look of a place she had loved so dearly. Her mother went the day before, and they both stayed some days with Miles in Edinburgh before they set out for Yorkshire. They had not been gone a week before we heard that the dear aunt to whom they were going had been seized with apoplexy, which had very much affected her mind. The next letter from Mrs. Taylor told us that her Elizabeth was ill, very feverish, and she was uneasy about her. Next day, Mary, who had been staying in Edinburgh for a few days, unexpectedly appeared at Auchindinny late at night, and with a countenance of deep distress told us that Elizabeth's complaint was typhus fever, and that she was in great danger. Margaret returned to Edinburgh in the carriage that brought Mary home, and she and Angus set off without delay to Tadcaster. The dear child knew her aunt Margaret, to whom she was warmly attached. She watched by her constautly, sharing with her mother the office of a nurse. But it pleased God to take her from them, and never did a purer or holier spirit return to Him who gave it. She had lived with us eleven years, and we could not remember when we lost her that she had ever said or done a thing to grieve us. She died on the 15th of December 1828, at the age of thirteen years and seven months, and was buried in a vault adjoining to that of the Hill family in the north aisle of Tadcaster church.

When Mary and I received accounts of her death we were watching by the deathbed of her grandfather. Mr. Fletcher's mind was so acute that we did not tell him of her death, he would have felt it so severely. Not many days before his death Mr. Turner, our family surgeon, came from Edinburgh to pay him a friendly visit. I happened to be out of the room when he arrived, but I found him giving Mr. Fletcher an account of the successful struggle the Greeks were making against their Turkish oppressors. I never saw Mr. Fletcher look more animated, and turning to me he said, "My dear, Mr. Turner says I must take some port wine, and you must take a glass with us, to wish success to the Greeks." I mention this as an instance of the public passion being strong in death. After that day he spoke little, but was in a placid, thankful, happy state of mind. He had always said he hoped he should die in the midst of his family. On the 19th of December I had a letter from Miles, expressing great distress in not being allowed by his medical men to come and see him, on account of his severe cough and the medical treatment thought necessary for it. His father said, in a strong and cheerful tone, " By no means ; write and tell him I entreat him not to come." Late that evening Angus arrived from Yorkshire ; he had set off from the funeral of his niece, and only reached Auchiudinny a few hours before his father died. Dear Mary and I had been the only members of his family that were about his bed, owing to the variety of our family afflictions at the time ; but when I told him Angus had come, though too weak to speak audibly, an expression of pleasure passed over his countenance. As he seemed disposed to sleep, Mary and I left him for a few hours in the charge of my son Angus, and an excellent maid of mine of the name of Brown, whom he liked much as a nurse, and who frequently read to him. Our good medical attendant from Penicuik, Mr. Renton, remained with us that night, and was in a room which opened into his. About two o'clock in the morning Angus came to tell us that all was over.

Thus closed a union of thirty-seven years of as much happiness as is commonly the portion of human life. During all that time I never experienced an unkind word or deed. from my husband; I never knew him do a thing that was not strictly honourable and high-principled. Considering the great disparity of our years, there was unusual sympathy between us. He had none of that narrow and paltry feeling which belongs to men of little minds, a desire of exercising power and authority in small matters. His indulgence towards me knew no bounds, and he secured my respect and affection by the virtues of his character, the soundness of his understanding, and the tenderness of his heart. It was my happiness to be able to sympathize completely in all his public feelings and opinions. If I had not done so, our union would have been far less happy ; for he lived in times when private interests were sacrificed to public principles by all who truly loved truth and justice, and had minds sufficiently enlightened and honesty sufficiently steadfast to prefer the public good to private and personal advancement.

[Miles A. Fletcher's letter to his mother, from bed, on the day of his father's funeral.

" *24th December* 1828.

"MY DEAREST MOTHER,—It was very kind of you to write to me. Be assured my ailment is yielding to Dr. Thomson's vigorous practice and great care. I cannot attempt to say how much the necessity of confinement to bed on this day distresses me, yet I know it is the course which would be most acceptable to the affectionate spirit now at rest. We have much of the purest pleasure in store in recalling recollections of the virtues which ennobled my father's character. They make me feel proud ; and although I cannot hope to adorn his name, yet I trust it will be transmitted by me without dishonour. I trust George is impressed, by some conversations we have had, in a way you would wish ; but I have not strength now to enlarge on a subject which at this solemn hour so fully engrosses me. My wife joins with me in warmly affectionate sympathy. —I am always your grateful and loving son,

"MILES A. FLETCHER."

It was during the first winter we spent at Auchindinny that we persuaded my mother to print her "Dramatic Sketches," which had been written at Callander a few years before. A selection from the many letters she received from true and loving friends about the Dramatic Sketches is here inserted :—

From Mrs. Grant of Laggan.

" Now I must tell you of the impression your dramas have left on my mind, though I cannot yet be said to have read them critically. I fear you will scarce consider it a compliment when I tell you that they far exceeded my expectations —not that I expected less, in some respects, than I found. I looked for exalted moral feeling, purity of sentiment, and the utmost purity of style, but—truth to say—I did not expect you to be so poetical, or to understand—what one might call the technical part—the management of the drama so well. The whole performance bears evident marks of being a transcript from your own mind, an abstract of those feelings and principles on which you have thought, spoken, and acted. I should think it a kind and friendly thing to point out any blemish that I might observe in your work, not with the view of altering or amending, but to prove my sincerity and try your patience. Now, I really can find nothing in the language or sentiments but what appears to me to be admirable as a composition. There is no prominence of striking or glowing passages, but the whole is finely and consistently sustained. There is a masculine strength in the language, yet the purity and delicacy of the thoughts expressed seem to belong to woman's softer breast. The characters are well sustained and sufficiently discriminated. 'Elidure,' I think, will please more generally. It is delightful to think such a character really existed ; to add life and colouring to such a portrait sketched by Milton must have been a delightful task ; and I could well suppose you to have luxuriated in it. Not seldom the practised and the professed and shameless selfishness of worldly characters has so wearied and disquieted me, that I feel a kind of triumph when I have any character, living or dead, to hold up for the honour of human nature as consistently actuated by noble motives. You have yourself, my dear friend, done me good service in this respect."

The Rev. Archibald Alison, her valued friend and pastor for very many years, wrote thus on the same subject :—

" I have waited until I heard of your return to Scotland to offer you my grateful thanks for the honour you have conferred upon me by the copy of your dramas, and for the delight you have given to me and mine by the perusal of them. We expected much, and even more than our expectations has been fulfilled. We have found in them everywhere the conceptions of a noble and exalted mind, in many passages much vigour, and in many others much felicity of poetic expression, and in all a facility in the management of tragic verse which would do honour to any dramatic author. I have found, however (for here I must speak in my own name, being happily the only critic in the family), a great unacquaintance with the craft of the drama, some negligence of the value of your own materials, and an ignorance, perhaps a disdain, of the art of setting them off by the common tricks of the stage. All this, however, if you wish to adapt them for representation, might be easily supplied. You have provided the gems, and a very inferior hand might set them, so as to give to their own natural brilliancy the advantages of artificial position. If you have no wish of this kind, you have at least the satisfaction of leaving to your grandchildren a domestic memorial which, in their eyes and in the eyes of those that follow them, will, I doubt not, be more valuable 'than all Bokhara's vaunted gold, than all the gems of Samarcand.'"

Joanna Baillie writes in August 1825 :—

"I have just risen from the second reading of your very pleasing dramas, and will no longer delay my immediate thanks to yourself, though I have written to your son on the subject, and begged of him to convey to you my grateful acknowledgments. I owe them for being kindly included amongst the friends to whom you give this token of regard, and I owe them for the pleasure I have received in perusing works of so much generous feeling and noble sentiment and principles clothed in such beautiful and harmonious verse. There cannot be a more perfect character as a mother and a queen than you have portrayed in 'Rowena;' and the entire rectitude and nobleness of it are so simply, naturally, and forcibly expressed, that it gives an originality which one does not often meet with in these days in dramatic subjects.

> 'What ! ask a noble nation to be slaves,—
> To crouch and fawn beneath a tyrant's feet,
> Because he was my son ?'

are noble and forcible lines, the spirit of which is sustained through the whole play, joined to great tenderness and affection. The flowers of poetry, too, which adorn both dramas, are pleasingly and happily introduced. If I were a play-going person I should probably prefer the second piece, which has more of dramatic effect ; but the first is my favourite, and I believe I shall have a good proportion of your readers to agree with me.   I read the first aloud to Mrs. Baillie and my sister as soon as I received the book, and they were both very much pleased, and beg me to offer you their thanks for that gratification.   I congratulate you very heartily on your success, and I congratulate those who will feel it more than you do,—Mr. Fletcher and your daughters."

From Lucy Aikin to Angus Fletcher, August 13, 1825.

" It is with real satisfaction, my dear sir, that I prepare to give you my sentiments on the 'Dramatic Sketches.'   Had they been sent to me anonymously I am certain that I should have discovered in them the spirit of my friend, that spirit which magnanimity and tenderness share between them so equally that neither of them encroaches on the other, but both blend into one noble and touching whole.   When I find in any work such evidence of a high soul, I really cannot descend to the minuteness of technical criticism.   I am satisfied with language which clearly and energetically conveys the thought, and I do not examine by rules of art the construction of the fable.   Your recommendation of reading the last first implies that it is your favourite, but here I differ from you ; the noble mother of ' Elidure ' is my friend's own self, and interests me more than all ; besides, the subject appears to me more interesting and more satisfactory, for I confess I have not so disciplined rebel nature as to have lost all pleasure in poetical justice.   I would in fiction at least take vengeance of the wicked first, and pity and forgive them after.   Besides, I can scarcely reconcile myself to the ruffian 'Dunstan' converted into a philosophic sage, and the grovelling superstition which he made the instrument of his pride and ambition changed into a benignant and beautiful faith, which has no temples throughout the world, even in this age, but the hearts of the purest and the most enlightened followers of a Divine philosophy.   But this affects not the intrinsic beauty of the characters, which is very striking.   I hope your dear mother will be encouraged to embody more of those high and lovely conceptions in verse. "

To E. F., on reading her "Dramatic Sketches."

Whose dreams are these? and art thou still the same
As erst when I beheld thee, lofty dame,
Some twenty years now past, when fancies high
And fire-fed thoughts illumed thy noble eye,
And patriot aims which seem for man designed,
With poesy and gentle heart combined,
And womanly romance, to make the sheen
Of thy discourse as beauteous as thy mien?
Why do thy mind and spirit show no trace
Of Time's dominion?   Has it spared thy face?
Come, show it me!   What wild delight to see
That aught of noble beauteous good can be
Immortal here.   I have not found them yet
Survive an hour, although I oft have set
My watch to measure them.   Oh! where are they,
The young enthusiasts, the spirits gay,
The brows unwritten on, the lips unstung
By grief, or not remembered?—tell me where
Is he, the rhapsodist once welcome there?
All, all are in the tomb—they are no more,
Who are not what they were, doth time restore?
No! though he comes with smiles, dispensing joys,
Alike his advent and his flight destroys,
And hope, and harmony, and bliss devour
Their favourites, victims, I have felt their power
And sorrows too, and but a wreck is left
Of hopes and fears, of peace and joy bereft.
Where are the happy beings I have known
Around thee? infant-blooms and blisses, flown.
Thy children now are matrons; a new race—
Their children, hope and revel in their place.
But thou art still the same; thy spirit's youth
Remains unbowed, enamoured still of truth;
Thy heart of dreams unchangeable, thine age
Not less romantic, nor thy youth less sage.
And worldly wisdom leaves untainted still
Thy pious mind, and innocence of will;

All this thy dramas show, and yet I deem
Thee less for poet formed, than poet's theme.
SINCLAIR CULLEN, 1826.

A characteristic letter from our Mother, and a fatherly P.S.

" *December* 1825.

" I must begin by scolding you for not sending your letter in time for the post-bag. Yesterday's post-bag was a blank to me. Then I will not scold dear aunty for wishing to keep you longer, but we must have you home before Christmas. Good Miss P. has agreed to come to aunt when you leave her. It will be four months since I parted from you, and indeed, indeed I cannot let you stay longer from home.

" This has been a barren week with us as well as with you, the snow, sleet, drizzling rain, and mist, so bad that Missy and I have had no walks together to the village. A letter from Miss Wesley about the Dramas has been the only gratifying circumstance. Truly, dear child, I begin to fear these gratifying letters are not for my soul's good; they please me more than they ought to please one who has lived more than half a century. If Margaret and you had allowed me to get a good trimming from some practised executioner, in the character of a scornful, contemptuous reviewer, it might have done me more good than all the flattering unction that I have taken to my soul. The way that I discover it has done me no good is from a feeling of disappointment, when no notice is taken of my little book by those to whom I have sent it. All who know me agree with Mrs. Grant, that the book is a metrical transcript of the author's mind. Still, like all other worldly gratifications, this has its dangers, if it makes me less distrustful of myself, less lowly-minded. I pray fervently against this temptation. On the whole, the plays have certainly met with much more praise than I or any of you expected; and if I know myself at all, much of the gratification their approval has afforded is the pleasure your father and all our children have had in it."

To this our father adds :—

" Tell our very kind aunt that we are very sorry to deprive

M

her of your society, but we have an unconquerable longing for your coming home after so long an absence. I hope you do not think of going to Ripon. If I thought you could bestow time to go there, I would not agree to your leaving aunt so soon. If you cannot get a companion in a post-chaise, my wish would certainly be that you should travel by yourselves in a chaise, and not go a mile in the dark. If you cannot think of this, the mail is certainly the safest.　　　　　A. F."

The following part of a letter from T. Campbell at this time shows how much he valued my mother's friendship, and also the tyranny exercised by the two leading Reviews of the day, as well as the pain their verdict inflicted on sensitive minds, even in this case, on one of such established fame as the author of " Gertrude of Wyoming " and " Hohenlinden :"—

Thomas Campbell to Mrs. Fletcher.

"Seymour St., London, *March* 1825.

" Is it very unmanly in me, my dear friend, to feel cut and sore at the hard injustice, as I think, which has been dealt to me in the Quarterly Review of Theodoric? Read the article, and either your opinion must have been converted, or I imagine you' will be indignant at the assertion that Theodoric is but a bold dragoon, and Julia and Constance are but so-and-so. I received your favourable opinion of the poem, my dear Mrs. Fletcher, with a degree of pride which has perhaps made my mind more sensitive than it would otherwise have been to this affront. It makes me feel the injustice of it to be the grosser. What ! has it touched your intellectual heart, and is a heartless reviewer to say uncontradicted that the work is uninteresting ? But I must say that I address you now as the being who best understood, and who I foresaw would best understand, all the moral beauty of my characters. Forgive this if it look like either vanity or flattery. It is certainly not meant to be the latter. Theodoric. was the production of what I may call the maturity of my moral feelings. All my life I have speculatively seen that the calm of mind produced by our cherishing the pure and kindly affections, and dismissing as far as it is possible all personal hatreds, is the only balm of this otherwise wretched existence. I believe a rebuke from yourself on the score of my being satirical was the first cause of my beginning to practise this truth. Imperfectly, I confess to you, I have practised it. I think I ought to say nothing for myself, but I ask your advice if anything can be said for me. It is no answer to say that Jeffrey's high praise is all set down to the score of his partiality for me. In fact, between ourselves, he does not understand the poem. Any one who can say that Constance is the same as Gertrude is obtuse on the subject. Constance is meant for a great moral character, with whom it was requisite to have been long acquainted

> 'Before the mind completely understood
> That mighty truth—how happy are the good.'

"These lines I knew would find an echo of sympathy in your mind. I have drawn the tears of approbation from your eyes, and from those of other women something resembling you in character. The only difficulty in the way of the office at which I hint is the repugnance which I can well imagine you will feel at giving publicity to your literary opinion ; but an expression of sincere approbation from some intellectual mind and heart is, I humbly think, due—though still I shall not be offended with you if you tell me the contrary.

"God bless you. I am already better for this confession of my feelings.—Yours, T. C."

PART IV.

About a month after my husband's death Mary and I left Auchindinny with many tears. It had been a blessed home to us for five years, and we left it uncertain as to our future plans, and with that feeling of desolateness which the breaking up of such a home involves. We had enjoyed much and we had suffered much there. We had formed several warm friendships among our poor neighbours, and we had enjoyed the visits of many valued friends, from far and near. Dear Mrs. Erskine, the widow of Henry Erskine and the sister of Sir Thomas Monro, was a frequent guest, a delightful companion to old and young. Mr. Fletcher delighted in her society, and so did my daughters. She cheered the latter years of her distinguished husband as no one else could have done, for she understood all his wit and wisdom, and supported him under many family trials by her unfailing sweetness and genuine piety. We had frequent visits from that delightful thinker, writer, and converser, Thomas Erskine of Linlathen, to whom we were so deeply indebted for the kind interest he took in my son Angus during the dangerous illness he had at Rome in 1827. T. Erskine and my old friend Mr. Clowes were more of kindred spirits than any men of spiritual natures I have met with in life. Dear Mrs. Grant of Laggan, and her daughter Mary, who had all *her* genius and more refinement, were often with us. We there first became acquainted with

Professor Sedgwick and Dr. Whewell, who came together to Auchindinny; and we used to benefit by the neighbourhood of the excellent family of Cowan at Penicuik, whose intimacy with Dr. Chalmers often brought him there, both to preach and shed the genial influence of his conversational powers among their friends and neighbours.

After spending a week with my son Miles in Edinburgh we joined Mrs. Taylor and Margaret at Tadcaster, taking my grandson, Archibald Taylor, with us. His mother had no wish to return to Edinburgh, and I felt it to be my first duty now to devote myself for the present to alleviate, if possible, the sufferings of the aunt who had taken a mother's care of me in my infancy.

I took lodgings at Thorp Arch, a pleasant village four miles from Tadcaster, where there was a good day-school at which my grandson could go on with his education, near his mother's lodgings. One of her sisters remained with her, and one with me by turns in my aunt's house, so that we were all within an easy reach of each other, and had the variety of frequent meetings.

[*To Dr. Francis Boott.*

"TADCASTER, *April* 1829.

" MY DEAR FRIEND,—I can no longer withhold my congratulations to you on the grand event—the Catholic Relief Bill. Who would have supposed that the Clare Election and the Irish Association would have opened the eyes of the blind and made the dumb to speak? The conquest of prejudice and the sacrifice of consistency to public good are honourable indeed to the present leaders in both Houses of Parliament. Truer patriotism than Wellington's and Peel's I do not remember, unless it is O'Connell's, who has nobly sacrificed popularity in declining to insist on his right to sit in Parliament in virtue of his late election rather than throw any impediment in the way of the great measure.

"But while we laud the public virtue of the champions of this Bill, what shall we say of the base artifices used to stir up the people against it? If the Church *is* in danger, it is her own sons who have by their unchristian spirit created that danger. A friend just returned from Ireland assures me he never saw that country so tranquil and contented. It is a generous people, and surely a grateful people. You would see a meeting has been held in Dublin to vote an estate to O'Connell as a reward for his public services, that he may be an independent Member of Parliament. The resolutions were moved alternately by Catholics and Protestants.

"Let us hear of yourself, of dear Mrs. Boott and your precious children. We are all recovering health and spirits after our great sorrows. We love each other so dearly that for each other's sake we do not dare to indulge in grief. Those we mourn are best honoured by our endeavouring best to discharge our remaining duties.

"You will be glad to hear your friend Angus is making good progress in his profession. He has been living happily and quietly for the last six weeks with our kind old friend Sir Robert Liston, who has fitted up a studio for him at Millburn Tower, and finds much interest in watching his progress. Sir Robert is now a lonely man ; his wife and he both loved Angus, and Angus venerates him, and they are good companions for each other."]

Three months thus passed on, and my aunt was soothed by my presence near her. Although unable to enjoy life any longer, she became less unhappy. Any immediate danger passed away, and we began to form some plans for the future. I was very desirous that my grandson should have the advantage of the best education that could be had, and where his mother could be near him. Dr. Arnold had been appointed head-master of Rugby School not long before, and after I read his pamphlet on "The Christian Duty of Conceding the Roman Catholic Claims," which was published about that time, I decided this was the school for *us*. Our cousin and friend, T. Shann, an old

Rugbeau who knew the neighbourhood, undertook to find a cottage for us within the school limits, where the boy could have the advantages of the education of Rugby and live at home with his mother.

I went to Rugby with my daughters Margaret and Mary, early in May, to make arrangements for the future, and we took possession of the cottage secured for us at Bilton the following day.

We found our cottage dwelling a peaceful and refreshing change to our.wearied spirits. We knew no one there; but "earth and sky" were blessings to us after a small country town street, and we soon experienced the greatest comfort and happiness in the society of Dr. and Mrs. Arnold, who came to see us shortly after we were settled at Bilton, she on her pony and he walking beside her.

I believe we were more than a week at Bilton before any one called on us, and my daughters began to amuse themselves by fearing that this new experience would not agree with my sociable tastes. Meantime, I cultivated the friendship of our good old landlord, Mr. Daniell, our subject of common interest being birds' nests, which he loved as much as I did, and kept carefully protected from the ruthless hands of village boys; but he pointed them out to me when I went out before breakfast into the little garden on the fine May mornings. He was a widower, and had no daughter, but he had a homely old housekeeper, who made him most comfortable, in the adjoining cottage to ours, and who paid him respectful attention. We did not know, for some time, that he had suffered a grief like that of "Old Michael." His only son, also the child of his age, had gone astray like Luke. My old friend, Mr. Daniell, belonged to the same class as the statesmen of Westmoreland; with greater kindness than they generally show, "*He* also had found a comfort in the strength of love." I am often reminded of him by our favourite neighbour, James Fleming of Grasmere.

An agreeable family, of the name of Boddington, lived very near our cottage, at Bilton Hall, formerly the residence of Joseph Addison after his marriage to Lady Warwick. These five sisters, all unmarried, lived together in great comfort. Their habits and modes of life were very different from ours, much more formal and precise. When we saw their fine powdered footman open their pew-door and arrange their Prayer-books in exact order, and the five ladies walk into church, we said to each other, "These ladies will not approve of us." It soon, however, proved otherwise. They called the following day. We returned it, were invited to the Hall, and, from being civil, they became kind and sociable. We found them amiable, intelligent, and well bred, with a good deal of individuality. To the poor they were exceedingly kind and judiciously helpful; and we always look back on their kindness to us, as strangers, with gratitude. When they first called on us, these ladies had a favourite niece staying with them, along with her father, Mr. Boddington. They went to their own home, in Shropshire, in a few days, before we had time to know what a treasure this niece was; but the impression had been made at first sight on my daughter Mary's imagination, and the aunts encouraged the friendship by bringing Gracilla Boddington to visit us, both at Keen Ground and afterwards in Kent, and a warm friendship was formed, not only between the young, but the old also, for I can truly say that we have both found a blessing in Gracilla's affection and society. She always reminded me of Milton's glorious sonnet "To a Virtuous Young Lady," beginning—

> "Lady that, in the prime of earliest youth,
> Wisely has shunned the broad way and the green."

It has been a great pleasure to me through life to make friends of the friends of my children, especially as time takes away my own, and thus make " relays of friendship " (as dear Benger used to say), and try to keep the heart young by adopting the interests of the present ; and it has been a joy to me to know how many of *my* friends my children have loved, and been loved by.

It was during this pleasant mouth of June that Margaret, Mary, and I made a sort of poetical pilgrimage to Olney and Weston, to trace the haunts of our beloved Cowper and his Mary.

[Letter to Mrs. Craig.

" BILTON, June 14, 1829.

" It is now almost six weeks since we came here, and it is not possible to imagine a place more suited to our purpose, or uniting more *agrémens* to our taste, than we have fouud here. Our cottage, indeed, is small ; but you know how happy even a large family can be in a small space. We have a sweet parlour, opening with a glass door into a grass plat and flower-garden,—shut in from, but not excluding, a sight of one of the prettiest of English villages. Our landlord (who has had a history) does everything possible to make us comfortable ; there never was so obliging a person. The Hall house, formerly the residence of Joseph Addison, is now inhabited by five maiden sisters of the name of Boddington. They are judiciously kind to the poor, especially in regard to education, and are very civil and attentive to us ; but our great delights in the way of society are Dr. and Mrs. Arnold. They are truly a charming couple. She reminds us continually of Madame de Bossi in her frankness, vivacity, and quickness of observation. She has the same sweetness of nature, and is not unlike her in personal appearance, but on a larger scale. Dr. Arnold is quite first-rate in talents, worth, and agreeableness. He published, three months ago, the best pamphlet that has appeared on the Christian duty of granting Catholic Emancipation, and is now at intervals of leisure writing notes for a new edition of Thucydides, a work he had undertaken before he was chosen head-master of Rugby. With all this learned and literary labour he is most diligent in his calling. In his own family he is delightful, always ready for conversation, liberal in politics, and high-toned in morals. He has published a volume of sermons, which we admire extremely, and we heard him preach in the School chapel a most excellent and impressive sermon to the boys. It is not, perhaps, the least of the merits of this agreeable couple that they have taken to us in the most cordial manner possible. We feel as if we had known them as many years as we have actually done weeks. Our next agreeable neighbours are the Moultries. He is the rector of Rugby, and married a niece of my dear friend Miss Fergusson, of Monkwood. They have also been most kind to us. Mr. Moultrie is a very able man, and an accomplished scholar and poet. We have made some pleasant excursions in the neighbourhood, for we have hired a double gig and a quiet horse for two months, that Mrs. Taylor when she comes may see a little farther than her feet would carry her. Our first expedition was one of thirty miles, to Olney in Buckinghamshire, to see the haunts of the poet Cowper. We traced him from his residence in the Market Place of that dull little town, one of the most unpoetical situations you can imagine, to the beautiful village of Weston, about two miles distant, where, in going to look for a house for Lady Hesketh, he found one which suited him and Mrs. Unwin."]

Before I returned to my post of duty at Tadcaster, the end of July, we spent a few days at the School House at Rugby, and partook of the home life of happiness enjoyed there by our new but already dear friends, Dr. and Mrs. Arnold.

It was a family custom retained from the Penrose household (Mrs. Arnold's old home) for each member of the family to repeat or read a favourite hymn before the children went to bed, and we were delighted to hear the hymns from "The Christian Year" repeated by little Jane Arnold and her brothers.

My daughters had become great admirers of "The Christian Year" before this time, and we then heard all about the college friendship and intimacy between Mr. Keble and Dr. Arnold, who always called him "dear old Keble," and they both spoke of him with peculiar love and admiration. Mr. Keble came as one of the Oxford Examiners of the school that summer to the Arnolds, and my daughters had the gratification of meeting him at the School House, as they remained a few weeks at Bilton after I left it. We still retained the cottage for the year we had taken it, although our family plans had been changed by Mrs. Taylor having decided to rejoin her husband, then employed in Ireland; her son was therefore placed at one of the master's houses in the town of Rugby.

In October 1829 I had a letter from our old friend Dr. John Davy, who had gone from Malta, where he was then stationed, to attend Sir H. Davy during a long illness he had at Rome, and was travelling home with his brother when Sir Humphry was seized by a severe attack of illness at Geneva, and died there on their homeward journey.

Dr. Davy offered me a visit, which I gladly accepted, having been in the habit of corresponding with him from the time he graduated at Edinburgh in 1814.

I had returned to Bilton for a few weeks to refresh my spirits before winter, Mary having taken my place at Tadcaster during my absence. Dr. Davy said he wished to read to me a MS. his brother had left to him for publication which he greatly admired. My dear old friend Miss Fergusson had joined my daughter Margaret and me at Bilton Cottage, and as we happened to be snowed up for some days early in the winter, we had full time to listen to and admire " The Consolations in Travel," read to us by the brother of the distinguished philosopher, and read with a degree of emotion at times which excited a new interest in the man who felt as he did the loss of his friend and brother. Dr. Davy went to London from Bilton to publish the volume, and asked permission to visit us again in Yorkshire on his way to Edinburgh, before his return to Malta.

On our way back to Tadcaster in December, Margaret and I paid a very interesting visit at the Parsonage at Bracebridge to Mr. and Mrs. Penrose.[1] She was my friend Mr. Cartwright's second daughter. She was at the time I speak of a happy wife, and the mother of three promising sons, a most delightful woman, with a lively, active, accomplished mind, and the most engaging sweetness and simplicity of manners. She had married Mrs. Arnold's eldest brother, a learned and estimable man. This renewal of intercourse was a great pleasure to me.

[*Extract from Mrs. John Penrose's Diary, after a visit from her Father's old friend.*

"BRACEBRIDGE, *December 19th*, 1829.

" We had the great gratification of a visit of two days from Mrs. Fletcher. Her appearance is so engaging, that the mere looking at her is itself a pleasure. In her youth she was brilliantly beautiful (she is about sixty) ; she retains so much symmetry of feature, so much fine expression of countenance, and so much grace of deportment, such a gentlewomanliness of manner, with such an expression of goodness, as make her absolutely lovely. She is rather fat than thin, and her beauty is matured more than faded. Her conversation is delightful, full of variety and anecdote. She is an enthusiast in politics, and on what is called the Liberal side, but there is such a feminineness in all she says and does, that even her politics could not alloy the charm of her agreeableness. She has a

[1] The " Mrs. Markham, author of School Histories."

most extensive acquaintance with literary persons, and her conversation is a stream of lively anecdote continually flowing."]

When we arrived at Tadcaster we were soon followed by Dr. Davy, whose correspondence and persuasion had overcome Margaret's hesitation to commit her happiness to his keeping. As he wished to see his friends in Edinburgh, and to settle some matters of business with my son Miles, Mary, who was going to visit her brother, accompanied Dr. Davy there. We had heard from Miles and his wife of his increased illness, but I had taken no serious alarm till Dr. Davy's return, when, in answer to my inquiries about him I saw by the expression of his countenance that there was great danger in his case, and he confessed he thought so. This was a terrible blow to me. Miles's life was infinitely precious and valuable to us all ; he was in the prime of life, then thirty-seven. My hopeful temper forbade despair of his recovery, and Mary's letters from Edinburgh were encouraging.

Dr. Davy left us for London in a few days, as his leave of absence from his professional duties at Malta was very limited. The marriage was fixed to take place on the 8th of March. A strange state of conflicting feelings takes place in a mother's heart in the approaching marriage of a beloved daughter. Her own loss is certain, the gain of happiness to her child must always be uncertain; but where there is soundness of principle and understanding, and great affectionateness of heart, marriage (always a lottery) seems the best chance of happiness for a woman who, when she has lost her parents and near domestic ties and duties in the paternal home, too often experiences " that hunger of the heart," that want of object in life, which nothing but a kind husband and affectionate children can supply. Hence it is that a mother sacrifices her own present to her daughter's prospective happiness, and with a sad but trusting hope gives up the first place in her child's affections to another.

Some weeks passed on in marriage preparations. Miles and Mary, and then Angus, arrived. If Miles's altered looks the year before had struck and pained me, this was much more the case when I saw him now. My hopes of his recovery were fainter, but in sympathy with the occasion that brought him he was in good spirits, and never complained of illness or pain. He gave his sister in marriage to Dr. Davy on the 8th of March 1830, in the same church where her parents had been united.

The wedded pair set off immediately after the ceremony, and Miles, Mary, and I posted the following day *en route* for London, while Angus went to Sir Robert Liston's kind home. We paid a short visit to our dear friends at Rugby on our way, and also at Oxford, which Miles much enjoyed. He had never been in London until now, and I was very desirous he should have the advice of Dr. Marshall Hall, who besides his great reputation at the time, was one of those who, I felt sure, would take a deep and friendly interest in the case. A successful London career had never weakened Dr. Hall's recollection of his student life in Edinburgh, where he thought I had been of some use to him, and he never failed to show his sense of this, by the most friendly attention and able professional aid on many occasions to different members of my family.

I took lodgings at Haike's Hotel, Duke Street, in the hope that dear Miles might have enjoyed seeing something of London in a quiet way, but he was quite unable for it, and was confined to his room by a sore throat when the Davys joined us. This however was an accidental ailment, not connected with his malady. He submitted with the most patient unselfishness to the disappointment of not seeing London when in it at last. With the most generous consideration for the indulgence of others, he habitually. exercised self-restraint, and was singularly inexpensive in his habits; while he had the greatest pleasure in making kind presents and in relieving the poor, he was as free from ostentation as he was from selfishness.

It was with the utmost reluctance that I could make up my mind to leave Miles ill and alone in London, and I proposed to remain with him and let Mary accompany the Davys to Paris, and return with our cousin, Mr. T. Shann, who was to be of our party. I remember the earnest way in which he begged me not to give up the plan of going to Paris, saying he especially wished me to go, as I might never again have an opportunity of seeing General Lafayette, and he knew we had good introductions to that great man ; besides, he added, " My wife is only too anxious to come, and I promise you to summon her, if I am not better, to-morrow." This decided me to go, and I heard of his wife having joined him when we arrived in Paris : she had, indeed, set off the day we left London.

I felt in a strange dream when I got to Paris, the scene, in my early married life, of such high hopes and bitter disappointments.. We all felt more disposed to turn to the living actors left of those times than to see sights ; and, to assist my memory, I have recourse to our journal at the time. Owing to Chevalier Masclet's kindness, we paid a most interesting visit to the Abbé Gregoire, and were not disappointed in the deportment and conversation of this venerable member of the Constituent Assembly, and known by them as L'Ami des Noirs. He seemed to be holding a sort of levée, and soon after our arrival a free African from Hayti was announced, a youth who was attending the University of Paris. The Abbé spoke of our Clarkson with great admiration and pleasure, and we felt it to be a real gain to have seen so beautiful an example of serene old age. He was, as Thomas Erskine told us, very much one's idea of Fénélon, courteous, polished, full of benevolence and kind feeling for good men of all countries and colours.

The Misses Garnet, some American ladies to whom we had brought letters of introduction, called to say General Lafayette would call on me at four o'clock. He came at that hour, and conversed most agreeably till six. We were all delighted with the mildness, benevolence, and ease with which this great and good man entered into conversation, expressing, without the least egotism, the most liberal and extensive views. He spoke of a new colony for the reception of liberated Negroes on the coast of Africa, called it " his daughter Liberia," and expressed the deepest interest in its success. We all went the same evening to a soirée at General Lafayette's, between nine and ten P.M. The suite of rooms, four of which were open, were much crowded, and the noise greater than at an English reception. Chairs were placed round the second room, close to the wall, where the ladies sat. The middle of the room was filled by men, vociferating with great energy to each other ; many of these were distinguished members of the Chamber of Deputies. We were introduced to Benjamin Constant, very intellectual-looking, but in feeble health. He had a sickly, melancholy appearance, like one weary of the world—and no wonder.

We continued to receive the kindest attention from the family of General Lafayette while we remained in Paris. His daughter, Madame De Lasteyrie, sometimes came to our hotel in the evening for an hour or two, and delighted to speak of her father. She said he enjoyed his retirement at La Grange extremely ; and there, surrounded by his grandchildren, and occupied with the cultivation of his estate, he passed a happy and serene old age.

There was something morally sublime in the contemplation of a character so pure and devoted as Lafayette's, so clear of party feeling, so free from egotism, so unspoiled by popularity, so unsoured by adversity and ingratitude.

We were at that time (April 1830) little aware that General Lafayette was again so soon to be placed at the head of the National Guards on the memorable three days of July in that year, when the destinies of France in the choice of an Executive Government were committed to those over whom he presided.

When we saw him he expressed his entire confidence and satisfaction at the enlightened state of public opinion in France; he said the people were now too well informed to admit of the Government taking measures subversive of their liberties; and that Frenchmen had paid too dearly for their rights not to know how to cherish them. The tone of General Lafayette's conversation was more remarkable for mildness, moderation, and good sense, than for eloquence or brilliancy, but it gave me the impression of earnestness, and honesty, and a hopefulness wonderful even to me after all he had seen and suffered. The opinions of Mignet the historian, whom we met, with several other distinguished literary men, at the evening receptions of Miss Clarke (now Madame Mohl) were more in accordance with the events which have since taken place at Paris than with the hopes of the sanguine general and patriot. Our journal records on Saturday, 9th April—" We met at Miss Clarke's, in the Rue Petite, St. Augustin, Mignet, the historian of the French Revolution." He is a man of about five-and-thirty, of a noble countenance, and very simple engaging manners. He has no other profession than that of literature. His society is much sought, but he prefers retirement, and he is indeed not a man of the world, but he is singularly animated and eloquent in conversation, not for

the sake of display, but from the interest he takes in the
subject of which he speaks.   He contended that nations,
no more than individuals, have been ever known to profit
by experience from the misfortunes of others.   He thought
the granting Catholic emancipation to Ireland was the only
exception.   The English Government *had* profited by the
experience of the Irish Rebellion of 1790.   Mignet is now
engaged in writing the History of Henry IV., and the
religious feuds of that period.   It is creditable to the
present state of society and manners in Paris to hear of
the high estimation in which men of real literary merit
are held.   Literature gives a man the first rank in society,
and wealth is not essential to him.   Bookmaking as a trade
meets with no encouragement.   The honour of a seat in
the National Institute, and a distinguished place in the
best scientific and literary circles, are the rewards of intellectual eminence in Paris.   Authorship in France seems
to be a more honourable than gainful profession.   The
copyright of books is much cheaper than works of the same
merit would be in England.   I was told that the law
which divides the property of families into equal shares is
gradually effecting a degree of equality which is not known
in the other countries of Europe.   So far as we could learn,
this division of property by the law of inheritance does not
relax industry nor lead to prodigality ; on the contrary, it
leads to moderation.

We saw a number of the so-called charitable institutions
of Paris supported by the State.   Many, such as the deaf
and dumb, and blind, were evidently beneficent and well
conducted ; but one did fill me with horror, and did more
to make me hopeless of the future of Paris, if not of France,
than anything I heard or saw there.   The first we went to
see was that known by the name of Les Enfans Trouvés.
Nothing could exceed the neatness of the apartments.   It

was truly a "whited sepulchre." Each infant was in a separate crib, and the curtains were white and clean, but there is no describing the effect of the little wailing cries of the poor deserted babes; the low faint sound of distress from all sides was most appalling. One of the *sœurs de la charité* was in the apartment; we involuntarily drew aside the curtains of one poor infant, whose low deep moanings were peculiarly affecting. The sister of charity lifted it up, and said, smiling, "It is dying." I besought her earnestly to give it some natural food, that of the breast, for the mouth of the child moved in search of it. She said, with much sweetness and composure, "It has a sore mouth, and would infect the nurse; it is dying." It was long before I could think of anything but the famished look of that miserable infant, and I left the institution with a firm persuasion that many children are suffered to perish there from inanition. I was powerless to do anything but write a letter to Madame De Pastoret, who gave us the order of admission. Count Philip Ugoni promised to translate and read my letter to her, as she had requested to have my opinion of that and the institution for young delinquents. The demoralizing effect of this institution is perhaps more to be reprobated than the indifference to human life which we observed within its walls. That there should be in Christian Europe, and in a city famed above all others for its civilisation and refinement, little less than seven thousand mothers every year capable of abandoning their infants at the moment of their birth, is a melancholy fact. It is not to be supposed that many of these mothers could bring themselves to put their children to a violent death with their own hands. This cruel institution, therefore, furnishes them with an apology for licentiousness. They send their superfluous offspring to an early grave within the precincts of this hospital, or to a life of sorrow and abandonment if

they are strong enough to live. We were told by one of
the managers of this institution that from twenty to thirty
infants were received every twenty-four hours; there were
eighty-seven when we visited the place, all of whom had
been received within the last three days. Every third day
these deserted babes are placed in hammocks, swung up
inside a large caravan, and sent into the country to be
nursed. Four hundred francs a year is given to the foster-
parent till they are twelve years old, and then the allow-
ance from the hospital ceases. We were told that one-third
die within the third day of their reception there. Many
of these mothers were supposed—from the dress in which
the children came—not to be in distressed circumstances,
but prefer this to the incumbrance and expense of a large
family.

[*To Mrs. Thomson.*

"LONDON, *May 4th*, 1830.

" I must leave Mary to give you the sequel of our adventures in Paris; she alleges I did not enjoy it sufficiently. The
fact is, it excited me too much. I never felt myself *old* till I
went to Paris. I wanted to find people to talk to me about
the Federation in the Champs de Mars—about the fall of the
Bastile—the scenes that took place at the Hôtel de Ville ;
but I could find no one that knew or cared about them, and in
vain we searched through many a shop and book-stall for ' Les
Jours de la Révolution,' the little book you recommended to
us. We had great enjoyment, however, in various ways, and
I shall enjoy it more at Bilton than I did in Paris. You will
be glad to hear that General De Lafayette entirely approves
of Fanny Wright's conduct in taking her Negroes to Hayti.
He gave her a letter of introduction to the President Boyer, of
whom he has a good opinion ; and he hopes by her energy and
the influence of her talents she will establish a good understanding between the Government of Hayti and that of the
United States, so as to facilitate the settlement of the Negroes

in that country.   He lamented her connexion with the Owens, but spoke of her with great respect and interest."]

Some weeks after our return to Yorkshire, in the summer of 1830, Mary went to pay a visit to Mrs. Taylor, in Ireland, and in September I set off for Scotland, having heard from Mrs. Miles Fletcher that Miles had been strongly advised by Dr. Marshall Hall to spend the winter in a milder climate, but that he would not consent to leave his boys, and that thus the hope of his health benefiting by the change recommended could not be accomplished.   This decided me at once to offer to take charge of the boys in their absence.   No time was to be lost, as the days were shortening, and I at once sent Angus to bring his sister · Mary from Ireland to meet me in Edinburgh; and my offer being gladly accepted by Miles and his wife, I set off at once.

I had not seen dear Miles from the time we had parted in London, and I was greatly shocked at the change in his appearance, though he was not uncheerful.   He was rejoiced to see me, and spoke hopefully of the benefit he expected to derive from going to Jersey.

On the 1st October 1830 I accompanied my dear Miles to enter his son Henry at the New Academy.   He was a cheerful little fellow, not quite eight years old; and I well remember his father's glistening eye as he saw him receive his ticket of admission and take the place his number gave him in the class.   Mary soon joined us from Ireland, and we entered on our unexpected duties.   It was a very mournful time for both of us; but we felt it was all we could do for one we dearly loved; and although we declined all invitations, we received much kind attention from old friends of all degrees, and had the pleasure of becoming intimate with Susan Ferrier, the good and agreeable author of " Marriage" and " Inheritance," novels of much humour and ability, and greatly admired at the time. Miss Ferrier took a most friendly interest in my grandsons for their mother's sake, whose intimate friend she had been from her early days.

Three months thus passed. My son's health did not improve; and, besides his desire to be at home, he wished to relieve me from the charge I had undertaken; and this was rendered more easy, as, from the change of Ministry, the Duke of Argyll had been appointed Keeper of the Great Seal for Scotland, and, without solicitation, he appointed Miles his Deputy Keeper. This was a very desirable event, as sickness had destroyed his prospects at the Bar. He wrote me a cheerful letter on reaching London, on his way home, and said that "his satisfaction on his appointment would be complete when he received my congratulations upon it." He and his wife paid a short visit to the dear old aunt who always delighted in him, on their way home, but he gave us so bad an account of her state that he did not urge my remaining many days, but asked me to leave Mary with him, which I did, she being at the time not able to travel from illness. My spirits were supported by feeling equal to the work God had appointed me to do—to watch over the kindest of friends to me and mine; and, as usual, she revived on my return to her, from the comfort of knowing I was near her.

[*To her daughter Mary, in Edinburgh.*

"TADCASTER, *May 7th,* 1831.

"I was indebted to Mrs. Dundas for procuring me a ticket for the High Sheriff's box on the hustings yesterday, for a most glorious day at York. Before I set out with Archy I had the very great satisfaction to receive the letter you sent me from Malta; mine has never appeared yet. Thank you, dearest Mary, for the relief your kind attention gave me,

but we have three long weeks to wait before we can hear of
her safety. We must pray, and trust in unfailing mercy.
Well, I have had many adventures since I wrote to you—first,
a call from Mr. Strickland, on his way to canvass the West
Riding—he was very agreeable, and full of kindly recollections
of us in early days at Edinburgh ; then, last Saturday, a
most friendly visit from Mrs. Dundas [1] after her husband's
election, offering me a seat on the hustings if she could get
tickets ; then, on Sunday, a long visit again from Mr. Strickland
on his return from his triumphal progress through the West
Riding, with divers amusing anecdotes and incidents that
occurred on his canvass. He took luncheon here, and left
me about five o'clock. Then the last fortnight has been full of
amusing episodes, stirring up a Reform committee in *Noodle-
dum*,[2] the sub-committee in the blue parlour of aunty's house.
The full committee held their meetings at Backhouse's Inn.
They actually raised subscriptions large enough to send such
of the seventy freeholders from Tadcaster as could not afford
to pay their own expenses if a poll had been demanded ; but
Mr. Duncombe, the Tory candidate, happily thought fit to quit
the field on Thursday, so that the immense tide of human
existence which rolled past this house from the West Riding
on Thursday afternoon, all Thursday night and yesterday
morning, were carried there by the impulse of enthusiastic
feeling in favour of the Reform Bill ; every one of that
immense multitude, five or six thousand at least, paying
their own expenses. Every wheeled carriage in Leeds was put
in requisition, and the number of carriages of every description
surpassed belief. Then the operatives on foot lined the road
and filled the streets of this town with their bands of music
and their shouts of triumph. On Thursday evening, as they
were passing, a heavy shower came on. All who had money
in their pockets took shelter in public-houses. Archy and I
observed two boys sheltering themselves under the gateway
opposite my aunt's house, with Reform colours—an orange card
—in their hats. The rain fell in torrents. We had just
finished our comfortable tea, and I sent Hannah to invite them
to tea in the kitchen. They were two young operatives,

1 Afterwards Countess of Zetland.   2 The family name for Tadcaster.

croppers, out of work, but well-dressed lads, who had set off to walk twenty-three miles without a shilling in their pockets. They enjoyed their repast much, and when the rain was over proceeded on their way to York. We reached York yesterday, soon after nine o'clock. Mrs. Dundas, Mrs. Lane (one of Lord Dundas's married daughters), Alexander Spiers of Elderslie, and I, proceeded straight to the hustings. The Castle Yard presented a noble sight ; not less than thirty thousand people, I was told, all of one mind. You will read the proceedings in the *Leeds Mercury* better than I can give them. Lord Morpeth is a most graceful and finished speaker. Sir J. Johnston gentlemanly, but rather feeble. Mr. Ramsden sensible and earnest, but not fluent. George Strickland manly, eloquent, and fearless. He was the most popular with the West Riding men. Good speeches were made by the proposers and seconders of the nominations, but the most touching of all was the anthem of 'God save the King,' sung by that assembled multitude uncovered, and with a religious fervency I never heard equalled in any place of worship. This was done simultaneously on the motion of Mr. Fawkes of Farnley, who is a most eloquent and impassioned speaker. The streets were so crowded it was not safe to return after the chairing of the members in a carriage, so we all walked from the hustings to Parsons' lodgings, where the Dundases are lodging, and then took leave of them. What strange doings at the Edinburgh election ! You want a safety-valve in Scotland. Oh how tranquil are popular elections even under the old system in England in comparison of the close system in Scotland ! I am in daily expectation of a visit from Sir Robert Liston, on his way down. I see a letter from Angus addressed to him here. God bless you, dearest Mary; I hope you are warmer than we are. We had a snowstorm yesterday. I am quite well, spite of all this excitement ; indeed, enjoying it greatly, as a Yorkshire freeholder ought to do."]

Mary joined me at Tadcaster in June, having left her brother and his wife at a beautifully-situated house they had taken in Fife for a year, within an easy distance of Edinburgh by steam. We remained with aunty, and enjoyed

many walks to Oxton and Wighill together. In the middle
of August I was persuaded to pay a visit at Mr. Brooke's of
Armitage Bridge, while Mary remained at the post of duty.
I was sitting in the drawing-room there, looking over a
large volume of Grose's Antiquities, when Catherine
Laycock was called out of the room ; she returned, looking
very sorrowful, and said, " Your Mary has come with bad
news." I said, "Is poor aunty dead ?" Mary, who had
followed, replied, " No, dear mother, but Miles is worse,
and wishes to see us." I did not sink, but instantly
prepared for our journey. It was Saturday, the 20th
August 1831. In half an hour we were on our way to
Edinburgh, posting day and night. We reached Borough
Bridge about midnight. I was so exhausted with sorrow
and fatigue that Mary persuaded me to throw myself on a
bed for an hour or two ; and we both felt strengthened by
it. About two A.M. we proceeded on our journey. That
day—Sunday the 21st—at three in the afternoon we
reached Percy's Cross, on the road between the vale of
Whittingham and Wooler, that very relic of antiquity
which at that precise hour the day before we had been
looking at and talking about while turning over Grose's
Antiquities. I mention this as a curious coincidence.

We travelled all Sunday night, and reached Edinburgh
soon after sunrise on Monday morning. On arriving at
11 Queen Street, Mary rang the bell, which was answered
by Angus, who had come there from Hillside to wait our
arrival. Our dearest Miles died on Saturday evening, the
20th August 1831. Though faint and exhausted, we
could not rest till we proceeded by the first steamboat to
Aberdour and Hillside. Charlotte Fletcher was perfectly
calm ; the relief of tears had not come, and she was
miserably worn out. Once, only once, I saw the remains
of my dear, excellent, and beautiful Miles, but so unlike

what he had been that I could scarcely have recognised a trace of resemblance. The funeral took place on the Thursday following. He was laid by his father and Grace, and a baby of his own, in the cemetery of the Calton Hill

In the darkest hour of sorrow some human comfort is often sent beyond that of the immediate family circle; and such we felt was the presence of Mary Campbell, an intimate friend of the poor widow, and also of ours, as her father had been one of my husband's earliest Edinburgh friends, and I was greatly attached to his eldest daughter, Mary, at the time I entered on my Edinburgh life. When Miles felt his last hours approaching, he sent for this Sister of Charity, " Santa Maria," as we always called her, to be with his wife, before our arrival; and she remained with us, and was of the greatest benefit to all, by the depth of her human sympathy and her divine love.

Letter on her son Miles's Death to Mrs. Davy at Malta, from E. F.

"HILLSIDE, *August* 1831.

[After giving an account of our journey from Yorkshire, travelling day and night, but arriving too late to see him alive, our mother says :—

"Dearest M., I could fill volumes with what is at the bottom of my heart about our dear, dear Miles, but I cannot now. I will send you a little memorial of him when time has mellowed my grief. It will then be soothing to me to remember him in the freshness and beauty of his youth, but he improved in character in *real life* every year he lived ; sickness and disappointment in his hopes of worldly prosperity most certainly fixed his heart on God. He read his Bible much, and there was a glowing light over his wasted features which showed the peace within."

James Wilson writes to Angus :—

"I had fondly hoped that his malady, though partaking of the nature of a mortal ailment, might have been so far subdued or prevented from increasing, as that he might have been spared even for years to gladden that circle in which, if I may judge from my own feelings, he never appeared without spreading joy and comfort.   To me during many years in which I had but few consolations, his presence was as sunshine to the earth, and I cannot help feeling, notwithstanding the blessings with which I am now surrounded, 'that my heart-strings are broken.'

"When we arrived here at seven in the morning on the 22d of August we found Charlotte up, and more composed than we could possibly have expected ; she continued so all that day, and Tuesday and Wednesday.   On Thursday, the funeral day, she became very ill ; her sensations were a lightness of the brain, which she thought indicated inflammation. She desired Dr. P— from Kirkcaldy to be sent for.   I was not present when he came, but Mary says she said to him with great composure, 'Now, doctor, I believe I am going to lose my senses ; I think inflammation of the brain is coming on.   If it is so, I entreat you to tell me honestly, for I have some directions to give and arrangements to make.'   He assured her the sensations she complained of were simply the effect of sleeplessness, grief, and fatigue, and that perfect repose would restore her.   Dr. Christison agreed with this opinion when he came, but she was in such a state of exhaustion that both her doctors were alarmed about her.   When her eyes were closed I never saw any living thing so deadly—so pale, emaciated, and unearthly.   Our anxiety and care of her made us in some measure forget our own deep affliction.   She is now able to be moved to a sofa while her bed is made ; she can converse a little, and is quite composed.   She reads her Bible much.   She is very sweet in her manners towards Mary and me.   I must leave M. with her, Charlotte clings to her so much."

M. F. says in the same letter :—

"Poor Charlotte is very unselfish in her sorrow, so willing to talk of all that is on her mind, and so soothed and gratified by the sympathy and the feeling of Miles's friends. She dwells constantly on the parts of his character which were indeed most striking :—'His truth in the inward parts,' his extreme delicacy of mind, his entire disinterestedness, and his love of promoting the happiness of others and finding his own in so doing. We are very thankful that he had the enjoyment of this place, and that the last objects his eyes rested upon were such scenes of beauty as can scarcely be surpassed in heaven. The last night he was up, he stood at the window to look at the moonlight on the sea ; and after he was in bed he said to Charlotte, 'I never saw a night that made such an impression on me as this.' We have often remarked his simple enjoyment in nature, and it seemed to have increased latterly in strength. I am now very, very glad I was with him so much last winter, although it has increased tenfold the sense of his loss personally to myself, yet it also increased in the same measure my appreciation of his character and my gratitude for his kindness and sympathy in all that concerns us. I felt, too, I was of use to him, as Charlotte was obliged to be absent for some weeks, owing to Rawdon's state of health, at her mother's house. I had not seen so much of dear Miles since his marriage, and it was impossible to be with him and watch his state of mind with regard to others, and himself, and not feel he was ripening for Heaven. His deep love for and gratitude to our mother quite satisfied me, as it would have done you.

"Dear Mary Campbell is with us still, and is an unspeakable comfort to the house in general. She has so much knowledge of human infirmity as never to be surprised at it, or impatient with it. She is most valuable to the boys just now, and also to Angus, and I am so glad our dearest mother has her near ; they can go back together in the family history farther than you or I, and they walk together about these lovely grounds. I am almost constantly in Charlotte's room, as Stewart, her maid, needs rest during the day-time."

To Miss Aikin, from Mrs. Fletcher.

" 1832.

" You know me too well to believe that I could either be un-mindful of you, or ungrateful for the kind expression of your sympathy which I received some weeks after it was written. I was then both ill and so sorrowful that I did not wish to distress my friends by my mournful communications, of various kinds. You knew my dear Miles in the freshness and beauty of his youth, and you were one of those who saw through the apparent carelessness and gaiety of his character,—saw that there was a fund of manly principle and good sense which would one day lead to valuable results. You were right. A higher and purer spirit never existed, and if he had laboured more in the acquirement of professional knowledge I should have had nothing to regret, but that he was taken away just when brighter prospects of professional success were opening before him. Latterly, for the last four years, the declining state of his health incapacitated him for continued application. He was a most beloved husband and father, son and brother, a most trusted and constant friend, a friend of the poor in the best sense, by taking trouble for them, and respected by all who knew him for the purity and integrity of his life. I have much comfort in the reflection that he lived to see better prospects opening on his country, and that no action of his public or private life was unworthy of his father's son."]

I remained with my aunt all winter : letters from Malta and from Mary in Edinburgh were my only pleasures ; but my duty at this time was a real pleasure to me, nor would I have exchanged my life at Tadcaster then for any other.

The more I saw of my aunt Mary Hill at this time, the more I revered the self-denial she practised, and the activity and extent of her benevolence. My visits at the Grange and to the poorhouse, early in the day, were my only visits. I discovered some abuses there, and got them remedied.

In the spring of 1832 Mary returned to me. Her

health was shattered ; but between her severe attacks of headache she recovered both her looks and vigour, and we went in May to pay a promised visit to our dear friend Mrs. Smith of Tent Lodge, Coniston.

It was at the time the Whigs, who had been striving hard for the first Reform Bill, were, by the vacillation of William the Fourth, compelled to resign, and they were for some weeks out of office. At this unexpected occurrence our Tory hostess rejoiced exceedingly, and then, when Lord Brougham left the Woolsack with his party, I offered a visit to my old and revered friend Mrs. Brougham, telling Mrs. Smith I was not so much afraid of her making an ungenerous use of her party triumph as I was of my own temper at her exultation. She replied, "By all means, my dear friend, go to Mrs. Brougham and condole with her, but make haste to come back again."

We stayed a few days with Mrs. Brougham and her agreeable daughter, both of whom received us with the most frank and hospitable kindness. Newspapers and letters from her sons came daily, and on the day we had fixed to leave her, news came that the tide had turned. The Whigs were again sent for, and the discussions on the clauses of the Reform Bill were resumed. We were much urged by Mrs. Brougham to remain another day, to see her receive a procession of Whigs and Reformers from Penrith, who had fixed on that day to come, with bands of music and colours flying, to hail the triumph of the good cause, and to sympathize with her in the share her gifted son had taken in the noble struggle. It was a strong temptation to both of us, but we felt we ought not to yield to our inclination to witness this demonstration at Brougham, but returned to our kind Tory lady at Coniston, in better spirits than when we left her, on public grounds.

[*To Mrs. Thomson, from Mrs. Fletcher.*

"TENT LODGE, CONISTON, *May 21st,* 1832.

" On our return from Brougham Hall on Saturday evening I had the satisfaction to find your kind letter. The very day we read in the newspaper that the Whig Ministry had resigned I wrote to offer Mrs. Brougham a visit. There was no one within my reach that could so fully and entirely enter into the grief and indignation I felt, not so much at Lord Grey's resignation, as at the monstrous audacity of the Duke of Wellington undertaking to form an administration to carry *the Bill* against which he had a few days before so strongly protested. Well, Mary and I said to each other, if the country, if the House of Commons, submit to this, England is not a country for an honest man to live in. Under these impressions we set forward last Thursday to Brougham, but at Keswick we met the welcome news that the Duke could not form an administration. That burst of honest and high feeling which prevailed in the House of Commons when John Wood brought in the Manchester petition, signed in three hours by twenty-five thousand persons, praying the House to refuse supplies till the Reform Bill was passed—when even the honest Tories scouted the idea of the Duke taking charge of the Reform Bill—that night's debate and the state of feeling in the country, as expressed universally at public meetings all over England and Scotland, set our hearts at rest, and we proceeded next day to Brougham, not to condole with, but to congratulate the Chancellor's mother on the proud position in which her son and his excellent compeers stood from the moment of their resignation. That was their point of glory, as Lord Brougham expressed it on taking leave of the Chancery Bar, 'To relinquish power at the call of public duty is not a misfortune but a glory.' The old lady was as happy as the noble-minded mother of so noble-minded a son deserves to be. We had heartfelt rejoicings together, and much pleasant chat about all our Edinburgh friends, and about what you would all be thinking and saying. Mrs. Brougham pressed us most kindly to prolong our visit, but we had promised to return here. The recall of the Grey Ministry was not absolutely secure when we left Brougham, but the

people had willed it, and *we* felt secure.   We found your letter
and the report of the Edinburgh meeting on our return to our
good Tory friend.   The spirit and intelligence of the Edinburgh
meeting is delightful.   Reform in Scotland and all the feeling
connected with it is, as you may believe, nearer my heart than
anything else connected with public affairs."]

In October of this year, 1832, I became very uneasy
about the state of Mary's health, from Dr. Thomson's
report of it, and, with my aunt's entire approval, I left her
under the care of a kind friend and her own excellent maid,
and joined Mary in Edinburgh when she returned there,
with her sister-in-law, from Fife, where she had been for
the last month for sea-air and quietness.

I had the good fortune to travel north with one of the
most remarkable men of his time—The Honourable Mount-
Stuart Elphinstone.   We had been some minutes in the
mail before we recognised each other, and then there was
a most animated and delightful discourse carried on for
eight hours, during which an infinite variety of subjects
were discussed.   He gave me much information quite new
to me about India.   His acquaintance with men and books
seemed equally extensive, liberal, and unprejudiced, and
we parted at Durham with an impression on my mind that
he was one of the most intelligent men it had ever been
my good fortune to meet, and beyond comparison, uniting
with this, the most engaging and prepossessing manners.
Bishop Heber, who was so well able to judge of the attainments of other men by the extent of his own, mentions
Mount-Stuart Elphinstone in his delightful Indian Journal as altogether the most accomplished man he had
ever known.   We saw him frequently after this, both
in Edinburgh and London, and always with renewed
pleasure.

We established ourselves in pleasant lodgings in Forres

Street, near Moray Place, where Angus joined us for the winter.

We received constant and tender attention from our old friends in Edinburgh, especially from all the Thomson family. Mrs. Thomson's loving sympathy much helped to cheer Mary's winter, as she was obliged to keep almost entirely in the recumbent position for several months.

It was during that winter, 1832-3, that the hustings were erected for the first time at the Cross of Edinburgh for the popular election of the members for the city, under the new Reform Bill. I often took my three grandsons, and explained to them how their grandfather and father would have rejoiced to see that day, for the sake of the improvement of their country and the security of its future freedom.

At length, in December 1832, came the day of election, and we were kindly invited by the Lord Advocate and Mrs. Jeffrey to their house in Moray Place, to see the members brought home in triumph. The citizens of Edinburgh did themselves honour in choosing two such representatives as James Abercromby, the Speaker of the House of Commons, and Francis Jeffrey, then Lord Advocate, men not less eminent for their talents than for their public spirit and courage in supporting the cause of civil and religious liberty, both in and out of Parliament. I scarcely felt equal to go, leaving Mary alone on that day in our lodgings. Our kind Mrs. Thomson secretly consulted her husband, and came with a cheery face early in the day to say Dr. Thomson allowed his patient to go with me to the chair or sofa offered her near the window by Mrs. Jeffrey. It was a glorious sight for us to see these truly honest men borne home amidst the acclamations of tens of thousands of their grateful and emancipated countrymen. We stood by them on the balcony of Mr.

Jeffrey's house while they shortly returned thanks to the people. Few events ever excited me more than those which took place in Edinburgh at that time. Mary, in the true spirit of a reformer's daughter, rose from the sofa to which she had been condemned for five months, to witness the joyful scene, and she did not in the least suffer from it. Nay, from that day she continued to be allowed more freedom of action and exercise, and about the middle of April was able to return with me to Tadcaster.

[Lord Cockburn's interesting "Memorials of his Own Time" close before this election of his friend Jeffrey, "his love for whom was passing the love of woman." He was more excited by joy on that day even than we were; and I well remember his way of rushing into the drawing-room, and looking round the crowd of Whig ladies and girls who were present, and calling out, "Where's Mrs. Fletcher? she's the woman that I want," and when my mother came from the window to meet him, they clasped each other's hands and had a good "greet" together; and not many words were said before there was a call for "Cockburn" from the crowd without, and he went to the balcony to respond to the call, and made a short speech of deep feeling which was cheered long and loudly.—M. R.

From Thomas Campbell to Mrs. Fletcher.

"London, *May* 18, 1833.

"I know that your interest in dear, yet glorious, though fallen Poland, will be a sufficient recommendation to her most illustrious poet, Niemskewitz, without a word from me; but as the venerable patriot and friend of Kosciusko also honours Thomas Campbell with his friendship, I cannot help giving myself the gratification of writing to you by him.

"I declare I can scarcely trust my thoughts with the melancholy subject of Poland. It has at different periods over-agitated me, even to the loss of health; and yet there are some of the Polish patriot exiles the sight and friendship of whom are a consolatory balm to my spirits. Among these, the most valued are my brother poets Niemskewitz and the Prince Czartorysky. It is some happiness to me to think that the chosen spirits of Scotland, and amongst them yourself, will testify your regard for a sacred cause, and for human worth, by attention to my venerable friend.

"I trust, my dear madam, that this will find you in good health. I am this day returning thanks to Providence for fairly feeling the return of that greatest of blessings. . . .

"I shall now resume the life of Mrs. Siddons, and shortly begin to print, so as to have it out for certainty in October. I am not sorry for the delay. It is no later than yesterday that I discovered a probability—almost near a certainty—that Shakespeare visited friends in the very town (Brecon in Wales) where Mrs. Siddons was born, and that he there found in a neighbouring glen, called 'The Valley of Fairy Puck,' the principal machinery of his 'Midsummer Night's Dream.'

"It would give me pleasure to hear from and to see your handwriting. I beg my best regards to all your family, and remain, after thirty years' friendship, your sincerely attached,

"THOS. CAMPBELL."

To Mrs. Davy, Malta.

"TADCASTER, 3d *May* 1833.

"We found good aunty shrunk into the least possible dimensions, but in a less suffering state than she was when I left her last October. Miss Hill is much bent in figure, but as much erect in mind as ever, and rejoicing in the effects she perceives of the Reform Bill in elevating the condition of the lower orders. She thought it was the first step towards the millennium!!! What would your Conservatives say of that opinion from a woman of eighty-one? They would say she was in her dotage; but I never saw her mind more entire, though the faculty of memory is somewhat impaired. I have been alarmed since I came here with the tone of the public press,— the coalition that seems to have taken place between the Conservative and Radical papers; they vie with each other in foul and scurrilous abuse of Ministers. The Conservatives are playing a dangerous game. They are making use of the Radicals to turn out the Whigs, not perceiving that by strengthening that party (the Radicals) they are destroying all those aristocratic associations in the minds of the people by means of which they calculate upon their own return to power. The fears of our Lord Advocate,[1] which his friends in Edinburgh imputed to his nervous timidity, had but too much foundation. He said the country had nothing now to fear from the Tory party, but very much to dread from popular and physical force, and he feared it would be impossible for any honest administration to satisfy the people, who had learned from the foolish conduct of the House of Peers last year to calculate upon their own strength, and to hold all other strength at defiance. He feared that spoliation, or, as he called it, levelling downward, would be the will of the great mass of operatives. This was in a conversation I had with him last November at Mr. John Cunningham's. I did not then think the people so unreasonable, but the speeches of O'Connell, Cobbett, Hume, etc., are of so inflammatory a character that I do fear Reform has come too late to prevent revolution. I am thankful however that it has come. It has organized a national guard in all the ten-pound voters, and I still hope that the selfish principle, if no better one, will influence the thinking and rational of all parties to rally round them."]

We found dear aunty quite as well as when I had left her five months before, and, as usual, delighted to see us again ; but Dr. Thomson told me that Mary's nerves had been so much affected by the complaint in her spine, and the reducing system necessary to subdue the inflammation, that she ought not to remain long in so melancholy a scene as my aunt's sick-room,—that good air was essential to her recovery. So in June our friend Mr. Harden took lodgings for us, for three months, at Thorney How, near Grasmere, to be near our dear friends the Arnolds, who were living that summer at Allan Bank, while their future home at Fox How was building. Our lodgings were in a

<hr>

[1] Francis Jeffrey.

simple farm-house, at that time furnished in the most homely manner; we were the first ladies who had inhabited it, as it was before Easedale was much known, except to such lovers of beauty as Wordsworth and De Quincey. We were greatly pleased with our quarters, and saw several of our friends there, for we never attached much importance to the size or appearance of our dwelling, so that it allowed us to exercise the pleasures of hospitality and enabled us to give a kindly welcome to our friends. Dear Mrs. Taylor and her little Mary joined us there, and added much to our happiness. Henry Fletcher paid us a long visit, and we had frequent intercourse with Wordsworth and his excellent wife, with Mr. Hamilton, who then lived at Rothay Cottage, at Rydal, and with our old friends the Hardens at Brathay Hall, and, above all, the Arnolds, who were our great attraction, to Grasmere and Easedale. We did not then foresee that so many happy years were in store for us at the little mountain farm called Lancrigg, which adjoined Thorney How, and which, from its sunny aspect and birch and oak copses, under Helm Craig, had for many years of Wordsworth's Grasmere life been a favourite summer haunt of the simple household of the bard, who then lived at Town End. Wordsworth and Dr. Arnold also were great admirers of the views from the Rock at Thorney How, and the poet, if depressed on first coming in, was often revived by a visit to the Rock, which his wife kindly suggested when she saw this was the case. It was that summer that the illness of his sister began; and those who know what they had always been to each other can well understand what it must have been to him to see that soul of life and light obscured. He was also cast down at this time by the state of public affairs, of which he took a very dark view; and what was the opening of new hope for the evils of the country to Dr. Arnold, and to us, was, to Wordsworth and his family, the end of England's glory. I have now lived to feel that we were both more in the right than our great poet at Rydal, and also the excellent and desponding Southey at Keswick, with whom I renewed an acquaintance formed long before, when we thought more alike on public matters.

[*To Mrs. Davy, Malta.*

"THORNEY HOW, 26*th July* 1833.

" On Wednesday afternoon we set forth to Keswick. Miss Southey followed us to the side of the lake with an invitation to drink tea with them. We all went. Southey is sadly altered since I saw him last ; his hair was quite white, but that was the least part of the alteration. . . . . . I never saw any one whose mind was in so morbid a state as that of this excellent poet and amiable man on the subject of the present political aspect of affairs in England. He is utterly desponding. He believes the downfall of the Church and the subversion of all law and government is at hand ; for in spite of all our endeavours to steer clear of politics, he slid unconsciously into the subject, and proclaimed his belief that the ruin of all that was sacred and venerable was impending. His state of mind presents a striking and curious contrast to General De Lafayette, in a letter I had from him, dated La Grange, July 16th, 1833. I think I told you that last winter I sent him a curious little book written by a Mr. Leonard, surgeon of a vessel employed by England on the coast of Africa for the prevention of the slave-trade. The ship or frigate was commanded by Captain Ramsay, who was in Edinburgh last winter, and he told Lady Grey that ' it was true to the very letter.' Mr. Leonard gives a most fearful picture of the enormities practised by the slave-ships to Spain, Portugal, and Brazil, under the tricolor flag of France, because they had not submitted to be searched by English vessels. On receiving this book the General put the question to the Minister of Marine, why France suffered such abominable cruelties to be perpetrated under her flag ? The Minister of Marine assured him that within the last six months a treaty had been signed between France and England in which the right of search was reciprocally agreed to ; and De Lafayette expresses the earnest hope that the example set by England in slave emancipation will ere long be followed by the United States and by all civilized nations. Miss Garnett says the General is rejoicing in the capture of the Miguelite fleet (his grandson had been for eighteen months in Don Pedro's army, a volunteer in the liberal cause of Portugal), and that he is now reposing after the fatigues of a long session of the Chamber of Deputies amid his family at La Grange."

"TADCASTER, *October* 23, 1833.

"Three days after we arrived here, Mary, Catherine Laycock, and I went to attend a county meeting at York, held to consider of some lasting tribute of respect for the memory of Mr. Wilberforce. The Archbishop presided, and opened the meeting in an elegant and short eulogium on the character of Wilberforce, especially his sincerely religious character, which manifested itself not in sectarian zeal or intolerant bigotry, but by soundness of principle and practical Christianity. He was followed by Lord Fitzwilliam, who declared he considered it one of the greatest blessings of his life to have been associated with Mr. Wilberforce in the representation of the county when he arrived at manhood, for that no man could live in habits of intimacy with him without being the better for it. People, his Lordship said, supposed that because Mr. Wilberforce was eminently pious he would be morose and severe towards others. The very contrary was the case ; and were he asked who was the happiest and most cheerful man he had ever known, he would say Mr. Wilberforce. Lord Morpeth followed in a very eloquent speech, on the part Wilberforce had taken in the slave trade, and on the happiness he expressed on his death-bed for having lived to see that great measure accomplished. He concluded this touching observation with these words, very emphatically uttered :—'Let me die the death of the righteous, and let my last end be like his.' Then spoke the Lord Chancellor. He had come all the way from Brougham to attend the meeting. He made a strong appeal to Mr. Wilberforce's native county, which he had so ably represented in six successive Parliaments, to erect a suitable tribute to the memory of that great and good man, not merely an inscription in brass or marble, but some institution which should have the instruction of the ignorant or the relief of the afflicted for its object,— some such monument to his name as Wilberforce himself would have chosen. ' It is true,' he said, ' we have not the evil of slavery in this country, but we have the monstrous evil of ignorance to a frightful extent, and ignorance is the fruitful parent of discord, intolerance, and vice.' It was one of the most interesting public meetings I ever attended. It was in the Music Hall at York, and the place was crowded up to the very door. Lord B. looked in good health. His speech was earnest, grave, and impressive. He seemed deeply impressed with the evils arising from the ignorance of the people; indeed, from Sir W. Hamilton's article in the July number of the Edinburgh Review, on education in Germany, it would appear that France and England are the worst educated nations in Europe."]

We returned to Tadcaster in September, and found our poor sufferer in much the same state; but so kind and touching was her reception of us, that I made a resolve then that nothing short of the most imperious duty, such as that which the care of Mary's health required, should tempt me to leave her again. Thank God, it was not necessary to do so, and we remained with her to the last. An increase of weakness and weariness came on, on the 24th of December, when I was sitting beside her, and she died on the morning of the 26th, 1833. I was standing by her bedside; her eyes were closed, and I said, " Dear aunt, I am beside you ; do you know 'your Bessy'?" She did not speak, but she pressed my hand, gave one short breath, and all was over. Thus passed away one of the purest spirits and kindest-hearted beings that ever lived. She had not a particle of selfishness in her nature, had great tenderness of heart, and strict integrity of life; her temper was excellent. She was the most dutiful of daughters, the kindest of sisters, the warmest and most constant of friends, and towards me personally, from the time I was six days old, when I lost my mother, she acted, with uniform affection, a mother's part. It was consoling to me to think that, after my marriage, the time she spent with us in Edinburgh was perhaps the most cheerful and animated of her life. She extended her affection towards all my children, and Mr. Fletcher always treated her with the most grateful love and respect. My daughters took by turns the office of cheering her old age; and though the sacrifice they made in leaving a home they dearly loved, and the attractions of Edinburgh society, was great, they never complained; they felt they were paying the large debt of gratitude their mother owed her, and the four last years of her life were cheered by my remaining with her whenever my duty to my children did not make a temporary absence indispensable. She was the kindest of neighbours; there was no gossip at her table; people who met nowhere else met there, and seemed to forget their small grievances towards each other in her presence, and it was truly observed by her nephew, Mr. Dawson of Wighill, on the day of her funeral, "that he never heard her speak ill of anybody." Her remains were laid in the north aisle of Wighill Church, by the side of those of her brother William. She was buried on the 31st of December 1833.

Early in February 1834, following dear aunty's death, Mary and I set off for London, in the hope of meeting Dr. and Mrs. Davy there in April.

We gave up the house at Tadcaster, and made our one-horse carriage our moveable home for some months, not wishing to fix on a new residence until the return of our Malta friends.

I had a strong desire to visit the last resting-place of

my dear friend Mrs. Brudenell, and to close the chapter of my early life by erecting a tablet to her memory in the parish church of Hougham, where she was interred near her children.

We paid a little visit to Mr. and Mrs. Penrose on our way. She was then ill of the malady which ended her sweet, intelligent, simple life. I remember her telling me it was worth while being ill to be so kindly nursed as she was by her husband. In the very small parsonage of Bracebridge this accomplished pair enjoyed the pleasures of refined and literary tastes and pursuits at home, although much cut off from congenial society.

Mrs. Penrose lent us the "Life of Crabbe," by his son George, then newly published, and we read it with great delight at Coleby, where we went next to pay a visit to the Miss Penroses, the amiable sisters of our dear Mrs. Arnold. On our way from their house to Grantham, we went through most singular by-ways and sandy lanes to find out the grave of my kind old friend Mrs. Brudenell. It was in the chancel of Hougham Church, where her unworthy husband had been rector. She was buried between her two boys, who died very young. It was more than sixty years since she had lived in Hougham Rectory, and I could not find a single villager living who remembered her. At Grantham, which we reached that evening, I ordered a marble tablet to be put up in Hougham Church to her memory. Hers were virtues that deserve to be commemorated. She had a generous heart and a deep sense of gratitude for benefits disinterestedly conferred upon her. This visit to her last resting-place was to me full of tender and melancholy recollections. She had gone to Hougham on her marriage, full of generous affection, hope, and confidence ; she was requited by neglect and heartless cruelty ; and there, after a life of much disquietude, she was laid at rest. We proceeded, by short journeys, suited to our mode of travelling, to London, which we reached on the 25th of March, and established ourselves in the lodgings which had been taken for us in Baker Street, Regent's Park, where we remained a month, and where we had the disappointment to learn that Dr. Davy had been obliged to remain at Malta for another year.

The month we spent in London was full of interest. Many of our dear Scotch friends were there and in office. Sir John A. Murray was then Lord Advocate, and we frequently met people of note at his house. On hearing from Sir John Murray that I was in London, Lord Brougham expressed a desire to take me to the Temple Church the following Sunday, and said he would call for us at the right time, with his daughter, as he wished to introduce her "to his early friend Mrs. Fletcher." This he did; and we made the best use of the drive in listening to his interesting conversation. The Lord Chancellor paid us much friendly attention, and proposed that we should go the following day to the House of Lords, where we might hear him speak on his favourite subject— the education of the working classes, which he did admirably. Another evening we heard him speak on the admission of Dissenters to Oxford and Cambridge without subscribing the Thirty-nine Articles. He was opposed by the fluent Bishop of Exeter (Phillpotts). Miss Brougham was of our party, to hear her father speak for the first time. It was interesting to watch her interest in what he said. She sat next me, her half-sister, Miss Spalding, on the other side. The young girl often said, "Oh, papa is too angry. Why is he so angry?" It was quite true; the excessive vehemence of the manner rather detracted from than added to the force of the matter.

We saw and heard at the same time the Great Duke, also Lords Grey and Holland, but heard no speaking either among Lords or Commons comparable to Lord Brougham's.

I saw a good deal at this time of my old Edinburgh early friend, John Allen, of Holland House notoriety, who had continued to correspond with my husband, and he repeated on this occasion of our meeting in London that he always traced to his conversations as a youth with Mr. Fletcher the opinions he had early formed and retained of constitutional liberty.

We saw a great deal of the dear Dr. Boott and his friendly happy circle in Gower Street; had some pleasant meetings and talks with Thomas Campbell and Allan Cunningham, and spent a delightful evening at Captain Gowan's with Mount-Stuart Elphinstone, certainly the most agreeable of men.

We were not sorry after some weeks of excitement to set off in our chaise-and-one for North Devon, where we had promised to pay a visit to Mr. and Mrs. Buckle, near Ilfracombe, and Mrs. Martin, who shared their home, then at Watermouth Castle, a large modern Castle beautifully situated near the Bristol Channel. From this agreeable resting-place we made excursions to Clovelly, a place of wonderful charm and oddity. It is built on a steep cliff. The one street rising from the bay forms a steep stair cut in the rocks, which are of most varied form and colouring, and beautifully clothed with rich vegetation as you advance up the *stair* street to the little village inn.

From Watermouth we went for a week to Lynmouth, the most perfectly beautiful place, we thought, we had ever seen; so much did we talk about it that we began to think our friends did not believe in such a place, and we agreed to abstain from its praises, except to each other, to avoid being considered " bores."

We travelled north, stopping at Cheltenham to rest and see our old friend Lady Williamson of Whitburn, and after that I went to meet Mrs. Taylor at Oxton, at the cottage I had furnished for Angus there, and Mary went along with Catherine Laycock to prepare a temporary home which had been secured for us near Hawkshead for a year by Mr. Harden, who with his family then lived also in that locality. This house, called Keen Ground, was by no means commodious or comfortable, but it was near the quaint little town of Hawkshead, endeared to me by many recollections of the first summer we spent in the lake district at Belmont. It was within an easy distance of my dear old friend Mrs. Smith, who, though now infirm in health, retained her warm affections and grace of manner. She made us acquainted with her favourite neighbours, the Miss Beevers, who lived, and still live, near the village of Coniston, and have continued the fast friends of our family from that time. They are the best of neighbours and most faithful of friends to all who come near them, rich or poor, old or young.

We passed the winter of 1834-5 at Keen Ground, and rejoiced in the return of the dear Arnolds to Fox How that winter, when we paid them a week's delightful visit about Christmas. We always found ourselves the better, as well as happier, for associating with them, there was so much elevation of purpose in all they thought and did; and then the home life at Rydal Mount was a great attraction to us, as well as the kindness we always received there.

In the May following (the 25th of May 1835) we had the great happiness of meeting our dear Margaret and her three eldest children at Kendal, and of bringing them back with us to Keen Ground. It is only those who have been separated from a beloved child for five years without any other intercourse but such as letters supply, who can know the happiness of a personal reunion. The heat of Malta had told on her constitution and looks, but she had the same bright animated expression of countenance, and all the tenderness of a mother had been added to the treasures of her heart's affections. Mrs. Taylor and her little Mary and my son Angus joined the family party. It was as happy a summer as the reunion of affectionate friends could make it, and so unwilling were Mary and I to lose sight again of Margaret and her family that when they left us in September we authorized Dr. Davy to take a cottage for us within an hour's drive of Fort Pitt, where Dr. Davy had been appointed the chief medical officer. We followed them in October, Mary taking Rugby on her way to Chatham, and I going to spend a month in the cottage at Oxton formerly occupied by my aunt, Mrs. Fretwell, and where I had established my aunt Dawson's faithful maid Hannah as housekeeper for Angus, so that he might always have a comfortable home to go to. She had married after her old mistress's death a young Methodist farmer, and the only sounds ever heard from their comfortable kitchen were hymns sung by this good couple at their evening devotions. It is strange that the month I spent at this time in my native village did not strengthen in the least the reminiscences of my childhood and youth. I had lived so intensely during the fifty years I had left that now almost ruinous house where I was born, and had left at eighteen, that it was more identified with my imagination as what it then was, cheerful and neat, with its trim garden in front, gay with flowers, and its well-trained fruit-trees on the walls, and its abundant orchard behind, than now in its forlorn, almost uninhabitable, state.

Mrs. Brudenell's cottage, where some of the gayest hours of my childhood were spent, was now inhabited by two peasants' families, hard-worked men. "Can this (I often said to myself) really be the place where the joyous years of my youth were spent? surely a blight has passed over it, so that they who knew and loved it once shall 'know it no more!'" It was mournful for me to feel that I was the last survivor of that once cheerful village. All its former inhabitants were gone, and they were replaced by a depressed, uncheerful-looking set of labourers, with slovenly wives and ragged children.

After spending our Christmas of 1835 at Fort Pitt, we entered upon our cottage home at Darland, which Mary and our Yorkshire maid had prepared for my reception. It was a beautifully planted and arranged little domain, an oasis in the desert; for nothing could be more destitute of beauty than the chalky hills all round the wooded enclosure where Darland was situated.

In compliment to the Davys, we had several visitors, but only made two friends—Dr. and Mrs. Richardson. He was the Arctic traveller, and then held a staff appointment at Melville Hospital at Chatham. She was a niece of Sir John Franklin, a large-hearted, lively, and most interesting woman. We got intimate at once; and as her health was very delicate, she used to come often in summer, with her baby Josephine, to us, for change of air, and he walked out in the evening, after the labours of the day were over. Mary and I used to say that Dr. Richardson's smile of recognition, when we drove through the ghastly streets of Chatham, was the only redeeming point in that dreary drive we took so often on our way to Fort Pitt.

On Saturday evening, the 18th of March 1837, Mary and I were sitting in our easy chairs at Darland, as far "into the fire" as the Scotch folk beg their friends to do, talking of some episodes of our past lives, and expecting a parcel of books from Chatham. The parcel came just at the right time, and contained the first volume of Lockhart's Life of our great townsman, Walter Scott. I believe it would be necessary to have lived, as we had done for the last year and a half, in cold and chalky Kent, to enjoy, as we did that night, the devouring of the volume,—the names of all so familiar to us, and the persons of most, as we used daily to meet them in the streets or the drawing-rooms of our beloved Edinburgh. To us this volume had all the interest of an old chronicle, so completely is our present life changed in its daily animation and interest. No doubt English readers will enjoy it, or think they do, but a dash of Scotch is necessary thoroughly to enjoy its charm.

[*To Mrs. Rathbone, Green Bank, Liverpool.*

"We have lately been reading the 'Life of Walter Scott' with deep interest; for though in matters of public feeling there was a great gulf between us, we always admired his genius, and the sweetness and kindness of his nature. The first sixty pages written by himself are quite refreshing, and Mr. Lockhart has very ably and skilfully filled up the outline. Never has a character formed by circumstances been more strikingly exemplified. He would probably have been an extraordinary man under any circumstances; but do we not owe his varied imagination to his early life at Sandy Knowe, and his listening there to the ballads and fairy lore of the old Tweedside shepherds?

"You cannot conceive what a delight it was to Mary as well as to me to read what is already published of these memoirs, in this arid land of chalky hills and official understandings. After lending the book to the Davys and Richardsons, no one else among our acquaintances here cared to have it, having no associations with either books or ballads."]

On the 1st of June 1836 we set off from Kent, accompanied by Angus, on a little tour to Switzerland. Having kept a journal of our tour, I need not repeat the impression it made on us here. Late as it was in life for me to set out on a Swiss tour (I was then sixty-six), I enjoyed it greatly, and so did my companions. It realized, and more than realized, all I had conceived of the grand and beautiful in Nature. We saw no form of society that seemed degraded by poverty or despotism, except that of Savoy, under the dominion of the King of Sardinia.

[The following letter, returned to me, is worth inserting here, relating to an interview which interested us all much with General La Harpe :]

To Mrs. Boott.

"Chatham, *August* 1836.

" I know it will give you and Dr. Boott pleasure to hear that we have got safely home after a most delightful excursion of two months, during which we traversed fully two thousand miles by land and water. By far the most interesting part of our tour was the month we passed in Switzerland, and we owed to Dr. Boott the highest gratification we could have had there, in an hour's animated conversation with his venerable and interesting friend, General La Harpe. We took the steamboat from Vevay to Lausanne, and we found the excellent old man in his dressing-gown in his library as serene and cheerful as if the world without had neither evil nor sorrow in it. As Dr. Boott's friends he received us not only with courtesy but kindness, and he evidently delighted to dwell on his personal obligations to the friendship of Dr. Boott and on the interest he took in him and you and all your children. We partook of a collation of fruit, cakes, and wine. He regretted his wife was from home. Every word he uttered impressed us with the liveliest respect and affection for him. When he uncovered a bust of the Emperor Alexander to show it to us, his voice faltered as he spoke of his many gracious and noble qualities, and he affirmed confidently that, had he lived, it was his full purpose

P

to give to Poland as free a constitution as she was capable of
enjoying or making a right use of.   While Mary and I were conversing, or rather listening to him, Angus asked his permission to
take the little sketch which accompanies this.   It does not do
him justice, but it has a considerable resemblance, and Angus has
great pleasure in sending it to Dr. Boott.   It happened to be the
week of the Tirage at Lausanne, when the best marksmen in
Switzerland meet annually in honour of William Tell and shoot at
a mark.   We saw the sharpshooters of the Pays de Vaud arrive,
about five hundred marksmen: every canton sends its quota.   It
is a voluntary service, but may be considered as the training of
an excellent militia for Helvetia.   We were enchanted with the
grandeur and beauty of the valleys of Lauterbrunnen and Grin-
delwald, and regretted that neither our travelling purse nor the
time we could spare admitted of our remaining another month
in these Alpine valleys.   We had a magnificent first sight of
Mont Blanc as we left Lausanne, on the clear bright evening of
the 29th of June.   The setting sun threw its last rays on that
majestic mountain, and its summit was unclouded, so that at
the distance of sixty miles we distinctly saw its form reflected
on the surface of the Lake of Geneva.   Lord Byron mentions
this fact in a note to one of his Cantos of ' Childe Harold,'
but I own that I thought it was a poetical licence till I saw
it with my own eyes.

" You will be glad, dear kind friends, to hear that Mary has
returned from her travels more robust in health than she has
been for six years.   This is a great blessing, delightfully earned
by exertions accompanied with an enjoyment we neither of us
can ever forget.   Angus enjoyed it too very highly, and the old
woman not less than any of the party.   God bless you, dear
friends."

We returned to Darland from our tour the last day of
July 1836, and found Mrs. Taylor, her son, and little
daughter Mary there.   In the autumn of that year we
made some pleasant excursions to the more picturesque
parts of Kent, and to places full of historical interest and
associations,—Penshurst, Knole, and Seven Oaks.   I was

disappointed not to find any monumental record of Algernon
Sidney in the beautiful churchyard of Penshurst, but his
epitaph is written in imperishable language in the annals
of his country. Our summer and autumn days were also
diversified by many family and friendly meetings in the
beautiful grounds and forests of Lord Darnley's place, near
Chatham.

We passed the winter of 1836-7 very quietly; but
found our habitation so cold in the severe winters of Kent
that we decided not to spend another winter there, but to
return to the neighbourhood of Edinburgh, where we had
still many interests and attractions which could never
pass away.

[From M. F.'s Note-book.

We had a most agreeable surprise on the 19th of August
1837. Mrs. Smith, of the dockyard, appeared at Darland
with Wordsworth and Dora. We did not even know the poet
had returned from his Italian tour. He looks somewhat
thinner and paler that when we left Lakeland, and, as he himself expresses it, 'is too home-sick to be comfortable,' but he
admired the arrangements of our little garden, and entered,
with his usual indulgence for Nature, into the merits of our
one large elm-tree. He confesses himself to have been too old
for a first visit to Italy, and that his visit with Crabbe
Robinson was too hurried for enjoyment; that at Rome he
had not time to get over his disappointment at the old and
new being jumbled together; and he thought the effect of the
Colosseum was lessened by the Popish ornaments being
obtruded into it. He mentioned the beauty of the flowers and
ferns that grew on its walls as its best attractions. He said
he knew too little to make Rome so enjoyable as it might have
been. He made the discovery, also, that he had no real taste
for sculpture, as he fell asleep before the Venus de Medici at
Florence. He was more impressed by the Apollo, because
there is mind there, but without mind he cannot be much
interested in mere form, torsos and other forms, which he

allows may be very interesting to students of Art.   He spoke
with most interest of the ruin at Nismes, and said he saw
nothing in Italy equal to the combined effect of the situation
and edifice of the Pont du Gard at Nismes.   Of the maritime
Alps route also, and of the Mediterranean generally, he spoke
with much delight.   In Vaucluse he had been in no degree
disappointed ; the colour of the stream and the beauty of the
flowers delighted him much.   He deplores the want of fine
timber in Italy, and the entire absence of gentlemen's country
houses and parks throughout the country of France.   These
observations chiefly took place on the Sunday evening which
he spent with us.   He remarked that he thought the French
peasant improved in a mere animal point of view ; that he
had formerly been much struck with the extreme feebleness of
frame among the French, but this was not the case now.   He
mentioned a tree which he had reposed under forty-eight years
ago near Liége as one of great size and beauty, and while on
this subject he branched off with interest on the comparative
merits of trees.   He admires the cypress of the south as a
beautiful spiral accompaniment to a landscape, but he holds
the yew higher as a 'fine creature.'   His conversation did not
become truly Wordsworthian, however, till he entered on the
"Life of Scott," three volumes of which he had read.   There
was so much feeling, wisdom, and elevation in all he said on
this subject, that, in his own words, we could truly say after
he left us,

> . . . . "So did he speak,
> The words he uttered shall not pass away,
> For they sank into me."

And yet to attempt to note them down seems hopeless.   He
said that it gave him pain to discover what sufferings Scott had
gone through from his connexion with printers, and the
unworthy shifts he had recourse to, to get rid of his quires of
unsold writings.   "It is cruel so to expose a great man's
weaknesses."   "Scott's sentiments (he said) sometimes shock
me ; and when I think of his free, frank manner, of what an open
creature he was, and then find that he was involved in all this
load of concealment and evasion, it gives me great pain,—it
must do so to all his friends.   The day before we parted he

spoke to me much of his portion of happiness in life, which he considered great; but it appeared to me at the time that he did not truly estimate his position as a man of genius. He appeared to think that the condition of an official under Government, or that of a country gentleman, was a higher one than that of a man of genius." This, Wordsworth said, was the more extraordinary from Scott having been born in the rank of a gentleman, and, therefore, he ought more truly to have estimated the real state of the case. Dr. Johnson had powerfully stated the truth on this subject, and Scott would have been a wiser and a happier man had he rested on his genius rather than on his accumulating acres and living beyond his means. Wordsworth then launched forth on the startling opinion pronounced by Scott on Johnson's Poem "On the Vanity of Human Wishes," being the finest poem in the language. He repeated two or three lines, and dissected them in the way he used to do some of Lord Byron's.]

In the spring of 1837 Mary and I spent a few weeks in London, and met with several interesting people. The first visit we paid was at the house of Mr. and Mrs. William Gray, in Great George Street, Westminster. I there met my dear school companion of other days, who was the mother of Mrs. Gray and the youngest daughter of Mr. Forster of Bolton. She was then the widow of General Ker, one of the claimants of the Roxburgh Dukedom and estates. The charm of her character and manners combined would have graced the high position which the Scottish Courts of Law gave to her husband, but which the House of Lords reversed after a ruinous lawsuit of many years. We renewed our youth together on this pleasant meeting among her grandchildren, and the loss of what the world most regards had in no degree lessened the sweetness of her spirit or the gaiety of her "innocent mirth." She returned with us to Kent at the end of our London visit.

It was during this visit at Mr. Gray's that I first saw

Giuseppe Mazzini. I can truly say that his character, and the cause to which he devoted his blighted youth and noble genius, gave, from the time I first formed his friendship, a new and increasing interest to my declining years.

A letter was brought to me one forenoon, some time in April, from Count Philip Ugoni, the friend of Madame De Bossi, who had been so useful to us in Paris, introducing to my special regard a young Italian exile who at that time was a friendless stranger in London. I was in Mary's room at the time, who was ill of influenza, but hastened down-stairs to receive the exile. I found in the drawing-room a young, slim, dark Italian gentleman of very prepossessing appearance. He could not then speak English, and I very imperfect French; but it was impossible not to be favourably impressed at once by his truth and his sadness. He told me he was an exile, and without endeavouring to excite my compassion, or dwelling at all on his wrongs or his circumstances, by relating any particulars of his past life, he said his present object was to obtain admission to some public library, that he might give himself to literary work. He looked so profoundly unhappy, and spoke so despondingly of the condition of his country, and of the genius of Chatterton with such high admiration, that I foolishly took it into my head, after he had left me, that he meditated suicide, and, under that impression, took the privilege of age and experience to write to him (when I sent him a letter that I thought would be useful for his present pursuits in London) a friendly exhortation against the weakness, as well as wickedness, of yielding to despair, while youth and talents and moral strength, which I felt he possessed, ought alone, independently of higher motives, to enable him to meet with fortitude his present adversity. The answer which I received to this letter convinced me how much I had mistaken his meaning, and formed the basis of our future friendship. It interested me much more than querulous complaints; and although we did not meet more than once again at this time, I was able to be of some use to his accomplished and excellent friend Ruffini, on our return to Edinburgh the following winter, and on our next visit to London we saw Mazzini frequently. We heard from Ruffini that besides the literary and patriotic work he engaged in, he devoted himself in the evening hours to the instruction of fifty or sixty Italian boys, who were traversing the streets of London all day, selling white mice, playing the hand-organ, or carrying plaster casts about for sale. These poor boys were sold for a certain number of years by their worthless parents to people as worthless, who employed without instructing them, and they were growing up both profligate and ignorant. Mazzini could not bear to see his countrymen thus degraded, not so much by poverty as by vice, and he devoted two hours every evening to teaching them to read and write, and imbuing them with some knowledge of their country's history, aud what it ought to be in future. All this I heard from Ruffini, as well as that he had become known to several cultivated people in London; but no inducements of pleasure or advantage could tempt him to quit his little Italian school for a single evening. Thus he became added to my list of heroes, and I insert his first letter to me in this part of my family history, that my great-grandchildren may learn from it the reason of my interest in the prophet of the future unity of Italy, Giuseppe Mazzini.

Mazzini's first letter in answer to mine.

" April 1837.

" MADAME,—You doubtless suppose that the frankness of your language displeased me or gave me some pain. Far from it ; I am grateful to you for it, as a mark of confidence and esteem. Perhaps I explained myself ill, perhaps also some of my expressions would require my life as a commentary to explain them ; but I desire much, madame, to rectify the impression which I have involuntarily given you. I am naturally *triste ;* I am rendered more so by my position, by what I have suffered—not so much by what I have personally suffered, as by what I have seen those I love and who love me suffer,—by the thousand causes which make exile bitter and life sterile in these days to us. I am, however, neither abased nor discouraged ; I only compared myself to your Chatterton in *fierté*, not in despondency. I believe, historically speaking, that the memory of Chatterton has been unjustly treated, but I also think that his despair was a weakness, and a consequence, as you remark, of an imperfect religious conception. I think also that his death would have been different had he lived in our days.

" Despair, neutralizing activity, appears to me the highest point of selfishness. He who despairs of things and of men, and whom despair makes inactive or leads to quit life, is a man who has wished only to enjoy, and has made that his chief thought ; not being able to do that, he destroys his life, either morally or materially, as the child does its plaything. Now, I do not consider life a game, but a very serious thing : it is an office to be fulfilled in the world ; it is a series of duties to be accomplished in our own improvement or that of others ; it is virtue, and not happiness, which ought to be the aim of life. If in following the ways of virtue we find happiness, so much the better ; but if we do not find it, it should make no difference in our pursuit. This life, in short, I consider but as the infancy of another, and when God placed us in the world He said, ' Work and do good according to the measure of your power and your knowledge ;' He did not say, 'Be happy.' For my own part, I do not believe in the happiness of the individual —in my own· perhaps less than in that of others,—but I should be the most cowardly and the most inconsistent of men if, on that account, I should neglect to serve my country or the cause of my faith. You see, madame, that I am far from that state which may be called one of despair. I shall then labour, and intend in some measure to follow your advice. I think seriously of occupying myself with a work the aim of which will be to make Italy known to your countrymen, such as I conceive it to be in its present state, and what it is likely to become. I shall write it in Italian, but I shall have it translated. It will be a long and difficult labour ; but although it is done through my imperfect means, some of the truths which it will contain may perhaps contribute to sow the seeds of sympathy between two nations, the one of which is already great and free, and the other must become so. I now wait for my books and papers to begin, and am at present engaged to contribute to a Journal, *Le Monde*.

" I thank you much, madame, for your kind offer of recommendation, should I wish for pupils. You judge rightly in supposing that, did I require it, I should not hesitate to give lessons in my native tongue ; there is nothing in that which would in the least degree offend me, and I thank you most cordially for your offers of assistance. Your kindness induces me to ask your exertions in favour of a young Italian at present in Edinburgh, whose name is Ruffini.

" GIUSEPPE MAZZINI."

[*Second Letter to Mrs. Fletcher.*

· "*April* 1840.

" Permit me to write to you, and permit me to make use for this time of a language which you know, and which is more familiar to me than yours. I write under the impression of a strong feeling of gratitude, and I feel a desire to let my pen go freely, to write as I used to speak to you, without stopping even for a moment to consider the form of my thoughts. I am always doubtful when I write in your language, which causes me a sort of painful feeling of restraint. Now, I wish to have pleasure in writing to you. I have first to thank you for the kindness with which you treat my friend Ruffini,[1] and

---

[1] Agostino Ruffini (the brother of Giovanni Ruffini, the author of "Doctor Antonio " and other works) passed eleven years of exile in Edinburgh ; and it is a comfort to think that this period was rendered as little painful as was possible in his circumstances by the respect and affection his virtues and talents inspired among all the friends he had there. He accepted the

then the remembrance which you have kept of me; and to me
it is delightful that it is through a tie of gratitude that I am
led to renew our acquaintance. I had a desire to do so, in
order to efface a painful feeling,—not in you, who are too kind
to remember what is wrong in others, but in myself. It
reproaches me for having, during so long a period, neglected
the first person who took an interest in me in London. I was,
when I had the honour of knowing you there, in a moral state
quite peculiar, tormented by a thousand chagrins, and brought
by a course of real causes to believe that my friendship or my
acquaintance could not give the least pleasure to any one, and
might easily become a burthen. I did not wish that, and so I
found myself imperiously drawn towards a melancholy isolation.
It was more a punishment to myself than a wrong done to
others. Yet it was wrong. The happiness, or unhappiness,
of our individual life should not interfere with our duties ; it
is not upon them, but upon the higher good, that our conduct
should depend. I understood that very soon, and I wished to
see you again, but you were I believe not in London, and I did
not know your place of residence. I spoke of you to the few
people whom I knew, among others to a man I much esteem,
and who said he knew you, Mr. Thomas Carlyle, but he did
not know your address at the time. I did not expect to find
you again in Edinburgh, doing good to me in the person of my
friend. As for him, I need not recommend him to you any
more ; I will only assure you that he deserves all that you can
do for him, and he is one of those whose sincere and lasting
gratitude is assured to every mark of benevolence and sympathy.
The flower of the souls of us exiles is faded, but, thanks to
God, the perfume has remained. Ruffini tells me you are
about to spend some time at the Lakes of Westmoreland, but
that you will let me know when you visit London. Till then,
madame, think sometimes of me ; and believe in the gratitude
and esteem of   GIUSEPPE MAZZINI."]

We passed the summer of 1837 at Darland, unmarked

amnesty of 1848 and returned to Piedmont, filled an office at Turin with
great ability and benefit to his country, and died of a very painful illness
at Taggia in 1855, mourned and loved in no common measure.

by any event, but in happy intercourse with our friends at Fort Pitt, and in increased intimacy with the Richardsons.

We remained in Kent till after the birth of dear little Humphry Davy, who was born on the 15th September 1837. We saw him christened and his mother recovered, and then set off for Yorkshire, travelling in our slow fashion, and taking Cambridge on our way.

It was towards the end of October when we reached Oxton, where we intended to remain for some weeks with Angus, to be near my aunt, Miss Hill. Angus, at his own desire, had then embarked in a speculation in London, on which he entered about that time; but we took possession of the cottage he had occupied, and the winter set in so early and so severely, one snowstorm after another, that we were compelled to remain there till the beginning of February 1838. Our trunks and books had been sent off to Edinburgh, and we were detained three weeks before it was possible to set off on our journey north. Our only resource was to send for materials to clothe the poor of the village, and we and our maidens set busily to work, and this saved us from all fretfulness and impatience, as is well observed by an anonymous writer in " Chambers's Journal" —" that impatience always springs from a bitterer root than itself." Now, this wholesome occupation of working for the poor counteracted the selfishness that would have made us impatient at our detention at Oxton.

We had a somewhat adventurous journey through the frozen piles of snow on each side of the roads by Wooler and Cornhill. The roads became heavier and deeper as we proceeded northward, and for many a weary mile we travelled through almost untracked snow, except such tracks as a few coal-carts made—dreariness and desolation on all sides of this Siberian landscape. Another day brought us to Lauder, and the following day we reached Edinburgh.

We were most kindly welcomed by our good friends Mr. and Mrs. Craig, in Great King Street, and their house was our hospitable and most agreeable home for several weeks, till we established ourselves at the pretty villa of Duncliffe, about two miles west of Edinburgh.

Our return to Edinburgh as residents, after an interval of ten years, could not fail to be attended with many touching remembrances. Many of those whom we had left aged were gone, the middle-aged had become grey-headed, and children then in the nursery had reached manhood. Many whom we had left hard-worked Advocates were now raised to the Bench. Foremost among these old friends were Lords Cockburn, Jeffrey, and Cuninghame. The Whigs were still in office, and Edinburgh still retained, in our eyes, its unrivalled beauty and unbounded hospitality. We had no reason to regret returning to a place where we still had many friends, and where we were received with so kindly a welcome.

We were most pleasantly situated at Duncliffe as to neighbours, about equal distances from Craigcrook and Belmont, where Lord Mackenzie then lived with his delightful wife and children—a home of rare cultivation, charm, and goodness combined. It was in September of that year we had the great pleasure of meeting Mrs. Fry at dinner at Lord Mackenzie's, and of attending a Friends' meeting at which she spoke, as well as at a meeting for constituting a female committee for visiting prisons. It was a great privilege to meet and be acquainted with Elizabeth Fry ; she was one of those rare spirits whom Milton describes in words that cannot die :—

> "Thy love is fixed, and zealously attends
> To fill thy odorous lamp with deeds of light,
> And hope that reaps not shame."

That winter of 1838-9 was passed most pleasantly at Duncliffe, where old friends came sociably to cheer our winter days, and Mary was actively engaged in visiting Bridewell and the House of Refuge.

On many snowy days, when no visitors were looked for, Lord Jeffrey was good enough to include Duncliffe in his walks after he left the Court of Session. His conversation, always full of intellectual variety and power, had become as remarkable for gentleness and kindness of feeling as it had always been for force. We met many agreeable strangers both at Craigcrook and at his winter home in Moray Place, and never failed to experience a large measure of his kindness, in spite of our differences of creed on Wordsworth and Joanna Baillie,—subjects now mutually avoided. This reminds me to say that my maternal vanity was fed by receiving, about this time, a very pleasant letter from Joanna Baillie, which I have put aside for the Family Memorials, and one from Mr. George Ticknor of Boston, along with two copies of the American edition of "Concealment," printed at Philadelphia. Mr. Ticknor says he had no hand in it ; he had sent a copy to the press at Boston from a conviction that it would be a very useful book for his countrywomen to read. When he met with this edition from the Philadelphia press, he stopped the New England one. Speaking of America after their late visit to England, in the same letter, Mr. Ticknor says :—

"We are, as you know, established in our circle again in our happy and prosperous country. I cannot tell you what a pleasure this is. Whatever may be said of us by persons of different views on the principles of government, it is fully admitted that we are unlike any other people,—I think growing more so by force of our free institutions,—so that we who have been born and bred here, and become attached to the country, are not likely to become substantially and equally happy anywhere else.   I am sure this is the case with me.   I have lived, at two different periods, eight years in Europe, and yet could never for a moment have the proper feeling of home or its true contentment while I was there."

This is a delightful testimony to the truth of country and home affections in an American of cultivated taste and real refinement.

[*From Joanna Baillie to Mrs. Fletcher.*

"1838.

"Your friendly letter of the 21st of May was more than I deserved.   I have long wished to tell you that I think Mrs. Davy's notices of Sir Walter's short abode at Malta are given with great delicacy and truth of observation; and there are no notices in the whole seven volumes that I like better—I ought rather to say so well.   How very touching it is to trace, as she gives it, the fading away of his mind and memory in the drive they took together in the country.   After praising Miss Austen and the other female authors, he says, ' And there is an Irish lady too' (I cannot tell you how these words went to my heart)—Maria Edgeworth, whom he had lived with and tra-velled with, and whose writings he would most undoubtedly have prized far beyond others.   The confusion of his ideas and the sweetness of his disposition are in this portion of his life more naturally marked perhaps than in any other.   So much was I pleased with your daughter's discriminating, modest statement, that I had intended writing to you forthwith upon the subject, when other things came in the way, and so my intention became one of those with which, as Sir Walter says in one of his letters, the ' pavement of hell ' is composed.

"Our neighbour, Mrs. Hoare, whose late excellent husband was one of the original committee, along with Clarkson, for the abolition of the slave-trade, is as little satisfied with the biographers of Mr. Wilberforce as you are.   Surely their father had honour and credit enough fairly won without robbing others to enrich him.   How richly have the lovers of biography been supplied of late in having two such men as Walter Scott and Wilberforce brought before them more or less skilfully, indeed with all the varied, extraordinary circumstances of their lives, cheerfulness and activity being the natural temperament of both."]

Early in the spring of 1839 we received alarming accounts of my aunt Hill's health. I had written to her some weeks before, mentioning our intention of visiting Mrs. Davy in May; and knowing she did not like to be troubled with guests in her house, I proposed to take lodgings at Thorp Arch, to be near her for a week or two. To this proposal I received no answer till I heard of her illness, and that she wished us to go to the Grange at once. We found her much reduced in strength, but care and good nursing brought her round, and before we set off for London I had the comfort of leaving with her a most respectable person as her companion and attendant. Miss Hill took leave of us cheerfully, and wished us to visit her on our return.

We had scarcely been a week in London and another at Fort Pitt before we were recalled to Yorkshire, by hearing that Miss Hill had fallen in her own drawing-room and dislocated her hip, which at her age was very dangerous. We set off the following day by railroad to Manchester (our first railway journey) and returned to the Grange early in June. We found my aunt in a state of great suffering, which she bore with wonderful patience. Her interest in the poor never diminished. I told her one morning I had no fewer than nineteen Irish haymakers already arrived in her back court that morning at breakfast. Her countenance brightened up as if I had told of a piece of good fortune. She loved the poor more and more as she approached nearer and nearer to God. She never was a great talker about religion, but every action of her life emanated from the pure love of God. She held the two great commandments—the love of God and her neighbour

—as the light and guide of life. She had many natural infirmities of temper to contend with, and she often mentioned with amusement an observation of a poor woman about her life when she was contrasting her own troubles with Miss Hill's freedom from them, " You have had a level life ;" but (she added) I told her *that* did not always follow, as she supposed ; that a " level " life had its trials and difficulties as great perhaps as many she had to bear, of a different kind—" trials from within."   She often said old age was to her the happiest portion of life, because repose came with it.

[Mrs. Fletcher to Mrs. Davy.

" The Grange, 1st July 1839.

" Still poor Miss Hill lingers in a state of great feebleness and suffering, but of much greater quietness and repose for herself and those around her than last week.   Yesterday our dear Mary and I set off for Leeds, at seven in the morning, and I saw her and Janet safe in and on the Kendal coach at ten.   It is quite a relief to me that this dear child is on the way to give and receive gratification she could not have had here.   She was most unwilling to leave me.   You once, dear Margaret, reminded me that I was more desirous to consult my children's pleasure than their performance of duty, and I did not venture to gainsay your gentle rebuke ; but in this case Mary has neglected no duty.   I am well, and able to perform the task that is before me.   It is plainly *my duty* to be here, because Miss Hill often asks for me, and if I am not by her bedside, I am in the garden or the hay-field, and can be with her in a moment.

" Among the treasures of old books Mary has found here, in the room we were never before permitted to enter, not the least valuable is an old black-letter Bible.   There is a Prologue to the Psalms (as it is called), by St. Basil the Great, worthy of all admiration.   I must give you a screed from it.   He says— ' Now whereas the Prophets have doctrines proper to them-

selves, and the Books of the Divine Hystorys written by themselves, and the Proverbial Books have their several kind of
exhortations, the Book of the Psalms comprehends in itself the
whole commodities of all their doctrines afore-said ; for it
prophecieth of things to come ; it recyteth the historys ; it
showeth laws for the government of life ; it teacheth what
ought to be done ; and, to be short, it is a common storehouse
of all good doctrine which doth aptly distribute matter to
every man peculiar to himself. . . . . . The Psalme is the rest
of the soule, the rodde of peace ; it stilleth and pacifieth the
raging billows of the mind ; it doth assuage and mollefie the
raging power and passion of the soule ; it maketh amitie where
was discorde ; it knitteth friends together ; it returneth enemies
to an unity again ; for who can long repute him as an enemy
with whom he joineth himself in lifting up his voice to God in
prayer ? Oh ! wise and marvelous device of our Heavenly
School-master, who should invent that we should so pleasantly
sing, and therefore profitably learn, whereby wholesome doctrine might be the deeper printed in us.'

"Now, I think you will admire St. Basil as much as we do.
Don't vex yourself about my loneliness, dear M., for with
the Psalms and St. Basil I am not lonely.   Then here is a
bright sunny day and a cheerful hay-field, for we began our
hay-harvest in the Crab Garth this morning."

Letter from Mrs. Fletcher to her daughter Mary at
Fox How.

"GRANGE, *July* 1839.

" I have just had your welcome letter of Tuesday.   You seem
to be in Paradise, with none but happy spirits about you.   I
can see you every minute at dear Fox How with our beloved
Mrs. Arnold, all her children about her except Jane ; but I can
scarcely imagine her without Dr. Arnold.   When does he return ?

" Well, dear child, I wrote to you on the 10th, the day of our
good aunt's release from suffering.   I desired Pannett to convene eight of the poorest of Miss Hill's tenants to carry her
remains from the churchyard gate to the family vault in Tadcaster Church on Saturday.   They had their breakfast at Betty
Leed's cottage.   Many of the most respectable inhabitants

followed the procession uninvited, and dressed in deep mourning.   Crowds of children gathered round the procession, and I truly believe there were many sincere and grateful mourners, both old and young.   Angus and I walked first, as mourners, George Fletcher and the Shanns also.

"Our Vicar gave us really an excellent funeral sermon the next day, from the words (14th Luke, 14th verse)—'For they cannot recompense thee, but thou shalt be recompensed at the resurrection of the just.'   He dwelt with much truth and very good taste on her devotion to the poor—to their moral and spiritual as well as their temporal interests ; on her calling together the maimed, the poor, and the blind, and not the rich neighbours.   In short, I had no idea of our Vicar being able to touch so many points of her character without exaggeration or false taste.   I shed many more tears at his sermon than at her deathbed ; for solemn and awful as it was, thankfulness for the mercy of God, in hearing her earnest prayers for deliverance from suffering, was the strongest emotion I felt at the moment, and tender respect and reverence for her memory have been my abiding feelings ever since.   Almost the only words she uttered for the last few days of her life were—'My Father's arms,' 'My Father's arms,' often repeated.   I think it was a mixed feeling of longing and reverence for her two strongest affections—her heavenly and her earthly Father. She longed for both in no common measure.

" Do you know, dear Mary, I am sometimes uncomfortable at the idea of this door being closed against the poor and miserable, to whom it has been opened for more than half a century ?   But I must compound with my conscience by making G— S— my almoner here to a liberal extent ; none knows better than he does who most need assistance, or will better administer it."]

It was during Mary's visit at Fox How at this time that she told me, in one of her letters, that the proprietor of the little mountain farm of Lancrigg had come to her a week before she left Fox How, to fulfil a promise he had made her, some years before, not to part with Lancrigg without letting us know. At that time he said, "I thought it never could be; but now it must be, for my sons have brought me into trouble."

I have requested Mary to copy here the part of the journal she kept for me at the time relating to this little episode, which led to such happy results, and which came to her, as to me, quite unsought; and had she not been in the neighbourhood at the time, we might not have heard of this little possession again.

Mary had seen a great deal of the Wordsworths, both at Fox How, their own Mount, and at Miss Fenwick's, who then lived at Gale House, Ambleside. She was an old and esteemed friend of mine during her Northumbrian life, and Mary paid her a visit at this time.

[*Extract from M. F.'s Notes.*

Fox How, *August* 1839.

Last evening I went to meet the Rydal Mount party at Miss Fenwick's. On consulting Mr. Wordsworth about the beautiful little farm of Lancrigg (now for sale), in Easedale, he entered into the subject most kindly, and offered to find out for us its real value. He described the tangled copse and a natural terrace under the crag as a very favourite resort of his and his sisters in bygone days, and said of the little "Rocky Well," "I know it by heart." He then asked Mrs. Wordsworth to look at his Miscellaneous Sonnets and read the one suggested to him there by the likeness of a rock to a sepulchral stone, in that hazel copse. This she did with much expression. At this time he wore a green shade, and his head was usually bent down, his eyes being weak. He remembered two or three lines of the Sonnet, not the whole. It begins—

> " Mark the concentred hazels that enclose
> Yon old grey stone protected from the ray
> Of noontide suns."

On Sunday, as we were going to Rydal Church, we met Wordsworth with an Italian gentleman of the name of Miers, whom he was going to put on the way to Grasmere. We walked a little way with them ; and as the poet, on Italian politics, is all we can desire, I asked him to inquire from Mr. Miers, who was going to dine at Rydal Mount, if he knew anything about Mazzini at Genoa.   Last night Mrs. Arnold and I sat with Mr. Wordsworth for above an hour, and he gave us many interesting particulars which he had heard from this Italian gentleman, with whom he had been much pleased.   He said he had asked him about Mazzini, and heard a very high character of him in every respect.   Mr. Miers said that shortly before leaving Italy he had called on the mother of Mazzini to ask her commands for her son.   She was not well, but she said, "Don't tell Giuseppe that you found me ill, but tell him that not a day of my life passes that I do not thank God for having given me such a son."   Mr. Miers added that "it was worthy of a Spartan mother ; but what made it so valuable was, that it was uttered by a Christian one."

Wordsworth spoke with strong and deep feeling of the present state of Italy and the crushing despotism of Austria, supported, as it is in secret, by Russia and Prussia.   There is no law of copyright in Italy, so that the more excellent a book is the less chance an author has of making anything of the fruits of his mind.   Wordsworth's discourse last night was varied, accurate, moral in its tone, and admirably descriptive of some scenes at Nismes especially,—not a trace of age or forgetfulness, not a link displaced in the chambers of imagery, or in the moral bearings of the subjects he was discussing.   I cannot think that Milton himself could have talked more loftily against despotism, or more excellently on truth and justice.]

Owing to Miss Hill's death it was not necessary for Mary to return to me in Yorkshire; and as soon as I had settled all my affairs, consequent on the succession to my aunt's property, I rejoined her at Duncliffe in September 1839.

We very soon entered on the possibility of the projected purchase of Lancrigg as a summer refreshment, and as her future home at my death, and as I cordially entered into the plan, we authorized Mr. Wordsworth to act as our agent in the affair, which he was most kindly pleased to undertake; and as few people have ever been so favoured as to have had such a poet as their man of business, or such a clerk as his beloved daughter Dora, I here insert her letter to my daughter on the final arrangements, received in October 1839 :—

From Dora Wordsworth to Mary F.

"RYDAL MOUNT, *October* 21*st*, 1839.

"My father, who is gone down to Calgarth, where he remains all night, requested me to inform you that this morning he had a long interview with old Rowlandson, which ended in his agreeing to purchase the property of Under Lancrigg for one thousand and thirty pounds, seventy pounds less than Mr. R. at first asked; but my father particularly desired that I might say the price 'was very handsome, and more than he was likely to get from any other person, and yet, duly weighing the interests of buyer and seller, his conscience allowed him to take the land at that price.' My father named to Mr. R. the time when it best suited Mrs. Fletcher to take possession. His reply was, 'The custom of the country is to pay down the purchase-money on the 14th February, when the purchaser comes into possession of the ploughed land, of the pasture land 26th April, of the houses 12th May; and it would not be convenient for me, on account of my farmer, to depart from this custom.' And my father ventured to say that, under these circumstances, doubtless Mrs. Fletcher would be willing to abide by the custom. My father desired me to express his great satisfaction at your becoming possessors of this little property, which has for so many years been so dear to him and his, and where so many happy hours have been passed by them; and his earnest wish that many years of like happy enjoyment may fall to your and Mrs. Fletcher's share, in which wish I most cordially unite, as would my mother and Miss Fenwick were they here, but they left Ambleside this morning for a three weeks' absence in the county of Durham, —my mother to her relatives at Stockton-upon-Tees, Miss Fenwick to hers at Whitton, where she is to meet Mr. Henry

Taylor and his bride, whom he is bringing down to introduce to his father and mother. They were married at Hastings on Thursday. Almost the last thing my mother said to me was, ' Be sure you write to me as soon as your father has completed the bargain with Rowlandson, that I may tell the pleasant news to Mrs. Arnold, and, indeed, we shall give pleasure to many by this " bit of news." ' Mr. Allen Harden looked so bright upon it to-day ; he is here on his return from Italy only for a few days."

In May 1840 I took lodgings at Thorney How, Grasmere, to enable us to superintend the alterations we intended to make at Lancrigg, so as to fit it for our summer quarters and Mary's future home. This furnished us with occupation and interest of a varied kind, assisted as we were by the advice and kindly interest taken in our new possession by Mr. Wordsworth and his ladies at the Mount.

[The following extracts from a family note-book, written at the time, may be worth inserting here as relating chiefly to our intercourse with the inmates of Rydal Mount after we became stateswomen in Easedale :—

From M. F.'s Note-book.

We reached Thorney How on the 1st June 1840, from Edinburgh. The day was bright and " beautiful exceedingly " when we reached our old mountain lodging and took possession of our bonny bit of earth adjoining to this little farm, which looked its best to welcome us. Mrs. Taylor, her Mary, and Angus had arrived some days before, and our old landlady of the summer 1833 gave us a kindly welcome.

It is a goodly corner we have lighted on " to bigge our-selves a bower in," and a dream of former days seems about to be realized without much effort on our part. So far it is safer than if it had been eagerly pursued. The beauty of Easedale is even greater than we remembered it to be, and Lancrigg so cheerful and innocent-looking, basking in the sun. I hope we shall not spoil it. The Wordsworth party were kind enough to call the day after we came, but we had gone to Green Head Ghyll to get a supply of bread from the chief baker of the place, and missed them.

On Thursday. we called at the Mount, and the following day, the 4th June, Wordsworth came to an early dinner here. He was in a very happy mood, and threw himself into the interests of our possession in a most engaging manner.

After dinner we all walked over the Intack part of Lancrigg to our boundary wall, and to the point the poet especially admires, as commanding the wild mountain view into Far Easedale on one side, and the more cultivated peep into the Vale of Grasmere on the other, with the church-tower, the lake, and the end of Loughrigg as the boundary, which is a kind of sun-dial from that point of view. We went through the West Copse, which led us past Kitty Crag to Far Easedale, and back to Thorney How by the flat part of the valley which goes by the name of Boothwaite, a favourite evening stroll of the poet.

After this we had many meetings of real business with several neighbours Wordsworth consulted, because, as he said, "They understand these things much better than I do." When we attempted to thank him for the trouble he was taking for us, he took leave, saying, "I always feel that those who receive a benefit kindly also confer a favour."

July 31st we spent at Rydal Mount, a bright evening. Mr. Henry Taylor[1] and his lovely wife came with Miss Fenwick. He is still very handsome, with much of thought and power in his countenance. Mr. Wordsworth told us of a visit they had a few days before from the Princes of Ashantee, and added, "They were very good company;" and the ladies spoke of the pleasing expression of the younger Prince. It is to be hoped they may escape being eaten by their subjects when they return. What a contrast a tea-party at Rydal Mount, perhaps the highest point in man's civilized life in all its bearings, and a cannibal carousal in the jungles of Ashantee! It would be very interesting to trace the progress of these two Princes, if one could really

---

[1] Author of "Philip Van Artevelde."

get near their minds. They are at present under the care of a judicious tutor of the name of Pyne.

The following evening we went to drink tea with our cousins the Williamsons,[1] at Mary Fisher's, where Mr. and Mrs. Wordsworth joined us, walking from and back to Rydal Mount over the fell way. Mary Fisher had been their servant in their early days at the cottage at Town End. After tea the conversation turned on Crabbe and his poetry. Wordsworth considers him a dull man in conversation. He said he did not either give information, nor did he enliven any subject by discussion. He spoke highly of his writings as admirable specimens of the kind, but he does not like the misanthropic vein which runs through them. He was surprised to hear from my mother that Crabbe's prose style was so stiff and artificial in his letters. He said that generally good writers of verse wrote good prose, especially good letters. "Cowper's letters are everything that letters can be, and many of Burns's are marvellous." His brother Gilbert, too, was an excellent prose writer. I attribute this very much to the method pursued by their father, and described by their tutor, Mr. Murdoch, a youth engaged to teach them. He details it in a letter in Dr. Currie's "Life of Burns."]

A few days after our return to Duncliffe we were followed by dear Margaret and her five children, Dr. Davy having been requested by Lord Palmerston to undertake a special service at Constantinople with the view of effecting some reform in the medical department of the Turkish army, which had been agreed upon between the British and Turkish Governments.

We spent a happy winter at Duncliffe with this addition

---

[1] Mr. and Mrs. Williamson. He was the only child of my mother's early friend and cousin, E. Dawson of Wighill, who married a Lincolnshire clergyman and died in 1800. The second wife of her son and my mother became intimate friends, and met frequently both at Lancrigg and at their home, Headingly Parsonage near Leeds. They now live at · Fairstowe near Bath, doing good which will live after them in the hearts of the many orphans her loving care has rescued from misery and ruin.

to our family, preferring to adopt the plan of joint house-keeping to having separate establishments.

Mary and I returned to Thorney How in April 1841, to expedite the proceedings of the dilatory workmen of the valley, who were highly amused at my Yorkshire activity in expecting them to be at work at seven A.M., and expressing surprise that the old men mounted the ladders and the young stood in idleness below. Our chief carpenter and man of affairs, old Edward W—, was a fine example both in look and manner of the Westmoreland artisan. He told us that in our absence he discovered one morning that the foundation of one of the walls of the old part of the house had given way in the night, and that it was necessary for the safety of the building that the wall should be taken down and a new foundation made. The reply of the builders was, " They 're nobbut women, they 'll niver find it out." Our protector replied, " It mun come down. If they are nobbut women, we munna be rogues."

Another of our Grasmere wallers amused us by his opinion of Mr. Wordsworth. My daughter, when enforcing her desire to have the chimneys like those in Troutbeck, said, " Mr. Wordsworth thinks they are the best for this country, and we must do what he tells us." " Yes," said the man, deliberately, " M'appen he *has* as much sense as most on us."

On the 16th of July 1841, the anniversary of the fiftieth year since my marriage, we took possession of our dear little Lancrigg home.

We spent a very pleasant autumn seeing much of our friends at Fox How and other kind neighbours; Hartley Coleridge, often coming in to share our early dinner, and who, with his gentle oddity and large range of contemplation over his own thoughts, always added something to our stock of ideas by these wandering visits. We never made

out whether he liked us or not, but we always made him
welcome.

Our pleasant villa at Duncliffe had during our absence
been sold in a somewhat illegal manner, so that we were
obliged to move, and I authorized Mrs. Davy to take the
large old-fashioned house of Murrayfield, which was nearer
Edinburgh, and which accommodated our united families
comfortably for the winter.

Dr. Davy returned from Constantinople and joined us at
Murrayfield in January 1842. A very few nights after his
return I met with a bad accident by a fall down stairs.
There was a deep cut and bruise on one side of my forehead, and I was some hours, perhaps days, under the impression that the injury might be of a serious nature, but
I bless God I never for a moment lost consciousness, and if
I were asked to mention three days of my active and
varied life I would wish to live over again, I think I should
say those three days that succeeded this accident, so intense
was the feeling of devout thankfulness that it had pleased
God to preserve my life and senses from sudden and afflicting disorder. My recovery was wonderfully rapid at the
time.

We returned to Lancrigg the end of April 1842 to complete the furnishing of the house and begin gardening
operations. Angus joined us soon after, and one day after
being overheated by a long walk as I was resting on the
sofa in the drawing-room and Angus was reading to me, I
was suddenly seized with a giddiness in the head, the room
and everything seemed whirling round me, and though I
never lost consciousness these attacks returned so frequently
as to alarm both myself and my family; the seizures were
so sudden and my helplessness under them so great as to
threaten danger. Dr. Davy had the great kindness to
come from Edinburgh to attend me; he remained with us

a month, and by his skill and attention, under the Divine blessing, the remedies applied proved successful. While this tendency to vertigo continued, I was not allowed either to read or write much, nor could I converse without feeling a heat of head which I had never experienced before my accident. It was a summer of uncommon beauty. I sat much under the oak-tree, and carriage exercise always agreed with me.

[It was during this time, when our dear mother was laid aside from her usually healthy and vigorous life for the first time in my recollection, that an event so mournful to our locality, and indeed to all England, occurred—Dr. Arnold's sudden death. We experienced on that occasion a pleasing mark of attention from one of our peasant neighbours, who lived between Rydal and Grasmere. The intelligence of this event reached the members of the Arnold family then at Fox How very early on Monday morning; and this neighbour, knowing of my mother's illness, and of the great intimacy that subsisted between us, and fearing she might hear it suddenly in one of her daily drives, walked to Lancrigg and reached it before 7 A.M. She asked to see me in my room. This enabled me, in some degree, to break the suddenness of the shock to my mother; and it was a pleasing testimony of the interest this neighbour took in both families. There was a long suspension at this time, owing to her illness, of any continuation in her family records of the sad events of that summer, for in August of the same year the two youngest little boys of Dr. and Mrs. Davy were cut off in one week by virulent scarlet fever, and interred in one grave in the West Church Cemetery in Edinburgh. In writing of it afterwards, our mother says, in 1844] :—

It was a sorrowful season; for not only had family affliction, in the death of the two dear little grandchildren, befallen us, but we had lost a neighbour and friend whom we both loved and honoured. This was no other than that great and good man, Dr. Arnold of Rugby. He died of

spasm of the heart, on the 12th June 1842, after a few hours
of acute suffering.　He was taken away in the midst of his
great usefulness and wonderful happiness, leaving a wife
and nine children—and such a wife! sharing his every
thought and devoting herself to his happiness with unequalled tenderness.　As I said in writing to her long before his death, and can now repeat, with more confirmed
conviction of their truth as applied to him than of any
man I have ever known, Milton's words—he lived in their
large Christian import—

"As ever in his Great Taskmaster's eye."

The sensation the death of this eminent scholar and truly
Christian philosopher produced in our valley was remarkable.　He had only spent a small part of the last eight
years of his life here, and yet, without popular manners,
his excellence, his gentle-heartedness, and genuine humility
of mind, had made the poor consider him their friend, and
the rich their genial and kind-hearted neighbour.

The return of his bereaved family to Fox How without
him, this sad, sad summer, was an affecting circumstance
to all of us.　*Their* light had indeed become dim, but was
not extinguished ; for his works and his life, written by a
faithful chronicler, will guide and comfort the lovers of
Christ and goodness so long as the English language
endures.

My friend Lord Jeffrey writes to me in a letter lately
received :—

["What you say of Arnold, and what I have been reading
of his correspondence, will make the neighbourhood still dearer
and more interesting to me when we make out our visit to you.
It is long since I have met with anything at once so loveable
and so exalted.　He was truly a noble creature ; with the
firmness of a hero, he had the softness of a woman, the devot-
edness and zeal of an apostle or a martyr, and the gentleness

and lowliness of a bashful child. I do not now wonder at what I used to think the exaggeration with which Mary used to speak of his character and the charm of his home life. It is sad to think that such an example and such a teacher should have been so early lost to the world.

"I feel, I believe, as you do as to poor T. Campbell ; and if I had not always all your indulgence for his faults, I am sure I am now disposed to remember nothing but his genius and his virtues, for I am quite aware that he had many virtues and endearing qualities, though they were more apt to give them-selves out to such gentle natures as yours than to those on whose 'pigeon livers' he could not so well rely. I am glad to see they mean to give him a monument in Westminster Abbey. I am now agitating for one at Glasgow also. God bless you.   FRANCIS JEFFREY."

We spent the winter of 1842-43 at Murrayfield very quietly, as prudence was strongly enforced on me since my late illness.

Lord Jeffrey and Mrs. Mackenzie were among our kindest and most frequent visitors, and we could scarcely have had any society more to our taste. Lord Cockburn also looked in upon us often, with his clear eyes and grand forehead still untouched by age or wrinkles.

We returned in April 1843 to Lancrigg, and as age was beginning to make me feel frequent journeys and the care of two houses somewhat irksome, we resolved henceforth to make Lancrigg our permanent summer and winter home.

We were decided to make this arrangement by Dr. and Mrs. Davy having resolved to sell their house in Edinburgh, where they had suffered so much, and to establish them-selves for the future in the Lake district. They bought a few acres of land a short distance from Ambleside, on the way to Rydal, and built an excellent house there, which was just finished and inhabited before Dr. Davy accepted an appointment offered to him in his own department in the

West Indies.   His mind was too active to be happy at his age without useful employment.

Thus, much to my contentment, it came to pass that we formed a little family colony in a district early endeared to us by frequent visits, by many enduring friendships, and, besides the abiding charm of the "everlasting hills," possessing a circle of people singularly free from the frivolities of fashionable life, while it combined still "plain living and high thinking" at the fountain-head[1] of that glorious Sonnet.   There was also more than ordinary cultivation among the gentlefolks, who were chiefly ladies, and much of honesty and independence among the working classes, with very little poverty and distress, except what intemperance produced.

The winter of 1843-44 was the first we spent in Easedale, and we found it by no means too sombre or solitary. There was a frequent intercourse between our friends of the Rydal valley, and Mrs. Davy and her children spent the Christmas week with us.   My grandson, Henry Fletcher, too was with us, and left us on the 22d January 1844, for his first term at Oxford.

We had the gratification in October 1844 of a visit from Dr. and Mrs. Alison.   Dr. Alison's is a character that deserves to be loved and honoured.   He has devoted his life to the health and comfort of the poor, and his means also, and the excellent pamphlet he published in 1840, on the destitution of the poor in Scotland, awakened all classes in that country to a sense of shame, and a desire to inquire into and remedy the abuses he was the first to disclose and make public.   In consequence of his book, associations were formed in Edinburgh, and in all the great towns in Scotland, to inquire into the statements he had made, and to apply to Parliament for a Poor Law for Scotland more

[1] Rydal Mount.

suited to the condition of the people, and to the increased wealth and ability of the higher classes. Dr. Alison will in after times be considered one of the greatest benefactors of his country, as he is now looked up to as the man most distinguished for personal and active exertions in the cause of humanity. We considered it a great honour to have such a man under our roof, and Mrs. Alison's talents, principles, and most agreeable manners, make her worthy to be his wife. It is one of the true pleasures of age to be able to continue the early friendship I·had for their accomplished father in the persons of two of his children, Dr. Alison and dear Mrs. Burge.

After the Alisons left us, the days shortened, and winter set in early, with more than usual severity. Henry Fletcher came from Oxford to spend his Christmas, and his cheerful temper cheered our winter fireside. My sailor grandson Archibald, who had just been promoted to the rank of lieutenant, joined his brother here on his way to Edinburgh. The brothers were delighted to meet again. Archibald's promotion was a joyful event, and his coming a great pleasure to us all.

We had some pleasant neighbourly gatherings at Christmas, and to keep my birthday in January, when games and charades were performed by young and old with great effect. Our pleasant neighbours, Mrs. Cookson and her daughters, assisted and enjoyed the fun, and I was glad to feel a growing intimacy and regard between Mrs. Cookson and myself. It is not often warm friendships are formed so late in life; but she commanded my respect and affection from the first by her dignified submission to altered circumstances, her active benevolence, and her motherly heart.

The Rev. Robert Graves, at that time and for several years the curate at Bowness, was a favourite guest at the family gatherings which took place on the 15th January to keep my birthday, and he was playfully designated my " poet laureate." He is a man much beloved, of wide sympathies and varied cultivation.

We never for a moment repented of our resolution " to marry the Lakes after flirting " with them so long.

[*To Mrs. Fletcher.*

ON THE SEVENTY-FIFTH ANNIVERSARY OF HER BIRTHDAY.

" Far to mine inward sense a solemn toll
  That word, thy *birthday*, Friend revered, conveys ;
  Yet when upon thy stately form I gaze,
  And drink thy glance,—bright efflux of a soul
  Whose charity still flows from pole to pole,
  Whose fire of youth still burns with kindling rays,—
  Scarce can my wondering mind believe thy days
  Five years have pass'd man's limitary goal.
  Time's Favourite art thou ; to thee we turn
  For memories of the great his depths conceal,
  Thine honouring friends ; nor these alone we learn,
  But fresh enthusiasm quaff and holy zeal.
  Then live, live on ; Heaven leave thee still below,
  To warm our old hearts with thy vernal glow.
                         " R. P. G.

" *January* 15, 1845."]

In April 1845 we made a railway expedition to London. At seventy-five I travelled from Lancaster to Euston station without fatigue. We spent three agreeable weeks with my dear old friend Mrs. Chapman at Blackheath Park. I went purposely to visit her; and it was delightful to see how happily and tranquilly she passes the evening of her days in the midst of her affectionate family, two sons and three daughters. It is instructive to see that, with much difference of opinion on religious points, they agree to differ without any abatement of love or respect towards each other.

We spent a pleasant hour or two with the Jeffreys at

their hotel in Brook Street, and met there the good old Whig Lord Lansdowne, who was very courteous and kind to an old Edinburgh Whig lady who could go back as far in her recollection of public events as he could himself.

We saw Mazzini frequently during this period, as my good friend was not afraid of him, and he was invited to join us more than once at Blackheath at luncheon, where his eloquence and the power he then had of expressing himself in good English was appreciated by all. He is a noble-minded creature, a man of great ability and elevated spirit, ready to undergo martyrdom for the deliverance of his country from the different tyrannies which crush it—north and south, east and west. He is not loud, but deep in the expression of patriotic feeling, and righteous in his hatred of oppression and injustice.

There is still a deep melancholy about the habitual expression of his fine countenance, but it is very different from what it was when I first saw him in 1837. He is evidently working for his country with more of hope than he then had. He gave us a little account of his Italian school, which still goes on, and spoke with deep feeling of the brothers Bandieri. When we told him how much we had liked Thomas Carlyle's letter about him at the time the opening of his letters was brought before Parliament, his face lighted up with pleasure, and he said, " Yes, and you do not know why it was so good of Carlyle to write it, for we had before that some differences of opinion which had led to some coolness between us, but when he saw I needed a friend he came to my support; that I call noble." He spoke of Sir James Graham's attack upon him in the House of Commons with perfect composure, saying that he felt it more for his friends than for himself.

We reached our dear home the end of May 1845, after this little peep into the busy world, and enjoyed a pleasant summer seeing several old friends, with the usual variety that summer brings with it at the Lakes—of agreeable strangers from distant lands.

We accepted the pressing invitation of our kind friends, the Miss Campbells, 35 Heriot Row, to go to Edinburgh in the spring of 1846, taking my granddaughter Grace Davy with us, that she might have the advantage of Edinburgh masters for a time. We reached Edinburgh on the 28th of February. We had no cause to complain of our wintry journey, and were most lovingly received by our warm-hearted friends.

On the morrow, Sunday, I was too tired to go to church, but after morning service we had several visitors, Lord Jeffrey, Mrs. Thomson, Dr. Allen Thomson, and others. If I had ever doubted the warmth and kindness of the Scottish character, this visit to Edinburgh would have convinced me of it.

The hospitalities and cordial welcomes of a whole winter were crowded into the two very agreeable months we spent under the roof of our hospitable friends. We scarcely made a single new acquaintance, nor did we wish it. We went to no public places of any sort, or to any fashionable parties, but our time was occupied from seven in the morning till ten at night, when I was glad to retire to bed. From seven till nine I wrote letters in bed by candle-light. We break-fasted at ten; after that till twelve I had a levée of humble friends, old servants, and pensioners, those who wished to tell me their family history and hear mine, without being objects of charity. After luncheon, the world, as it may be called, flocked in upon us, and none of those whom we had known ever so slightly failed to pay us this mark of personal regard on our return to Edinburgh. We dined out three or four times a week, attending Lord Jeffrey's most pleasant soirées to which he gave us the *entrée*, and also Lady

Murray's, at both of which we met many I had known in the nursery, now eminent barristers.

One of our highest gratifications during this visit to Edinburgh was to hear Dr. Chalmers address his humble congregation in the Tanners' Warehouse in the West Port, where he has assembled a ragged school for week-day teaching, and it is used as a place of worship on Sundays. It is near the scene of the Burke murders. The persons, old and young, who are gathered together there, never probably before heard the word of God, or were taught to feel their relation to Him as immortal beings.

We breakfasted with Dr. and Mrs. Chalmers at Morningside the day after he completed his sixty-sixth birthday. His morning prayer was beautiful, one of its petitions I remember, "Give us, O Lord, such holy dispositions on this side of death as may fit us for the blessedness Thou hast prepared on the other side of death for those who love and do Thy truth here, in lowliness of mind."

Dr. Chalmers spoke with great interest of the Lakes and of Wordsworth, asking many questions about him, and returning to it when other subjects were introduced. He said he took a walk from Fife to Westmoreland in 1797, and he afterwards visited Rydal Mount in 1817. He said, " I always felt attracted to Wordsworth by his love for the common people." In speaking of Grasmere he said, with a sweet glow of countenance for a man of sixty-six, " There is an intense loveliness about that place." He spoke very warmly of Dr. Arnold's sermons, and said they contained Evangelical doctrine without the phraseology which often weakens the effect of the most important truths.

We saw for the last time our faithful friend of many, many years, Dr. Thomson of Morland. His mind in his eightieth year was in full vigour, and it was a mind of great strength and energy, with much warmth and generosity of feeling.

We spent a most agreeable day at Belmont. Lord Mackenzie's conversation has increased in richness and flow, and in a quiet humour peculiarly his own ; his wife as charming as ever, and all the intercourse we had with Lord Cuninghame and his wife, and many other dear friends of "auld lang syne," made us rejoice we had undertaken this journey once more to experience afresh the feelings of gratitude towards those with whom we lived, and all who received us so lovingly.

In the autumn of 1846 we had several agreeable visitors, one American lady, Margaret Fuller, and two friends with her, spent some hours here. She struck us as very original, with great powers of expression and genuine enthusiasm for what is good and beautiful, which always attracts me much. She is neither English, Scotch, nor Irish, but it is pleasant to be able to communicate in our own tongue so freely as one can do with an agreeable American woman of genius.

In September, Sir John Richardson paid us a week's visit on his way to see his venerable mother at Dumfries. We had not met since the death of his excellent wife a year and a half before this time. He spoke much about the different characters of his children, and we felt that besides his many fine qualities, he united in a remarkable degree the tenderness of a mother's feelings towards them, with a father's anxiety for their good and happiness.

After passing a pleasant and peaceful winter at Lancrigg, Mary and I joined Mrs. Davy and her daughters at Leamington, in February 1847, almost a new scene to all of us ; but good masters for the girls were to be had there, the object of our going.

After paying several short visits on the south coast, and also in Yorkshire, Mary and I reached our beloved Lancrigg on May 17th, 1847.

Easedale was in the perfection of its early beauty, and we never felt it so much as on this occasion, or enjoyed the blessing of its repose more thankfully.

The preparations for Mary's marriage so occupied the time that intervened before that event was to take place—the 4th of August—that we saw less company than usual, and I have little to relate except the calm anticipation of a marriage, that was for a time to separate me from my affectionate and constant companion ; but I felt we should be little apart in the body, and not at all in spirit, and that in her union with so amiable a companion as Sir John Richardson I confided her to one who would greatly add to her happiness as well as to my own.

[*To Mrs. Chapman, from Mrs. Fletcher.*

"*June 26th*, 1847.

" I ought to have thanked you before this for the affectionate congratulations I received from you on the happy prospects that are opening for my dear Mary.   Hers, as Joanna Baillie writes in her congratulatory letter, is ' both a reasonable and romantic marriage ;' and this description of it accords with Mary's character, which is at once reasonable and romantic—reasonable in her estimate of the value of things, and romantic in her standard of what is requisite in character to interest her affections ; hence she has always been a fastidious person, and, fortunately, Sir J. Richardson happens to possess the qualities to which she has always attached most importance.   You, my dear friend, who know what we are to each other, will feel for me, as many do ; but I am more delivered from *self* on this occasion than I ever expected to be, and I can assure your motherly heart that Sir John does not wish us to be separated at all, but that in winter at least I should make my home at Haslar for the future.   Mrs. Davy claims me for the alternate winters, and the summer months I shall spend at Lancrigg as usual, if God so wills it ; but it is presumptuous to look forward at seventy-seven.

"I ought to tell you, my dear old friend, that Sir John

Richardson frankly told us that in case no intelligence concerning the fate of the Franklin Expedition reached England by the return of the whale-ships this autumn, or by their own return, which he fully expects, he had promised to conduct a searching boat expedition to set forth in the spring of 1848. This is the only cloud in the distance ; but if Mary is willing to undertake the charge that would then devolve upon her, it is not for me to gainsay so generous a resolution."

Letter from Lord Jeffrey.

"E. I. COLLEGE, *Tuesday*, 11*th May* 1847.

"MY EVER DEAR MRS. FLETCHER,—It always makes me happier and better to get a letter from you, for it makes me think more favourably of our common nature, and of myself also, both as belonging to it and as capable of being gratified by finding it so loveable.　Generally, too, it lets me see that the most truly loveable are the most surely happy, and this, I need scarcely say, is peculiarly the case with your last most kind, most pleasing, and most amiable communication.　You have told me everything so frankly, so reasonably, so gently, and so naturally, that I enter at once into all your feelings, and rejoice in your joy, as cordially as if I had always had the same interests and anxieties as to the objects to which they relate.

"Do assure my dear Mary of the entire sympathy I have in her prospects of happiness, and of my confidence in their being realized.　I always thought her rather too difficult and disdainful of our poor rough sex, and am very glad that she has at last found one to reconcile her to it, and much obliged to Sir John Richardson for having procured us that indulgence.

"I hope to see both her and you once more before I die ; but it cannot, unfortunately, be now. . . .—With all love, and respect, and good wishes, and blessings, believe me always, my dear Mrs. Fletcher, very affectionately yours,

"F. JEFFREY."]

After the marriage took place (on the 4th of August), and the wedding guests had dispersed, I courted repose, and Margaret, with her usual attention to my wishes and comfort, invited the whole party to spend the evening at

Lesketh How, leaving dear Mrs. Taylor to stay quietly with me at Lancrigg. Days and weeks passed on, enlivened by letters from the married pair on their tour through Holland and on the Rhine, where they paid an interesting visit at Pastor Fliedner's Institution at Kaiserswerth, Sir John having a hope of getting some change made in the nursing arrangements at Haslar Hospital.

Mrs. Taylor, her daughter, and Angus, formed my home circle. Some very agreeable neighbours, of the name of Broadley, took lodgings at Thorney How that autumn. We found them a great acquisition, and met frequently in a pleasant way. Our autumn passed pleasantly, and every exertion was made by those with me to lessen my feelings of regret, or rather of want, in the loss of her who, as Wordsworth used to observe, was my " inseparable companion."

[From Mrs. Fletcher, to her daughter Mary.

" *September* 1847.

" I have been reading with great interest Mr. Brooks' successful action against a fleet of pirates off Borneo. I see that great and good man is coming home to have his Governorship of Labuan ratified. If he is at Portsmouth I hope Sir John and he may meet ; he is a noble specimen of what disinterested courage and humanity can achieve. I think your husband and he are kindred spirits.

" I took a turn before breakfast this morning, and stood at your favourite point at the gate looking into Easedale. I also took leave of poor Wifie,[1] but hope to see her again at Haslar and you on her back. I gave Joseph strict charges to see her safe in her box at Oxenholme. Mrs. Arnold came with the Lesketh How party yesterday to dinner. I see how much she misses you when she comes here, dear Mary. To me you are so constantly present that I think I miss you less when I am in company than when I am alone, and *could* have a quiet chat with you ; but in or out of company I bless God for having

[1] A favourite grey pony.

provided you with objects of affection and opportunities of usefulness which will be of such value to you after my death. This hope and belief cheers and supports me continually, and prevents my complaining of our temporary separation."]

At the end of October, when my other children left me, I went to Lesketh How. It was a cheerful, pleasant winter. Mrs. Davy and her dear girls did all that affection and sympathy can do to cheer the occasional languor of age, and I bless God for having given me such a child as Margaret, fulfilling as she does the duties of a Christian daughter, wife, and mother.

[*From letter to her daughter Mary.*

" *November.24th*, 1847.

" We went this evening to drink tea at Rydal Mount, and found the dear old couple *tête-à-tête*. Mrs. Arnold went with us. Mr. Wordsworth was more like his former self than I have seen him since Dora's death. He showed us two letters he had had this week from ladies he had never seen or heard of,—one in prose, the other in verse. The former said she was the wife of a hard-worked London solicitor with five children. She found her greatest solace for all her cares and troubles in his ' Excursion.' She compared herself to a wearied traveller seated by a dusty roadside, tired and thirsty, when lo ! a fountain of fresh water sprang up by her side ; she drank of it freely, was refreshed and strengthened to pursue her journey. This was the effect ' The Excursion' produced on her mind and feelings. The other letter was from a solitary single woman, who describes herself as one who has survived all her kindred and the friends of her youth, and, seated on the sandy beach at Southport, she can forget all her sorrows when she has a volume of Wordsworth in her hand. Some of the lines are very good, and reminded us of Crabbe. Mrs. Arnold told him a gentleman at Oxford had made Susy read to him Wordsworth's Poem of ' Lycoris,' and we begged him to read it to us. He said it was suggested to him one day at Ullswater, in the year 1817, by seeing two white sunny clouds reflected in the lake. 'They looked (he said) like two swans.' He read the poem twice over, in his most beautiful and impressive manner. It describes a feeling quite familiar to me,—the preference the young have for autumn and the old for spring."]

Lesketh How, 15th January 1848.—I bless God for having permitted me to see this seventy-eighth birthday in the possession of all my mental faculties, and in bodily health less infirm than is common to persons of my age. I have through this long life experienced so many mercies, that my heart is full, but not full enough, of thankfulness and love towards that Being who created and redeemed me. Blessed be His name. From infancy I have been an object of tender love to all my family and relations that watched over me. I had the kindest and tenderest of husbands, and now, in my seventy-ninth year, I am blessed with most dutiful and affectionate children and grandchildren, and many most attached friends. This day I received testimonies of this love and respect from dear Margaret and her three children, from Mrs. Taylor and her Mary, from my own Mary and her excellent husband Sir John Richardson (whose letter I shall keep while I live), and from my son Angus, who never forgets his mother's birthday.

On the 19th of February 1848, Mrs. Davy and I and her two daughters set off in the train from Birthwaite to Liverpool. We were most kindly welcomed by Mrs. Rathbone and her excellent husband at Green Bank, and spent three days most agreeably with them. They are people whose whole lives have left a track-life to those who follow them, both of them being constantly occupied in seeking and finding opportunities of doing good. They unite with all the most active principles of the Christian character, the most liberal opinions, and a spirit of charity and good-will to those who differ from them in religious opinions.

Mrs. Rathbone introduced me to a most remarkable character, "Catherine of Liverpool," the well-known washer-woman, who, after helping all her poor neighbours to keep themselves clean, while she herself was toiling for her daily bread and supporting her aged mother, and making her house a refuge for many an orphan child, is now, through the influence of Mrs. Rathbone, placed at the head of a great washing establishment for the poor. Catherine is an Irishwoman, and a Methodist, and has all the fluency and cheerfulness of her countrywomen, with all the Christian love of God and her neighbour which John Wesley taught his followers as the main evidence and test of their religion. It did one's heart good to hear Catherine pour out her gratitude to Mrs. Rathbone when that lady was not within hearing.

From Green Bank we went the first day to Rugby to see Archy Davy, and the following day (the 23d) reached the Euston Square station, where Angus met us; and we found waiting for us, in the lodgings taken in Weymouth Street, dear Mrs. Taylor and her daughter, Sir John Richardson, and my own Mary, who were on a visit to Lady Franklin. A gladder heart than mine was not that day in London, to have my four surviving children and my excellent son-in-law, Sir John Richardson, and three dear great-grandchildren all about me, in health and comfort, and all making merry at my expense when I insisted, after my journey, on setting forth before dinner to make my-self "*braw*" by buying a cap and bonnet in Regent Street.

I had not seen my dear Mary since I had parted with her on her marriage-day, the 4th of August. We were so glad to meet again, that the traces of anxiety on the near prospect of parting with her husband were that day not predominant in her speaking countenance.

[Part of letter to Mrs. Stark, from Mrs. Fletcher.

"HASLAR, *March 26th*, 1848.

"The public and private events that have filled the last five weeks since we left Lesketh How and reached this place leave me at a loss how to write to you at this the first leisure hour I have been able to command. . . . I remained with our assembled family party a week in London, dining out nowhere but at Lady Franklin's, where the Richardsons were on a visit. On the evening of the 24th, at Lady Franklin's soirée, Dr. Boott came in and gave us the first news of the French revolution—that is, the news of the tocsin sounding in the streets of Paris, the tricolor waving as of old, the fraternization of the people, and the military helmets (*not heads*) carried on poles through the streets, and the people rushing into the Chamber of Deputies, crying '*Vive la République.*' We were struck dumb with this astounding intelligence. Mr. Carlyle was sitting by me at the time. I looked at him, hoping he would speak. He said not a word, but broke out into a loud laugh, and rose and left the house, to devour the journals, which that night were filled with news from Paris.

"I had engaged Mazzini to breakfast with us the following morning, and he came ; by that time the flight of the King and of Guizot was known, and the excitement had become excessive. It was beautiful to hear Mazzini's eloquent and simple lamentation over the moral degradation of Guizot. 'It was from his lectures,' he said, 'I first learned to love civil and religious liberty ; and that such a man should truckle to the base measures of Louis Philippe is deplorable.' I asked Mazzini what effect this would produce in Italy. 'The most glorious effect,' he answered ; 'the fall of the French monarchy is the restoration and union of Italy.

"We heard a few days after this Mazzini had left London for Paris ; and he is one of those master spirits destined, I trust, not only to serve but to save his country. He is a determined and uncompromising republican, but so true a lover of justice and humanity that he will take no part with those who do not make these their principles of action. . . .

"As to French affairs, I cannot pretend to see or understand how the financial difficulties are to be got over. Lamartine immortalized himself at first by abolishing the punishment of death for all political offences; but my great hope is in the ascendency of Odillon Barrot over the National Guard and the middle classes.   His extraordinary freedom from selfishness and party spirit in yielding to and even supporting the Provisional Government till the elections are over, when they resign their power to the will of the National Assembly, is above all praise. If all this can be accomplished without anarchy and bloodshed, it will be owing to the moderation of Odillon Barrot and his friends, who stand in the position the Gironde held in 1792.

"What a beautiful manifestation does this contrast of 1848 to 1792 make as to the improvement and progress of Europe in the last sixty years!   Tell Mrs. Bannatyne, with my kind love, that I rejoice she has lived to make this glorious comparison.   It is a comfort to us both to know that the smallest services those we loved best rendered to the good cause in those days of cowardly oppression, when they, and honest men like them, never shrank from the maintenance of high principles, that such service then, tells now in the different reception that England and Scotland gave to this over that state of things in France in 1792.   But I must quit this most engrossing subject, and come down from my hobby to private matters.

"Sir John Richardson left us last Monday, and was to sail yesterday from Liverpool to New York.   He gave me a short sketch of his route, which I sent to my granddaughter, desiring her to make a copy to send to you.

"As Sir Edward Parry told me yesterday, 'I think no man ever set out in a truer missionary spirit, or made a more generous sacrifice of private happiness than he has done,' and I am thankful to say his wife fully participates in the unselfishness of his conduct.   The separation has been and is a very great trial to her.   I thought her looking very ill and anxious when I came, but she is calm, subdued, and not uncheerful. She is devoted to the children, and they cling round her with confiding affection.   She and I have the heart-intercourse we always had, and I am thankful.   I think I told you Sir John had kindly proposed to take Thorney How for the governess and children during the time of his absence, so that we might be as little separated as possible. Lancrigg would not hold us all with my other summer guests.

" I return with Margaret in April, and Mary joins me in May with her little flock. The Admiralty allow Sir John the use of the house here should Westmoreland not agree with the children. I have not written so long a letter for many months, so, dear friend, you must take the quantity instead of the quality. God bless you all. E. F."]

Lancrigg, 14th January 1849.—To-morrow, if it please God to spare me till then, I shall have completed my seventy-ninth birthday, and entered upon the eightieth year of my life. This is a solemn thought, and ought to excite in me the deepest thankfulness to God for having been permitted to enjoy so much health of body and mind at so advanced a period. I have not been without my share of trials and disappointments, or deep sorrows, but they have been accompanied with many alleviations. I have loved much, and have had the happiness to be much beloved, as a daughter, wife, and mother. These are the crowning mercies of God in my pilgrimage hitherto, but my soul longs for a more intimate communion with God. I delight to do His will, and rejoice in the spirit of thankfulness for " the goodness and mercy " which " have followed me all the days of my life," but I deplore the sinfulness of my nature : I am too apt to be disturbed by trifles, am too impatient, and not sufficiently attentive to the feelings of others. I have too much self-love, and am not so humble-minded as I would desire to be. Oh my God, Thou who knowest my infirmities, have mercy upon me ; pardon my transgressions in thought, word, and deed; make me to feel habitually that " I am poor and needy, but that Thou carest for me ; " and in the trial that awaits me, the parting with my dear and dutiful child Mary, who has been my affectionate companion from her childhood, grant that I

may submit without repining to a separation that she feels
not less than I do, but which it is plainly her duty to do,
and mine to suffer. It is a more grievous separation than
that occasioned by her marriage, because she then had a
cheerful and happy home to go to, and the companionship
of her husband to cheer and support her. Now her anxieties about his safety are aggravated by her sorrow for poor
Josephine Richardson's illness and her concern for me;
but God, who knows the singleness of her heart and the
integrity of her purpose to do her duty, will support and
bless her.

Lancrigg, April 21, 1849.—Towards the end of December 1848 a joyful event occurred: Dr. Davy returned
safely and in good health from Barbadoes, and the thankfulness and gladness of heart thus afforded to my dear
Margaret was visible in her countenance and the improvement of her health and spirits.

Another event conducive to my tranquillity of mind
and domestic happiness occurred. Angus had been invited
by the Colonization Society in London to accompany some
deputies from their committee to visit the large manufacturing towns of Yorkshire for the purpose of promoting emi-
gration to Australia for the unemployed operatives. The
Chartists opposed the meetings held at Leeds for this purpose; at Huddersfield, however, the deputies secured a
patient hearing, which was much owing to the personal
influence of Mr. W. E. Forster, of Bradford, who is considered by all parties as the poor man's friend, so that his
approbation of the views of the Colonization Society induced
about ninety hand-loom combers to volunteer to emigrate
under the auspices of the Society. Angus offered me a visit,
and brought with him at my request his kind friend Mr.
Forster, to spend a week at Lancrigg. Mr. Forster had
been first made known to us by Mrs. Charles Fox, of Fal-

mouth. On this occasion he brought with him a novel then just published, "Mary Barton." Mr. Forster did not know by whom it was written, nor did we know for some months after this, but we were at once struck with its power and pathos, and it was with infinite pleasure I heard that it was written by the daughter of one whom I both loved and reverenced in my early married life in Edinburgh, so that I had a twofold pleasure in making Mrs. Gaskell's acquaintance through Miss M. Beever, who knew her at Manchester, and who told me she always asked about me with interest. Thus by these seeming chances are people brought into contact with those who are associated with much that is of interest in their past lives.

My dear Mary set off for her Haslar home with the three younger children, as their sister was unable to leave the good medical care she had at home. This separation was a great trial to us both, but we submitted to it without complaining, and Miss Craik, who had joined me at Lancrigg, kindly agreed to remain with me till the end of March, and Angus agreed to remain with me for the winter. Miss Craik, the daughter of one of my oldest friends, proved a most pleasant companion to both of us. She has a most intelligent mind, always in pursuit of knowledge; great sweetness of temper, and quick sympathies. We had a quiet but by no means an uncheerful winter.

Towards the end of March I was conscious of an excessive activity of mind, even amounting to a painful degree of restlessness, like a person who, on the eve of a long journey, remembers to have left many needful things undone, and feeling the shortness of time to do them in, is in a continual hurry and state of unrest. About the end of March I used to awake every night with a distracting pain in my head. I certainly thought (notwithstanding Dr. Davy's opinion that the symptoms were not alarming) that I had not long to live; and I bless God, humbly and fervently, that in the moments of extremest pain, when death would have been most welcome, I had a strong persuasion that the severe suffering He permitted me to experience was but a new proof of His Fatherly love and mercy. I had, through faith in the blessed promises of His Son, made my peace with Him, so that I had no fear of death; but my heart had fainted under the terror of the bodily agony that commonly precedes the separation of soul and body, and the thought of parting with my dear children was often overwhelming. Now I perceived the goodness of God in sending me this sharp pain to wean me from life and disarm death of all its bodily terrors. The only desire of my heart was to assemble all my children about me, that I might see them once more before my mind was utterly gone. They came most affectionately at my call, and before long the pains gradually subsided. I got more sleep, and by this 23d of April 1849, I record with thankfulness my comparative restoration to health.

On the 1st of May 1849, after this illness, I rose much refreshed. It was a glorious morning, the first day of summer according to my calendar. When I looked out of the window, at six in the morning, a crowd of poetical images and recollections filled my mind; and though I could not express them poetically, I set down my thoughts in measured lines as follows:—

COMPOSED IN THE EARLY MORNING OF MAY 1ST, 1849, BY E. F.

> HAIL! glorious day, in Spring's fresh verdure clad,
> Queen of the year, all Nature worships thee.
> Last eve, at twilight's close, I marked the swift
> And wingèd harbingers of summer days
> Flock to their clay-built homes beneath the eaves,
> Wearied with flight; and at the morning's dawn
> They give thee welcome, while the " wandering voice"

Had travelled long, and far, to join his notes
To the glad gush of song that hails thy coming.
The little lambs skip with fantastic glee,
And the green carpet with which earth is clothed
Is spangled o'er with flowers of brilliant hue.
Time was when I, a happy village child,
With sportive gladness ranged the flowery fields
To gather garlands for this festive day ;
The scented cowslip, purple orchis joined,
And wild blue hyacinth, with primrose tufts,
For votive offerings at each cottage door.
That eighty summers have not dimmed the sense
Of these pure pleasures—God, be thine the praise !

[*Part of letter from Mrs. Fletcher to Sir J. Richardson.*

"1849.

"I little expected once more to feel the same deep interest in any event which my dear husband and I did feel in the French revolution of 1789, before France had committed savage cruelty, and when all good men rejoiced in the destruction of a grinding despotism, the fruits of which were bitterness and ashes ; but the Roman Republic has roused the same high hopes and the same deep interests for the restoration of that noble people. We hear that Mazzini is actively employed in exhorting the people and restraining them from acts of violence."

To her daughter Mary.

"LESKETH How, *8th July* 1849.

"I have to thank you for two most welcome letters. Alas for Rome ! I knew how you would feel when you read 'The French in Rome;' but Mr. Price gave me some comfort ; he said, 'You may be sure the noble defence of the Roman people will have an imperishable influence on the future state of Italy. Formerly the Italians could not depend on each other ; now that distrust is vanished. All true friends of freedom will understand each other, and it will be in vain for Austria or the united despots to crush the spirit *that* defence has manifested.' There is still great comfort in this hope, and it is nobler in the Assembly and the Triumvirate to spare a massacre than to immolate thousands of innocent victims on the shrine of national independence. Those who have fallen will not have fallen in vain if their fate shall rivet the love of liberty and hatred of oppression on their surviving countrymen."

To the Same.

" Yesterday, about two o'clock, we drove off to call on Mrs. Gaskell at Millbrow, and found her, with her two friendly inmates and fine children, looking bright and happy. She has a noble countenance, intelligent and modest. She received us, as she always does, with that expression of heartfelt cordiality the Richardsons did at Chatham. She came back with us to dinner. The Palmses came to tea, and were delighted to meet the writer of ' Mary Barton.'"

To the Same.

"Thou art thy father's own daughter. The lines are beautiful, full of high and noble feeling. . . . I will not believe that Mazzini has fled, but if he has fled from so base, so perfidious an enemy, it is not that he fears death, but that he has still faith in the good cause, and he may yet serve it and fulfil his high mission, for if there ever was a soldier that took righteousness for his breastplate, that soldier is Mazzini.

"I expect every moment the car to be announced that is to take the children and me to Lancrigg to meet Mrs. Gaskell and her party to take luncheon there. They are to go to Easedale Tarn after it, while I take repose. Dear Lancrigg! you are, if possible, more present to me there than anywhere else, and I cling to it."]

Soon after her return to Fox How in September 1849, Mrs. Arnold asked me to meet her distinguished guest, the Chevalier Bunsen, who, with his wife and daughters and one son, was staying with her for a few days. The very high estimation Dr. Arnold formed of the Chevalier's talents and goodness made us very anxious to see him.

His countenance beams with benevolence, and his conversation is full of good feeling, intelligence, and liberality. I was glad to hear him reprobate the interference of France in the affairs of Italy, and speaking of Mazzini he said, "He is a man of very great ability, perfectly honest, and purely disinterested, but I do consider him a fanatic in politics." He thinks highly of the national character of the Italians, and very lowly of the French. "The French have no faith in anything; they change their political principles as easily as the colour of their cockade; to-day it is blue, to-morrow red, and the next day tricolor." He seemed to think free institutions quite incompatible with Papal domination, and did not risk an opinion as to what might be the final result of the liberal movement in Italy. For Kossuth and his brave Hungarian compatriots he expressed great admiration and sympathy. All he said was expressive of candour, liberality, and good faith, and I felt it a new obligation to Mrs. Arnold that she had allowed us to meet this excellent man.

About three weeks later we set off for Mr. Williamson's parsonage, near Leeds. It was here I had the very great satisfaction of learning accidentally from the schoolmaster that Sir John Richardson had reached Lake Superior on his homeward route. This cheering intelligence had appeared in the *Times* of that morning. He had not been heard of for more than twelve months, and I well knew the happiness this intelligence would convey to all at Haslar. We spent two days most agreeably with our kind friends at Headingley, and on Thursday evening reached Rugby, where I found a letter from Mary, who had received a telegraphic despatch from the Admiralty with the joyful news. Next day she met me with a light heart in London, and we remained with our good friend Dr. Boott till we left town on Tuesday the 30th of October for Haslar. On the

Sunday I went to hear Mr. Gurney preach in Marylebone, called for Madame Mohl at Mrs. Reid's, and drove to see our excellent old friends, the Miss Baillies, at Hampstead. Miss Joanna told us her sister was ninety, herself, I believe being eighty-six, and both still enjoying life with thankfulness. We dined that day with dear Mrs. Taylor, and on the next I went with Dr. Boott to see the Nineveh marbles at the British Museum, and the model lodging-houses for the poor near St. Giles. That district looked more dirty and unwholesome than any of the wynds in Edinburgh, and the cholera had prevailed there to a frightful degree, while out of fourteen hundred inhabitants of the model lodgings in its neighbourhood there had not been one case.

On our reaching Haslar the little boys clung round their mamma's neck with such eagerness that they fairly brought her to the ground on the threshold of her own door.

On Monday, the 5th of November, Mary had a telegraphic despatch that the *Hibernia* had reached Liverpool. It was Sir John's birthday, and we had hoped he might have spent it with us, but he did not reach London till Tuesday night. Next day he had to report himself at the Admiralty, where he was detained some hours, and where he met with Sir James Ross, who had appeared there that day on his return from the Arctic Expedition. Of course we were all on the *qui vive* as the hour of the arrival of the train approached, and at eight o'clock on the 8th of November Sir John was joyfully received at his happy home. We all thought him looking better and younger than when he went away. There never were more heartfelt prayers of thankfulness than those he read to his family *that* night.

[*Part of letter to Mrs. Arnold, Fox How, from
Mrs. Fletcher.*

"HASLAR, *Nov.* 8, 1849.

" Some hours' detention at the Admiralty makes us doubtful
whether our dear traveller may reach his happy home till to-
morrow. In the meantime I begin a letter to you, which I
shall leave open till I can tell you he is actually under his own
roof. The lively sympathy Mary meets with from all her
neighbours and friends here is really most delightful. Sir
John Richardson has been prayed for by name in the parish
church at Alverstoke during the whole of his perilous travel
by land and water ; and the warm-heartedness expressed on
all occasions by his sailor shipmates and brother officers here
makes one really think there is a freshness of feeling in the
sailor's heart that is not to be found in the same degree
among landsmen.

" How glad we are, dear friend, to hear of your delightful
letters from all your absent sons ; but your dear William is
my hero now, and you know I am much addicted to hero-worship. There is not any one to whom I have mentioned the
voluntary labour of the young soldier in the work of education that has not been struck with this energetic trait of his
father's son.'

" A telegram has just come from the Admiralty to say that
Sir John *may* be here to-night.

" I write with many joyful interruptions from friends coming
in with hearty congratulations. Good news circulates through
Haslar with telegraphic speed."

To Mrs. Boott, from Mrs. Fletcher.

"HASLAR, *November* 10*th*, 1849.

" Before I rise I must indulge myself in thanking you for
the sweet note I received from you yesterday. I do not know
a holier or happier feeling than that of gratitude towards those
we love and honour. Both Mary and I left your house with
that delightful feeling. Our traveller arrived by the late train
on Wednesday night. I had my pen in hand to tell you the

good news yesterday, but was interrupted before the post-horn sounded. He came in while his children were dancing to the tune of—

'There's nae luck about the house,'

and you may believe his entrance did not spoil our mirth, though it gave it a more subdued and quiet character. He is, thank God, in perfect health ; nor could we extort from him a single complaint of the hardships and privations he has suffered."

"HASLAR, *January 30th*, 1850.

"MY DEAR MRS. BURGE,—I have wished to write to you, but had not courage to enter on the subject uppermost in my mind—the dreadful loss your dear brother and all of you have met with in the death of dear Mrs. Alison. She was a rare creature, a very gifted woman. I always admired but never knew her well till after Dr. Alison's publication of his pamphlet about the poor, in the year 1840. I saw how very deeply her heart was in *that* work, and how she was affected by the moral effect it produced ; for it was truly a revelation of the condition of humanity which no one had previously believed in or suspected; it led to great results, and she lived in the deep interests her husband had roused in the thinking part of the community. She said she 'was a proud woman in seeing his labours so appreciated.' Then came his illness; and the fine spirit that had been so elated was severely stricken, but not crushed ; her sensibilities were so acute that she suffered more from anxiety than most others equally attached would have done. I cannot regret she took that last journey to England, because she did it for *his* sake, and the pulmonary complaint was too deeply fixed to be curable. We were much comforted to hear how calmly and how like a Christian your brother bears his great affliction. Pray offer him our kindest and most respectful sympathy. Within the last few days I have lost another friend whom I most sincerely lament—Lord Jeffrey. I cannot now think of Edinburgh without Mrs. Alison and Lord Jeffrey without a depression of spirit which I thought nothing less than a family bereavement would have occasioned.

"My old age is cheered by the great happiness I see in this household. Since the return of my excellent son-in-law, Mary is one of the happiest of women. I never saw a mind more finely balanced than Sir John's ; with all the enthusiasm that led him, on a principle of duty and affection, to undertake his arduous expedition, he has the kindest, gentlest heart, and the most sweet and cheerful temper, with a fund of information. I hope to remain here till the first week in March, after which I intend, please God, to join the Davys for six weeks in London."

From Mrs. Fletcher to Mrs. Davy.

"HASLAR, 1*st February* 1850.

"The death of Lord Jeffrey is indeed a mournful event to me. Though so little in advance of him in years, I had always considered him a young man, young in the vigorous powers of his mind, and young in the gentleness and kindness of his heart—this last quality had been gaining strength by the exercise of home affections ; and it is impossible to have seen him with his grandchildren climbing on his knee without loving ,the affectionateness of his disposition as much as one always admired the brilliancy of his talents. If I, who have for many years seen so little of him, feel the sadness of this stroke, what must it be to his home and 'inner circle,' as he used to call that of his familiar friends. It is about fifty years since I first met him at James Grahame's ; brilliancy in conversation was then his great attraction, and flippancy his great defect. It was probably the secret ambition of those who conversed with him that made them afraid of him ; I know this from experience. He delighted in checking aspiring or ambitious women, as he used to call Mrs. Millar and me—'women that *would* plague him with rational conversation '—and for many years of our early acquaintance I feared more than I liked him. Just in proportion as I aspired less, I gained more of his esteem and respect ; and latterly there was, as you know, a perfectly friendly feeling tacitly established between us. The country owes him and his coadjutors a vast debt of gratitude for their fearless and noble advocacy of civil and political freedom in the great questions of liberty of conscience, freedom of the press, general education, abolition of exclusive privileges, abolition of the slave-trade, and a hundred other subjects, where the emancipation of the public mind from the trammels of slavish prejudice may be traced to the influence of the *Edinburgh Review*.

" I believe Jeffrey was a happier man in his age than in his youth, though I could not help thinking, at the time I saw him borne on the shoulders of the people when he was chosen member for Edinburgh in the winter of 1832, that that was the most splendid conjuncture of his fate. Many were the glad tears that were shed on that occasion, when the triumph of the good cause he had so bravely advocated was attested by the people's choice. He took it all so calmly ; and he became a humbler and therefore a greater man the more he was distinguished. I shall never forget the last earnest conversation I had with him, after having heard on all sides on our return to Edinburgh of his unequalled reputation as a Judge. I said, ' I rejoice, Lord Jeffrey, to have lived to know that the Court of Session possesses the confidence of the country.' He answered with great animation, ' Yes, Mrs. Fletcher, but if it had not been for *the indomitable courage* of your husband, in the worst of times, when he and one or two more maintained the independence of the Bar, we younger men would have been trampled on and the Court of Session would never have enjoyed the confidence of the country.' I have registered this saying of Lord Jeffrey in my heart of hearts, and I would have you engraft it on that of your children."]

March 1850.—We spent a very agreeable evening at Mr. Wedgwood's, where we met Sir Robert Inglis, who recognised me as an old Edinburgh acquaintance, and Madame Pulzky, the charming wife of a Hungarian patriot, who had been the secretary of the distinguished Kossuth. He had sacrificed immense possessions in this noble cause, and this heroic woman had followed him into exile. Her father, a rich banker at Vienna, furnished them with the means of living in very humble lodgings, and yet not a regret or complaint escaped her. She had with difficulty avoided the horrors of captivity in an Austrian prison with her three little boys. Their flight was arranged and

accomplished by the courage of a gentleman who acted as her husband's principal steward, and who attended them in the assumed character of a common servant. Madame Pulzky is a very attractive person, very pretty, and combining much intelligence and energy of character with the most engaging gentleness of manners. We became well acquainted, and saw her often.

At dear Mary's earnest desire I sat for my picture to Mr. Richmond, a most agreeable man and very distinguished artist. We met him at Mr. Gurney's, at whose house we spent a delightful evening at dinner.

We dined also one day at Lady Davy's. She called one morning and politely asked me whom I should like best to meet. I said, "Rogers the poet," whom I had never seen. "Certainly," she said, "you shall meet him on Wednesday, if you will all come and dine with me." She kindly brought him, however, next day to call upon me, and I found Mr. Rogers most courteous, lively, and conversable. But a day or two after he was seized with a fit of the gout; so Lady Davy said, to console me for the disappointment, she had asked Lord Lansdowne to meet us. I sat next the Lord President of the Council, whom I remembered in Edinburgh above fifty years before, when he was Lord Henry Petty, and lived with Dugald Stewart. He had the greatest reverence for that excellent man, and spoke of his Edinburgh life and of his friends Horner, Jeffrey, and Playfair, with much interest and kind-heartedness.

I had the honour of a call from Mr. Cobden and his agreeable wife, brought by a very pleasing friend of Mrs. Gaskell, Mrs. Schwabe, who had eagerly sought Mrs. Gaskell's acquaintance after reading "Mary Barton."

The last day we spent in London was one of the busiest. I went to take my last sitting at Mr. Richmond's, from thence to call on the Dowager Lady Grey; found her mind as active in benevolent pursuits and as acute as ever, and was much interested in the wide circle of her philanthropic interests. She is a wonderful person of eighty-five. From her house we drove to Lambeth Palace, a striking old building.

April 1850.—We reached Lesketh How on the 8th, and heard distressing accounts of Mr. Wordsworth's dangerous state. He continued to sink daily, and died on the 23d of April 1850, about three weeks after he completed his eightieth year. Although no one had expected his recovery for several weeks, it is not easy to describe the mournful feeling his death occasioned. It was a personal loss; every one who had enjoyed his society and friendship felt there was much taken out of life that was most worth living for. To himself it was a blessed change, for his grief for the loss of Dora, his only daughter, was incurable; and though his devoted wife had lost everything that made life precious when she lost him, yet such was the unselfishness of her love towards him that I verily believe she was thankful he had not been left to be the survivor. She watched by him day and night, and saw him laid in his grave on Saturday, the 27th of April, in Grasmere churchyard.

[*From Mrs. Fletcher to her daughter Mary.*

"*April* 26, 1850.

" Mrs. Davy had a message by James Dixon to say if she and Dr. Davy wished to see the remains they might go to Rydal Mount. They went accordingly. Dr. D. advised me not to go, he thought I might be too much excited. They were both much struck by the likeness of the countenance, in the deep repose of death, to that of Dante. The expression was much more feminine than it had been in life—very like his sister. She bears this sad loss with unexpected calmness. She is drawn about as usual in her chair. She was heard to say, as she passed the door where the body lay, ' O death, where is thy sting? O grave, where is thy victory?' Dear Mrs. Wordsworth has all the earthly support she can have ; her two sons are with her, and heavenly support is mercifully given her. She is able in calm resignation to occupy herself with household duties much as usual. The funeral is to take place to-morrow. It has, as you truly say, been a great privilege to have seen this great and good man so nearly. I think it may be said of him ' that he did justly, loved mercy, and walked humbly with his God.' The funeral is to be very private— only Dr. Davy invited from this house. Margaret, the girls, and I intend to drive to Grasmere an hour before, to Mr. Jefferies', and we shall go into the church before it arrives."

To the Same.

"*1st May* 1850.

" Did I not, dear child, give you a detailed account of the funeral? If I did not, it must have been from the impression that Margaret had done so, when we returned from that mournful scene. We met Mr. and Mrs. Barker[1] on the way to Grasmere Church. They only heard of our great poet's death as they came the day before, and could not resist the desire to pay this last tribute of respect to his memory.

"The same simultaneous feeling filled the old church of Grasmere with unbidden but most sure mourners. When Mrs. Wordsworth, supported by her two sons, followed the coffin into the church, I should not have recognised her figure, it was so bowed down with grief ; but she bore it calmly, and I stood opposite to her when she bent over the grave. When she was seated in the carriage on leaving the churchyard, Mr. Quillinan told us they feared she would have fainted. She did not, however, and after she returned home she resumed such firmness and composure that she joined them at tea, and made it for them.

" Every Grasmere face you know of the upper grade was at the funeral, but I was sorry not to see any of the peasantry, he was so peculiarly the poor man's friend. James Fleming was there, and the Greens. I had intended to go on that day to Lancrigg, but really, after the solemn scene in Grasmere

---

[1] Present Bishop of Sydney, and his wife.

churchyard, I could not give my mind to household cares and troubles, so we returned straight to Lesketh How and passed the evening quietly.　I slept little that night, and in the morning I put into measured lines the thoughts that had kept me waking, which one of the girls is to copy for you."]

THOUGHTS ON LEAVING GRASMERE CHURCHYARD, APRIL 27, 1850,
AFTER THE FUNERAL OF WILLIAM WORDSWORTH.

WE saw him laid within the quiet grave,
Near to the yew he planted.　'Twas a day
Of most rare brightness, and the little birds
Sang no sad requiem o'er the hallowed spot :
'Twas as they welcomed him to his last home.
All Nature glowed instinct with tender love
For him, her fervent worshipper, no more
To chant her praises 'mid her mountain wilds,
Her streams and valleys, " vocal thro' his song."
There lives not one whose pilgrimage on earth
Has been more blest, by God's especial grace,
In stirring Heaven-ward thoughts in fellow-men.
His was no narrow creed ; he loved mankind
Because God's law is love ; and many hearts
In loneliness and grief have felt his power
Work like a charm within them, lifting high
Their thoughts from earthly aims and sordid cares
To life's great purpose for the world to come.
Sweet was the privilege of those who shared
His daily converse, marked his blameless course,
And learned the true philosophy of life
Under his teaching, simple, but sublime.
Peace to his honoured memory ; peace to those
Who cherish fervently within their souls
The beautiful realities he taught.

[*Letter from J. Baillie.*

" MY DEAR MRS. FLETCHER,—Your Thoughts on Leaving Grasmere Churchyard are so touching and so just that I cannot delay one moment expressing my sympathy.　They do indeed express the peculiar worth, simplicity, and wisdom of the man, and nobody will pass through that place of graves without feeling it deeply. William Wordsworth taught much in his own peculiar way, and we were not quite aware how much and how effectually he taught till his noble lesson was nearly drawing to a close.

" Many thanks to you for sending us a copy of these lines, and for letting us know how his excellent wife, Mrs. Wordsworth, bears up under her severe affliction. She was a mate worthy of him or any man, and his sister too, such a devoted, noble being as scarcely any other man ever possessed. . . .

" To have a grandson and *his* son returning from India on a three years' furlough is indeed an uncommon event. May this great-grandchild arrive in safety and be a blessing to you all ! The boy will think his great-granddame a young beauty if you look as well on his arrival as when I saw you last. . . .

" The air is mild and delightful on our hill, and we breathe it with thankfulness, though in the course of nature we cannot expect, and should not desire, to breathe it long.

" With all kind wishes to yourself and your distinguished family, I remain, my dear Mrs. Fletcher, affectionately yours,

" J. BAILLIE.

" HAMPSTEAD, *Tuesday Morning, June 11th,* [1850.]"

The following letter, addressed to Harriet Martineau, on the subject of Somerset, the Negro boy, was written about this period, and was, I believe, inserted at Miss Martineau's desire, in some Anti-slavery periodical either here or in America :—

Mrs. Fletcher to Harriet Martineau.

" LANCRIGG, 1850.

" DEAR MISS MARTINEAU,—It has been said that the noblest act of the British Parliament was that which gave twenty millions of British gold to purchase the freedom of eighty thousand slaves in the British colonies. I think it was a still nobler act of national justice and humanity when in the case of Somerset, in May 1772, it was decided by the verdict of a London jury that the moment a slave set foot on English ground he was free !

"In the summer of 1807, when I resided with my family in Northumberland, I had the good fortune to meet with an intelligent old lady, Mrs. Judith Sharp, the sister of Granville Sharp. She gave me many interesting anecdotes of her brother. Though descended from an old family in the county of Northumberland, Mr. Sharp was himself a shopkeeper in Cheapside. In one of his early morning walks in the suburbs of London, he met a poor negro boy; and observing that his head was bound with a bloody handkerchief, he asked what accident had befallen him. The boy simply said, 'It was Massa did it.' On questioning him further, Mr. Sharp learned that the poor slave had been sent as a present from a slaveholder in Jamaica to his brother, a merchant in London, and that this London slaveholder had, in a moment of brutal anger, struck the boy a desperate blow on the head with some sharp instrument. The boy ran away, and had been some days begging in the streets, having no one to protect or take care of him. Mr. Sharp took him to the nearest hospital, had his wounds examined and dressed, left him under medical care for some days, and when all danger from the wounds was over, he took him to his own home, and bade him remain in his service, at the same time acquainting his former master where he was to be found. The ruffian claimed him as his property. This was exactly what Mr. Sharp wished. He defended the negro's right to freedom before a jury in Westminster Hall; and Lord Mansfield had the honour to record there the immortal verdict which became from that day the law of England. Not many days after that great event was known throughout all London, Mrs. Judith Sharp told me a lady was sitting in her balcony overlooking the Thames between London Bridge and the West India Docks; she saw a small vessel hurrying towards these docks, and heard a piercing cry, and the name of 'Granville Sharp! Granville Sharp!' loudly shrieked as the vessel passed rapidly below her balcony. It instantly struck her—'This must be a kidnapped negro;' and, without a moment's delay, this energetic woman went straight to the Lord Mayor, made an affidavit of what she had seen and heard, and obtained a warrant to search every vessel in the West India Docks for him who had cried so loudly on Granville Sharp for mercy. After some hours' search, a young negro was found concealed under an empty hogshead, his hands and feet tied together, and his mouth bandaged. This victim of avarice and cruelty was instantly liberated by that glorious verdict of a London jury.

"Oh that America would learn this lesson before it is too late to avert a servile war—that she would learn to 'be just and fear not.' Had George Washington lived in our days, his magnanimous spirit would have taken the side of Negro Emancipation as fearlessly as he did that of American Independence. He did not live up to that period of social progress which some of the enlightened Americans of the Northern States have now reached. In his day, the mother country, who boasted herself free, was not ashamed to carry on the slave-trade, and to curse her possessions in the Southern States of America by leaving them the legacy of that most foul and impious traffic. But a greater than Washington will yet arise in America, a man capable of making a great personal sacrifice of property in human beings, one that will not only plead the Negroes' cause in Congress, but will risk all personal consequences, and will hold out the right hand of fellowship to such a noble effort of humanity and justice. Such a day, I trust, is not far distant in America, when Mrs. Chapman, you, and many others, who have laboured in this most righteous cause, will find their reward in its accomplishment. —I am, dear Miss Martineau, truly and respectfully yours,

" Eliza Fletcher."]

I remained with my friends at Lesketh How till the 4th of May 1850, on which day Margaret came with me to Lancrigg and remained with me some days, leaving Grace and Sissy alternately to be my companions before Mary and Sir John, Josephine, and little Edward, arrived. It was a happy arrival; Mary's cheerful countenance denoted a heart at ease, and Sir John and Josephine expressed cordial admiration of Lancrigg. Mary and he employed themselves actively in thinning the shrubberies a few days after they came. Josephine and Eddy explored their favourite copses, and Lancrigg was a scene of much enjoyment to us all.   When, after three weeks, Sir John's leave of absence expired, he returned to Haslar with Josephine, and Mary and I had some weeks of *tête-à-tête.*

[A large family gathering assembled at Lancrigg during the summer of 1850.   The party from India arrived there on the 11th August, her eldest grandson George Fletcher, his wife and child.   It was then our mother first saw her little great-grandson Miles Angus.   She says of him at the time, "Dear little Miles is the handsomest and most sweet-tempered and engaging child of his age I have ever seen."   After we returned to Haslar our mother had a pleasant little visit from Alfred Tennyson, who spent that summer with his wife at Tent Lodge, Coniston.   His visit was much appreciated by all at Lancrigg.

From Mrs. Fletcher to her daughter Mary.

" *October* 16*th,* 1850.

" We were so fortunate as to meet our little postman Dove at the Town End yesterday, on our way to Coniston, and got from him your delightful packet.   Pray give Sir John my best thanks for his share of it.   Mr. James Marshall read it aloud to the pleasant coterie round the fireside at his own house, Lord Monteagle being an earnest listener, as well as Aubrey de Vere.   The party at the Marshalls' were, Lord and Lady Monteagle, Lady de Vere and her agreeable son Aubrey, with whose travels in Greece we have lately been much delighted.

" Lord Monteagle is very animated and pleasant, and has much Irish humour.   He spoke with enthusiasm of the wonderful energy of Mrs. Chisholm, through whose individual exertions no less than 15,000 emigrants, chiefly Irish, have been sent to Australia, and once when she was accompanying about 1500 Irish emigrants through a narrow defile, up the country, she was told there was a fight begun between the Connaughtmen and the Tipperary boys, and that they blocked up the way, on which she speedily rode onward and told them, they should not fight there, but if they *must* fight, they should climb the mountain and descend into the plain below and fight out their battle, as they would have room enough without obstructing their neighbours. They were heartily ashamed of themselves, and cheered their commander with a hearty cheer.

"We were very sorry to find Mr. and Mrs. Tennyson had left Tent Lodge on Monday, as I hoped to see them again. I like to hear her talk of your husband, which she does *con amore.*

"I like 'In Memoriam' better the more I read it, but I want you beside me very much when I do."

From Lord Cockburn to Mrs. Fletcher.

"EDINBURGH, *November* 1850.

"MY DEAR MRS. FLETCHER,—I am very sensible of your kindness; I am not just so strong as I was, but am getting rapidly better. The Life is, so far as scheming and preparing are concerned, advancing, but nothing has yet been done in the way of actual writing, or indeed could have been done, but I do hope to finish some Memoir of Jeffrey and his times which may not be unworthy of either.

"The Scotch bull is expected to be roaring in a few days. Our Calvinistic souls are to be put under the charge of seven Bishops. Sawney will make a terrible uproar, because Bishops, no matter of what sort, are hereditarily odious to him. It was they who squeezed his thumbs and his legs a few years ago. Whatever the law or the policy may be, it is an unfortunate occurrence. It will revive sectarian hatreds and increase the difficulties of general education. But on these matters the human mind has not advanced one inch during the last five hundred years, and considering the nature of that mind it may be doubted if it will advance one inch in the next five hundred years.—Yours very faithfully,

"H. COCKBURN."

Lesketh How, 1st January 1851.—How many mercies have I experienced since last New Year's Day! Oh that I were sufficiently thankful for God's loving-kindness towards me in all His dispensations! I will not say the last year has been *without* its trials, troubles, and disappointments, for who can expect to escape from them?

8th March 1851.—It will be a fortnight to-morrow since Mrs. Joanna Baillie died, at the age of eighty-nine. It is just fifty years this summer since Miss Millar introduced me to the pleasure and privilege of her acquaintance. She was truly a woman of genius, original in her conceptions, full of brilliant imagination, elevation of mind, and turn for humour. Her taste was simple, and her affections strong and tender, with most unaffected and unpretending manners. She was much sought by the literary, the fashionable, and the learned world, and could count on her list of friends all the distinguished writers of the age in which she lived, yet she was perfectly unspoiled by the homage paid her, and loved her. old friends with unchangeable affection. She died peacefully after a few hours' illness—Sunday the 23d of February. It is a satisfaction to me that Angus, being in London at the time, was allowed by her nephew, William Baillie, to take a cast from her face after death, so that the lineaments of her fine countenance may be preserved in marble. Angus has been superintending another work of art, a medallion of Wordsworth, to be executed by Mr. Woolner, and placed in Grasmere Church; thus he has the privilege of assisting to perpetuate the memory of two great poets.

Lancrigg, 25th August 1851.—Some old friends have taken us on their way to the Crystal Palace. Among these were Mr. and Mrs. John Mylne and their two nice little girls. Mrs. Mylne read me a review she had written some years ago on the subject of female education. It. is remarkably able, and I know few women who could have written it. Then we had the pleasure of Mrs. Stirling's delightful society for two or three days. There is a freshness and animation, an originality and gentle-heartedness about her that is most engaging. Our next beloved guest was dear Catherine Hughes, who, I verily believe, loves me like a daughter, and I feel her as such, more than any one out of my own family.

On the 13th of September 1851, Mrs. Taylor, her daughter, and I, set off on our Scottish expedition. To see my venerable friend Miss Millar once more in her own house, was one of the principal objects of my journey, and to attend Henry Fletcher's wedding was another. After I left Milheugh on the 19th, I reached Doune, where, at Old Newton, kind good Miss MacNab had provided everything for our comfort. The profound quietness, the pure dry air, and lovely scenery, have agreed with me so well that I feel much better than when I set out.

On the 1st of October we paid a most agreeable visit to our friends, the Miss Spiers', at Laurel Hill. There we found six amiable sisters living in the most perfect domestic harmony, and occupied in doing good.

On the 6th of October we left Old Newton, and reached Edinburgh, where, after gliding swiftly under the Castle rock and through the Mound, we found Henry Fletcher and Charlotte Monro waiting for us. Mrs. Taylor had parted from us at Dunblane, preferring a lonely sketching tour in the Highlands to our wedding festivities. I was affectionately received at 35 Heriot Row, and saved from fatigue by the watchful kindness of our friends there.

On Saturday I went with Angus to pay visits, not to the living, but to the family burial-place on the Calton Hill, where so many dear to us were laid at rest, and from thence to see the spot where our little darlings, Humphry and John Miles Davy, were laid in one grave. On Sunday evening Mrs. Stirling went with me to see the grave of Jeffrey. Nobody entered so entirely into my

Italian sympathies as Mrs. Stirling. She is delightfully agreeable.

On Tuesday came the marriage. Dr. Alison kindly sent his carriage to take me to St. John's. There was a large party of Charlotte Monro's family and friends. Henry had only his old grandmother in her white silk bonnet, his uncle Angus, brother George, and cousin Mary. The much-beloved Dean Ramsay, long the friend and pastor of the bride, officiated on this happy occasion. The bride was becomingly dressed, and looked well; dear Henry very interesting in the calm happiness of his deportment.

My farewell visit to Edinburgh was not blemished by one dark spot or painful recollection. I had seen many valued friends for the last time; all very, very kind, some very affectionate. I had the happiness to see Mrs. Burge and her incomparable niece, once more in their former happy home, and of infinite value to Dr. Alison.

I stayed a few days to rest at Lesketh, and on the 8th of November set off with Mrs. Davy *en route* for Haslar. Most kindly received at Headingley Parsonage; stayed there all Sunday, and reached Mr. and Mrs. W. E. Forster's, near Bradford, by four o'clock; admired the views from Rawdon, but still more the domestic peace and happiness that prevail in. that happy home. Next day we went to Manchester, dined with our delightful friend Mrs. Gaskell, with whom Margaret, Angus, and I took up our quarters; and we went to a great Hungarian meeting that same day at five o'clock; it was held in the Free Trade Hall, and there were seven thousand persons present. Kossuth, the great Hungarian patriot, was hailed by universal acclamation. After a speech from the chairman, and a much better one from Mr. Bright, Kossuth rose, and with extraordinary eloquence, notwithstanding

his foreign accent and idiom, he delighted the audience
with a clear, straightforward statement of the wrongs that
Hungary has endured from the House of Hapsburg, and of
its determination to shake off the yoke, if England and
America, by peaceful intervention, would stop the encroach-
ments of Russian and Austrian despotism. Kossuth's
appearance is very interesting; he is not above the middle
size, slender in person, but dignified in deportment, his
countenance highly intellectual, the expression mild and
firm, that of a man of genius. I sat there five hours, but
when his speech was finished we left the meeting, and it
seemed that my *extreme old age* served me in place of rank,
so little was I annoyed by any pressure of the crowd, who
considerately made way for me. It was delightful to
witness the interest the masses in this great town of
Manchester took, in the foreign politics of this great man,
and it is only under the government of so much beloved
a Sovereign as Queen Victoria, with a Liberal Cabinet and
a reformed House of Commons, that such a meeting could
be held with perfect safety, though Kossuth did not utter
a sentiment to which a constitutional Englishman might
not respond with perfect loyalty. In the days of George
the Fourth, when great discontent with the Government
and disaffection to the personal character of the Sovereign
prevailed, it would scarcely have been safe.

At Mrs. Gaskell's we had the great pleasure next day
at breakfast of meeting Thomas Wright, a philanthropist
of no ordinary cast of mind, profoundly pious and humble-
minded, with the most energetic devotion to the principle
of doing good. He devotes every hour he can spare from
his employment, that of overseer of an iron-foundry, to
visiting the prison, and doing all he can to reclaim convicts
from their evil ways. He has been the means, under God's
grace, of reclaiming more than four hundred, and is so self-

denied that he seldom allows himself more than four hours out of the twenty-four for sleep.. He is a hale man at sixty-six years of age.

On arriving in London I had the happiness to meet Mary from Haslar, and we had both the very great pleasure of finding Gracilla Boddington in the same hotel. She came to us the next morning when Mazzini was with us, and was much struck, as I had been formerly, with the likeness of his countenance to the St. Francis of Guido.

[*From M. R.'s Note-book.*

November 16th, 1851.

I had not seen Mazzini for several years until yesterday, and was never more struck with the increase of happiness resulting from having proved himself a man of action as well as a man of thought. The melancholy grace, the sickness of the heart, the indescribable look of suffering for others which had struck me so much six years ago, had disappeared, and he is now a man full of experience, patience, and hope, one fitted to inspire that confidence which he himself feels, and infuse life and hope into his country. The treachery of France to the cause of the people has unfortunately thrown him more than he himself desires into association with the party of Ledru Rollin, of whose character he has no high opinion, *un grand gamin*, easily led to good or evil by the impulse of the moment. He did not deny the position advanced by Dr. Boott, that a popular movement in France was likely to lead to the most frightful excesses, that the feelings of the employed against their employers were most ferocious and bloody ; but it is evident that he feels and knows that things cannot go. on in France as they are now doing, and he said, " We a little trust in Providence that more good will come out of the evil than we can at present perceive. There is indeed no one man in France to meet its wants, but I hope some man will appear to appeal to what is good, and save her from what we all so much dread.' He mentioned two men in whom he had some hope. One was

Carnot. He knew all the leaders of the Republican party, but had no confidence in any one but Ledru Rollin with regard to Italy. In speaking of him, Mazzini mentioned various little traits which we should call very French, when one considers the amount of suffering that must follow even the best revolution. Mazzini said, Ledru Rollin and he were each smoking cigars, with a little dog on the sofa between them ; it showed signs of discomfort. " Poor little dog," said Ledru Rollin, " it suffers, let us put away our cigars." He said he was doing all he could to impress the Frenchman with his own views : " He *is* a Frenchman, and I always feel it, but he is the only hope for Italy out of itself. I do not want the help of France, I only want them to let us alone, and that cannot be accomplished till the troops are withdrawn by a power friendly to us, as a defeat would never be forgiven by the French."

Mazzini has no expectation of the day of Cavaignac or Lamartine coming round again. The first he said justly lost his influence by his unnecessary slaughter of the populace in the insurrection of May 1848. He might have quelled it at once, but he allowed it to go a certain length to do the thing with greater military effect. This they never can forgive. Mazzini gave a shrug of decided hopelessness when Lamartine was mentioned, but he did not deal at all in personal invective, even against the President. His mind seems too full of hope about Italy to admit of gloomy ideas about other countries, and one ought to place one's-self in the Italian, not the French position, when one talks with him. The dungeons of Naples make as strong a case for the necessity of a change with all its attendant horrors as Dr. Boott's Lyons anecdote was felt by him to be a convincing argument for leaving things as they are. Mazzini said Mr. Gladstone's letters had been of much use in this country in rousing the attention of the humane to the real state of things, and he considers Italy already ripe for a change, and spoke, half seriously, half in playfulness, of hoisting his flag on the Quirinal this time next year, and of his hope of seeing my mother there. When Dr. Boott spoke of his power of attaching others to himself, he said, " It is because I trust them. They had been so long told they were a poor, wretched people, fit only to be slaves, that they began to believe it, but I gave them a new life by telling them they were men and brothers." He said a remarkable proof had been given of the attachment of the Roman shopkeepers to him when a great friend of his went there. She could not get any accounts sent to her. He spoke of Kossuth with much interest, said that they had long interviews with each other in London, four or five hours at a time, and that they understood each other completely. He rejoiced in the demonstrations then going on as a new feature in the English life, one which was much required. It is impossible to convey by notes an impression of Mazzini's conversation, so much of his eloquence depends on his look, his attitude, what he says and what he does *not* say, for a great man in full possession of a great subject is often to be quite as much admired for what he does not say as for what he does, and this one feels very much with Mazzini ; rancour and distrust and anger, even against evil, seem to be extinguished in him.]

On the 15th of November 1851 Mary and I reached Haslar, and I have passed two months of great quietness and tranquillity, in the enjoyment of excellent health, receiving the most constant kindness and minute attention to my comfort from dearest Mary and her excellent husband, while Josephine is always my ready and kind amanuensis.

January 1852.—About thirty friends and neighbours were invited to celebrate my eighty-second birthday, on the 15th of this month. Sir John, assisted by Sir Edward Parry, put forth his strength in enacting charades; they had been experienced in this innocent amusement, having, during the long nights of an Arctic winter, often resorted to masquerades and pantomimic exhibitions to divert and cheer the ship's company in their dark and dismal abode amid regions of "thick-ribbed ice." Music and singing intervened between the acts, and after supper Sir Edward Parry prefaced his toast to my health by a very affecting allusion to the many mercies that had been spared to me in my long pilgrimage—such a speech as filled my eyes with tears and my heart with thankfulness.

[*To Mrs. Arnold, from Mrs. Fletcher.*

"HASLAR HOSPITAL, *January* 1852.

"If it pleases God to spare you to complete your eighty-second year, as I have done, you will be surprised, as well as deeply thankful, that you have not been made to feel you have lived too long.

"Dear Margaret told me joyfully you had consented to be one of her birthday guests on the 15th, and your own dear letter of kind congratulations is tied up apart with those of my children and grandchildren ; for you know *you* became one of my children from the time you adopted me as a mother in my short solitude at Bilton in 1829, and you have never since disappointed the claim that adoption gave you to my love and gratitude. . . .

"I dare not trust myself to speak of France, that self-destroyed country. I lost all sympathy with them when they allowed a government chosen by universal suffrage to send an army for the subjugation of Italy. That was an act of unmitigated oppression and injustice. The submission to the *coup-d'état* is an act of national suicide, an utter extinction of all that can elevate or uphold the dignity or worth of man in his political relations. I never was so hopeless of Continental affairs ; but I still trust that British statesmen will take warning, and, by timely extension of safe measures of reform in Parliament, ward off revolutionary dangers. I still put faith in Lord John's honesty of purpose and courage."

To Mrs. Davy, from Mrs. Fletcher.

"HASLAR, *7th January* 1852.

"You will receive this on your fifty-fourth birthday. A blessed day it was to me, and has been till this time. I well remember dear aunty bringing you to me when you were first washed and dressed, saying, 'I have brought you a dark-eyed daughter,' and you opened your large dark eyes, the first that had been seen in our flock, and aunty pronounced you like my mother, from your eyes, and then you first nestled in my bosom, my little dark-eyed daughter. It was a day of thankfulness to God, and such you have made it ever since. May He continue to preserve and bless you for ever and ever!

"We have finished the first volume of Southey's Life and Letters. We like his autobiography, but were disappointed in his letters. Oh how inferior to Cowper's letters! There is a want of the playfulness of youth, and so poetical a mind as his should have betrayed itself in the open confidence of friendship. He was 'so pure in heart' he had nothing to conceal, but he does not seem to have anything to tell but what is passing through his mind in preparation for the press. He overtasked himself as a literary drudge, and in his case above all others you see how unfortunate it was he had no other profession, and made poetry his working machine rather than his delightful recreation. I think some of his political enthusiasm must have been suppressed. It is impossible, feeling so strongly as he did the public interests that occupied minds much less fervid and elevated than his, that he should not have written more eloquently on these subjects to his bosom friends than appears in these letters. I think the prudence and perhaps the prejudices of his biographer has induced him to suppress the political ebullitions of his mind from 1793 to 1800."

To Mrs. Davy.

"HASLAR, *January 17th*, 1852.

". . . I have so much to thank you and my dear oes[1] for, in these packets I received on my birthday, that I know not what to say, except that I received them all with a grateful and thankful heart ; grateful for all your kindness, and thankful that God in sparing me to such a great old age had been merciful in giving me so many affectionate children and grandchildren, and had extended to me the capacity of enjoying the

---

[1] *Oes*, the Scotch name for grandchildren.

many proofs of love and tenderness I am continually receiving from them."

To the Same.

" HASLAR, *February* 1852.

" Yesterday, the day being mild, Josephine and I went to visit Titchfield Castle, the birthplace of the daughter of ' the virtuous Southampton,' Lady Rachel Russell. I sat with the gamekeeper of the Delmé family, an old man of eighty-one, who has been forty-six years in the family of the present owner, Squire Delmé, while Josephine walked about. He was garrulous about the greatness of the Delmés, but when I asked him if he had ever heard of Lady Rachel Russell, he said, ' No ; you see, madam, I don't know Latin, but I have been gamekeeper to the Delmés for near fifty years.'

" He showed us a very accurate model of the ancient castle, two feet long, and told us it was made out of the corks that were drawn from Squire Delmé's cellars by that gentleman's butler, and added with a sigh, ' Oh they were grand cellars ! I knew them well.' He showed us an oak-tree four hundred years old ; saying that painters often came to paint it. We did not get home till four o'clock, when Mary had something warm ready for me, and I went to lie down till six, and was ready to appear at a dinner of doctors. I heard of another castle to go and see, Porchester, a Roman castle *said* to have been constructed by Julius Cæsar at the time of his invasion.

" To Porchester then we must go, must go."

In addition to the castle-hunting described in these letters during this last winter my mother spent at Haslar, we took a day at Winchester and visited the shrine of Jane Austen, with even more interest than that of William of Wickham. We talked over the happy days of reading aloud the delightful novels of Jane Austen, when the author was as little known as that of Waverley, and when some of our party gave our mother the name of Miss Bates, from the favourable view she took of all the human race and the events of the world.]

The month of March was passed very agreeably at

Haslar, Mary and I taking daily drives from twelve till two, never being twice prevented by cold weather. We saw many lambs this month playing in the fields; took a cold dinner with us one day to Midfield; it was a bright day, and we enjoyed it much.

On the 19th of April Mary and I bade adieu to Haslar, and arrived at a late dinner the same day at Peasemore, travelling by railroad through a very interesting country new to us, by Reading, Newbury, etc. We found Henry and his excellent wife in a beautiful cottage, the *beau-idéal* of a curate's abode in its combination of simplicity and elegance. I never saw a happier couple; the absence of vanity and the cultivation of cheerful contentment are the human elements of this happiness, along with the confidence, esteem, and affection that subsist between them. This visit was a real happiness to me, as it afforded a confirmation of my good opinion of, and regard for, both parties.

Sir John Richardson joined us at Lancrigg in May 1852, and employed himself for several hours of every day in directing a labourer to make walks through the south copse, an extension of our rambles I had long wished for, but never could have accomplished it so successfully without his good taste and active engineering. Another field of his judicious improvements was in the high terrace, commanding the most beautiful view of Easedale, till, at the end of nine dry weeks, came deluges of rain, and all outdoor work was interrupted.

On the 12th of August Jane Fletcher and her two children came, she looking delicate, but the children lively and in good health. I never regretted impaired strength and ability for exertion more than in not being able to play more with these dear children. When Mary left me, Mrs. Taylor's watchful attention to my health and comfort never ceased; she scarcely ever left me for half an hour. The extreme heat of the weather for some weeks affected my sleep, but I thank God my many restless hours were without pain or acute suffering; and though I was less disposed for the pleasures of conversation, I enjoyed the visits of many friends this summer. On the 15th of September 1852, James Wilson and his family came to Thorney How. It is refreshing to meet an old friend with unchanged feelings of respect and kindness on both sides. It was also a happiness to us to receive a visit from Henry and Charlotte Fletcher, and while they were with us we collected as many friends and neighbours as we could to hear her sing. On one of these days in September, Sir Edward and Lady Parry, with five more of their party, came to us from Keswick. It was a very enjoyable day, and I had most kindly letters from them both, proving that the pleasure it afforded was reciprocal.

Christmas Day, 1852.—Two months have passed very serenely and cheerfully; I could not have had companions more desirous of promoting my comfort and happiness than Angus and Miss MacNab. She is a most agreeable inmate, as well as an attached and faithful friend.

A short visit from George before his embarkation for India has gladdened my heart, by his affectionate manners towards me and all his relations.

I pray fervently to be more deeply sensible of all the mercies I have experienced during the past year. Sometimes I have a painful feeling of being useless, and a mere cumberer of the earth; but I know this is an ungrateful and unholy feeling, and I always combat it. It is not a meet preparation for "the company of saints made perfect;" it is worldly and selfish. Lord, give me grace to resign myself wholly to Thy will in thankfulness.

[Lord Cockburn to Mrs. Fletcher.

"EDINBURGH, 12*th* March 1852.

" A copy of Jeffrey's Life, which is to be published on Tuesday, leaves this to-morrow morning addressed to you.

" There are some things not in it which you will miss ; but I found it absolutely necessary to confine it to purely personal matter, and there are some things in it which I hope you will like.

"My object has solely been to unfold the character of our late friend, and by doing so, to give the public better reasons for loving him than it had before.

" How little soever may be thought of the first volume, I cannot doubt that the second, written entirely by Jeffrey, must impart undivided delight. If there be better letters in the English language, I have never seen them.

" I wish I had an hour's dialogue with you on the state of the world. The general opinion in this Northern region, deducting Radicals and Tories, is strongly against the new Reform Bill, and seems to all good Whigs to introduce what is practically universal suffrage, and this they think a thing only to be liked by County Tories and Town Radicals.

" A terrible retribution surely awaits, and sooner than they think, the tyrants of the Continent. I, knowing the ever young benevolence of your heart, talk of these things to you, because I know they interest you.

" Farewell. Though absent, be assured of the respect and affection in which you are held by all your Edinburgh friends, by none more sincerely than by me.—Yours faithfully,

" H. COCKBURN."]

ON THE UNION AND COMPANIONSHIP BETWEEN WORDSWORTH AND HIS SISTER, AFTER READING HER GRASMERE JOURNAL.

BY MRS. FLETCHER, AGED EIGHTY-TWO.

IF in thine inmost soul there chance to dwell
Aught of the poetry of human life,
Take thou this book, and with a humble heart
Follow these pilgrims in their joyous walk ;

And mark their high commission,—not to domes
Of pomp Baronial, or gay Fashion's haunts,
Where worldlings gather, but to rural homes,
To cottages and hearths where kindness dwelt,
They bent their way ; and not a gentle breeze
Inhaled in all their wanderings, not a flower
Blooming by hedge-wayside, or mountain rill,
But lent its inspiration, scent, and sound,
Deepening the inward music of their hearts.
She touched the chord and *he* gave forth its tone ;
Without her, he had idly gazed and dreamed
In *Fancy's* region of celestial things ;
But she by sympathy disclosed the might
That slumbered in his soul, and drew it thence,
In richest numbers of subduing power
To soften, harmonize, and soothe mankind ;
Nor less to elevate, and point the way
To Truth Divine,—not with polemic skill,
But sought from Nature and the human heart,
With sacred wisdom from the fount of God.]

June 9th, 1853.—Dear Catherine Hughes came to me
early in April, and remained till the 2d of May.   She
was a most cheerful and affectionate companion, and helped
me greatly in shaping the little garden ; she also exerted
much energy and bodily labour, as well as good taste, in
ornamenting the avenue with primroses, daffodils, and
sundry wild-flowers.

My causes of thankfulness to Almighty God are more
numerous than words can tell, more in number than the
hairs of my head, more unceasing than the breath I draw.
Let my whole remaining life be one hymn of thankfulness,
till I am permitted to join in that blessed privilege in the
life everlasting.

January 2d, 1854.—I have entered upon another year,
the eighty-fourth, of my pilgrimage. I am fully sensible of
all my unworthiness of the least of God's mercies, but the

want of continual praise and thankfulness weighs upon me most. A new cause of rejoicing occurred when, on the 25th of November, I received a letter from the Lord Chancellor (Lord Cranworth) telling me that on the urgent request of Lord Brougham, he had appointed my grandson, the Rev. Henry Fletcher, to the Rectory of North Stoke, near Bath. My first feeling and expression was—Now I see why it has pleased God to prolong my life, that I might live to see dear Henry in a position of independence and usefulness. I was greatly pleased that Lord Brougham had obtained this for Henry, expressly on the ground of the strong claim given by his grandfather's labours in the cause of Reform.

I had likewise, about the same time, the comfort of hearing that Archibald had, through the influence of the Duke of Argyll, been appointed to the post of Lieutenant-Ordinary of the Devonport dockyard, thus placing him on full pay, and in a situation favourable to a married man with a family. Here was another great cause of thankfulness.

[*To Mrs. Fletcher.*

ON HER EIGHTY-FOURTH BIRTHDAY, SUNDAY, JANUARY 15, 1854.

" DEAR venerated Friend, with welcome true,
  With trembling joy, we hail thy natal day,
  Bright with a Sabbath's sanctity, and pay
  To Him, who bids another year renew
  This festival beloved, thanks largely due :
  For not in vain He grants thy lengthen'd stay,
  For which we've fondly pray'd, for which we pray.
  Blessings still crown thee, and thy pathway strew !
  Still through thine eye thy heart sends forth its beams
  Of kindling love, more sacred hour by hour ;
  Still from thy chasten'd zeal, thy mind's young power,
  Thy steadfast faith, a holier virtue streams :

Thus blessing, thus be blest, till thou art given
A birthday and a Sabbath both in heaven !
" R. P. G."

[*Part of a letter to Mrs. Hughes.*

" I don't suppose Dr. Davy thinks there are any alarming symptoms in my present case of influenza ; but, on the very borders of eighty-four, I cannot help feeling that I am walking through 'the valley of the shadow of death.' God be praised, I can say with the Psalmist, ' I will fear no evil, for Thou art with me, Thy rod and Thy staff they comfort me.' Humbly trusting in the mercy of God through my Redeemer, I have no fear of death except the mortal conflict ; but my gracious God, whose goodness and mercy have followed me all the days of my life, will support me in that awful hour. I will trust in Him, whether I live or die, for ever and ever. I am going to rise, and go down to the drawing-room to meet my friends from Lesketh How. E. F.

" *January* 1854."

Letter to Mrs. Arnold.

" LANCRIGG, *January* 1854.

" Yes, dearest Mrs. Arnold, I did rejoice with you in spirit, for all the blessings that surrounded you on New Year's Day. Long may you be the centre and bond of so much family concord and affection. You well deserve to be so.

"I think I told you Angus had given me an animated description of the family party at Fox How, the day you kindly allowed him to join it.

" I heard of you shivering (as you must have done) yesterday, by poor Mary Fisher's grave. I hope you have not suffered by that act of sympathy with Mrs. Wordsworth and of respect for the departed. I long for Dr. Davy to give you leave to come some day in the warm carriage with Margaret. I long to hear all you have to tell me of your dear ones.

" Mary writes to me cheerfully, full of hope that we shall meet once more. God grant it may be so. She is at the post of duty. Mine is to ' stand and wait,' supported by the ' rod and staff,' the sure support of the aged pilgrim.

U

"I had a restless, feverish night, but am better since morning. I can only add love, much love, to the children who are with you, from your affectionate friend of five-and-twenty years' standing.   ELIZA FLETCHER."

From Mazzini, after his Mother's death.

1853 or 1854.

"DEAR MRS. FLETCHER,—It is very late that I acknowledge your kind, affectionate note ; but I acknowledged it then with a grateful heart.   I could not write on the subject of your letter, but every word that came to me from friends in that hour of need did good to me, and is recorded in my soul to be never forgotten.   My mother's death has left a blank in my life that nothing can fill.   She was a warm patriot, shared in my belief, praised my efforts ; and the dream of my individual life was—that of meeting her once more on this earth in the joy of triumph—to be able to tell her, ' You see that we have not been living separate and lonely for an illusion.'   And this dream has vanished ; but if anything can soothe such a grief, it is the soft expression of truefelt sympathy for her and for myself, and of that I have had more than I ever dreamt of deserving.   My own native town, and my second country, England, have become dearer to me since then.   Do not fear that I shall now think less of my own life or embrace desperate schemes of insurrection. I feel my mother as near me as before—more sacred than before ; and I feel bound to avoid everything that she would blame or mourn about ; but even if I had not that feeling watching within me, I would never compromise in an imprudent attempt the progress of my country, and the life of the numbers who would follow me, without calculating the chances of success."

"DEAR MRS. FLETCHER,—Your note to Miss C. and the article of Mr. Greg would make me despair about my ever being able to see England take a correct view of the Italian question.   What practical hopes can you derive from Piedmont enjoying pure constitutional liberty ?   That the example will act on the other Italian provinces ?   There is no need of that. Italy is morally ripe, and the love of nationality is far more powerful in Lombardy, in Rome, and elsewhere, than in Piedmont ; or that the King of Piedmont will set himself one day at the head of the Italian crusade ? *That* is impossible. No king ever will or can initiate a revolutionary movement, exactly for the same reason which makes the ambition of Louis Napoleon shrink from war as soon as its prosecution becomes impossible without a land campaign which would join the nationalities. The king of Piedmont cannot overthrow the tyrant of Naples, much less the Pope. It is only through a popular insurrection that such things can be done. It is only through a national movement that the Italian nation can be founded. Let us, then, continuously work towards such a movement. It is my aim ; the task of my life and of those who side by me. We do not agitate against Piedmont or its king. We endeavour to rouse the nation. But to rally, as you say, around the Piedmontese flag would amount simply to accept inertness as a law, to condemn ourselves to immobility, and to content ourselves with a fragment of Italy. We really cannot ; we want Italian unity ; the king of Piedmont cannot give it to us; we must try, therefore, to conquer it ourselves. It is only *after* a popular national movement that a path for the Sardinian king might open ; it was only *after* the Lombard insurrection that Charles Albert was enabled to march ; he never would have initiated the struggle. That is the true position of the question. Fifty times we have said to all the sections of the Party, ' Adjourn all discussions, and work towards the common aim ; if *you* want the Sardinian monarchy to lead the crusade, let the crusade be. You must *act* before, then claim the help of monarchical Piedmont.' The men who declare the *nation* will spring from the Sardinian monarchy are *tout bonnement* renouncing all hopes and practical schemes. They have broken the unity of the great national party ; they divert the mind of our young people from the simple logical method which they ought to pursue to hopes which prove deceptions. Since 1848, Piedmont has done nothing for the Italian cause. There has not been a single step in advance ; there has only been a dangerous duality established when one single idea was fermenting. The *national* cause would have been better felt and understood had the same level of oppression remained upon *all* the Italian populations. English people cannot understand this ; they believe that a question of *nationality* is solved in the same way as a question of *liberty ;* it is a fundamental error. I have no party feeling, no personal hope or aim, nothing that can overcloud or deviate my mind ; I may, of course, be mistaken, but mine is a matter of deep conviction, and it is impossible for me to modify or alter it. Though sorry that I cannot on this point agree with you, I am glad, my dear friend, that your note has afforded me an opportunity of writing again to you, whom I love and revere more than my silence would indicate. May God prolong your life until the dawning of our national liberty appears ! and remember that you have here a grateful and sincere friend in

" JOSEPH MAZZINI."

In March 1854 I spent a fortnight with dear Margaret at her pleasant How. I continually blessed God to see her walk in His ways, an example to her mother and to all who observe her. Dr. Davy was most kindly attentive to my health. I missed the cheerful faces of the girls; but their amusing letters from Edinburgh, Archibald's weekly reports of his studies and progress at Cambridge, with my precious Mary's letters from Haslar, kept my heart in wholesome exercise. My warm-hearted friend, Catherine Hughes, returned with me to Lancrigg. We can go back with mutual interest over her earliest days to my excellent aunt Dawson's admirable and unselfish character. She was very fond of Catherine.

Sunday, May 7, 1854.—Yesterday Mrs. Davy brought Mrs. Wordsworth to dinner. It is always a pleasure to see the placid old age of dear Mrs. Wordsworth. Hers has been a life of duty, and is now an old age of repose, while her affections are kept in constant exercise by the tender interest she takes in her grandchildren.

Mrs. Arnold has been called away to see her youngest son before his embarkation for Australia. She is a most tender mother and a most faithful friend ; hers is a character in which it is not easy to find a fault. How often have I to repeat that most comprehensive prayer of the Psalmist—"Create in me a clean heart, O God, and renew a right spirit within me," for I am too often " careful and troubled about many things " that are of no importance, while I fear I fail to " keep my heart with all diligence." I am humbled with the consciousness of making small, if any, spiritual progress, while I see my juniors suddenly called to their eternal home. The unexpected death of that truly great and good man, Lord Cockburn, has affected me deeply. His was a righteous life, and " a righteous God loveth righteousness." I am thankful he lived long enough to raise an imperishable monument to the memory of his friend Lord Jeffrey, in doing which his own great talents and love of freedom and goodness are identified with his subject.

[*To Mrs. Hughes.*

"*April* 29th, 1854.

" It would require a much longer scroll than I am able to fill, my dearest Catherine, to tell you how much we miss you, and how often we talk about you, of your animated social qualities, of your affectionate sympathy in all our thoughts and feelings. We like to trace you in all our walks and wanderings, and are sorry you did not stay long enough to see your primrose bed in the avenue in all its glory, for really it has come out much more gaily than you or I gave it credit for. The peony has made little or no progress since you left us this day fortnight. Mary has had only one attack of headache, and I one very bad night, but am now pretty well again, as well as a sad heart will let me, for I received accounts of the death of a dear old friend yesterday—Lord Cockburn. Mr. Fletcher and I always honoured and loved him for the inflexible integrity of his character, and the warmth and bene-volence of his heart. His death will be deeply and widely mourned in Scotland. He has not left his equal behind him. You know he laid me under everlasting obligation by his just and discriminating sketch of Mr. Fletcher's character in his admirable 'Life of Jeffrey.' I have not slept since four this morning, thinking over the many interesting traits of his character, and the noble stand he made against the insolence and oppression of a corrupt faction fifty years ago. He died at seventy-six, in the full possession of his vigorous faculties. I am thankful to have dearest Mary with me when I received the shock of this sudden intelligence. It is a solemn admoni-tion. He was seven years my junior. May God prepare me for the awful summons, come when it may. I know I am not unremembered in your prayers, dear child.—Your truly attached and faithful friend, E. FLETCHER."

June 24th, 1854.—Nearly two months have glided away since I have found time to make an entry in this Journal. After two months of uninterrupted enjoyment during the finest spring weather I ever remember in this country, seeing my dear Mary enjoying her garden and improve in health and cheerfulness, after her anxiety about Edward all winter, she was suddenly called away to attend Beatrice in scarlet-fever, near London. Not called away by her kind and most indulgent husband, for he was him-self attending his sick child, and did not wish Mary to shorten her stay at Lancrigg, but her own sense of duty decided her to exchange the delights of her mountain home for Beatrice's sick-chamber. She was right, and I did not dare to say a word to detain her. She happily found the child convalescent.

It is remarkable how trials come in the very direction where they are most felt. If Sir John Richardson has an inordinate affection, it is in his paternal relation. He has always had not only a father's but a mother's love and

care for his children,—a patient, watchful, tender, and
untiring love and forbearance that few, even kind, fathers
have ; and his faith and patience have been severely tried
by their delicacy of health, and frequently by their alarming illness. All this he has borne with uncomplaining
resignation; the strength of his character is exemplified by
his patient submission to the will of God.

I have been greatly delighted within the last few days
with a speech of old Lord Lyndhurst, which reminded me
of the manly and fervid eloquence of Charles Fox. It was
not merely a declamatory exhibition of patriotic feeling,
but a profound and heartfelt appeal to the highest moral
principles that can actuate the government of nations, an
indignant reprobation of the unprincipled and audacious
attempt of Russia to trample on the freedom and civilisation of Europe.

We have had most pleasing intercourse with Mrs.
Empson. I never saw a more conscientious and devoted
mother, and we all thought her the most unworldly person
we had met with for a long time. No ambitious views for
her children ; that they may be good and happy is her only
aim. She drank tea with us twice, and brought her children with her. It was a great pleasure to me to seek birds'
nests with Frank Jeffrey Empson, a very amiable and intelligent boy ; at ten years old he is well read in Shakespeare.

On the 21st of August I had the very great gratification
to meet Lord John Russell at luncheon at Fox How. This
truly honest and able statesman stopped at Low Wood Inn
with his family, on their way to Scotland, after the fatigues
of the session. Mr. Hodgson heard he was there, and
crossed the lake from Brathay to ask him to address a
meeting on opening a school at Skelwith Bridge. Lord
John cordially accepted the invitation. Mrs. Davy only
heard of this at two o'clock, and despatched her courier,

Mrs. Peel, with the news to us. We had not half done dinner; down went our knives and forks, and up flew William to bring down the horses from The Brow, harness them, and drive with all despatch to Skelwith. We arrived just before Lord John began to speak. He looked at me with something like a look of recognition; but it was forty-four years since I had seen him, when he was a youth in Edinburgh, and used to come sometimes with Mr. Playfair to our evening parties in Castle Street. Hard work has pressed upon him still more than years, and has given him a worn and weary look. He said he believed good teaching to be more important than the number of schools, for as is the schoolmaster so will be the school. He quoted a schoolmaster of great experience, who recommended a spacious playground. "And here," said Lord John, "your pupils have the mountains for their playground." He paid a deserved tribute of respect to the memory of Dr. Arnold, and when afterwards told that his widow was in the room, said, " May I be introduced to her ?" She invited him to luncheon the Monday following, and had the great kindness to ask Margaret and me to meet him. I was gratified to find he had not forgotten our former acquaintance in Edinburgh. He spoke of those days with much interest, of Playfair and Dugald Stewart especially. When I told him Lord Cockburn's son-in-law, Mr. Cleghorn, had lately told me Lord Cockburn had left a historical account of Scotland, in what might be called the reign of terror, his face lighted up with a radiant smile, and he said, "Yes, even Dugald Stewart was afraid," adding, "No man but Cockburn could have done it; we sent for him to consult him about the Reform Bill for Scotland." Lord John is a man of few words, but I did not feel that there was anything of *hauteur* or repulsiveness in his demeanour. There is not a shade of vanity or egotism about him.

[During the winter of 1854-55, it was thought best by all her children, as well as by herself, that our mother should be nearer medical advice during the cold season than she was at Lancrigg, and near those who could more easily reach her from Lesketh How and Fox How.

During the period of the Crimean War she felt most keenly both for the country and individual friends. She had taken a most active part in promoting the association of ladies at Grasmere the preceding winter in aid of the comforts to be sent to the wounded men ; and she was able, by her abounding sympathy, to cheer the anxiety of the young wife of a most deserving soldier, who had come to spend the time of her husband's absence in the Crimea with her father at Grasmere. The husband of this person was then a sergeant, and he distinguished himself so much by conduct and bravery that an officer's commission was offered to him, and a request at the same time from the officers of his regiment that he should remain in it. His grateful wife has often told me since that she does not know how she could have got through that time but for the " dear old lady at Lancrigg." She took all her husband's letters to read to her, and they cried over them together, and much was explained to her about the war. I fear I always felt in this war, as in most others, like old Kaspar—that " what they killed each other for I never could make out." I saw my mother settled at Springfield Lodge, a · good house, nearly opposite the gate at Lesketh How. Before I returned to Haslar her favourite friend Miss MacNab came to spend the winter with her there.]

Springfield Lodge, 10th January 1855.—I have much reason to rejoice at having come to live so near Lesketh How. Springfield has agreed with me in all respects, and I have been cheered within the last ten days by letters telling me of Archibald's appointment to the command of a gunboat in the Black Sea. May he be preserved in the day of battle, and may he be enabled to do his duty, and, if occasion serve, to distinguish himself in his country's service.

I never in my long life remember anything like the national gloom and almost despondency, increased by the accounts of the miserable condition of our brave troops in the Crimea.

[*Part of letter from Mrs. Fletcher to her daughter Mary.*

"SPRINGFIELD, *January* 10*th*, 1855.

" I sit down boiling with indignation against the inhabitants of Portsmouth and its vicinity, for not .giving a more fitting reception to the maimed and mutilated men who came home in the *Himalaya.*

" I have just been reading that article in the *Evening Mail,* describing the shameful neglect these brave men experienced ; and beg you will write, if possible, to contradict such a report of national ingratitude and want of all right feeling, not only in officials but in the whole mass of the people, who ought to have poured out and vied with each other in proving their sense of the strong claim these brave men had upon their sympathy.   I can imagine, though I cannot forgive, the miserable jealousy and little formalities which would prevent naval officials from taking any active part in disembarking military men, otherwise we know dear Sir John would have been foremost to help them, and I wonder you, dearest Mary, were not there ; I am sure your old mother would have gone down to the jetty, in defiance of all military etiquette, to hail these poor fellows."

Sir John Richardson's reply to Mrs. Fletcher.

"*January* 12*th*, 1855.

" I read with much interest your sound and hearty burst of indignation on reading the *Times'* account of the landing of the invalids from the *Himalaya.*   There is more on the same subject in the papers of to-day, and, indeed, such occurrences are, I fear, almost inseparable from war, and from the peculiar organisation of our boasted civilisation.   Boards and bodies are constituted for particular duties, and everything would be deranged, and matters rendered much worse, if their action were interfered with by bystanders.

"I did not hear of it till this morning, and having occasion to be in the dockyard to-day, I inquired about the cause of delay, and learned that the officers of the *Himalaya*, being of the merchant service, had not sent notice of the ship coming into harbour to the Governor of the garrison, from whose office the orders for the landing and directions for fatigue-parties would have issued. Pending the arrival of these the tide was falling, and the draught of water of the *Himalaya* being very great, her officers were desirous of drawing off from the jetty into deeper water, and therefore hurried the sick on shore with their baggage, which had to be inspected by the Custom-house authorities.

"The greater part of the *Himalaya's* passengers were women and children, and the helplessness of the class that accompany the army would scarcely be believed were it not witnessed; cleanliness and order are out of the question, and I can well believe that the deck was filthy beyond description. A merchant seaman, improperly sent on shore in a helpless condition, was hawked about the streets until he found an asylum in the workhouse, where he died next morning. To-day a much larger body of invalids were on board the *Avon*, alongside the wharf. There was no want of proper officers to attend to them, but they were kept judiciously on board until everything was ready, the ship clean within, and the invalids cheerful and content with their treatment. The more helpless had their dinners on board, and were taken to the Army Hospital in omnibuses, cabs, and bearers; while the greater number were directed to sleep on board, and to go next morning to Chatham. The *Sampson* has also brought invalids, and I suppose that now we shall have a continual influx, till between twenty and thirty thousand of our grand army come home disabled by sickness or wounds."

Mrs. Fletcher to her daughter Mary.

"SPRINGFIELD, *February 9th,* 1855.

"I was in hopes your last letter, received yesterday, would have brought the decision of the Admiralty respecting Sir John's appointment. I admire his and your composure about it, and

I am astonished at my own ; for, without feeling less interest
in all that relates to his and your health and happiness, I feel
less occupied about the improved position this office would
afford you than I should have done some years since.   I dare
not hope that this proceeds from my being less worldly-minded,
but I think extreme age has blunted the keenness of my per-
ceptions and desires.

" The late providential event, which surely must paralyse the
whole Russian Empire, while it gives light and hope to the
rest of the world, I hope and pray may be met by the Allies
in a right spirit—I mean in a Christian spirit—a moral and
chivalrous spirit.   Our arch-enemy[1] has been stricken down,
not by the strength of hostile armies, not by the energy or
exertion of political combinations, but by the hand of God
Himself ; and we should not presume on this manifestation of
justice and mercy by proudly demanding more stringent terms
of peace *now* than we should have demanded of the author of
our national calamities.   We should show our sense of this
providential interposition by our moderation and sense of
justice, not by proud defiance, or by any act that can prolong
the unhappy contest in which we are engaged.   I would fain
hope that this event may lead to an armistice, and prevent that
greatest of horrors—the storming of Sebastopol."

The first part of this letter relates to the office just then
vacated by the retirement of Sir William Burnett, Head of the
Medical Department of the Naval service.   Sir John Richardson sent in his claims for the office ; but a junior officer was
appointed, on which my husband, feeling that he retarded the
promotion of those under him at Haslar Hospital, retired from
his active public service,' and henceforth made Lancrigg his
home.   The first summer after his retirement we spent in
Scotland, chiefly in the beautiful neighbourhood of Achray and
the Trossachs, and joined my mother in the beginning of
winter, 1855-56, at Lancrigg.

[1] The Czar Nicholas.

To her daughter Mary.

"I can but write you a line this morning, for you know better than I can tell you how much real sympathy I feel for Sir John and you on this sad occasion, knowing as I do that in the natural grief you both experience in the loss of so very dear an object of tender love, you will bless God for his deliverance from a life of so much suffering, and in the unspeakable blessedness he is now enjoying. 'In my Father's house are many mansions.' His spirit was well fitted to inhabit that nearest to his Saviour, for I think it was the most loving little heart I have ever known.

"This I imagine will be the funeral day. Thank dear Josephine for her note, received yesterday ; it was very sweet and touching. Could not Sir John ask leave to come down with you, if it were but for a week ? I think the change might do him good. I know his entire submission to the will of God, and that you will not leave him till you can do it consistently with your duty. I am well cared for from Lesketh How, but I never more ardently wished to see you. I hope dear Mrs. Kendal will be with you all this sad day. I liked to hear of the primroses coming from the Isle of Wight, from dear Miss Stott, and his father placing them round the little still pale face. May God support and bless you all.

"E. F."]

18th March 1855.—Since my last entry in this journal I have entered on my eighty-sixth year, and have most abundant cause of thankfulness for the many blessings that attend this long pilgrimage—for health of body and mind, and for the most affectionate and tender care I experience from those near and those absent.

Public affairs continue gloomy, and I never remember a time of such painful excitement. Our soldiers and sailors are men of indomitable courage, but we seem to want a Wellington and a Nelson. The compassionate and generous feeling of the country towards the sufferers is beautiful, and the self-devotion of Miss Nightingale and her associates is above all praise, and marks an epoch in the history of our beloved country. Towards our Lady the Queen I have a feeling of profound loyalty; she is both the Queen and the friend of her suffering people.

April 11th.—To-morrow I expect my Mary. She has suffered much since I parted from her in the illness and death of her darling little Edward, whom she had adopted with a true mother's fondness.

[I joined my dear mother at Springfield at the time she expected me, and, while Lancrigg was preparing for us, remained with her there. Mrs. Davy records in her Note-book at this time the following impression of her good looks and spirits before they set off on a little foreign tour on the 25th of April of this spring :—

From Mrs. Davy's Note-book.

"We all ran down to Springfield to have the last words and kisses from dearest Gran.; but so active was her love and sympathy with our outset, that just as we were getting into the carriage, at 12 o'clock, April 25th, she, with aunt Mary, appeared before our door. It was a sweet, genial morning, but Gran.'s face looked more sweet and genial still."

To her daughter Mary, in the Highlands.

"Lancrigg, 1855.

"I had a great treat on Saturday morning, for half an hour. Our dear Mrs. Arnold brought Arthur Stanley to see me. It does one's heart good to see a man devoting all his powers to his Master's service. He is so animated, so agreeable, so unspoiled by his high reputation, so child-like in simplicity, and so vigorous in his conceptions, and candid in his constructions. We had only a few words about Lord John Russell as he was getting into the car. He said 'it was too wide a field to enter upon, that Lord John had committed some mistakes ; but I believe,' he said, 'that you and I shall live to see him again

Prime Minister at the desire of the people.' The car drove off, leaving me this drop of comfort.

"*September* 1855."

Lancrigg, 18th September 1855.—In May it pleased God to bring me through a severe attack of bronchitis, and I am thankful to say I have been in better health since than I was before my illness. The tender attentions I received from all my children made me feel that I had not lived too long.

I made few new acquaintances this summer, but was cheered by the visits of our dear old friend, James Wilson. There is something inexpressibly reviving in the company of one who recalls former happy reminiscences.

October 29th, 1855.—This is my last month of house-keeping. I never liked the details of that vocation, and hence I always enjoyed the freedom and ease of living at an inn. Henceforward Mary's inn at Lancrigg will be my headquarters. Goodness and mercy have followed me all the days of my life. Pray God I may never lose the bless-ing of a thankful spirit, and that all my children, when they lay me in " our grave,"[1] may be thankful that I end my long pilgrimage in peace among them. I trust in the mercy of God that, through the merits of Christ, He will take me to his everlasting kingdom of righteousness when I can no longer be useful or satisfactory to those who love me best on earth.

January 2d, 1856.—It has pleased Almighty God to permit me to live to see another year, and to bless me with more health and contentment of mind than I have experienced for several years past.

March 14th.—Public affairs look most promising in the prospect of peace. How true is that sentence in one of

[1] We chose the spot together, and she always called it " our grave."

the beautiful Collects of our Church's ritual, " The hearts of Kings are in thy rule and governance." The fate of nations is determined by that will which can alone bring good out of evil.

I am rejoicing in George's appointment at Chittagong as a proof of his deserts, and cheered by Sir E. Lyons' excellent report of Archibald's professional character.

August 2d, 1856.—The deep interest I have taken in Lord Cockburn's "Memorials" has been a new era in my existence. This delightful book has refreshed my spirit, improved my health, and, I verily believe, will continue to cheer and lengthen my life.

August 16th.—Our domestic sorrows have been increased by the increasing sufferings of poor Josephine. She affords a remarkable example of patience, employing every waking hour of the day, and even sometimes at midnight, in reading, using her needle, or knitting. She is always cheerful; and once, when I ventured to express sympathy in her sufferings, she gently rebuked me, and, with a placid smile, said, " Yes, but you know whom the Lord loveth He chasteneth." Sir John's great sorrow on her account is supported with manly as well as with Christian resignation. He sits in a room adjoining that which she occupies, and through the open door he can see and hear her while he employs himself in writing a scientific article of considerable research in natural history. He gets books from the British Museum. My dearest Mary neglects no part of her duties to me and the sick-room, and is mercifully supported under her great trials.

[*To Mrs. Arnold.*

"*October* 10*th*, 1856.

" I cannot tell you how much we all enjoyed the pleasure Mr. Stanley's visit gave us yesterday; I only regretted dear

Mary was not here to share it with us.   We accompanied him in
his most interesting Scottish tour, from the venerable site of St.
Andrews and the historical records of the old Covenanters to
the romantic haunts of Burns and the grave of Helen Walker.[1]

"Then his exceeding admiration of Edinburgh, tracing its
real resemblance in national features to the Athens of ancient
Greece; his liberal view of the Scottish Church and Church-
men; and above all, his estimation of the intelligence of the
Scottish peasantry.   All this, given with his own peculiar
earnestness and simplicity of manner, made us exclaim, when
the door closed upon him, 'Well, there is but one Arthur
Stanley in the world.'

"I think much of you, my dear friend, and rejoice that you
will have all your daughters with you to-day."]

October 20th, 1856.—It was judged best for me to go
to Lesketh How as poor Josephine's last days drew near;
so in the beginning of September, after Dr. and Mrs. Davy
had set off on their Highland tour, Mrs. Taylor and I
went to stay with the dear girls.   Josephine died without
a struggle on the evening of the 8th September, and a more
pure, patient, uncomplaining spirit never went to its everlasting home.

[Parts of one or two of my mother's letters to a correspond-
ent in Edinburgh she much valued, of a younger generation,
are inserted here, on a subject near her heart:—

Mrs. Fletcher to Montgomery Bell, Esq.

"June 5th, 1856.

" MY DEAR MR. BELL,—Your kind letter, received this
morning, has anticipated my intention of writing to tell you
how exceedingly I and all my family have been delighted with
Lord Cockburn's 'Memorials.'   On seeing the book advertised, I wrote to Messrs. Black to send me a copy the moment
it was out, and it arrived a few days ago.   I don't know when

---

[1] Jeanie Deans.

I have been so much refreshed and exhilarated as in reading
it.　The passage you transcribe was particularly gratifying to
me ; it is so true and so characteristic of him whom it describes.
Lord Cockburn is, indeed, most happy in the truth of his portraits.　He might have dwelt more fully on the hardships
and difficulties that beset the few Whig members of the Bar
between the years 1791 and 1800. . . . It is a delightful
book ; and since there is no other literary monument of Lord
Cockburn's great ability and integrity, these 'Memorials'
will attest them."

To the Same.

1856.

"The more I reflect on the great public good the late Lord
Cockburn did in his lifetime, and the great value of 'Memorials
of His Time,' lately published, the more strongly I am convinced of the debt due by his countrymen to his memory.
Now, I do not know whether any monument has been or is
likely to be erected to his memory in Edinburgh ; if not, it
occurs to me that with the approbation of his family, it would
be well for the friends of Reform to raise such a sum, by subscription, as would afford an annual prize of a gold medal to
such a scholar of the New Academy (the Institution which
originated with Lord Cockburn) as should write the best Essay
on Constitutional Freedom, or other historical subjects, and be
most approved by the Directors of the Academy, and that such
a prize should be called the Cockburn Medal.　This idea has
haunted me ever since I read the 'Memorials.'

"Your views of the public results of this war delight me
exceedingly—the moral and religious amelioration and social
improvement that may arise out of it.　God grant your hopes
may be prophetic ; I am a willing disciple of your hopeful
school ; to despair of a just cause is to deny a wise and good
Providence.　I do not envy those who can read of our good
Queen reviewing her noble fleet with dry eyes ; it is good for
her children to have heard the cheers of her gallant men at
Spithead."

Lancrigg, 15th January 1857.—It has pleased our most

gracious God to permit me to enter on this eighty-eighth year of my long life in better health, and more freedom from infirmity in mind and body, than is usual at so advanced an age. I have no doubt my life has been prolonged, as I am sure my happiness has been greatly promoted, by the family arrangements that have been made, in my freedom from household cares.

March 12th.—I have passed nearly three months of this new year in surprising health and happiness, feeling the infirmities of my very advanced age, but feeling in a still greater measure the mercy of God in preserving to me my faculties of mental enjoyment in no common degree; feebleness of limbs, and some degree of deafness, remind me of old age, but my heart is I think as young as ever.

April 24th, 1857.—Since my last entry in this Journal I have experienced the greatest anxiety on account of the alarming illness of my dear grandchild, Elizabeth Davy. I had presumptuously hoped that none of those I tenderly love might be called to suffer deeply before I am to be called hence; but our merciful Father has seen fit to give me another trial of faith and patience.

May 24th, 1857.—We saw dear Lizzie the day after her parents and Grace brought her home; so sadly changed was her appearance that I should scarcely have known her. She did not keep her bed entirely for more than a week, but symptoms of rapid consumption appeared, and her strength sank rapidly. There was a great increase of gentleness, lowliness of mind, and great consideration for others : nothing could exceed her humility. Deeply as I felt the loss, and dearly as I loved the sufferer, when I lost all hope of her recovery I was thankful for her release. O Lord, let us not forget all Thy mercies, while we endeavour to bow to Thy chastisements.

October 6th, 1857.—After two months I resume my

Journal.   On the 7th August, Sir John, Mary, and Beatrice, set off for Ireland, paying some pleasant visits in Yorkshire on the way.   Sir John attended the meeting of the British Association, where he met many of his scientific friends, and received an honorary degree from Trinity College, Dublin. Mary was unwilling to go on my account, but I insisted on her doing so, and they have all much enjoyed their tour and cheered me by their letters.   The miserable state of India weighs me down, and dwells upon my mind with fearful terror.   I feel a sad want of faith and hope on that subject, and pray God to give me that "peace which passeth understanding."

[This was the last entry in her Journal, but I had many letters from her on our tour, expressing the warm interest she felt in all we heard and saw, especially in the Reformatory for boys established by her new neighbour and much-esteemed friend, Mr. Wheatley Balme, at whose Yorkshire home we paid a short visit.   We also visited Mr. Brooke and Miss Laycock, near Huddersfield, and saw the distribution of prizes to the young mechanics, given by Lord Granville with an encouraging address.

From Mrs. Fletcher to her daughter Mary.

"*August* 1857.

"I have just read your yesterday's letter, not without tears at your account of the distribution of prizes, especially of that pale-faced young mechanic who had written the best essay on English literature.   That lad, if he lives, will henceforth distinguish himself.   Do get his name and present occupation. Those shouts of sympathetic feeling will never be forgotten by those who gained the prizes, and will be strong incentives to those who strive to gain them in future."

Mrs. Fletcher to Mrs. Stark.

"LANCRIGG, *October 11th,* 1857.

"MY DEAR FRIEND,—Many thanks to you for remembering me amidst your many anxieties and tender sympathies for suffering friends. I feel for them and you most deeply. I see many well-informed people take a less gloomy view of Indian affairs than I do. My only comfort is in the belief that a 'righteous God loveth righteousness,' and that He has power to bring good out of evil. Never was there such a trial of faith and hope as this sad state of India. ·

"My own bodily health is good, and I pray against despondency ; for in my eighty-eighth year I can make little effort. You would not know me, I am so changed in mind and temperament. You will pray for me. All the circumstances of my home are the happiest possible, and I am very grateful for it."

When we returned to Lancrigg, the end of September, we were received with even more than my mother's usual warmth and thankfulness of affection. The weather was very fine, and she sat with me and others a good deal in the open air, and took a lively interest in hearing of the different people we had seen, especially her old friend Mr. Craig and his daughter Sarah, in Tipperary, Dr. Livingstone, then about to return to his great mission in Africa, Lady Parry, whom we had seen in Wicklow, and many others. I had not, however, been long or much alone with my mother before I became aware that the hopeful buoyancy of her spirit was affected in a way I had never before seen it. The excellent maid who always slept in her room told me that she had observed a change in her a few days before our return from Ireland. At the age of eighty-seven it should not have excited any surprise, as the very intensity of her feelings made it more remarkable that the spring of hopefulness had lasted so long, than that it should now in some degree fail. The variety of private sorrows and public troubles, in which she had taken so deep an interest, during the last years of her life, doubtless did contribute to the end which was approaching. We could not but feel "that the silver cord of her existence *was* loosed, that the golden bowl *was* broken," although we never lost the hope of her revival until the middle of January. After that her bodily weakness increased; she kept chiefly in bed, and died from the exhaustion of nature, without any bodily pain, and in a gentle sleep, on the morning of the 5th of February 1858.

The following note from our kind friend, the Rev. R. P. Graves, expresses truly what we desired fervently to feel at the time—"That it was well :"—

"Dove Nest, Windermere, *February 5th*, 1858.

" My dear Lady Richardson,—I have just heard that God has taken to Himself your dear, good, noble mother. 'It is well,' and we must all feel thankful to Him that her decline was not longer protracted. Her own rest is come ; and yet we need not think of her as gone from us, for I am sure she will still live in our hearts, and her example, looked back upon, continue to animate our lives. I cannot therefore speak as a mourner, though feeling deeply all she has been to the many circles which looked to her as to a centre ; and I earnestly trust that those nearest to her, and to whom she was most precious, will be enabled to give her back to God with thankfulness far exceeding their sorrow. I shall be very desirous to hear that you and dear Mrs. Davy have not suffered in health by the trial you have been going through.　　　　R. P. Graves."]

CONCLUDING CHAPTER.

At the time of my mother's death, now seventeen years ago, one who had known her only during the latter years of her life, wrote thus to a mutual friend concerning her approaching death :—" I am very sorry to hear nothing more hopeful from Lancrigg; but the balance is not all on the mournful side. A mission so fulfilled, and such a mission, is not a common thing. Merely to have seen her must have kept many people from doing much mischief, if it has not led them to do some little bit of good—' Life is real, life is earnest,' was so plainly and attractively preached by her look alone."

If such was the impression of a thoughtful observer, who had only known her slightly, and if it be responded to by all who came nearer to her, and most of all by those to whom life lost most of its sunshine when she left it, it seems at once due to her memory and the cause of goodness to endeavour to bring together the records of a social influence so extensive and so penetrating as hers.

The reminiscences written by herself were begun, at my request, when she was nearly seventy, and give a vivid picture of her simple childhood and youth, the events of which stood out in her recollection as a green vista of summer days, spent among the fields and flowers of a small unknown hamlet in the plain of York. She continued to note down at intervals her joys and her sorrows until nearly the close of her life; but after her marriage her life became one so full of public and private interests, and her sphere of usefulness was so extended, that her reminiscences, although full of the impress of her faith, love, and hope, fail, perhaps, in giving so distinct an impression of her whole character as may be gathered from some of her letters written at the time to those who shared her thoughts and feelings on passing events of interest and affection.

It was the earnest desire of my dear sister, Mrs. Davy, as well as my own, that these Memorials of our mother should be printed for her descendants; and my sister undertook to select some letters, and to add her own recollections, which went back five years earlier than mine relating to the Edinburgh period. This my sister was able to do before her illness and death, which occurred in 1869. Since then a succession of family sorrows have made me delay the preparation of these Memorials for the press; but now that my own day is far spent, I am desirous to accomplish the work before I go hence, feeling sure that I can in no other way leave so precious a legacy to her great-grandchildren as the example her noble, truthful, loving, and consistent life sets before them. Hers cannot perhaps be considered a religious autobiography in the ordinary sense of that term, but it is because we believe that hers was in very truth a life devoted to God's service and her neighbours' good, that we desire to have a record of it left in print for her descendants.

My mother's view of the social duties of a Christian led her to the conviction that exclusiveness was a defect rather than a merit, and although she had many intimate friends among those who held different opinions on these points, it was a striking proof of the consistency with which she was able to carry out her principle of living above the commonplace estimate of social life in England, while mixing freely in it, that I believe no one ever suspected her of what is called *worldliness* in her intercourse with society. She so little suspected this in others that it ceased to exist in her presence. She called out the reality of those she conversed with by the intuitive sympathy she felt and expressed for what was real, beautiful, and true, and by her no less strongly expressed scorn for what was base, frivolous, and sordid. She had not by nature what is often mistaken by the other sex for sweetness of temper, the clinging, yielding temperament which submits patiently to injustice and neglect ; and had she been united to one less affectionate, and less high-toned than herself, she might have been supremely miserable, but her wealth of "saving common sense" prevented her "miscellaneous impulses" from leading her astray. She could not have attached herself strongly to any one who had not the great qualities she most valued,—earnestness of purpose and singleness of heart. She was loved by men and women as few so beautiful have been ; for if it be true that beauty in their own sex excites the envy of women rather than their affection, it was one of her felicities to form an exception to this axiom. The affection of good women formed a great part of the happiness of her life, and she scattered flowers and interests over the paths of many who, from temperament or circumstances, might not have enjoyed some of the pleasures she was enabled to bring within their reach.

The secret of my mother's influence was well expressed by her early friend, Dr. Kilvington, of Ripon, as she herself records it, and it may be called the key-note of her whole life. He says in one of his letters to her at the age of seventeen, "I have never known any one so tenderly and truly and universally beloved as you are, and I believe it arises from your capacity of loving." As this loving heart was God's special gift to her, so she gave her heart to Him in as large a measure as can be said of any human being. She lived in the habitual fear and love of God, fear of offending Him, and joy in loving Him. Her fear of offending God was shown in the unmurmuring submission with which she bore great sorrows, and her joy in loving her Father in Heaven, by the overflowing gratitude with which she expressed her sense of His daily mercies. Of her it might be said with truth, "She rejoiced to see a Divine will moving in all things, and so it came to pass that her common thoughts were piety, and her life gratitude."

The bright sunshine of winter or summer, good tidings either of a public or private nature, called out these fervent ejaculations of thankfulness to "God the Giver of all good things." If tidings of a melancholy nature reached her, her first impulse was to alleviate, if possible, the present suffering, and then to find out all the points of comfort in the case before her. It would be difficult to select any special instances of this thankfulness of heart; it seemed so much a part of herself that, when it ceased, she died.

She had been an early riser from her childhood, and continued to be so until nearly eighty; and so wide and varied were her interests, that every day seemed to bring its work along with it, so that life never lost its practical or its poetical aspect where she was. After she ceased to join the family breakfast-table, the activity of the mind continued in full force from the early hour at which she awoke until ten at night. She occupied herself for hours before others in the house were astir, in reading or writing, or devising liberal things for the good or enjoyment of others. Perhaps one of the most vivid recollections that we have of her, in her latter years, is her appearance in bed before breakfast on a fine spring or summer morning, her face still radiant from the morning reading of her favourite Psalms. The tones in which she would repeat, after the morning kiss, "Bless the Lord, O my soul, and forget not all His benefits," the bright, healthy complexion, so unlike that of age in general, the mingled look of purity and intellect her eye expressed as she looked into the eyes of those she loved for the sympathy which, thank God, she never failed to receive, and then the thoughts and feelings of the night, the sad ones disappearing in the utterance of them and the hopeful ones taking their place, with her plans for the day, which always included some attention to the wants and feelings of others, rich or poor,—this picture rises to the memory, as the habitual state during an old age which was as free as her whole life had been from bodily or mental infirmity, and which continued to be her frame of mind until five months before her death.

The minute and affectionate interest she took in her poorer neighbours was a very marked feature in her character, very early formed, and continued through her busy life to the end. If she had adopted the mother of a family as a friend, this interest, from sympathy with her, was carried out towards every member of the household, children and grandchildren; and if any of them were settled at a distance, either in England, Scotland, or Ireland, New Zealand or Australia, India or America, she found she had some friend there, to whom she could recommend them, or from whom she could learn some tidings of them to cheer the mother's or the granny's heart. In talking about them, she rarely made a mistake about their names. Several have mentioned this to me with surprise and pleasure, that their Willys, and Johnnys, and Marys were so distinctly remembered by her in her great age.

The impression she made on servants who were capable of understanding her character was also a striking point in her social influence; many of them have since told me that although she was a faithful reprover of their faults, and not what could be called an unexacting mistress, that scarcely a day passes since they left her service that they do not think of her with gratitude, and feel proud to have been in the same house with her so long. The feeling so common with servants of having a separate code of morals for themselves and their masters, was one she exceedingly disliked; she endeavoured to make them feel that she loved them as children of a common Master, and earnestly desired to raise them to her standard of feeling and action; and where she was understood by her domestics, the impression she made on them was as permanent as on every other class of persons she associated with.

None are now left who remember my mother in her early married life, but I have received some recollections of her from two members of the same family—Mr. Bannatyne, of Glasgow, and his sister, Mrs. Stark, one of her most valued friends and correspondents for fifty years. Mrs. Stark's reminiscences were sent to me soon after my mother's death, and Mr. Bannatyne's were copied from his Note-book and sent to me after his death by his widow.

Mrs. Stark says :—" You will feel, I am sure, everything that remains to you of your dearest mother so strongly and vividly impressed that when your sister and you are together you will call up the remembrance, as if you saw it in a stereoscope, and little things will float before you hardly noted at the time. There was always a purpose and a character in everything she said and did. From the time I first knew her, her kindness and condescension (I was going to say to me, but she would not have liked that word) engaged and charmed me, and, as her whole noble nature unfolded to me, won my whole heart.

"We had heard of Mrs. Fletcher before, but I think it must have been about 1803 when your father and she came to spend an evening with us at my uncle Dugald Stewart's, where I was on a visit with my parents. Our father and yours were friends before. How well I remember her and all the conversation of that supper-table, the very place she sat, with her blue gown and brilliant look. I had not been much in company, but we, my dear father and mother and I, were all to go to a ball at Miss Coates's, where we should see Mrs. Fletcher again. To see her seemed to me enough. Henry Brougham was there, and Robert Owen, and many other notabilities. I watched every one who had the happiness to be near her, and particularly when her face was lighted up in conversation with my father or mother; but she spoke to *me* so kindly, and told me to come and see her when I went to Edinburgh ; and so I did ; and from that day, ever, ever on, she drew me to love and admire her more and more.

"Soon after I went to my Edinburgh home she gave it her blessing, and your father and she used to be our inmates at the cottage at Kirkhill."

From Mr. Bannatyne's Note-book.

"GLASGOW, 21st *February* 1858.

"Mrs. Fletcher is dead, at a very advanced age. I trust some day justice will be done in some of the autobiographies of distinguished men, probably in Brougham's, to this very remarkable woman. Throughout life I have never known a purer, a more elevated, a more amiable spirit. Her beautiful countenance and majestic air were combined with the most attractive kindliness. Her full and commanding voice and faultless speech live, like every other distinguishing feature, in the memory of all who were privileged to know her, and most of all in the memory of those who were permitted to call her a friend ; and these were not few, for never was there a mind better attuned, not only to general benevolence, but to warm personal attachments. She busied herself through life in promoting liberty and truth and holiness. Her enthusiasm in favour of the rights of man, at a period when this country was threatened with despotic rule by an oligarchy, raised up many violent and bitter opponents ; but I doubt whether she ever had an enemy. Her disinterestedness and candour disarmed those who might otherwise, in times of the greatest excitement, have yielded themselves up to personal hostility, even against a woman. It was my happiness, as a boy, to have had the opportunity of intimately knowing Mrs. Fletcher."

It was early in this century that she became intimate with Henry Brougham, during the period he passed in Edinburgh, before he left the Scotch Bar. They seldom met in after years, but he never ceased to make her feel that she retained that place in his respect and friendship which his young imagination had assigned her.

In Lord Brougham's introduction to his own speech on Burgh Reform in Scotland, when he notices with high praise my father's exertions in that cause, he takes occasion to pay a tribute to my mother. He compares her to two women of most heroic and tender natures—Madame Roland and Lucy Hutchinson ; and if we add to them Lady Grizzel Baillie (her own favourite heroine), we have, as nearly as possible, the combination of qualities which made up her moral and intellectual nature in the estimation of those who knew her best.

I remember, when on a visit to Mrs. Brougham in 1832, my mother's expressing her fervent sympathy with the mother of such a man, one who had so largely benefited his country, and had at the same time been so affectionate a son and brother, and she added—"I fear, my dear friend, my head could not have stood such a trial of happiness as yours has done;" while the mother of Brougham, with her quiet smile and look of grand simplicity, replied—"I must say Henry never forgets his old mother."

Mrs. Brougham told us also on this visit to Brougham Hall that the time she felt most elated, and had fears for her own head, was when her son Henry was returned Member for Yorkshire, without possessing an acre of ground in the county. She took us to see the picture presented to her on that occasion of Henry Brougham by the freeholders of Yorkshire. I remember she told me then, when we were alone, that her son always considered that my mother's friendship had been of great use to him as a young man, that her entire absence of personal vanity astonished him, and that she never failed to rouse him to noble aims for the honour and good of his country.

This testimony from his venerable mother, who was truth itself, gives additional interest to the last letter he wrote to mine, on hearing from Mrs. Arnold, at Kendal, of his old friend's serious illness. I cannot resist inserting it in this closing chapter, as there is a gentle and tender tone about it, which is pleasant to associate with one who filled so prominent a place in England's Parliamentary history during fifty years of this century.

From Lord Brougham.

"My dear old Friend,—It gave me great pleasure indeed to see Mrs. Arnold and her daughter here, from the respect I, in common with all, had for Dr. Arnold; but it was no little abatement of this gratification to hear from her of your having been ailing. I hope and trust that you are getting round, and I shall be most truly obliged to you if you will desire some one to give me a few lines directed to London, where (D.V.) I hope to arrive this evening, merely to let me know how you are. The pleasure I have in seeing once more my old Kendal friends (alas! I may say those of them who remain) has been greatly increased by finding them so right and so zealous in their opinions upon the new attempts to revive the infernal slave-trade under a new name. What I stated last July in the House of Lords on this subject proves to have been rather under than over the truth, and I well know that of the many subjects connected with human rights and duties on which you and I have always agreed (indeed, I know of none on which we ever differed), there has been none nearer to your heart than this.—Ever your affectionate   H. BROUGHAM.

"KENDAL, *Tuesday, Nov.* 11, 1857."

The Impressions made on a Granddaughter as a Child.

"The concern she showed if any of her grandchildren failed in due deference to her never had a shadow of petty exactingness, but was always plainly for themselves, as being a defect of character where she would fain have seen nothing but good. If she ever fancied there had been the least trace of personal vexation in the most deserved reproof, she would before long ask a little girl's pardon as for undue vehemence, to the delighted wonder of the rest and the utter melting of the culprit herself.

"Her sympathy with the young in all their joys had the rare quality of not requiring that the joy should be one she herself would have chosen, her imagination always helping her heart to enter into the needs of widely differing characters. Her intuitive wisdom also kept her from expecting exact agreement with even her most cherished forms of opinion, content if she saw any kindling of enthusiasm for what was unquestionably good, any sign of quiet dutifulness; and many who in a different age and among other surroundings may have been led to varying conclusions must yet feel how much of any love of goodness and hatred of evil there may be in them was kindled and fostered by her. How much of the delight in books, and Nature, and human life, came to them through the touch of her inspiring ardour ! Her very look and tone, amidst the simplest country pleasures, could teach (unconsciously at the time) high lessons of love and thankfulness, so that an afternoon's nutting by the stream, an evening's stroll through the meadows when the bog-bean was in its prime, a drive home from some loving family gathering, can all be remembered after nearly forty years, far more surely than the mere charm of the outward pictures. Lasting, too, ought to have been the impressions, on the one hand, of honest indignation, and, on the other, of the dignity of the true simplicities of life, of unselfish frugalities, and most un-pretending and thoughtful charities—points in which the stately ' matriarch,' eloquent on some theme of politics, or poetry, or philanthropy, still kept the heart of the little Oxton child.

" One of the ways in which she tried to cherish and direct little children's natural delight in giving was by making the power and the permission to bestow alms a much-coveted reward. The impression as of a beneficent being she made even on the youngest, and when she herself was a very young grandmother, is well shown by the recorded words of a tiny brother and sister, who, after giving the history of a happy holiday by the sea, wound up with—' Then we said our prayers and went to bed, and *speaked* about God and grandmamma.' "

The following extract from Margaret Fuller's book, " At Home and Abroad," was lately sent to me by a friend. It is a wonderfully true picture of the outward form revealing the inner woman to an observer of genius. The mistake made in it is quite pardonable in a foreigner, and even in an American, that of believing my mother to be Scotch, and, like the old ladies, admired by Burns and Scott. It is very difficult for travellers to find out accurately the distinctive difference between English, Scotch, and Irish ladies of marked characters, although perfectly known among ourselves.

From "At Home and Abroad," by Margaret Fuller, Ossoli.

"AMBLESIDE, *Aug.* 27, 1846.

"We also met a fine specimen of the noble, intelligent Scotch-woman, such as Walter Scott and Burns knew how to prize. Seventy-six years have passed over her head, only to prove in her the truth of my theory, that we need never grow old. She was 'brought up' in the animated and intellectual circle of Edinburgh, in youth an apt disciple, in her prime a bright ornament of that society. She had been an only child, a cherished wife, an adored mother, unspoiled by love in any of these relations, because that love was founded on knowledge. In childhood she had warmly sympathized in the spirit that animated the American Revolution, and Washington had been her hero : later, the interest of her husband in every struggle for freedom had cherished her own. She had known in the course of her long life many eminent men, and sympathized now in the triumph of the people over the Corn Laws, as she had in the American victories, with as much ardour as when a girl, though with a wiser mind. Her eye was full of light, her manner and gesture of dignity ; her voice rich, sonorous, and finely modulated ; her tide of talk marked by candour and justice, showing in every sentence her ripe experience and her noble genial nature. Dear to memory will be the sight of her in the beautiful seclusion of her home among the mountains, a picturesque, flower-wreathed dwelling, where affection, tranquillity, and wisdom were the gods of the hearth to whom was offered no vain oblation. Grant us more such women, Time ! Grant to men to reverence, to seek for such !"

My mother, who died at eighty-eight, had survived all her own contemporary friends, but her affections were so young and her sympathy "so radiant," as Mrs. Arnold used to say, that she made many friends among the middle-aged and young when they met in London, or when they visited the Lakes on a summer holiday. Among those she most valued were the Rev. Hampden Gurney, Frederick Maurice, Alexander Scott, and especially Mr. Stanley, now Dean of

Westminster, whom she had known when he was a Rugby sixth-form boy. Mr. H. Gurney, writing of her to Mrs. Arnold at the time of her death, says, "I had heard of Mrs. Fletcher's hopeless illness, so it was a relief to hear from you that she had reached the Land where the Sun of Righteousness shines without a cloud. I am thankful to have known so grand a specimen of noble womanhood." To the same friend Mr. Stanley wrote at the time : "I had heard of Mrs. Fletcher's death from young William Wordsworth at Oxford. She had certainly to the very last nourished and renewed her strength, 'mounted up with wings as an eagle.' How much there is to be thankful for, in every such case that one has known of a character living on for so many years without leaving behind any recollection of littleness, and so very much of excellence and beauty."

To me also Mr. Stanley wrote, after a visit to Lancrigg, from Fox How, on his return from his tour to the Holy Land with the Prince of Wales, when I sent him a photograph of my mother :—

"Many thanks for the photograph, which I shall value highly as a memorial of the character which I used to regard as a personification beyond any other I had ever seen of Christian Hope. Indeed, I fully entered into your feeling, and was grateful to you for at once speaking so freely on a grief, which is not increased but greatly lightened by being always remembered. I went to your mother's grave in Grasmere Churchyard, and was much struck with the texts. It was of her, as indeed of my own dear mother, so true, that the eye and the ear, of any who had eyes to see or ears to hear, so immediately received what was within."

Hope was indeed the " anchor of her soul " from youth to age. She quoted four lines to me in one of the last letters I had from her, when hope was beginning to give way but love still remained.　I do not yet know who wrote them, but they very much express her habitual state of mind, and with them I close this book :—

"For who has aught to love, and lives aright,
　Will never in the darkest strait despair,
For out of love exhales a living light,
　The light of love, that spends itself in prayer."

MEMOIR OF GRACE FLETCHER.

BY HER MOTHER.

———◆———

July 15th, 1817.

MY DEAR CHILDREN,—The desire of my heart is to preserve some memorial of your beloved sister, some record or testimony of her many rare and admirable qualities ; and this not for her sake only, but for yours, that amidst the temptations, sorrows, or vissicitudes of life, you may have, as it were, a sort of sanctuary to retire into, where your anxious and troubled spirits may repose on the contemplation of a character which is endeared to you by many tender recollections.

Grace was born on the 23d of May 1796, and in her infancy she was more remarkable for gentleness and docility of temper than for quickness of apprehension or extraordinary parts. I early observed, however, uncommon disinterestedness of character—a preference of others to herself ; and this was shown in the exultation with which she ran home from school to tell of her sister's superior scholarship. It was never of herself she boasted ; and though less accustomed to attract notice than my two elder children, she never discovered envy or jealousy on that account. Being one day much caressed by an old lady, on my asking her why she thought that lady had been so kind to her, she answered, with much simplicity, " I know why, mamma : because I am clumsy and have not a pretty face."

In the summer of 1802, my two elder children went to Yorkshire, and Grace was the eldest of the four that remained with me. She was then six years old, and this seniority made her more the companion of my walks than she had hitherto

been, and perhaps more the object of my attention. We lived
during that summer at the village of Dalmeny, about nine
miles from Edinburgh. Grace and I began to botanize together, and I was surprised at the readiness of her apprehension and her quickness in discovering new plants and leaves.
She had great delight in this amusement. She had before
this time made little progress in reading, but she used to sit
on my knee for hours together listening to stories and recitations of poetry, entreating for a repetition of them again and
again. This summer seemed to be an era in her mental
existence. I used to find her in a quiet corner, reading with
intense and passionate delight all kinds of stories and works of
fancy. Nor was her imagination merely passive; for when at
play with the other children, she was inventive, lively, and
affectionate. When she was eight years old I engaged a
governess highly recommended to me for integrity of principle
and useful habits. This lady remained with me nearly five
years, and I found her useful in many respects; but the sternness of her temper did not suit some of my children; and if
this part of my life were to occur again, I would act differently,
and I have often reproached myself with the tears I suffered
to be shed in the school-room. I had hitherto pursued no
system with my children but to make them happy, and
endeavour to make them good. I was their play-fellow,
their most intimate companion, but I had neither time nor
patience to be their teacher; and as I was quite satisfied with
their teacher's integrity of purpose and usefulness of habits
and aims, I reconciled myself to her defect of temper as an
evil which my indulgence would mitigate and counteract.

Grace, more than any of the rest, was the victim of this
severity. She never complained, but after expiating her little
faults by tears and submission, consoled herself by taking
possession of a large chair in her mother's room, and there
with some favourite book (not seldom Plutarch's Lives, or
Shakespeare), she forgot her cares and sorrows, and had her
favourite passages to read to me when I came in. I could at
this moment think I see her, her countenance beaming with
delight, and coiled up in the chair waiting for my return.

In June 1806 we all went to the Lakes. Though the

pleasures arising from beautiful scenery are not early expressed
by children, they are long remembered. This summer was
full of enjoyment. Every new walk afforded a new pleasure.
Lakes and mountains were objects of poetical association, and
Coniston and Windermere were never forgotten.

There was a little rocky bit where caves were easily imagined,
in a copse wood behind Belmont House, and there my happy
children spent hours of that real enjoyment which none but free
and cherished children know. In this cave they enacted many
adventurous histories which produced much innocent mirth.

When winter returned, the school-room in Edinburgh became perhaps the more irksome from the freedom and enjoyment of the preceding summer ; but in July 1807 we all went
to a new scene at Hebburn, in Northumberland, and they
again enjoyed the pleasures of the country, and Shetland
ponies, and an old border tower, where we had a school in
which they assisted, and where the governess worked with us
with hearty good-will.

Grace returned at this time, with her kind aunt Dawson, to
Yorkshire, and the correspondence with home awakened in
her, at eleven years old, an unusual amount of· sensibility and
tenderness of feeling. The sweetness of her disposition made
her much an object of affection to the friends she was with ;
and an intimate correspondence with her mother cultivated
her taste, and cherished that desire of intellectual improvement which the irksome lessons of the school-room had a
tendency to repress.

After I parted with the governess a different plan was
pursued. A small class was formed among some favourite
friends of my children, and masters of real ability came to our
respective houses to give lessons, which greatly advanced the
desire for knowledge in all my daughters. Grace's decided
talent for art began to show itself, and she had instruction in
drawing from busts, from Henning the artist, before he went
to London.

The great intimacy formed about this time with the youngest
daughter of Mr. Mackenzie ("The Man of Feeling ") and some
other good and intellectual companions, were of great advantage to my girls, and led them early to appreciate the blessings

of friendship with their own sex, and to discuss their innocent desires and imaginations as only equals in age and taste can do.

In the autumn of 1810 I went with my eldest daughter to London, and during the following winter Grace and Margaret became more than ever my companions, and, pursuing their studies together, they made considerable progress in Latin and Italian, while their intimacy and attachment to each other was greatly increased by the sympathy of tastes and the mutual enjoyment of their cheerful and happy home.

It was about this period of her life that Grace became intimately known to my friend, Mrs. Millar, whose opinion of her talents and early development of thought and understanding was expressed to me with all the warmth of generous admiration. Her visits also at Milheugh to the daughters of the celebrated Professor Millar, of Glasgow, increased her ardour and love of knowledge, and excited her to a degree she had never before experienced. Her letters to me from thence were written in a strain of enthusiastic enjoyment. She used to speak of this visit at Milheugh as the acme of her intellectual existence. The extent and variety of knowledge that was pointed out to her on subjects of taste, politics, and morals made her feel, she said, how she had before trifled away time, and when each day closed on these delightful speculations she used to lie awake whole hours to revolve the great things she hoped one day to acccomplish. The humour and fun of some members of that Scottish sisterhood formed no small part of the enjoyment of the visit, as well as the explorations daily made of the lovely glens and burns in the beautiful neighbourhood of Bothwell and Hamilton.

From these enchanting visions and animating scenes she was recalled home by the illness of her father, and in his sickroom she exerted herself with all that assiduity and tenderness could suggest. The sweetness of her attentions and the cheerfulness of her services could not be exceeded, and I found in her the kindest and firmest support under all my anxieties.

In the winter of 1812 we were favoured by a visit from Miss Aikin, whose literary attainments, and whose lively, varied, and powerful talents, furnished her with inexhaustible sources of conversation. In these our beloved Grace shared very largely. She became a peculiar object of Miss Aikin's attention and regard. They read and conversed together, and the desire of making more classical proficiency was the result of her intercourse with this accomplished woman. She resumed the study of Latin, and though it was sometimes interrupted by more favourite pursuits, it never afterwards ceased to engage a share of her attention.

In the summer of 1812 she accompanied her father, mother, and youngest sister into Yorkshire, and Margaret and she resumed their favourite pursuits together with a pleasure heightened, if possible, by their late separation.

In the autumn of that year these sisters were present at a York county election, and stood for several hours in the crowd near the hustings to hear the speeches of the different candidates. It might seem extraordinary that girls of fifteen and sixteen should enjoy this species of amusement, and yet I do not exaggerate in saying that there was not among all the auditors then present one heart that beat higher to the sentiments of genuine freedom and enlightened patriotism than that of the person whose character I am now portraying. Grace remained in Yorkshire all the following winter, cheering by the sweetness of her engaging manners the kind old friends whose quiet and unvaried hours formed a striking contrast with the gaiety and animation of an Edinburgh winter. During some weeks of this winter she had the happiness to be the guest of Mrs. Millar (who then resided at the village of Fulford, near York), and certainly no one out of her own family ever obtained so strong an influence over her mind and affections. This was in a great measure from the power of sympathy. This quality, so engaging to the young, produced an intimacy which rarely exists between persons of such different ages. Mrs. Millar has much vivacity of temper and feeling, with a strong and tender capacity of affection. Her eloquent conversation and engaging manners, and, above all, her elevation of mind and quickness of sensibility, gave her unbounded influence over every human heart that was capable of comprehending her. Over that of our beloved Grace she exercised an influence that was almost maternal, and she repaid this homage by the most perfect affection for her adopted child.

Grace was peculiarly alive to feelings of compassion, and it was not with her a passive and inactive feeling. During the winter of this year a poor American woman was taken ill when passing through Tadcaster on her way to Hull, the settlement of her husband, a seafaring man, who had died in the south of England. No sooner did our dear Grace hear of this unhappy stranger than she visited her in one of those haunts of wretchedness which afford a night's shelter to the wandering poor. Ann Tucker was the poor woman's name. She was in the last stage of consumption, and the fatigue of a long journey on foot had brought on symptoms of premature child-birth. Under these circumstances of severe distress the parish officers of Tadcaster were desirous to hasten the poor woman forward on her journey, that she might reach her husband's settlement before her child was born. Grace was shocked by the barbarity of their conduct ; and after expostulating with them, and threatening to lay the case before the neighbouring Justices of the Peace, she accomplished the object she had at heart, and personally attended the removal of this poor woman from her wretched lodging to a comfortable room in the parish workhouse, where Ann Tucker was shortly afterwards delivered of a male child. Grace continued to visit her poor patient at least once every day for several weeks. She read to her, soothed and comforted her by compassionate attentions, and took her such articles of food as suited better with her sickly palate than that which the workhouse afforded. This young woman was gentle, pious, affectionate, and grateful (Grace could never speak of her tenderness to her child without emotion) ; but she became at last so feeble and emaciated that she grew regardless even of her child, and sank away almost without a struggle. Henry Tucker, the infant of this poor woman, then became an object of no ordinary interest. Grace had promised his mother to see that he was taken care of ; and as long as she remained at Tadcaster, not a day passed without her visiting him. The intrepid humanity that could lead a girl of seventeen to contend with the ruggedness of parish officers, and personally rescue a human being from such suffering, requires no comment. But this was not the only instance of her benevolence. She was constantly alive to every claim of pity, and yet she discriminated judiciously between the really needful and the imposing beggar.

In the winter of that year, during her residence at Tadcaster, she made considerable proficiency in painting, and finished a good copy of the picture of a Jewish Rabbi.

In the spring of 1813 she returned to Edinburgh, with a mind enriched by more extensive reading. Such of her letters as have been preserved mark the progress of her vigorous understanding at this period.

On the 14th of June 1813, our whole family removed to Park Hall, a small property which Mr. Fletcher had purchased, and Grace enjoyed highly the mountain scenery of that part of Stirlingshire. While her sisters amused themselves with sketching landscapes, she used to draw groups of cottage children, and not unfrequently found good picturesque subjects for her pencil in the old beggars whom we met with in our rambles. She engaged ardently with her sisters in teaching an evening school, attended by some village children; and it would not be easy to find a family that realized more pleasure than ours did that summer in the enjoyment of beautiful scenery, in the happiness of family affection, and in the luxury of doing good. We were at that time living in a very small house, cheaply furnished by a village carpenter. We were too happy to feel any desire for the gratifications of vanity or to envy those who possessed them. It was a summer of uninterrupted happiness till we were deprived of Margaret's society. She went into Yorkshire in the autumn of 1813, and I, accompanied by my two eldest children, went to pay a long promised visit to Mrs. Glasgow, at Mount Greenan, in Ayrshire. Grace, during this time, remained at Park Hall with her father and her youngest brother and sister. In the following winter she remained in Edinburgh, and partook more than formerly of general society, where her engaging manners and animated conversation made her an object of attention wherever she was known.

The summer of 1814 was one of deep interest to our whole family. On the 16th of July, in that year, Grace's eldest sister was married to Mr. Taylor, and such an event could not happen in a family so tenderly united without much anxious solicitude for her future happiness. Immediately after that event the family returned to Park Hall, where Grace resumed her habits of active benevolence, and shared with her sisters in the task of instructing village children. She likewise pursued her favourite amusement of painting with less interruption than in town. She took a portrait of her father, and one of her youngest brother. The former was an excellent likeness, but her taste was so superior to her execution, that she was always dissatisfied with her performances, and often threw aside her pencil in despair of overcoming the impediments which a female artist must always feel from the want of scientific instruction. Some of her sketches, however, made during this summer, of old beggars and cottage children, were excellent, and obtained the unqualified approbation of some good judges of drawing.

In December 1814 she again left her beloved home to cheer that of her friends at Tadcaster. I shall never forget the sadness of her countenance as I saw her seated in the mail-coach that was to convey her away from Edinburgh. It was a dreary day in December, the snow was falling heavily, the sky was dark and lowering; she suppressed the expression of her feelings, but she sank back in her seat, pale and almost faint with grief at the thought of leaving those she loved so dearly. She was fortunate in having as the companions of her journey friends who knew how to value her. In a few days she wrote me an animated account of her journey, and a cheerful view of her feelings and occupations at Tadcaster. She was so naturally disposed to happiness that all the refinement of her character did not render her fastidious. It was the happiness of others, not her own, that she was always aiming at, and this was the secret of her contentment and cheerfulness of temper. She employed herself during this winter in painting the portraits of her uncle and aunt, and succeeded so well that Mr. Williams, an Edinburgh artist, assured her friends that there were not above two artists there who could have executed them better. There was, however, in the tone of her letters this winter a more pensive expression, more longing for congenial society, and more indulgence of cherished recollections connected with home than formerly. On observing this, I proposed that she should spend a month or two amongst friends in London, so that a variety of new objects and an enlarged sphere of observation might exhilarate and amuse her. To this proposal she was less inclined to assent than might have been expected from one so young and so alive to the gratifications of taste. But it separated her further from the home of her affections, it prolonged that separation, it carried her among strangers of distinguished intellectual character before whom she dreaded to appear without the support she was accustomed to derive from her own family. Ever disinterested in her purposes and feelings, she objected strongly to the expense this journey would occasion ; but her friend Mrs. Millar (with whom she passed a delightful week this winter) seconded her mother's wishes in reconciling her to it, and accident favoured its accomplishment, by giving her the opportunity of travelling with Dr. and Mrs. Brunton. The delight she experienced from this journey, and her sensibility to the kindness she received from her excellent friend and companion, Mrs. Brunton, and from others whom to know is to revere, is best expressed in her own letters, and the impression which her gentle manners and cultivated mind produced on them is best to be collected from their communications to her mother. She spent six weeks in London, part of the time in lodgings with Mrs. Brunton, who daily accompanied her to such exhibitions as strangers most desire to see in London. At Mrs. Barbauld's Grace enjoyed the highest and most refined pleasures of society, and Miss Aikin's affectionate reception of her was warmly and gratefully remembered. One of her own letters from Mrs. Barbauld's house gives her feelings at the time better than her mother can record them :—

From G. F.'s letter to her Mother.

"STOKE NEWINGTON, *June* 1815.

"DEAREST OF MINNIES,—I left Hampstead with great regret on Monday, and came to town for one day and night, which I passed at Dr. Baillie's. There was a large party in the evening, where I did not know many people, but where Mrs. Joanna was very kind in coming to speak to me very often ; indeed, I am truly grateful to her for her constant kindness

and attention.   The next morning she took me to see a part
of the town I had not before been in—Hyde Park and Picca-
dilly.   I was pleased to find such a place as the Park, where
the poorest inhabitants of this overgrown and dismal metropolis may see the trees and green grass, and have some chance
of feeling that a good Spirit formed the universe.   After our
return, Mrs. Baillie kindly pressed me to stay ; but as I had
fixed to dine at Mrs. Barbauld's that day, I declined.   She
then insisted upon sending me in her carriage, and Mrs.
Joanna Baillie was so good as to ' accompany me.   Mrs.
Barbauld received me most kindly, and I have passed with her
a week of a most quiet and gratifying kind of enjoyment.
The dreadful fear I had of Mrs. Joanna Baillie, the hopelessness of pleasing her, gave a feeling of constraint which I
hoped I had got over, but which, whenever I saw her composed figure enter the room, returned with painful force ; yet
I have seldom seen any human being that excites stronger
feelings of respect ; and there is something so extraordinary
in the union of such excellent poetic genius and such simplicity, and even plainness of manner, that your attention is constantly alive to every word she utters, hoping you may hear
some poetical or elevated sentiment.   She is one illustration
of Miss Benger's theory about complicated characters ; there
is so much left to the imagination, you *must* feel great
interest.   But, to return to Mrs. Barbauld : there is in her so
much indulgence for the fancies and even follies of youth, that
in one week I feel more at ease in her society, and more attached to her, than I could be to Mrs. Joanna Baillie in years.
Enthusiasm has not departed from the character of Mrs.
Barbauld, but has left such deep traces, that you find many of
her feelings and opinions still tinged with its magic.   In Mrs.
Joanna Baillie that glowing, elevating sentiment has dwelt in
such impervious depths, and pursued such secret paths, that
the passing eye might think her uninfluenced by its spells.

    " Miss Aikin seemed very happy to see me.   We meet al-
most every day.   Dr. and Mrs. Brunton dined here on Friday,
and were pleased with their visit to Mrs. Barbauld, and Mrs.
B. liked them.

    " Owen came on Sunday and dined with us.   You would see

his Bill had gone through the second reading ; but it cannot pass this session.   Mrs. Barbauld thinks him visionary, but he had not sufficient time to unfold all his ideas, and then he will beat anybody (papa would say) by exhausting their patience.

"Maggie tells me our dear Mrs. Millar is with you.   How delightful that will be for you !   I imagine you wandering up to the burn this beautiful day, or some other pleasant place. Dearest mamma, pray do not venture to ride the stupid starting pony.   I tremble whenever I think of the escape you had last summer, even with your trusty squire Angus by your side.   Is darling Molly very busy with some little plan of her own ? Now let me answer your questions.   I was present at the 'Family Legend,' and was much discomposed to see it so ill acted—very inferior to the Edinburgh representation.   Mrs. Barclay looked ill, and acted worse.   As it was a benefit night, no disapprobation was shown, and Mrs. J. Baillie, who was present, was so good-natured as to be pleased.   Lord Byron, who is now one of the Directors of Drury Lane, wishes to bring on the stage another of her plays, I believe 'De Montfort.'   He thinks it would be better adapted for the stage were she to give some stronger motive for the hatred of De Montfort against Rezenvelt.   In reading it you do not perceive the want of this, considering the proud, irritable character of De Montfort, but the spectators, particularly in the galleries, require some evident insult or cause of resentment."

At the Miss Baillies' house, Grace met Lord and Lady Byron during the one year of their union.   She admired the sweetness of Lady Byron's looks, and the unaffectedness of her manners, while she was struck by the gloom of Lord Byron's fine but melancholy countenance.

She had great delight in the pictures she saw in London and in Mr. Angerstein's collection ; she studied them with the eye of an artist and the taste of an amateur, but she knew no other rules of judging than those which her own pure taste prescribed.   Murillo was decidedly her favourite.   His pictures had, she thought, more of poetry, as well as nature, in them than those of any other artists she saw.

Grace was much urged by Mrs. Barbauld to prolong her

visit at Newington; but her uncle and aunt having fixed to set
off for Scotland in the beginning of July, she hastened down
to join them, and arrived with them at Park Hall on the 9th
of July 1815.   This was a happy meeting with her family,
from whom she had been separated for eight months.   She had
much to tell of all she had seen and felt, and she used to say
that her London life had been so crowded with gratifications
that she enjoyed it more on recollection than at the time; but
what she most delighted to remember was the kindness she
met with from persons whose genius and virtue gave them the
highest rank in her estimate of human character.   She had too
much feeling and too much imagination to be at ease in the
presence of such persons as Mrs. Barbauld and Joanna Baillie.
Their genuine modesty made her feel, as she expressed it, a
sort of self-annihilation; but this feeling of reverence for what
is really great and good so much resembles the sublimity of
devotional feeling, that it is delightful to minds such as hers.

From London and all its wonderful varieties she returned
more fond than ever of her home and home society.   The
summer was passed chiefly at Park Hall, from which she and
Margaret made an excursion to see the Lakes of Monteith and
the Trossachs, and their impression of this beautiful scenery is
still preserved in a letter which I received from them while on
a visit at Mr. and Mrs. Taylor's house at Bourtree Hill, in
Ayrshire.

During this summer Grace began a picture of her mother and
youngest sister, which was finished during the ensuing winter in
Edinburgh, to which place all the family returned in November.

In the course of this winter Grace was present at the performance of the Oratorio of the " Messiah," the first musical
festival ever held in Edinburgh, and she was deeply touched
by the sublime and affecting music of Handel, sung by Marconi
and Braham, especially by the words sung with peculiar expression and simplicity by Madame Marconi—" He was despised
and rejected of men, a Man of sorrows and acquainted with
grief."   Grace had never before felt the power of music in its
highest degree.   She had a very sweet and expressive voice, and
had her musical taste been earlier cultivated, I think she might
have excelled in that accomplishment as much as in painting.

She saw her little niece, Elizabeth Taylor, for the first time, this winter, and this new object of affection excited the most tender interest in her heart.

About the same time she formed an intimate acquaintance with Miss Wilkes, a most agreeable American lady, the niece of Monsieur Simond ; and during the whole of this winter Grace enjoyed the pleasures of Edinburgh society with an animation peculiar to herself, for it was not in crowds that she delighted, hers was not that exterior gaiety which requires strong excitement, and which often hides an aching heart, it was the gaiety of intelligence, benevolence, and peace. At Mrs. Elizabeth Hamilton's she was always a welcome and cherished visitor ; but it was at home that her cheerfulness diffused itself most sweetly.

The loss of our excellent friend, Mrs. E. Hamilton,[1] who died at Harrogate on the 23d of July, affected Grace extremely. Many were the happy hours which she had passed in her delightful society. Mrs. Hamilton had early discovered her uncommon character, and had honoured her with distinguished regard. During this summer she amused herself with painting. She improved and completed the pictures of her mother and youngest sister, painted the year before, and enjoyed much some parts of Yorkshire, and its beautiful villages, with those feelings of benevolence which delight in witnessing the comforts of the poor.

On the 7th of October 1816, Grace, with her mother and her brother Angus, left her kind aunt and youngest sister to return to Edinburgh. They paid several pleasant visits on the way in the county of Durham ; spent some days with Lady Williamson, at Whitburn Hall, and Mrs. Millar, who then lived near that place, and reached home on the 19th of October 1816. She said on that day she had never enjoyed a journey so much. As the carriage drove up the Canongate of Edinburgh, while the clock of the Tron Church was striking eight, she exclaimed, " Oh ! how rejoiced I am to see once more ' mine ain romantic town.' "

Before the return of the rest of the family from Park Hall she urged me strongly to form a resolution against engaging in

---

[1] Author of "Cottagers of Glenburnie," and " Life of Agrippina."

the turmoil of large parties, either at home or abroad, during the winter. She suggested that her father's delicate state of health made it proper to abstain from these engagements, and that the enjoyment they afforded was quite inadequate to the expense, trouble, and vexation in which they involved us. " Let us avoid crowds," she said, " and enjoy society."   Her sister Margaret heartily agreed with her in this request ; and on one occasion, when a too great facility had made me yield to the request of a lady to join an evening party at her house, Grace brought me a pen, and, putting it into my hand, entreated me to retract my engagement and keep firm to my resolution of avoiding evening parties.   Thus did her firmness, prudence, and discretion establish a regulation in the family highly favour-able in every respect to its comfort, ease, and real enjoyment. But while she avoided crowds, she enjoyed the real pleasures of society with a zest and vivacity more than usual.   It seemed as if she had a presentiment that she had not long to live, and that the last months of her life should be as full of usefulness and rational enjoyment as possible.   If I could mention any period of her life in which a deeper feeling of habitual piety seemed to influence her whole conduct, it was this winter. She had always possessed devotional feelings and a firm belief in the truths of Christianity ; but those peculiar views, which are in the best sense of the word evangelical, seemed now to be gaining on her mind.   They were strengthened by her intimacy with Mrs. Brunton, and while they served to form a habit of practical piety, they did not narrow her mind, nor 'limit her charity and toleration for the religious opinions of those who differed from her.   The duties of humanity were never neglected, nor were they ever suffered to interfere with the duties of home.   Three or four days of every week she and her sister Margaret attended the House of Industry, or the Lancasterian School, but from these she always returned home before two o'clock, to accompany her mother if she chose to go out.

During this winter our family became acquainted with Mrs. Wilson (the widow of Theobald Wolfe Tone), whose character and fate interested Grace in an uncommon degree.   She admired her talents, and loved her for the noble-mindedness

and generous enthusiasm of her character. They became
friends, and she offered to paint a picture of young Tone from
a portrait of him which his mother had, and which had been
injured in the carriage. The desire of gratifying this devoted
mother was an object which she had much at heart, and the
painting of young Tone's picture excited her extremely. She
succeeded well in finishing it, but an accident occurred in the
varnishing of the picture which destroyed her whole labour.
Instead of being disconcerted by this, she said, after mentioning
the accident to me, "Don't mind, dear mamma; I hope I shall
be able to do a better." She began another, but did not live
to finish it. She likewise left an unfinished likeness of her
father. The mornings that were not devoted to the superintendence of the House of Industry were employed in reading
and painting. The evenings were given to domestic society,
where she diffused a cheerfulness and sweetness to which no
description can do justice.

In one of their visits in the month of March this year (1817)
to the House of Industry, Grace and Margaret met a crowd
in the Canongate, occasioned by the screams of a child of seven
years old, which a woman was leading to the Charity Workhouse.
They followed the woman, and learned that she had reared the
deserted orphan from infancy, but that the time was now come
when the managers of the poor had thought fit to take it from
her, according to the general rule, and place it in the Charity
Workhouse. The child, however, had repeatedly run home to
her kind old friend, and neither threats, punishments, nor
bribes, could detain her in the workhouse. The pertinacious
fondness of this child for her nurse interested the two sisters ;
they followed her to the workhouse, and, by strong recommenda-
tions of kindness to the matron, and by promises of reward to
the child, and by gaining for her permission to pay a weekly
visit to the nurse, they hoped to reconcile her to her fate ; but
in this they were disappointed : they found she had again
escaped the vigilance of the matron, that she refused food, and
that, even when reduced to great debility by typhus fever, she
had gone, in the midst of a stormy night, to her nurse's door
and begged to be admitted. The sensibility and affectionateness of this unfortunate child touched Grace's heart ; she left

no exertion untried to obtain her removal from the workhouse, and by the influence of her excellent friends, Dr. and Mrs. Brunton, she had the comfort of seeing her placed as a town pensioner in the house of the nurse she had loved so dearly. Whether or not it was in visiting this poor child that our beloved Grace caught the fever of which she died, God only knows. She was about her Divine Master's business—she was walking in His steps and doing His commandments. When could she have been fitter to appear in the presence of her Father and her God? The activity and universality of her benevolence could only be equalled by the disinterestedness, gentleness, and sweetness of her temper.

On the Sunday before she was taken ill, she walked out for some time with me and her sister Margaret; and speaking of the past winter, she said—"When have we passed so happy and so undisturbed a winter? This has been owing to its quietness." She used to speak much and tenderly of her absent sisters and her excellent aunt, and delighted herself with the playfulness of her little niece, Elizabeth Taylor, who was our inmate this winter.

The first thing Grace did every morning was to visit the nursery and bring the child in her arms to my bedroom. The child reposed on her tenderness, and always showed her marked preference. Her affection for this engaging infant seemed to afford her great increase of happiness.

On the Monday before her illness began she accompanied me to dine with Mrs. Craik. She entered warmly into an argument against negro slavery, and supported her views on that subject ably and eloquently, in opposition to a gentleman who had lately returned from the West Indies.

On the morning of the day following (Tuesday) she accompanied me to the House of Industry, and visited her little orphan protegée at the house of her nurse, and in the evening she went to see Kemble act "Hamlet," the last time he performed that character in Edinburgh. I never saw her enjoy anything with more animation. Her taste in acting was exquisite.

On Wednesday she employed herself in painting the second picture of young Tone, and in the evening accompanied me and her sister to Mrs. Brunton's. She was in excellent spirits, and she at all times enjoyed Mrs. Brunton's society extremely.

On Thursday, after spending some hours at the picture of her father, she went out to dispose of tickets for a benefit concert for Miss Derby, a deserving young woman who had been recommended to us by some English friends, and expressed a wish to go herself to the concert, having never, she said, attended one in Edinburgh before. In the evening we were at home, and quite alone, and Grace read to us most beautifully some of the finest passages from Young's "Night Thoughts." Her voice, in reading, was touching and expressive, and her taste correct and elegant.

On Friday evening she accompanied me and a small party of friends to Miss Derby's concert, and returned in high spirits and much pleased with the evening's performance, for though her taste for music had been little cultivated, she felt its power strongly.

On Saturday she accompanied her father and Mrs. Wilson on a little drive to the country, and, on coming home, reminded me of some visits which we had reproached ourselves with not having paid. On these visits she accompanied me, and afterwards enjoyed the society of a few friends at dinner, and of Mr. and Mrs. Wilson in the evening. It was remarked by Dr. Anderson, who was one of the party, that he never saw Grace more animated, intelligent, and pleasing. At night, after the party had left us, she read aloud Southey's "Wat Tyler" (then newly published), which was interrupted by much mirth and laughter.

On the following morning (Sunday) she rose earlier than the rest of the family, and, after breakfast, went with Miss Wright (a friend of mine lately arrived from the country) to hear Mr. Grey preach at a small chapel in the Old Town. When Margaret and I returned from our attendance at the Episcopal Chapel, we found her in the drawing-room. She complained of headache and weariness, and said the heat of the small and crowded place of worship she had been in had made her feel faint, and that now she felt cold and disposed to shivering. I recommended her to lie down in bed, but she said she hoped to be better after dinner. She went down to dinner with us, and took tea in the drawing-room, but retired early. Next day she kept her bed, still complaining of headache ; and at night, on rising for a little while to have her bed made, she fainted. I sent immediately for our family doctor, Mr. Turner, but, in spite of the remedies he applied, she became every day more hot, restless, and uneasy, especially during the night.

On Friday morning she sent for me, and said, " Oh, mamma, I have had a dreadful night, but I think I could sleep in your arms." I laid myself down beside her. She said, " Let us pray ;" and she slowly and distinctly repeated the Lord's Prayer. She then laid her head on my breast, and seemed to sleep quietly for a few minutes. On raising her head again, she said, " Dearest mother, I have had my first sleep where I had my first food." Soon afterwards there was an increase of heat and headache, which was not removed by the application of more leeches to the temples. During the whole of the day (Friday) her restlessness and anxiety increased, and towards night high delirium came on.

The symptoms of typhus fever (for such it was now declared to be) kept increasing all Saturday. During the continuance of the delirium she constantly entreated to be taken home, and anxiously asked, " Why she was suffered to lie in the streets ; why she was not suffered to go home." And once when I told her she *was* at home, at that dear home where she had spent so many happy evenings, she looked earnestly in my face, and pressing my hand, said, " Dearest mother, you know how I dote upon those evenings."

On Monday morning the pulse fell considerably, and the blister seemed to have had good effect. Her feverish delirium subsided. She appeared all that day in a state of stupor, with low mutterings.

On Tuesday Dr. Thomson thought her decidedly better. On that night, when I was sitting by her bedside, she said— " Bring a candle, and let the light shine full on mamma's face, that I may see her." When the candle was brought, she fixed her eyes on me with an expression of tender earnestness for a few minutes, as if to search my thoughts, or, perhaps, to look her last. At this time she seemed not to recognise any of the rest who attended her ; but whenever I approached her bed she stretched out her arms, and once she said—"Dearest mother, if I should die, I do not suffer excessive pain."

On Wednesday she appeared worse than the day before, and Dr. Gregory was called. He did not conceal from me that the danger was extreme. He ordered wine in considerable quantity to support her. For three days it appeared to agree with her well, and there was no increase of any dangerous symptom. After the first sleep procured by an opiate, she said—"Oh, how inexpressibly happy do I feel!" Never, amid the wanderings of delirium, did a word escape her that was at variance with the piety and purity of her whole life. Once she clasped her hands, as if in an attitude of prayer, and said, "Give us, Lord, the spirit of love, that we may delight to do Thy will, and of discernment, that—that," and she seemed to lose all recollection, and again relapsed into muttering delirium.

On Sunday and Monday, the 13th and 14th of April, the headache and depression increased. On Tuesday she seemed easier, and our hopes revived. That evening, however, as I was sitting by her bedside, the stomach rejected the wine given. The next day this symptom increased. All hope was now over. She passed a day of great suffering from sickness, and there was no interruption to the delirium ; but her voice was strong, and I was not aware that all would so soon be over. "Mamma, mamma," were the last words she uttered.

She died on Wednesday night, at ten o'clock, April 16th, 1817. Dr. Thomson, whose kindness on that occasion can never be forgotten by us, remained with us for four hours, and did not leave us till she had breathed her last.

Never was there such tender, dutiful, fond, and respectful affection as her whole short life exemplified. Thankful to God for having given me such a child, and still for sparing me so many blessings in those that remain, may we be enabled so to live that, when time shall be no more, we may be reunited to her in a blessed immortality.

MEMOIR OF ARCHIBALD FLETCHER,

ADVOCATE,

WITH A SKETCH OF THE POLITICAL STATE OF FEELING IN EDINBURGH FROM 1791 TO 1815.

BY HIS WIDOW.

---

*Character given of Archibald Fletcher, Esq., by Lord Cockburn,
in his " Life of Lord Jeffrey," vol. i. p. 90.*

" A pure and firm patriot.   Throughout all the changes
that occurred in his long life, he was the same,—never neglect-
ing any opportunity of resisting oppression, in whatever quarter
of the globe it might be practised or threatened, ashamed of
no romance of public virtue,—always ready to lead, but, from
modesty, much readier to follow, his Whig party in every
conflict of principle,—and all with perfect candour and
immoveable moderation.

" He was almost the father, and was certainly the most
persevering champion, of burgh reform in Scotland.   But
indeed his whole life, devoted as it was to the promotion of
every scheme calculated to diffuse knowledge and to advance
liberty in every region of the world, was applied with especial
zeal and steadiness to the elevation of his native country."

" BILTON COTTAGE, NEAR RUGBY, *May* 21*st*, 1829.

" MY DEAR GRANDCHILDREN,—You were all so young
when you lost your excellent grandfather that I have thought
it right to give you a short account of him, both for your
satisfaction and improvement.   I might have made this

Memoir of his useful and honourable life much longer, yet my object being to interest and impress your hearts with veneration for his memory rather than to give a minute detail of the narrative of his life, I hope you will accept it, imperfect as it is, with my prayers, that it may please God that you may all so live as to be worthy representatives of him, both in his public and private life.—I am, dear children, your affectionate grandmother,   ELIZA FLETCHER."

ARCHIBALD FLETCHER was born at Pooble, in Glenlyon, in Perthshire, in the year 1746.   His father, Angus Fletcher, was a younger brother of Archibald Fletcher, Esq., of Bernice and Dunans, in Argyllshire : and their ancestors were, according to the tradition of the country, the first who had raised smoke or boiled water on the braes of Glenorchy.

In that wild and mountainous district the Fletchers had been a numerous and warlike clan for many centuries; and near to Loch Auchalader there may still be seen the mossy cairns where the bones of the fierce Macdonalds and M'Inlaisters were interred, after a deadly feud fought near that spot many hundred years ago, on account of some disputed ground which each clan claimed as their rightful inheritance. The patronymic of M'Inlaister, translated from the Gaelic, signifies " Man of the Arrow."   Whether the Fletchers were of old celebrated for making, or for using, arrows is uncertain ; but the Stewarts of Appin, a very powerful clan in feudal times, found the M'Inlaisters such useful allies in battle, that they formed a treaty of alliance with them in the fourteenth century, and bound themselves to espouse the interests of their clan in all their hostile encounters, on condition of receiving their help in times of need.

Angus Fletcher was twice married.   He had four children by his first marriage.   Archibald, your grandfather, was the eldest son by his second wife, Grace M'Naughton.   She was a woman of most noble nature, affectionate dispositions, strong sense, and fervent piety.   She lost her husband when her six children were very young.   It may be supposed that the property of a Highland tacksman, eighty years ago, would not be considerable when divided between a widow and ten children. But their mother, notwithstanding her second marriage, proved so faithful a guardian of their little property, that she was enabled to give her sons the education of gentlemen. Archibald used to delight in the recollections of his Highland boyhood. His favourite sport was spearing salmon by torchlight; and often, with his little troop of brothers, he used to leap from a height into a peat moss breast-high, and then spring into a mountain stream to wade and splash amidst the torrent. I never could discover that he had any taste for pastoral life; it was too inanimate and tranquil for his ardent temperament. He used, when quite a boy, to delight in listening to the tales and songs of wandering bards who frequented his mother's farm, but these were tales of battles; and he well remembered his joyful anticipations when any of the family were to be newly clothed, because the itinerant tailor of Glenlyon had a vast store of Ossianic lore, and Archibald used to sit by his side the day through, listening to the poems of Ossian, and the tales of ghosts and fairies. His imagination, however, was not so much capti-vated by the marvellous as his moral taste was elevated by the sublime. He delighted, even then, in the generosity and magnanimity of Fingal and his heroic times, and never to the last hour of his life could he read or hear of a noble action without being moved to tears. This high tone of feeling, fostered no doubt by the legends of the tailor bard, was likewise cultivated by his mother's habitual piety and unworldly turn of mind. She was profoundly acquainted with her Bible, and she made its pure and holy precepts the guide of her life. Her dwelling was at least ten miles from the parish church, and on the Sabbath afternoon many of the neighbouring cottars who were unable to walk so far, assembled on a hill-side in summer, or in a shieling near her house, and there, seated in the midst of them, she read to them from her English Bible, translating into Gaelic the parables of the Saviour, or the prophetic portions of the Old Testament, or the patriarchal histories so well suited to interest her shepherd clansmen.

There was then no translation of the Bible into the Gaelic tongue; it was to these poor Highlanders a sealed book. Mrs.

M'Diarmid exercised the office of a home missionary among her neighbours from a principle of pure love to God, and from an earnest desire to do them good, neither arrogating any merit nor expecting any reward. This gratuitous exercise of the holiest charity had its reward however in the affection and respect of her little flock, who had such confidence in her judgment and kindness that they consulted her in all their difficulties. Nothing could exceed the harmony that prevailed in her numerous family, and the impartiality of her conduct towards her own children and those of her first and second husbands.

Archibald's first separation from this excellent mother was when he went to the Grammar School at Kenmore, in Breadalbane. He was then about ten years old, and there he began to learn English and Latin Grammar at the same time, and soon distinguished himself as an aspiring and industrious scholar. He was removed at thirteen to the High School of Perth, where his academical ardour was still more excited by keener competition. Being one morning too late in making his appearance at school, his master degraded him to the bottom of the class as a punishment; his heart was hot with indignation at this supposed injustice, but restraining the expression of his feelings, in a few minutes afterwards, by a fortunate superiority in scholarship, he regained his place at the top of the class. The boys cheered him very loudly, and then, giving way to the passionate expression of mingled feelings, he burst into tears. From that moment, he used to say, he dated his devotion to popular feelings and his hatred of injustice.

As Archibald's small patrimony was nearly exhausted by the expense of his education, and his inclination led him to prefer the profession of the Law, he was placed at sixteen in the office of Mr. Grant, a writer in Edinburgh, and from that time was wholly dependent on his own exertions. Mr. Grant formed so high an opinion of his worth and talents that he appointed him by will sole executor in trust for his affairs, and recommended him as confidential clerk to the then Lord Advocate, Sir James Montgomery. Sir James had too just an estimation of his merits to allow him to continue long in a subordinate capacity. He became his zealous friend, ·and recommended him to Mr. Wilson of Howden, with whom, after serving a regular apprenticeship, he became an active and efficient partner. He took advantage of the good libraries and good society of Edinburgh to cultivate his mind and improve his taste. It was during this period of his laborious professional life, when assiduous attention to his duties recommended him to every one in whose employment he was engaged, that for several years he used to rise at four o'clock in the morning to study Greek ; and he found time, when the labours of the day had concluded, to attend literary and debating societies, and exercised his pen in the composition of various ingenious essays, chiefly on metaphysical and literary subjects. He attended at this time the lectures of Professor Adam Fergusson, who so ably filled the Moral Philosophy chair in the University of Edinburgh, and while attending that class became acquainted with Mr. Dugald Stewart, in whose deservedly high reputation he afterwards always took the most cordial interest.

It was about the year 1778 that the regiment of M'Cra Highlanders mutinied and refused to embark at Leith for America. They maintained that they had been enlisted for home service only, and that Government had broken faith with them in proposing to send them abroad. These furious mutineers posted themselves on Arthur's Seat, and obstinately refused to obey the orders of their commanding officers. In this alarming emergency, Mr. Archibald Fletcher was chosen to negotiate with them. His perfect acquaintance with the Erse language, and his high reputation for talents and integrity, qualified him for this difficult and delicate mediation, and entitled him to the confidence of both parties. He was suffered to approach the mutineers with a flag of truce. Not one of them could speak a word of English, while many of their officers were equally ignorant of Erse. This negotiation lasted several days before Mr. Fletcher was able to reconcile the claims of the opposite parties. He did, however, prevail on the mutineers to lay down their arms, and the Government agreed to accept their limited services to Ireland, from which they were afterwards drafted into other volunteer corps to serve in America during the war.

On the expiration of his apprenticeship, Mr. Fletcher entered into partnership with Mr. Wilson, and became a member of the Society of Writers to the Signet. About this time the Faculty of Advocates attempted to establish a regulation that no man above twenty-seven years of age should become a member of their body. Mr. Fletcher wrote a very able pamphlet on the subject, addressed to the Society of Writers to the Signet, exposing the illiberality of this regulation, and ascribed it to an aristocratical spirit of exclusion, alike injurious to the aspirations of young men of talent and to the interests of the Scottish Bar, which ought to be open to all candidates qualified by education and character for that honourable profession. This essay obtained for the author the thanks of the Society of Writers to the Signet. The irony and sound argument it contained bore so severely against the exclusionists in the Faculty of Advocates, that they withdrew the proposed regulation, and never afterwards attempted to enforce it. The liberality of principle and eloquence of composition which distinguished this publication obtained for Mr. Fletcher the friendship of the Honourable Henry Erskine, whose high birth and gifted understanding alike made him averse to adopt the vulgar distinctions that the exclusionists aimed at. From that time Mr. Erskine, then holding the first rank at the Scottish Bar, honoured Mr. Fletcher with his most cordial friendship. Soon after this pamphlet had attained its object, Mr. Fletcher published an " Essay on Church Patronage," a subject at that time warmly contested in the General Assembly. He took the popular side of the question, and demonstrated by the most conclusive reasoning that the choice of the minister of each parish ought, according to the laws of the Church, to be vested in the parishioners who were members of the Church of Scotland. He exposed the servility of spirit which the present system of Church-patronage produced, showing that it converted the servant of God and the faithful pastor of His flock (which a Christian minister should be) into a time-serving and worldly-minded dependant on the favour of the great. He proved also that the exercise of their rights in the choice of their religious teachers would accustom the people to reflection, and raise them in their own esteem, and thus prepare them for a due estimation of all the civil and political rights that belonged to them as a nation of free men.' The " Essay on Patronage " was written in a fearless spirit, and with great vigour and elegance of style, and the argument was enforced by the happiest illustrations to prove the benefits of freedom, both civil and religious.

About this time Mr. Fletcher was one of the founders of the Juridical Society and a constituent member of the Highland Society. To the business of both he devoted much of his leisure time.

It was during the American War that his attention was first directed to Politics, and he then acquainted himself extensively with the history of nations, and the manner in which different forms of government had influenced the human character. From that period political science was his favourite object ; I might almost say it became his passion ; for he perceived that there was no effectual means of improving the condition of mankind but by a wise and just government. He hailed the establishment of American Independence as one of those great events that serve to teach practical wisdom and moderation to old Governments, and as an experiment of Republican principles under circumstances much more favourable to their development than the ancient Republics had enjoyed.

From that time Mr. Fletcher became an ardent admirer of Mr. Fox ; but his love of liberty did not confine itself to abstract speculation. In the year 1784 he became a member of a Society the object of which was to inquire into and reform the abuses of the Scottish burghs, the close system of a self-elected and irresponsible magistracy which prevailed then being, as he conceived, the root and hotbed of all political delinquency, as it separates the interests of the governors from those of the governed, and indulges the selfish and corrupt principles of mankind at the expense of the public good. To the object of Scottish burgh reform Mr. Fletcher for some time, in a great degree, concentrated his exertions, and his gratuitous labours in that cause were for several years intense and unremitting. He was chosen Secretary to the Edinburgh Society of Burgh Reform, and opened an active and extensive correspondence with the Liberal promoters of that measure in every burgh in

Scotland. The delegates from these burghs met annually in Edinburgh ; and after their secretary had collected a vast mass of evidence proving the corruption of the system and the monstrous abuses to which it led, he was desired to draw " The Principles of the Bill for Burgh Reform in Scotland " to be submitted to Parliament.

In February 1787 Mr. Fletcher, accompanied by some other gentlemen, was sent to London as delegate from the Scottish burghs. It was then he became personally acquainted with Mr. Fox and the other distinguished leaders of the Whig party. Mr. Fox expressed his decided approbation of the views of the Scottish burgh reformers, but lamented that he should not have leisure that session to do justice to their cause. He recommended the delegates to wait on Mr. Sheridan and commit their important business to him. They did so. Mr. Sheridan readily undertook to be their champion, and at an early period of the session obtained a Committee of the House of Commons to inquire into the grievances. Mr. Fletcher was in daily attendance on this Committee, and from what he then saw of the leading Whigs, both in public and private society, he was convinced of the integrity of their public principles, as well as delighted with their candour and freedom from the bitterness of party spirit. In no society did he ever hear the talents and merits of Mr. Pitt more justly valued than in that of his rival statesmen.

It was while on his way to London, in 1787, with a mind intensely occupied by the subject of this mission, that Mr. Fletcher first met the lady who became his wife in 1791. It might be supposed that having lived a bachelor above forty years, and with a character formed by long habits of professional life, as well as a mind directed to political and abstract speculation, Mr. Fletcher might have had little indulgence for one whose age and pursuits were so different from his own ; but the contrary was remarkably the case. He was in the best sense of the word a most indulgent husband. He liberally admitted his wife to a participation of his intellectual stores, and exalted her aims by cultivating her sympathy in his own extensive views and elevated purposes.

In the years that followed, from 1791 to 1800, we experienced much of that strong excitement which the early period of the French Revolution produced. Mr. Fletcher hailed the first dawn of liberty in France as the harbinger of good not only to that country but to the whole of Europe. He deprecated all foreign interference in the political affairs of a nation that struggled constitutionally to be free. He heartily co-operated with the Whig party in Edinburgh, and attended every anniversary of the fall of the Bastile since the glorious day on which it fell, the 14th July 1789.

He took a deep interest in the deliberations of the Constituent Assembly, and· admired the abstract principles of the Gironde party, while he condemned their want of vigour in not punishing the authors of that bloody day (the 10th of August 1792), and the still bloodier which followed on the 1st and 2d of September ; for while he deeply cherished the principles of rational liberty, he heartily deplored the excesses committed in its name.

Mr. Fletcher attributed the power and mischievous influence of the Jacobin faction in France in great measure to the foreign interference which had been directed against the proceedings of the Constituent Assembly. The coalition of crowned heads encouraged the hopes of the Court faction and the anti-Revolutionists, while the violent party among the Republicans became alarmed by the threats of the Duke of Brunswick and the flight of the King after he had solemnly sworn to be faithful to the nation and the law. These circumstances combined to excite the public mind to a state of political distrust and delirium, of which bad men took advantage ; hence the Jacobins attained an ascendency over the moderate and enlightened Girondists, and "The Reign of Terror" succeeded to that of law and justice.

These opinions, which Mr. Fletcher declared on all occasions, were so hostile to those of the political faction which at that time governed Scotland, that his pecuniary interests as a barrister were considerably affected by them ; for such was the servility of the public mind at that time, that it was not considered safe to trust a Whig lawyer with the management of a case, from the supposed prejudices of the Judges against their holding those opinions. Mr. Fletcher always maintained that this was an unfounded slander on the Scotch Judges, and that however much in some instances they might have recommended themselves to seats on the Bench by political servility, he never knew them violate the integrity of justice from political prejudices against any member of the Bar. Certain it is, however, that the Whig lawyers at that time were comparatively briefless, and that agents were instructed not to employ their own brother if they chanced to be opposed to the Minister of the day.

Although conscious that it would have made no difference in my husband's line of conduct at this time, when we were often reduced to our last guinea in " our Reign of Terror," it was my happiness to delight in the uncompromising principles on which he acted ; and he has often said to me that the support he derived from my sympathy in these trying times was most consolatory to his mind.

Although Mr. Fletcher declined to become a member of the British Convention, from his disapprobation of Universal Suffrage and Annual Parliaments which they advocated, and from a conviction that such claims would increase the alarm among the higher orders, and therefore strengthen Mr. Pitt's administration, he never shrank from being the professional advocate of those unfortunate and misguided men who suffered for such intemperate opinions. He acted gratuitously as counsel for Joseph Gerald, and others, accused of sedition ; and when party spirit was at its height of intolerance, and the Honourable Henry Erskine was deprived of the Deanship of the Faculty of Advocates by a vote of the majority of that body, in 1796, on account of being present at a meeting the object of which was to oppose what were called the " Gagging Bills," Mr. Fletcher was one of the courageous thirty-eight who formed the minority of the Faculty of Advocates on that occasion.

At this time he took an active part, as a member of the Edinburgh Committee, for the Abolition of the Slave Trade, and never lost sight of the business of the Society for the Improvement of the Highlands. His labours in the cause of Burgh Reform were suspended owing to the alarm for what were called " French principles," which operated unfavourably on all questions of reform ; and Parliamentary Reform, once Mr. Pitt's favourite measure, was now included in the cry against all dangerous innovations.

While party feelings divided friends, and even members of the same family from each other, Mr. Fletcher continued to hold so high a place for personal integrity, his patriotism was so much without pretension, and his conduct so wholly free from the imputation of sinister motives of any kind, that, though he suffered professionally from the political panic of the times, he never had a personal enemy, and he began to find his professional emoluments gradually increasing. His law-papers were considered models, both in perspicuity of style and acuteness of reasoning ; whatever he did was done with the zeal and energy of an upright purpose, and perhaps there never existed in any mind more of the capacity of submission to the drudgery of labour in the performance of professional duty united to independence of spirit and unpretending dignity of character.

Almost the only part of Mr. Pitt's administration which Mr. Fletcher heartily approved was the Irish Union ; and he gave that statesman great credit for retiring from office when he could not redeem the pledge he had given for Catholic emancipation. For that great measure my husband was a zealous and uncompromising advocate, identified, as he considered it to be, with the tranquillity and safety of the whole British Empire, and no less an act of policy than of justice.

He rejoiced in the formation of a Whig administration in 1806, and was, perhaps, one of the most disinterested men of his party in that feeling, for he had formed no ambitious expectations of promotion.

The death of Mr. Fox, which happened in September 1806, was an event Mr. Fletcher deplored, in common with every friend of constitutional liberty. He had early admired that great statesman for his vigorous opposition to the American War, and still more for his consistent and manly resistance to all interference in the internal affairs of France at the beginning of the Revolution. He was one of the fourteen gentlemen who met to celebrate Mr. Fox's birthday on the 24th of January 1797, after his name had been erased from his Majesty's Privy Council for his determined opposition to the French War. This little meeting was composed of courageous spirits, for it was known at the time that the names of the fourteen assembled on that occasion were sent to Government as dangerous and disloyal subjects. Mr. Fletcher rejoiced, however, that Fox had been in office long enough to accomplish the object nearest his heart,—the abolition of the African Slave Trade ; though his honest endeavours to obtain honourable terms of peace with France were frustrated by the arrogant and unreasonable demands of Napoleon Buonaparte.

Mr. Fletcher was at this time so indignant at the tone of defiance and threatened invasion assumed by France, that he thought it was every man's duty to arm in defence of national honour. With this feeling he entered as an ensign in the Highland corps of volunteers. His soldierly accoutrements were a subject of much amusement to his family and friends. His quiet manners, and studious, sedentary habits, accorded ill with the pomp and circumstance of regimental duty, but he set about the acquirement of a military step and deportment with as much zeal and earnestness as if the defence of the country had depended on his individual exertions ; and at a mock battle at Leith, when it was assigned to that part of the Highland corps to which he was attached to fall back for a time before an invading enemy, he declared with characteristic simplicity, that " he never could command Highlanders to retreat, and that, if he did, he hoped they would disobey him." He quitted his law-papers at the hour of drill without showing the least annoyance at such interruptions, for as his old friend Lord Buchan observed, " Fletcher buckles on his sword in the true spirit of a civic soldier."

In the enjoyment of perfect domestic happiness, and in consideration for the welfare and comfort of every member of his family, he never was surpassed by any one. His children can never forget his quiet sympathy in all their pleasures, his anxiety that they should enjoy every advantage of liberal education, his tenderness towards them when they were sick, and the great indulgence and reasonableness of his habitual conduct towards them. To his servants he was the most kind and indulgent of masters, and to the poor and afflicted his nature was so compassionate that he would have divided with them his last shilling.

One instance of Mr. Fletcher's compassionate disposition is

well remembered in his family. A miserable female culprit had been detected in the act of stealing from his premises, and in the absence of their master and mistress his servants had secured her until the police were summoned to take her before a magistrate. Mr. Fletcher, on coming home, would not interfere with the course of justice, but going quietly to the place where she was in custody he gave her a loaf of bread, saying, "Take that, poor woman; you look hungry; I dare say it was that that made you steal." He was ever ready to be the poor man's advocate, and used to think his time well employed when he could professionally assist the indigent or oppressed with his advice and exertions.

The unjust aggressions of the French Government in Spain made him rejoice in the assistance rendered to that nation by the British Government in 1808. He took a strong interest in the Peninsular War, because he considered the cause of Spain to be just, and he hailed the peace so dearly purchased in 1814, as it secured the fall of that military despotism which Napoleon had established on the ruins of the French Republic.

The violation of the Charter by Louis XVIII., and the enthusiasm with which the army and the people of France received their exiled Emperor on his return from Elba, gave rise to mingled feelings of hope and apprehension. Of hope, that the Chamber of Deputies would so limit the power of Napoleon that not his will but the law on which he had dared to trample should thenceforward govern France; and of apprehension that Napoleon was not of a character, any more than the Bourbons, to profit by the misfortunes he had experienced. The hundred days justified these apprehensions, and France, notwithstanding her apparent devotion to this "spoiled child of victory," had now so little confidence in his justice or invincibility that instead of the four hundred thousand that had followed him to Moscow in pursuit of glory, scarcely one hundred thousand could be found to rally round him on the plains of Waterloo, when nothing less than national independence was at stake.

The battle of Waterloo was so proud a day for Great Britain that Mr. Fletcher rejoiced in it with true patriotic feeling; but he did not rejoice without trembling, lest that confederacy of armed powers which prevailed over the fortunes of one military despot should forget what was due to France and to the rest of Europe. The formation of the Holy Alliance confirmed these fears. That league of Kings, allied for the express purpose of perpetuating the abuses of old governments and repressing the spirit of civil and religious liberty whenever it should appear, enlisted among its adherents the Government of England. Mr. Fletcher deprecated this union as the most disgraceful that England could have formed. From this coalition, and not from the spirit of its own laws and institutions, he attributed the harsh and ungenerous treatment of our fallen enemy Napoleon Buonaparte, whose sufferings at St. Helena ought, in his opinion, to have been made as little severe as was consistent with the peace and safety of Europe.

In the spring of 1816 infirm health obliged Mr. Fletcher to retire from the Bar, just when the emoluments of his practice began to reward the diligence of his professional life. So long as health permitted he never complained of the fatigue of labour ; he loved his profession and delighted in the energetic exercise of his mental faculties, but when obliged to relinquish it, he did so without a murmur, and retired during the summer months to his farm in Stirlingshire, where some additions had been made to the house. The employment of planting, draining, and improving the soil supplied to his active mind a substitute for professional employment.

In the spring of 1817 Mr. Fletcher had the misfortune to lose his second daughter ; this was the first great blow to his domestic happiness. She was in her twenty-first year, and had all the gracious and endearing qualities that a highly-gifted understanding and a most affectionate disposition could bestow. He followed her remains to the grave, a true mourner, and never afterwards could mention her name without the tenderest emotion.

After Mr. Fletcher ceased to be able to superintend his farming concerns with pleasure to him, it was thought best to part with the property in Stirlingshire ; and in the spring of 1824 he took a lease of Auchindinny House and grounds, on the banks of the Esk, and there his family had the comfort of seeing him enjoy a serene and healthy old age. Reading, conversation with his family, and benevolent projects, were his chief pleasures. He was uniformly cheerful and contented, and his interest in public affairs continued unabated. Till within a short time of his death his eyesight was so good that he could read without glasses. Here I could recount his many touching expressions of gratitude to God for the blessing of our union, for our happiness in each other and in our children, but these are sacred subjects. He delighted in the playfulness of his grandchildren, and loved to see them all about him. He was confined by his last illness only a few weeks to bed, and those who faithfully attended him can testify how patiently he bore the wearisome days and nights of increasing debility, and how considerate he was of others. He had no acute bodily suffering, and his mind was in a composed and heavenly frame, for thankfulness seemed to be his habitual state of feeling. He died at half-past two o'clock in the morning of the 20th December 1828.

His remains were attended to the grave by many faithful friends. He was interred in the family burial-ground, on the Calton Hill, on Wednesday the 24th of December 1828.

Sacred

TO THE MEMORY OF ARCHIBALD FLETCHER, ADVOCATE.

HE DEVOTED THE ENERGY

OF A VIGOROUS, BENEVOLENT, AND DISINTERESTED SPIRIT

TO THE CAUSE OF CIVIL AND RELIGIOUS LIBERTY.

HE DIED DECEMBER 20TH, 1828,

AGED 82.

Sacred also to the Memory of his Daughter,

GRACE FLETCHER,

WHO DIED THE 16TH OF APRIL, 1817,

AGED 20.

BLESSED ARE THE PURE IN HEART,
FOR THEY SHALL SEE GOD.

*Extract from Lord Brougham's Introduction on Burgh
Reform, relating to Archibald Fletcher's exertions in that
cause, in the Collected Edition of his Speeches.*

" To both the state of its parliamentary and its municipal
constitution the attention of Scotland had, at different times
during a long course of years, been directed by some very able,
virtuous, and patriotic persons whose labours were unremitting
for the removal of the abuses thus pointed out and traced to
their source, and who, in the time of alarm that followed the
earlier scenes of the French Revolution, were fated to see
the fruit of their labours blighted long before it was ripe.
Among these eminent patriots the first place is due to
Archibald Fletcher, a learned, experienced, and industrious
lawyer, one of the most upright men that ever adorned the
profession, and a man of such stern and resolute firmness in
public principle as is very rarely found united with the
amiable character which endeared him to private society.
Devoted from his earliest youth to the cause of civil liberty,
his mind had become deeply imbued with a sense of the
corruption which had crept into our constitution and disfigured
its original excellence.   His zeal for the maintenance of these
principles, and his anxiety for the renovation of British liberty,
were, if possible, still further excited by the matrimonial
union which he entered into with a lady of Whig family in
Yorkshire (one of the most accomplished of her sex, who, with
the utmost purity of life that can dignify and enhance female
charms, combined the inflexible principles and deep political
feeling of a Hutchinson or a Roland); and he devoted to the
great work of reforming the Scottish elective system, both as
regarded its parliamentary and municipal branches, every hour
which could be spared from the claims of his clients.   The
proceedings in the Convention of Royal Burghs, the bills
introduced by the Crown lawyers for reforming the scheme
of their accounting, the motions for Scotch reform made by
Mr. Sheridan, were all intimately connected with his unremitting and most useful labours, nor could anything but the
alarm raised by the deplorable turn of French affairs have prevented some important measures, at least of Burgh Reform,

from being adopted nearly fifty years ago. Although his life was protracted to the extreme period of the life of man, he was not permitted to see the triumph of the cause to which he had been devoted, and for which his latest prayers were offered."

THE END.

EDINBURGH : PRINTED BY THOMAS AND ARCHIBALD CONSTABLE, PRINTERS TO THE QUEEN, AND TO THE UNIVERSITY.

www.ingramcontent.com/pod-product-compliance
Lightning Source LLC
Chambersburg PA
CBHW021529110726

47902CB00004B/806